W9-BFS-032

THE WALLS OF BYZANTIUM

THE MISTRA CHRONICLES

JAMES HENEAGE

HERON
BOOKS

First published in Great Britain in 2013 by Heron Books
An imprint of Quercus Editions Ltd

55 Baker Street
7th Floor, South Block
London W1U 8EW

Copyright © 2013 James Heneage

The moral right of James Heneage to be
identified as the author of this work has been
asserted in accordance with the Copyright,
Designs and Patents Act, 1988.

All rights reserved. No part of this publication
may be reproduced or transmitted in any form
or by any means, electronic or mechanical,
including photocopy, recording, or any
information storage and retrieval system,
without permission in writing from the publisher.

A CIP catalogue record for this book is available
from the British Library

HB ISBN 978 1 78206 111 3
TPB ISBN 978 1 78206 112 0
EBOOK ISBN 978 1 78206 113 7

This book is a work of fiction. Names, characters,
places and events portrayed in it, while at times based on historical
figures and places, are the product of the author's imagination.

10 9 8 7 6 5 4 3 2 1

Printed and bound in Australia by Griffin Press

Typeset by Ellipsis Digital Limited, Glasgow

To Charlotte

CONTENTS

PROLOGUE

CONSTANTINOPLE, 12 APRIL 1204

At first he didn't hear them.

Alexios V, Emperor of Byzantium, heard only hoofbeats from his balcony overlooking the Hippodrome. The ghosts of chariot-eers past.

The cough came again and the Emperor turned.

Standing between the pillars were four men of his Varangian Guard. All were over six feet tall and had fair hair that fell in plaits either side of faces cracked with fatigue. They carried axes and their armour was spattered with blood.

The Varangopouli. Thank God for the Varangopouli. Give me an army such as these.

'Where are the Franks?' he asked.

A Varangian stepped forward. His voice was hollow with exhaustion. 'Within the city, Majesty. They managed to enter through one of the sea gates. They got behind us.'

There was a pause. Metal scraped on metal as one of them shifted pressure from a wound.

'The Guard stood firm, lord.'

The moon emerged from behind a cloud and its light fell upon eyes that hadn't closed in days. Alexios had known the commander of his guard for thirty years. He put his hand on his shoulder.

'I don't doubt it, Siward. When has it not?'

A woman's scream came from below, then the crash of a falling building. The Emperor looked down.

'A hundred and forty years, Siward. You, your father, his father . . . all those years.' He looked up and smiled. 'Now your Emperor needs one more service.'

Alexios stepped forward and looked at each man in turn. 'Follow me,' he said.

The five men's footsteps echoed through the corridors of the empty palace until they arrived at a courtyard silhouetted by flame. They walked across it to a small door. The Emperor pushed it open and led them down a steep flight of steps, worn with age.

At the bottom, Siward took a torch from its sconce and lit their way across a hall to a door in the far wall. The Emperor reached up to the heavy lintel and moved a stone engraved with a double-headed eagle.

Slowly, slowly, the door creaked open and they entered a large, circular room fetid with dust. Lifting the torch, Siward looked around him and saw dismembered heads stare out from the shadows. Constantine, Gratian, Justinian and Basil the Bulgar-slayer. Eight centuries of emperors looked out from their plinths with disdain.

In the centre of the room was a plain altar.

The Emperor turned. 'Move the altar. There's a passage beneath.'

In a square next to the great church of Hagia Sophia in Constantinople stood the much smaller church of St Olaf, the church of the Varangopouli. Beside it was a narrow street that led to the Harbour of Hormisdas.

The Franks had yet to reach this part of the city, but they were near. Sounds of fighting were coming from the direction of the Iron Gate, where they'd made a second breach in the walls.

The church door opened and, one by one, the Varangians stepped into the street, silently fanning out to form a wall of shields. Then a single casket appeared, supported on poles carried by four palace servants.

Siward brushed the dust from his cloak and raked the street with his axe-head. He looked behind. The casket had reached a small square and its carriers were hurrying towards a sea gate that opened on to the harbour jetty beyond.

But someone was there before them.

A merchant and his wife were on their knees, pleading with the soldiers guarding the gate to let them through. The woman held part of her dress to her mouth against smoke that billowed from a street behind.

Siward backed towards them, then stopped to listen. There were men on the other side of the smoke.

'*Saint Denis et Montjoie!*'

A score of wraiths rose up, monstrous, metal figures emerging beneath a banner of lilies. They held shields and maces and fierce animals reared high on their helmets. The four Varangians were outnumbered five to one but there were no better soldiers in the world. Their axes swung and sliced their way through the finest Milanese armour and the Franks fell at their feet, their skulls crushed and their limbs pumping blood on to the stone. And as they fought, the men backed inch by inch towards the open gate. The casket was through but they were running out of time.

The merchant and his wife were pressed against the wall between the Varangians and the gate, transfixed by the slaughter.

'Get away!' yelled Siward.

The woman fell to her knees, clutching his leg in her terror. Siward glanced down at her.

I cannot save her but I can save the casket.

He reached down and hauled the woman to her feet. She was pretty enough. He flung her towards the French. She fell at their feet, her dress rucked up to reveal a thigh. It was enough. One of the Franks leant down and tore open her bodice. Wrenching open his visor, he fell on her as his companions roared.

'Now!' yelled Siward, and the four Varangians turned and ran through the gate, barring it behind them.

On the jetty, the boat was ready to sail. It was a squat, round-bottomed merchant vessel that flew the flag of Venice. Siward looked up.

Will it fool them?

The casket was on board and the sailors stood ready to cast off. The Varangians boarded and the ship was pushed out into the Propontis, the wind snapping its sails taut as they were hauled up the mast. Gathering speed, they passed platforms with giant engines of war manned by half-naked men who cheered as their fireballs exploded against the city walls. Siward saw another part of the sea wall slide into the sea.

It won't be long now.

He looked out to sea. His ancestors had sailed this way in their longboats from an island far to the west, an island shrouded in mist called *England*. They had passed the deep ruins of Troy and into the Sea of Marmara to arrive at the fabled

4

city of Miklagard as the dawn had ignited the gold of its palaces and churches. They had sailed to escape the Normans who had killed their king, put an arrow through his eye. They had come to seek service with an emperor who needed men of courage and skill to fight his own Normans. They had come with hatred in their hearts and they had become the first English Varangians.

Now they were sailing away. Siward looked down at his sword, at the dragon's head that was its pommel. It was all he was taking with him.

Except the casket.

A sudden gust billowed the sails and the ship lurched forward. Then it was through the blockade and heading for the open sea. He hauled himself to his feet and called out to the captain: 'You know your course?'

The man shook his head. 'South only,' he shouted. 'They said you'd tell me where.'

Siward took one last look at the city. It could have been the salt spray or tears that clouded his eyes. Then he turned his head to the south.

'Mistra,' he said. 'We sail to Mistra.'

PART ONE

MISTRA

CHAPTER ONE

THE CITY OF MONEMVASIA, SPRING 1392

For birds migrating south that day, the journey down the coastline to Cape Maleas offered a view unchanged since their species
began.

On one side, the deep, deep blue of the Mirtoon Sea spread
its unabbreviated calm out to the horizon. On the other, the
Despotate of Mistra offered mile after mile of rugged hinterland, wild with forest and mountain.

Until Monemvasia.

There, the Greek Peloponnese extended a crooked finger into
the sea and on its knuckle perched a city where twenty thousand souls bustled within walls that seemed to grow out of the
rocks beneath them.

Scattered across the sea were the white sails of merchantmen waiting in the roads to enter the city's port to the north
and, closer in, closer to the rocks on which the city stood, were
the figures of four boys lying on their backs in the water.

One of these was Luke Magoris. He was looking up at the
walls of Monemvasia and thinking.

Twenty thousand of us living in this labyrinth and that many cats.
How do we sleep at night?

9

It was a thought that had occurred to him before.

Matthew, Nikolas and Arcadius had for once stopped talking and were too far away for attack. Luke turned his body so that the entirety of the city lay cradled between his feet.

Above its wall, rising from the rocks from which Luke had just dived, sat the jumble of small houses that made up the lower town, nudged by the splashes of oleander and bougain-villeia that sprouted between. Small rooms led on to small balconies, and the houses crowded the steep slopes like an audience taking its seats. A wash of early sunshine bathed the mosaic of a million terracotta tiles and lit, to a dazzling white, the bell tower of the Elkomenos Church. And above, immense and implacable, sat the pitted rock of the Goulas.

The Goulas.

Was there anything so magnificent in the world? Its sheer sides rose from the skirts of the lower town, deep-scarred by the stairway that twisted its way up its face.

Luke's gaze travelled up the stairs until it reached the walls above. In this light it was difficult to see what was made by man and what by God until armour flashed from the ramparts. Above, on a gently rising plateau, lay the mansions, churches and gardens of the upper town, where the richest of the city's inhabitants had their homes.

At the very summit sat the squat, reassuring spectacle of the citadel, home to the city's small garrison and supposedly impregnable. From its tower flew two standards, limp symbols of the split loyalties of this little city. In a fresher wind, one would show the double-headed eagle of the Byzantine Empire, the other the black castle of the Mamonas family.

Luke looked down at his body as it was swayed by the passing waves, enjoying the warm current that fingered his back like velvet. He was tall for his sixteen years and had a powerful physique to match. His father's lessons in the art of fighting had given him broad shoulders and muscular arms. His legs, meanwhile, were long but bowed from time spent on horseback. His father was a Varangian Guardsman and had told him that the Varangians had always fought on foot, surrounding the Emperor with a shield of iron on the battlefield. But, from birth, Luke had shown an extraordinary ability with horses. So Pavlos Mamonas, Archon of Monemvasia and by far its richest citizen, had decreed that his Varangian training should be interspersed with time spent at the Mamonas stud.

Luke dipped his head back into the water, throwing it forward to look directly into the sun, spray hitting the sea around him like pebbles. He tilted his body, swinging it back round so that his feet faced south.

South to Cape Maleas and round it to Mistra. Where I should be now.

Someone spoke.

'Can you see the beacon from there?'

It was Matthew, closest of the friends and nearest to Luke in age. He had swum up to him so that their heads were almost touching.

'It's been lit for days,' he continued. 'The Turks must be almost at Mistra's walls.' He paused to blow water from his nose. 'Our fathers should've let us go.'

Our fathers. My father.

Luke had been so careful that morning. He'd taken an age to creep down the wooden staircase, avoiding the creaking step. He'd taken the sword silently from the chest, and then tiptoed through the door of the house on to the steps to the street below. One of his shoes had been loose and, so narrow was the

11

alley, he'd been able to stretch a hand to the opposite wall to pull it on.

He'd picked his way through the shortening shadows, his cheek brushing jasmine tumbling from a neighbour's wall, to arrive at a small square where a mulberry tree offered shade to a lizard darting from stone to warming stone.

Only then had something broken the still of the sleeping city. The voice of his father, Joseph.

'You've taken your birthday present early, Luke,' he'd said, pointing at the sword. His voice was low, always low. 'Couldn't you have waited for me to give it to you?'

Silence.

'Were you going to Mistra?'

Luke had nodded.

'With the other three?'

He'd nodded again, and found his voice. 'The beacon's been lit for three days. The Despot needs us.'

'You?' One eyebrow had lifted in surprise. 'Four Varangian boys barely sprouting beards? You think so?'

'You've taught us to fight, Father. We can help. Our loyalty is to the empire.'

'Your loyalty is to the Archon of Monemvasia.'

'Which is part of the empire. Father, we're not bound by any oath to the Mamonas family as you are.'

Joseph had nodded then, his hand stroking the enormous beard that lay on his chest like a blazon. 'But you owe some loyalty to me, Luke. Enough at least not to sneak away like a thief. With my sword.'

'Which was to be mine on my sixteenth birthday. Today.'

Then they'd stood and stared at each other, Luke seeing the broken nose, the long mane of straw hair that, unplaited, fell to his father's waist, the blue eyes he'd been graced to inherit which came from some island far, far to the west.

'We are Varangians, Luke,' Joseph had said quietly, 'whether sworn or not. I am here to guard the Archon as you will be one day. We're not free to take sides.'

'Not even when our Despot has an army of Turks marching to destroy our capital at Mistra?'

'Not even then.'

Now, he lay upon his back and felt the sun on his eyelids and thought about his father and the complicated business of duty. His head bumped against Matthew's.

'I must return to the house,' he said, turning on to his front. 'If we're not going to Mistra then I'd better get up to the Mamonas twins. They want to ride out to the stud.'

Inside the house, his mother had laid out Luke's riding clothes on the table: leather breeches with an extra layer on the insides to protect his thighs and new boots of untreated hide that still stank of the tanner's yard. His father had put the sword back in the chest and locked it.

A lunch of bread, cream cheese and salted pork lay in a napkin next to a bowl of dried figs stuffed with chestnuts: Luke's favourite. He stretched out to take a handful while his mother's back was turned and wrapped them quickly in a napkin.

'The figs will make you bilious,' Rachel said, 'and I was saving them for tonight.'

She swung round, laughing. 'Oh, take them. I can make more.'

How he loved that laugh. It had cast its spell over the two men of the family since Luke's first day on earth. In her mid-thirties, Rachel's unlined face still radiated the beauty that comes from inner calm. Everything about her was gentle.

Luke hugged her.

'Silly boy!' She smiled, her chin against his chest as she looked up at her son. 'Joseph, tell this thieving Varangian to get up to the palace or we'll have no food at all to put on the table!'

Joseph walked over to his son and put hand on his shoulder before he could leave the house.

'I know that you're eager to fight for the Empire, Luke,' he said gently. 'It's what you've spent all your life training to do. When the time is right you can go to Mistra, but not today.'

'So why not Constantinople? They say there are still Varangians there.'

Joseph sighed. 'You know why. We Varangians are here for a reason.'

Varangian.

For centuries the Varangians had guarded the Emperor in Constantinople with unquestioning loyalty. In the Great Palace, they'd stood either side of the monumental bronze doors that led into its interior. When the Emperor gave audience, seated on the elevating throne that held ambassadors in such awe, they'd assembled around his sacred person, always bearing those great axes, their *distralia*, on their right shoulders. The Guard Commander was called *Akolouthos*, which meant 'follower', since he was the person allowed nearest to the Emperor on official occasions. Indeed, so trusted was he that the great keys of the city were given to him whenever the Emperor went away.

The Varangians had grown rich in the service of their emperor. When a city was taken, it was the Varangians who'd had first pick of the spoils. When a new emperor came to the throne, it was the Varangians who'd been permitted to fill their helmets with gold.

Luke knew that, on a night of fire and ruin, a treasure had been brought to Mistra by four Varangians, led by his ancestor, and buried somewhere on its hill. It was a treasure they said might save the empire one day, a treasure the Varangians and their descendents had vowed to guard until it was needed. It was the reason why they were still there. When the Norman Villehouardin had conquered the Peleponnese and built his citadel at Mistra, their sons had been forced to go to Monemvasia. But the secret of where the treasure lay buried in Mistra stayed with them, passed from father to son through the generations.

Until.

Until when? When had the chain been broken? Luke wasn't sure. Somehow the secret of where it was had been lost so that now no one quite knew what was history and what myth.

Tonight, the four Varangians and their sons would meet as they did once a year to talk about myth and history and an island on the edge of the world called *England*. And they would renew their oath of loyalty to an empire that had given them a home.

On reaching the alleyway outside his house, Luke broke into an easy run, taking two at a time the steps that led up to the *mesi odos*, the cobbled central street of the town. The shops and taverns were still boarded up and sleepy traders mumbled greetings as he passed.

He reached the square that formed the crossroads with the street that led from the sea gate to the upper town. At the church of Christ Elkomenos, he turned left, nearly colliding with a water seller who was filling cups suspended on a rope around her neck.

Luke rounded a corner and saw before him the steps to the upper town. Soon he was catching his breath at the top, leaning against the balcony that overlooked the maze of streets below and the sea beyond. Here there were fewer people, fewer cats and much less noise. Here you weren't brushed by pack-mules as you walked, or stopped by street hawkers trying to sell their wares. Here you could rest on a stone bench beneath the shade of a mulberry tree or sit for a moment on the cool edge of a fountain to collect your thoughts. And here you could gain an uninterrupted view of the vast canvas of sea on which were painted the motionless sails of vessels, large and small, which passed Monemvasia in the endless barter of continents, a barter in which his city played its important part.

Luke breathed in deeply. The plateau and surrounding mountains and valleys were covered in a spring blanket of narcissi, hyacinths and violets and the heady smell was all around him. What a difference from the lower town, where a waft of wind could pick up the stench of the tanneries, lime kilns and slaughterhouses that stood outside the walls. No wonder the Goulas was known as Manexie Kalessie, 'castle of flowers', and no wonder the rich chose to live here.

Luke crossed the square and started up the paved street towards the Panagia Hodegetria, the church that had provided a landmark for sailors for centuries. On either side of the street were the walls of great villas, the tops of cypress trees promising cool gardens within.

No one was up at this time except the old praetor, whose job it was to keep the streets of the upper town clean and lit at night. He was busy extinguishing the wicks of oil lamps along the walls. He knew Luke of old.

'Wrong way for the palace,' he said.

'I'm to meet them at the citadel today,' said Luke, stopping to catch his breath, 'and they say the fleet is returned to Palea.'

'It's there all right. But the Archon won't send it to help Mistra.'

The old man turned, wiping oil from his hands with a rag. 'You might tell them there's a beacon alight. As if they haven't seen it.' The man spat and turned back to his lamp.

That the Archon was unpopular in the city, Luke knew. What he hadn't realised was just how much the citizens supported their new Despot, Theodore, sent to rule over them by his brother, the Emperor Manuel in Constantinople. Now the beacons had been lit and the people wanted to march to help defend their capital.

As I tried to do this morning.

By now Luke had arrived at the church and he climbed the rocks behind it, carefully avoiding a gossamer-thin spider's web that stretched between two mulberry bushes. He bent to look at the beads of sparkling dew that hung from every taut thread and marvelled that anything so tenuous could resist the elements.

Perhaps the Empire can survive after all.

Looking away, he saw the blue expanse of the Mirtoon Sea before him, the coast to his left rising sharply as it swept round the edge of Monemvasia Bay. A mist still clung to the water and Luke strained his eyes to see the masts of the twelve galleys that were all that remained of the once-glorious Imperial Navy.

He shifted his gaze to the north, where the deep-water port of Kiparissi lay. Once it had contained shipyards that used the oak and pine from Mount Parnon, and the iron from the furnaces at Voutamas, to create ships of strength and beauty. The men of Monemvasia had provided much of the manpower for the navy but since the Emperor Andronikos had disbanded the fleet a hundred years ago, there were barely sufficient ships to protect the merchantmen that plied the shipping lanes to Constantinople, let alone fight the Turks.

Now most of the ships that Luke saw crossing the bay flew the winged lion of Venice, huge galleys with three banks of oars on either side whose sweeps dipped to the beat of a drum.

Wiping the sweat from his neck, Luke ran along the path that edged the north face of the rock. To his left the plateau fell away to fields containing neat rows of wheat and vegetables and the public cisterns. Luke hoped they were full.

Soon he was climbing the final slope to the rock on which the citadel stood. His path led round to the north edge of the plateau from where he could see the bridge that linked the island of Monemvasia to the mainland. The drawbridge at its centre was being lifted to allow a boat through to the jetties and quays beyond. Ships laden with wine, oil, silk, cochineal and the fruit of the Laconian soil would be waiting to leave.

'Luke!'

He looked up to see a familiar face leaning over the battlement.

'Late as usual, damn you!' shouted Damian Mamonas. The Archon's heir was a year older than Luke and stood to inherit the vast Mamonas empire. The knowledge made him arrogant. 'My father is on the verge of not letting us ride to Sikia with the Turks on the march. Wait there. I'll get Zoe.'

Zoe Mamonas: Damian's twin in everything but temperament. While Damian was lazy, arrogant and shallow, Zoe had depths beyond the reach of man, or at least any man who'd tried to bind her in marriage these recent years. Zoe had rejected any suitor that might have eased the pain of knowing that she would inherit nothing.

They didn't meet any Turks on the ride to Sikia and, if they had, the Turks would have been hard pressed to catch them. Like Luke, Damian and Zoe rode well, and all three were mounted on the best horses that the Mamonas stable had to offer.

They had met the horses at the town gate and had trotted through the outer town where lay the Jewish quarter and homes of the poorest inhabitants. Here were the glass factories, metal workshops and pottery kilns and Zoe held a handkerchief to her nose until they'd reached the custom houses and warehouses which clustered around the bridge. Crossing it, they'd come to the open field reserved for feast-day fairs, where you could watch bear baiting or buy a plate of suckling lamb, fresh from the spit. There you could find exotic goods from the outside world, the latest books and weapons from Florence or marten fur from the lands of the Golden Horde. And it was there that Luke felt, most strongly, the pull of somewhere else.

Once clear of the field, all three spurred their horses into a canter as the road began its gentle rise into the mountains of the hinterland. The going was easy since rain had not fallen for weeks and a fine red dust rose beneath them.

Luke rode behind Zoe, watching her lash the flanks of her horse, her jet-black hair flung out behind like a pennant. Neither she nor Damian had spoken more than a sentence to him since they'd mounted.

By now the riders had reached a deep gorge that split the mountain in two and they could hear the rush of a river far beneath them to their left. The path narrowed and vanished around a series of blind bends ahead. Something told Luke that there was traffic around the next corner. He was sure of it.

'Slow down!'

The twins were riding fast and, if they'd even heard, paid no heed. It was a miracle that they didn't hit the wagon. Both riders swerved to the left, their horses' hooves close to the edge of the gorge, then yelled at the wagoner as he cowered against the mountainside.

It took five miles for Luke to catch up with them and only then because Damian and his sister had stopped to look over a long valley stretching out before them.

Vineyards of startling green against rich vermilion earth marched in perfect rows as far as the eye could see. Occasional watermills, wine presses beside them, followed the course of a thin string of river that wound its way through the valley. Flocks of starlings circled above, lifted by gusts of wind. In the distance, the village of Sikia sat on the only hill in the landscape. And beyond the village lay the Mamonas stud.

'Malvasia,' murmured Damian. 'Our wealth laid out like a banquet before us.'

'Which will disappear if the Turks overrun the despotate,' said Luke. 'Why won't your father fight?'

Damian looked at him. 'And what makes you think the Turks will bother Monemvasia?'

'Because, Damian,' replied Luke, 'they've bothered every other part of the Byzantine Empire these past years. Hadn't you noticed there isn't very much of it left? Just our little Despotate of Mistra and Constantinople itself?'

Zoe smiled. 'I hear you tried to get to Mistra yourself this morning.'

There was no doubt that Zoe was beautiful. Her long hair

framed an olive-skinned face with heavy-lidded eyes and a full, sensuous mouth. She had the dark grace of the panther.

She continued: 'When we were young you told us that you became a Varangian on your sixteenth birthday. Which is today. Were you going to Mistra to defend it or to find your treasure?'

'It's myth, Zoe.'

Luke kicked his horse down the winding path that led to the valley's bottom and on to a wider road that ran past its vineyards.

It was a question he'd asked himself. Why had he wanted to go to Mistra that morning? He supposed it was what his father had spoken of: some ancient bond between Varangian and empire that he'd always seemed to feel so much more keenly than his friends. He looked around him at a different empire.

Malvasia wine: famed throughout the world for its taste and exorbitant price, the secret of how it was made known to only a few and was jealously guarded. It was the most valuable export of the city of Monemvasia, and the Mamonas family owned most of the vineyards that produced it. It was to be found on the tables of kings and cardinals throughout Europe. The English called it 'Malmsey', the French 'vinum Malvasie'. Even the Ottoman Sultan, forbidden by his religion to enjoy the fruit of the grape, was said to have a craving for it. And every Venetian merchantman that left the ports of Monemvasia, its holds creaking with the weight of oak barrels, added to the enormous wealth of the Mamonas family.

Within an hour they had reached the outskirts of Sikia and Damian led them on to a path that wound its way up through explosions of yellow broom to the walled enclosure of the Mamonas stud.

As they approached, the gates swung open to reveal a series

21

of paddocks surrounded by outbuildings. Inside, they dismounted, handed their reins to waiting grooms and walked towards a stout man who was hurrying over to greet them, beckoning to servants in his wake bearing trays of cool drinks.

The man bowed deeply. 'Welcome, welcome, my lord Damian and my lady Zoe. You do us honour with your visit. Would that your great father could find time to come here more often.'

Damian exchanged a glance with his sister. They took the drinks.

'Arsenius, thank you. My father, alas, has the welfare of our city to look to,' said Damian imperiously. 'So you have us instead. I hear you have a new stallion. Is it fine?'

Arsenius bowed again. 'It is indeed fine, lord. Fine but fiery. We have not been able to place a saddle on its back nor a bit in its mouth. It is very strong and not biddable.' He paused and glanced at Luke. 'We have waited for Luke to speak to it, to see if his way will calm it.'

Irritation darkened Damian's face. 'It sounds as if it might make a good destrier to sell to some Norman knight,' he said. 'Luke knows little of such animals. Let me see him.'

Arsenius looked at Luke, who gave the slightest of shrugs.

The party walked between the paddocks until they reached one in which a single horse stood cropping the grass. At their approach, it raised its head and stared at them, every fibre in its powerful body taut, expectant. It began to back away, its eyes darting from side to side, searching for escape.

Arsenius shook his head. 'I will go and get help. Just in case.'

The three of them were alone with the horse.

Luke moved next to Damian. 'Let me go first, Damian,' he whispered. 'This one looks truly wild. Let me talk to it.'

Damian was transfixed by the animal. He didn't reply.

22

'Let me talk to it,' Luke tried again. 'Then you can come. But let me go first.'

Damian looked at Luke but he didn't see him.

Zoe was standing next to her brother. She frowned.

'You forget yourself, Luke,' she said quietly. 'If my brother wishes to approach the horse, he will do so.'

Luke shook his head and, with infinite care, climbed into the paddock. But Damian had heard his sister and, a moment later, vaulted the fence to land heavily beside him.

Luke spun round.

One of us will now die.

The horse screamed as it reared, pawing the air with its hooves. Luke backed away, not taking his eyes off it. One step. Two steps. Slowly.

Damian stood where he was, his body rigid with horror.

The stallion swung its neck violently to the left, to the right. Its eyes shone with madness and foam ringed its nostrils. Then it lowered its great head. Its hooves raked the ground, dust rising around it.

It's going to charge. Sweet Jesus, it's going to charge.

Luke turned to Damian. His voice was low, urgent. 'Damian, get out of the ring. Get out of the ring now!'

Still Damian stood his ground, hypnotised.

But it was too late. The stallion, centuries of destrier blood pumping through its veins, did what its instinct dictated. It charged.

For Luke, what happened next stretched out to eternity. In slow motion he dived towards Damian, landing heavily behind him. He rolled on to his side, trying to drag the boy with him but it was too late. The stallion's hooves were on top of Damian, trampling him into the ground.

Damian screamed as the hooves hit his legs, his arms, his body.

He must die. He must surely die.

Four grooms had come running to the ring and launched themselves at the horse. One of them threw a rope around its neck while the others managed to hobble its forelegs. Eventually the stallion was wrestled to the ground.

Silence.

Luke peered through the settling dust. Damian lay face up in the paddock, the red earth around him pooling into a deeper red. He lay absolutely still.

Oh my God.

CHAPTER TWO

THE CITY OF MISTRA, SPRING 1392

The darkness in the hole was complete and heavy, clinging to the little girl like a thing from hell. She felt it all around her, closing in with its searching tentacles, clawing its way into her soul with its foul presence. It stroked her hair and sent shivers up her spine with its reeking breath. It moaned with ghastly insistence, rising to a shrill scream when it felt itself denied.

Never before had she felt such fear.

She was curled into a little ball, her head sheltered beneath her hands in supplication to a God she knew had abandoned her for her disobedience.

I swear by my brother's life I will never again disobey my mother. Let me see the morning and I will be good. I swear it.

The next morning seemed an impossibility. It felt like hours since that awful crash outside had told her that the storm had brought a branch down at the entrance to her hiding place. At first she'd tried to push it away, using all the weight of her seven-year-old body. But as it had refused to budge, she'd felt the first surges of panic rise up in her, quickening her heartbeat to a tempo that seemed to convulse her whole being.

Help. Help me. Help me. Help me.

But the panic had taken her voice. And the noise of the storm outside, as it ebbed and surged through the roots of the giant tree, drowned any tiny sound she could muster.

Please Father Jesus make Alexis come. I will never be bad again. I swear on his life.

To swear on her brother's life was to promise a lot. There was no one more worshipped in Anna's world than her only brother, three years her senior and idolatrously close to her God. But her brother didn't know of this hiding place. One of the few secrets she kept from him was this little cave she'd found amidst the roots of the oak that grew in the corner of the Peribleptos Monastery walls. And she hadn't told him for the very good reason that it provided the perfect hiding place in their games. Not even the monks who taught them knew about it.

Now she wished, with all her heart, that he knew of this place.

What was that noise?

She had heard a scratching noise. She was sure of it. It came from the entrance. It was closer than the storm. It came again.

They are coming for me.

She turned away from the sound and began to tear at the earth, clawing great handfuls from the blackness in front of her to escape whatever was coming. Dirt flew into her hair, her eyes, her mouth, engulfing her as she scrambled to get away.

Father Jesus, Alexis, Mother Mary . . . help me, help me, help me.

Then she felt air.

Miraculously, her fingers were free and she felt air on her palms.

Freedom!

She threw every last ounce of effort into widening the hole

she'd created. She brought her other arm up and pulled aside the earth and grass to make the smallest of windows. She hoisted herself up and looked into the night, lifting her nose to breathe in the scent of pine.

Then she screamed.

Two eyes, yellow and beyond evil, were staring into hers.

Anna shivered. The night was warm but the memory of that night was still vivid. She'd managed to block it for so many years and it was only in these days of terrible suspense, as the Ottoman army bore down on her city, that it had risen unbidden from the depths of her unconscious.

Had she kept her promise to God? No, she could not claim that. Had she obeyed her mother without question from that moment onward? Assuredly not.

But then had her crime been so terrible? All she had wanted was to see the Despot and his new Despoena, Bartolomea.

But her mother had forbidden her. She'd taken her hand and led her past the honey cakes, plums and spiced chestnuts, past the partridge and quail in saffron with fried mushrooms, past hares baked in wine and grey mullet from Rhegis, past everything that Bartolomea would eat without her.

Once in bed, she'd determined that she would see the new Despoena, whatever it took, and she'd climbed out of her window and on to the branches of an apple tree.

But just as Bartolomea's delicate toe emerged from her litter, the branch had snapped and Anna had fallen on to a clothes line from which hung some of her mother's finest dresses.

So Anna had run away to the one place she knew she would not be found.

Now, eight years on, it was night again and a new fear was

all around her. Anna was standing on the balcony of her house in the city of Mistra, looking out over the Vale of Sparta where the lights of countless campfires studded the darkness like fireflies and the conversation of fifty thousand Turks drifted up the hill in a single whisper.

Around her, filling the streets, squares, balconies and battlements of their small city, stood people looking on in silent vigil.

Anna felt a presence behind her.

Her brother was watching her. 'Are you frightened?' he asked quietly.

Anna turned to look at him. She smiled. 'Do you remember when you found me, all those years past, wandering outside the city walls in my nightdress?'

Alexis nodded.

'Do you remember I said then that I couldn't remember what happened to me that night?'

Her brother nodded again.

'Well, I've remembered.'

She turned back to look over the valley, and Alexis moved to stand next to her at the balustrade. Below them, far out on the plain, a deep drum had begun to beat. Then the squeak of heavy wheels could be heard between its thumps, and from among the campfires emerged horsemen holding torches aloft. Behind them rolled the engines of destruction: trebuchets, mangonels and tall, multi-tiered platforms with dripping hides hung from their sides. Anna had never seen such monsters.

'And this is more terrifying?'

'No,' she replied. 'You see, this I understand. The Turks want our empire because it's the last fortress to defend Christendom. Once they have it, then they can conquer the rest of the world.'

Alexis took his sister in his arms. 'Anna, all that is left of the Empire is Constantinople and our little despotate. That's all there is. We just have to hold them off long enough for the armies of Christendom to gather and drive them back.'

Anna shivered. She pressed her cheek against the hard buttons that ran up the front of his tunic. 'Will I go into the Sultan's harem?' she asked.

Alexis laughed. 'No, the Turks don't enslave the well born, and our family is the most honourable in the despotate. You'll be safe, I promise you.'

But eight years ago Anna had made a promise to God and not kept her faith.

'Will Emperor Manuel in Constantinople not come to our aid?' she asked.

'The Emperor has no money,' Alexis replied. 'No emperor has had any money since the Franks pillaged Constantinople two hundred years ago.'

'But surely Mistra has money?' asked Anna.

'Yes,' said Alexis, 'we're rich. But not rich enough.'

'What about Monemvasia?' pursued Anna. 'You're always telling me that the Mamonases are one of the richest families in the world. Surely the Archon will come to our aid?'

Alexis turned to look up the hill, to the very top where the citadel's bulk was silhouetted by a giant beacon blazing from its tallest tower.

'That beacon was lit a week ago,' he said. 'It's fifty miles to Monemvasia and there are beacons on every hill between. They'll have seen the signal for days now but still we've had no word.'

Brother and sister were silent for a long while. The siege engines had stopped in front of the campfires and, if anything, seemed more menacing in silhouette. Great boulders would be hurled from the trebuchets tomorrow, boulders that would make short work of the city's walls.

But did the Turks have cannon? Anna's father, Simon Laskaris, was Protostrator of Mistra, second only in rank to the Despot. He had been urging Theodore for years now to invest in these new machines that used some form of igniting powder to hurl a stone. Indeed, a Hungarian had presented himself at the court only three years past, ready to sell this new technology. But the Despot had merely laughed and waved the man away. He'd rather use the money for new churches.

Anna said, 'So Bayezid means to conquer the world?'

Her brother nodded. 'This Sultan is far more warlike than his father. He has boasted that he will water his horse at the altar of St Peter's in Rome. '

Anna shuddered at the thought of such desecration. Rome might be the seat of a Catholic Pope but he was still a Christian.

Just then a light gust of wind lifted the cooking of a thousand campfires.

'Come, Anna,' Alexis said. 'We're in God's hands now. Let's go inside and see what our mother has for us to eat.'

Anna did sleep that night. So quiet and well disciplined was the Ottoman host that only the neighs of their horses and the sound of mallet on tent peg disturbed the rest of those citizens of Mistra that lay abed.

When dawn came, it was as if a city of tents had risen from the ground in the night. The people of Mistra, emerging sleepily from their bedrooms, wondered at the sight before them. Even the cats were silent.

This was order indeed. For as far as the eye could see there were row upon row of tents, with streets and squares laid out between them and corrals for the horses on the banks of the Evrotas River. At their centre stood a gigantic pavilion, made up of silks of every colour imaginable. It had gardens around it with rows of fruit trees in tubs and caged birds suspended from their branches and neat lawns on either side with borders of tulips gently swaying in the dawn breeze.

Ten minutes later, the Protostrator Simon Laskaris and his daughter were hurrying up the streets on their way to the citadel. The streets were full of jostling crowds anxious for news or simply there to fill amphorae with the water they'd need for the siege. Simon was pleased to see that the praetors, whom he'd ordered be armed the night before, were keeping some sort of order in the queues for the wellheads. The city's population was already swelled to triple its normal size by the influx of refugees from the countryside.

When she'd heard that her father wanted her to accompany him to meet the Despot, Anna had guessed that he wanted her with him to amuse the Despoena while the men talked. In fact he'd been so impressed by her calm at dinner on the previous evening that he wanted her with him as an example to the city.

And it seemed to be working. People stopped to bow to the Protostrator and stare at the girl striding behind him. They were used to seeing Anna chasing her brother through the streets with a catapult. They knew her as a tomboy, with mud on her knees, the women secretly worrying for the day they knew she would be forced to make some illustrious marriage.

But here she was dressed as a woman.

Anna Laskaris had Norman blood in her veins and it showed

31

in the cascade of hair, soft and red as fox fur, that fell to her waist and in the two malachite eyes that stared out on the world from a face traced with the lightest patina of freckles. Dressed in a chemise of the finest white lawn and with the plaits of her hair braided with flowers, she radiated calm.

They arrived at the citadel to find the Despot already dressed in armour, his breastplate burnished to a perfect sheen. With him was the Despoena Bartolomea, who hurried over to greet them. 'Anna, you look ravishing! How many soldiers did you distract from their important work on your way up? Come, let's go and feed my marmoset and you can tell me how things are. That man' – she nodded in the direction of her husband – 'tells me nothing.'

The Despot, however, was not to be cheered by the sight of Anna. When the women left, he was still arguing with a Frankish knight over a scroll that lay on the table between them. Eventually, the Despot ripped it in two, handing one half to the knight who bowed stiffly and left.

'Normans!' said Theodore. 'They can't write and they won't do anything unless you pay them.' He looked down. 'Get up, Simon. I can't talk to you down there.'

Laskaris rose from his knee.

'It's their way of sealing a contract,' said the Despot, pulling a chair to the table. 'You put your mark on the paper and then tear it in two. They claim their money when we join the two bits later. Ingenious. Wine?'

The Protostator took the goblet.

'Sweet wine from Mount Ganos.' The Despot raised his glass and drained it in a gulp. He wiped his beard and looked suddenly at his friend. 'Do we still have Mount Ganos, Simon?' he asked.

'I fear not, Majesty. Most of Thrace belongs to Bayezid now.'

The Despot sighed. 'Well at least we'll still have the Malvasia, assuming those Mamonas pirates haven't sold the last barrel to the Sultan. Did you know they sell it to the Sultan?'

'I had heard something,' murmured the Protostrator, sipping his wine.

'Horses too, I gather,' went on the Despot. 'Since the Turk took Adrianopolis for his capital and renamed it Edirne, they've been doing regular business there. The Sultan wants to build up his cavalry and Mamonas has access to Outremer stock. Apparently they're fast and fierce. Destriers that bite their way into battle.' He paused. 'Anyway, we can't afford them any more than we can cannon. Let's go outside and see what's going on.'

The Despot took the arm of his Protostrator and led him from the chamber, up the winding steps and out on to the top of the tower.

The Vale of Sparta stretched out before them in miniature. Simon Laskaris had woken every morning of his forty-eight years to the reassuring sight of that huge plain with its farms, orchards, vineyards, olive groves and the bright ribbon of the Evrotas River winding its way through it all. It was a world of green, ordered prosperity, a world in balance, a world worth fighting for.

Now he saw smoke rising across the plain. Closer to, he saw the tanneries and storehouses alight and tiny Turkish soldiers running to set fire to houses in the Albanian and Jewish quarters.

'St Demetrius,' said the Despot suddenly.

'Majesty?'

'He's our patron saint, isn't he? Have we done enough praying to him, do you think, Simon? Should I organise a procession or something?'

'Highness, he was also patron saint of Thessaloniki.'

Theodore considered this, stroking his long beard. Thessaloniki, north of the Peloponnese, had fallen five years ago. He looked down at the square in front of the palace below. It was a place he'd wanted to be the new Athens, a place where children would sit at the feet of philosophers and learn of reason. It was a place he loved.

'The Turks are a very conservative people,' he said. 'Their religion leaves very little room for doubt. They won't keep our square.'

'No, lord,' agreed the Protostrator. 'And the cathedral will become a mosque.'

Both men were silent for a while, each contemplating what this future held for them.

'Well, no time for conjecture, Simon. What do we do?'

The Protostrator turned back to the plain and pointed at the gigantic pavilion in the centre of the camp. 'Two Horsehairs, Majesty,' he said. 'Which means that someone other than the Sultan is leading this army.'

In the little square of beaten earth outside the entrance to the pavilion stood a single lance driven into the ground. At its top, moving gently in the breeze, were two horse-tails.

'The Grand Vizier, do you think?'

'No, I hear he is in Serres with his master. I think we may have one of Bayezid's sons before us. Perhaps the eldest, Suelyman.'

'Is that good or bad?'

Laskaris shrugged. 'It is the janissaries who will decide the battle,' he said. 'Look at them! Have you seen such a sight?'

They both looked down at the gardens before the pavilion where groups of men with tall white hats, each sprouting an extravagant plume, stood talking to each other. They seemed in no hurry to begin anything.

'Why should we fear them?' said the Despot. 'They look like peacocks.'

'Peacocks perhaps,' said the Protostrator, 'but also machines of war. The Sultan's father came up with the idea and it's ingenious. Every four years they send their men into the villages of Rumelia and take Christian boys aged between eight and fifteen from their families. They indoctrinate them in Islam and train them for war. They call it the *Devshirme*.'

'But they're slaves!' protested the Despot.

'Indeed, lord. But never were there prouder slaves. Look at them. They're the best. An élite fighting force that doesn't know fear.'

'And what do we have? Two thousand demoralised Albanian mercenaries and a handful of greedy Norman knights.' He glanced at the Protostrator. 'We need Varangians. That's what we need. And their gold which, apparently, is buried here somewhere.' Theodore sighed. 'But it's no more than legend,' he said miserably. 'There are four Varangians in the service of Mamonas, but they won't fight for us.'

'It's not they who won't fight, but their archon,' said Laskaris. 'We'll have to bind Pavlos Mamonas to our cause if we are ever to get these Turks off our plain. We need him.'

The Despot nodded gloomily. 'As always, Simon, you're right. My brother the Emperor sees it the same way. He's sent gold to bribe the bastards since they won't be shamed into helping us. But I can't see how we can get the message to Monemvasia. We're surrounded. If only we had cannon.'

The Protostrator was about to reply when there was a distraction from the plain below. A warehouse had exploded and tiny, burning Turks were running towards the river.

Anna was at the top of the staircase, holding her breath. Having got bored of the marmoset, she had come to find her father and had overheard most of the conversation. She coughed.

'Anna!' cried Theodore. 'What a sight you are! Simon, we should put her image on every banner in the city. It will remind us what we're fighting for.'

Anna stepped forward to be kissed. But she wasn't really concentrating. A very daring idea was taking shape in her fifteen-year-old mind.

Five minutes later, Anna was running back to her house as fast as the crowds would allow. The Laskaris house, one of the largest in Mistra, was situated in the lower town within its own walled garden and orchard. It was about as far from the citadel as any house could be.

At last she stood, panting, in front of the tall gates with the heavy coat of arms above the archway, listening for any signs of life. There was none. It seemed that her mother had taken the servants up to the palace for safety.

She climbed the broad stone steps to the front door and pushed it open. The triclinium was empty of all furniture and tapestries and her short breaths came back to her as echoes. The vivid wall scenes from Greek mythology seemed gaudy without the divans from which her mother's aristocratic friends would swap court gossip. And without the rich carpets, the marble floor felt cold beneath the soles of her shoes. All that remained was a solitary prie-dieu and the hollow sound of the fountain that played in an alcove at the other end of the room.

Through the tall, curtainless windows she could see the houses of her beloved city climbing the hill to escape the Turk. She felt emboldened.

I can save this city.

She straightened, clenched her fists and ran up the staircase to her room, pulling off the chemise as she went. After frantic searching, she found riding breeches and some stout leather boots. She pulled them on with one hand while tearing the flowers from her hair with the other. She ran to her brother's room and found a doublet and the riding hat he sometimes wore. Finding a mirror, she looked into it and smiled.

From girl to boy. From Mistra to Monemvasia. Now I need courage.

At the gates of the Peribleptos monastery, Anna flattened herself against the wall, nervously peering around it to see if her way was clear. A monk was hurriedly pulling plants from the little herb garden to make potions for the wounded. At the smithy beyond, two more were hammering swords into shape before plunging them into a cauldron of water while another carried blocks of ice from the underground ice house to keep it freezing. The buildings stood hard against the city walls and, looking up, Anna could see soldiers on the ramparts clearing the machicolations of weeds so that boiling water could be poured on to the heads of the attackers. From the kitchens behind the scriptorium came the smell of baking bread, and a cart stood at its door waiting to take it to the city's storehouses.

Then she saw it.

The old oak tree stood in the corner made by the city wall and the refectory. This was the first time she'd seen it since that night and it sent a shock of fear coursing through her body.

I have to do this. I'm the only one who can.

She drew a deep breath and half ran, half crawled along the walls until she was lying facing the tree. Fighting down her panic, she parted its roots and slipped inside.

Immediately she felt terror. She was inside the hole and there was no turning back. All the horrors of that night came back to her. The blood was pounding in her temples and she felt faint. She was shaking uncontrollably.

Sweet Virgin Mary, help me.

But she couldn't move; her limbs were paralysed.

It's just a hole.

She managed to reach out an arm, feeling for the earth in front of her, praying that it was still loose.

There it was. Softer to the touch. Easily moved.

Her fingers scrabbled their way through, pulling it into the hole until she could see daylight beyond.

Freedom.

The opening grew wider and soon was big enough for her to crawl through. Stretching her body, she used all her strength to wriggle her way up and out and collapsed, exhausted, on the grass. The smell of pine and wild garlic smelt better than any meal. It was the smell of the forest, of deliverance, of a fear conquered. Gradually her senses cleared. She needed to think. She needed to be careful.

She rolled over on to her front and looked up at the ramparts. No sign of the soldiers. She looked down the hill towards the plain. No Turks as yet. They'd yet to surround the city after all.

Finally she looked into the forest that climbed the slope outside the city walls. All was quiet.

Bringing her fingers to her lips, she let out a low whistle. There was a pause and then she heard an answering neigh.

Anna allowed herself the briefest of smiles. All was going to plan. Looking once more up to the ramparts to check that she hadn't been seen, she crawled on to the edge of the trees and then rolled forward into a ditch that would hide her from view while she collected her thoughts.

To travel the fifty miles to Monemvasia, she would first have to climb the hill, then drop down the other side into the deep valley between Mistra and the slopes of Mount Taygetos. She knew that she could pick up a path there that wound round the back until it joined the Monemvasia road some three miles further on.

But where are the Turks?

Anna picked herself up, brushing the pine needles from her brother's doublet, and whistled again. Again came the reply.

She pushed her way through the branches of the trees until she came to a small clearing where a ruined hut stood, its broken beams pointing up to the sky like teeth. Stones lay in a jumble all around it and, amongst them, a tethered pony patiently cropped the grass, its tail languidly swishing flies.

Pallas.

Anna smiled. She'd had Pallas since birth and he was old now but he'd have to make one final effort today. If he got her there, she would give him the most comfortable berth in Monemvasia.

She went over to the pony and stroked his neck, untying him and leading him through the trees to the path beyond. When they reached it, she stopped, looked around and listened, shushing Pallas, who had begun to eat noisily again. She could hear nothing but the sounds of the forest and the occasional birdcall echoing through the trees. They were alone.

Slowly and carefully, she got on to the pony and was pleased to see that he could still take her weight. She urged him into a slow trot, her feet barely clearing the ground, her back jarring against his unsaddled back. She climbed the path, moving deeper into the forest. A red butterfly danced before her in dust that floated in a shaft of sunlight and Pallas gave a familiar snort of satisfaction. Anna began to feel safer.

At the top of the hill, the path plunged deep into the valley and then veered sharply eastwards, the trees gradually clearing to reveal the sheer sides of rock that backed the hill of Mistra to her right. The citadel, with its beacon still burning, was just visible at the top.

On her left, the forests of Mount Taygetos gave way to scree on its upper slopes. She looked further up to the snowline that never melted, even in summer, and then beyond to the distant peak soaring into the clouds. Anna remembered playing with Alexis on those slopes when they were young and she closed her eyes as the sun reappeared from behind a cloud and bathed her in new warmth.

Then she heard it.

The unmistakable twang of a bowstring and the sound of an arrow in flight. A heartbeat later, it was embedded in a tree inches from Pallas's head.

The pony stopped suddenly and Anna was flung across his neck. She looked up, her heart racing, and saw a flash of horse and rider between the trees to her left. She saw rich colour: silk with mail. Not Greek. Not Norman.

The sunlight was blinding her and she shielded her eyes. There was nothing there.

The crack of a branch and a mocking laugh told her that the danger was now on her right. Another arrow hit the tree behind her as she tried to wheel Pallas to see her assailant.

40

'Who are you?' she called, angry at the fear in her voice. 'I'm not alone. There are soldiers behind me!'

Again came the laugh and a third arrow thudded into the ground beside her, causing the pony to rear. Anna was thrown from his back and landed heavily on the ground, hitting her head hard. All went black.

A moment later, she came to and heard the rustle of mail as someone dismounted very close to where she was lying. She opened her eyes but they had dust in them and she couldn't see properly. She wiped it away with her hand and looked up at the figure bent over her.

Two yellow eyes stared into hers.

In the square in front of the palace, the Despot and his Protostator sat on the wall and looked out over the plain.

The sun was at its zenith and, although a breeze had arisen, both felt uncomfortably hot in their armour. They had taken the precaution of sitting in the shade of one of the fruit trees which lined the square and, in better times, might have provided the headrest for some sleeping philosopher. Simon Laskaris could feel the sweat coursing down his back. He wasn't used to wearing armour.

The Ottoman army had at last deployed, in one expert movement of dust and silence, into a vast crescent behind the siege engines. In the centre stood the massed ranks of the *bashibozouk* irregulars, who would rush forward to die in their thousands against the city walls, the cry of 'Allahu Akhbar' on their lips and a vision of black-eyed houris before their eyes. Behind them, in perfect order, stood the ranks of the janissary regiments, each with its standard and its aura of invincibility. On either wing of the crescent stood the *sipahi* cavalry dressed in their skins with their bows resting on their saddles, great quivers of arrows slung by their sides.

The only sounds that came from this army of fifty thousand were the snap of banner and the jangle of harness.

Simon Laskaris mopped his forehead. The cloth smelt of his wife and he breathed in its fragrance. He wondered where his daughter had disappeared to. He moved his gaze to the soldiers on the battlements. Would they really die for a city that wasn't even theirs? Probably not.

Theodore seemed to read his thoughts. 'Will they fight?'

'Yes,' he answered. 'With you amongst them, lord, they'll fight.'

The Despot sighed. 'And when I retire to the citadel, Simon? Will they fight then, do you think?'

The Protostator leant forward. 'We've discussed this many times, lord. Your duty to your people is to survive to rebuild this city once the Turks have gone. This is probably just a raid. They'll ransack the lower town and then leave.'

'Where are your family?' asked the Despot. 'Are they safe in the citadel?'

'I hope so, lord. Except Alexis. That's him now.'

Running up the steps to the square came his son. He was dressed in full armour but his head was bare.

How young he looks.

The boy dropped to one knee. 'Majesty, I have news from the Turks,' he said between pants.

Theodore lifted him to his feet. 'Nothing that won't wait for you to recover your breath, Alexis. Sit down and drink some water.'

Alexis sat on the wall and drained the water brought to him in one gulp. He ran his hands through his hair and flicked away the sweat. 'Thank you, Majesty. It's a steep climb.'

'Yes, Alexis. Steep for us, steep for the Turk. Now, what do they say?'

Alexis pointed up at the flag that flew from the palace tower. 'Their message is this, lord. If, by lowering our standard, you signify the surrender of Mistra and your vassalage to the Sultan Bayezid, then the city will be spared.'

'And if we choose not to?' asked the Despot.

'Then the city will be taken and all will be put to the sword.'

Theodore was silent for a long time, stroking his beard.

'How old are you, Alexis?' he asked at last.

'Eighteen, lord. Nearly nineteen.'

The Despot smiled and considered the person who came closest in the world to being his own son. God had not granted him and the Despoena the blessing of children.

'And how would you feel if you knew that those eighteen . . . no, nineteen years were the last of this thousand-year empire?'

Alexis glanced at his father, who was standing next to them listening. Then he looked straight into the eyes of his ruler. 'We must fight, Majesty. We have our walls, we have our valour and, above all, we have our God. We can win.'

'And our citadel, Alexis,' added Theodore. 'Don't forget the citadel,'

'Indeed, lord. And it cannot be taken. The ground is too steep for their engines. Even if they succeed in taking the lower town, we will attack them from above.'

Theodore templed his hands and brought them to his mouth. 'Who commands their army?' he asked.

'We're not sure, sire. Some say it is Suleyman, eldest son to the Sultan. But no one has seen him.'

The Despot pondered this. 'Tell the heralds to say this to

Prince Suleyman, if indeed it is he: that Christian Mistra will remain Christian. Tell him that Mistra will stand.'

Alexis sprang to his feet, delight creased into every corner of his face.

'Oh, and another thing, Alexis,' said the Despot. 'I want you to carry the message yourself. You will be herald.'

'But, Majesty, you know that the herald does not fight. I—'

Simon Laskaris had stepped forward. 'You will do as the Despot has ordered, Alexis,' he said quietly.

The boy looked from one to the other of them, opening and closing his mouth. Then he frowned, picked up his helmet and saluted. He began to turn but stopped in front of his father.

'Goodbye, Father,' he said simply, embracing Simon Laskaris with all the strength he possessed.

Then he was gone.

Theodore glanced up at his oldest friend, still standing looking after his son. 'Yes, Simon,' he said quietly. 'Mistra will stand. God help us.'

Soon afterwards, Alexis was cantering towards the Ottoman army. He delivered the message with as much flourish as he could muster and then wheeled his horse around and trotted back to the city walls. He felt the gaze of twenty thousand citizens on him as he rode. What would they say when they knew of their despot's decision?

Alexis was angry to be left out of the fighting. Heralds were expected to sit out the battle so as to be there to acknowledge the victor. Now flies were buzzing around his horse's head and the heat was searing. He hated this inaction. He hated the silence before the first rock was launched at the walls above him, before the scream of 'Allahu Akbar' set the bashibozouks in motion. And, most of all, he hated the fact that he'd have to ride to one side and do nothing to stop them.

Then he heard something. Not a rock in flight but the sound of many men in voiceless movement. The bashibozouks to his front were opening their ranks to let someone through.

Alexis could see a spiral of dust far behind them moving towards the front of the army. There was a single rider approaching.

He strained his eyes to see better, leaning forward in his saddle and shielding them with his hand. He was nearly blinded with sweat.

The rider came closer, his mail catching the sun through gaps in the dust cloud and his harness clanking to the heavy rhythm of his hooves.

Now the bashibozouks were bowing as he passed through them and suddenly the rider had broken through their front rank and his ebony black mare was performing a practised rear. The dust settled around him and all was still again.

Alexis gasped. He could not believe what he was seeing. There, perhaps four hundred paces to his front, was the most magnificent warrior he had ever seen. He was clad from head to toe in shimmering gold mail. Even the tall, spiked dome of his helmet was gold. Whether or not he wore a breastplate, Alexis couldn't see. For, seated in front of him on the horse, was his sister Anna.

She seemed to be dressed in his doublet, and his riding hat sat crookedly on her disordered hair. She was covered in dust and stared miserably at the ground. The warrior's arm held her firmly to his front and his shoulders above were rising and falling. He was laughing.

Then, in fluent Greek, he addressed the city walls. 'People of Mistra! I have here one of your prettier citizens!'

Anna struggled against his arm but he tightened his hold.

'I found her outside the city walls, trying to get help from Monemvasia, I believe.' He paused while his mare wheeled. The extra passenger was making it skittish. 'I am Prince Suleyman,' he continued, his voice rising. 'Eldest son to Bayezid, whom some call Yildirim.'

The city held its breath.

'I have an army of fifty thousand on this plain and siege engines which will demolish your city within minutes. Your despot says you will stand against us. But will you stand and watch this beautiful hostage die?'

The first sound, then, came from the city. It was a low murmur of anguish and fear that rippled across it like rain.

On the palace square, the Protostrator had fallen to his knees, his head in his hands. The Despot was no longer with him, having taken up a position on the city walls. Then Simon stood, helped to his feet by two of the Guard. If his daughter was to die, then he wanted one last look at her.

But Anna had no intention of dying.

With all her strength, she drove her heels into the flanks of the mare, which started just enough for Suleyman to release his grip. In one fluid movement, she threw her leg over the horse's neck and vaulted to the ground.

Then she began to run as fast as she could towards the city walls.

At the same moment, her brother snapped out of his shock and spurred his horse towards her, urging it forward with every muscle in his body.

The city held its breath and watched as brother and sister

raced towards each other, the ground between them closing with unnatural slowness.

Suleyman had by now reined in his mare and, for a brief moment, looked in amazement at the scene taking place before his eyes. Then he dug his spurs into the sides of his horse and it sprang forward after the girl.

The two riders reached her almost simultaneously, both pulling their mounts to a stop in a cloud of dust either side of Anna.

'Who are you?' Suleyman demanded of Alexis, his hand resting on the jewelled pommel of his sword.

'I am her brother,' shouted Alexis over his sister. 'And you'll have to kill me first before you touch a hair on her head!'

Sipahi cavalry were closing in on the scene and Suleyman raised his hand to halt them.

'I'm sure that can be arranged. Don't you feel a touch outnumbered?'

Alexis shot him a furious glance. 'And don't you feel a touch ashamed, terrorising a girl of fifteen?'

Suleyman glanced down at Anna. 'Fifteen? I had hoped for older. No matter, she will grow.' He looked back at Alexis. 'I'm sorry, I don't know your name.'

Anna stepped forward. She had her brother's cap in her hand. 'Alexis,' she said. 'Alexis Laskaris and he is twice the man of you.'

Suleyman smiled. 'Laskaris?' he asked. 'Laskaris, as in the Protostrator Laskaris?'

Sister and brother exchanged glances.

'So,' said Suleyman softly, 'it seems I have two valuable hostages for the price of one. What good fortune!' He turned to Alexis. 'Can you tell me why your city is so stubborn, Alexis Laskaris? You know you can't win.'

But it was Anna who answered again. She was standing with her legs apart and her hands on her hips. There was colour beneath the freckles of her face, colour to match her hair.

'You are right. You can take our lower town,' she said. 'But you will never take the citadel. Look at it!' She pointed above the city walls. 'It's impregnable! And it has cannon.'

'Cannon—?'

But Anna hadn't finished. 'What would Yildirim say if you were to return with only half your army?'

Suleyman snorted. 'I can lay waste your lower town and not bother with your citadel.'

'And where is the honour in that?' she asked. 'Is that what Saladin would have done?'

There was a long pause. Then Suleyman threw back his head and laughed. 'Saladin!' he cried. 'Very good. But he was Egyptian and I am a Turk.' He studied Anna for a tense moment. He looked at the bustle of red hair, the wide, defiant eyes, the set jaw and the fifteen-year-old body poised to burst into its full blaze of beauty. He would like to see that.

He smiled. 'You are an extraordinary girl,' he said, bowing from the saddle.

And then he turned his horse and cantered away.

Simon Laskaris had watched all this with a mounting sense of foreboding. It seemed that both of his children were now to be taken hostage and he cursed himself for allowing Alexis outside the city walls. But something unexpected was going on in the plain below. Instead of seizing his children, Suleyman appeared to be conversing with them – and Anna was doing much of the talking.

Then, to his astonishment, he saw Suleyman ride back to his

lines, only slowing to issue a command to the sipahis that had ridden out to escort him. And, miracle upon miracles, the whole Ottoman army turned around and began to march back to its tents, the siege engines rumbling slowly behind them.

It seemed to the Protostrator that a tiny wind had risen across the hillside of Mistra as twenty thousand breaths were released below him and a city's population looked down at its children and saw a future before them. Then, little by little, the wind rose to a roar, a roar of such jubilation that it seemed the very stones of the houses might be lifted from their mortar.

The city of Mistra was saved.

And out there on the plain below stood its saviours, hand in hand.

CHAPTER THREE

MONEMVASIA, SPRING 1392

Luke had never been inside the Mamonas Palace. In all the years he'd passed under its imposing gateway to meet Damian and Zoe, he'd not once been invited inside.

But he didn't mind. The courtyards, with their fountains and gardens, were cool after the climb and anything that delayed an encounter with the twins was a blessing. The gardeners, too, were always good for gossip and reliable in gauging the mood of their young master and mistress.

But today he would enter the palace and he was not looking forward to it.

Luke and his father Joseph stood together in the entrance hall and waited in silence. Conversation between the two had been difficult since Luke had come home two days before to recount what had happened at the stud. His father didn't know what to say to his son. He entirely accepted Luke's version of events but he also knew the Archon. The wait for news from the palace had been nerve-racking. Was Damian maimed for life?

Other worries had kept Luke awake over the past two nights: the beautiful stallion for one. Despite its wildness, the horse had sparked something inside Luke and he longed to see it again. But had they let it live? And then there was Zoe. She'd come to him once Damian had been lifted, screaming, on to the litter to bring him home. He remembered the conversation vividly.

'You could have stopped that.'

'What? Zoe, don't be ridiculous. You saw what happened.'

'I and no one else.' She'd paused. 'I want to know about the Varangian treasure.'

'You're blackmailing me?' He'd laughed then. It was too absurd. 'I told you, it's myth.'

And she'd shrugged and walked away.

Now he waited. To distract himself, Luke looked around. Sitting amongst spacious orchards on the Goulas of Monemvasia, the Mamonas Palace was of an opulence unmatched anywhere in the city. An enormous marble gateway led into a series of courtyards of Moorish design inspired by Pavlos Mamonas's visit to the Alhambra Palace in Spain. Central fountains played into pools in which lily pads gently floated. Gravel paths edged with fruit trees surrounded them, fronting borders full of flowers collected from the many countries in which the family sold its wine. Marble benches stood in the cool shade beneath the trees.

The entrance hall was circular and domed, with large, arched alcoves each holding an exquisite vessel of coloured Venetian glass. A shaft of light from an aperture at the apex of the dome threw their reds, blues, greens and yellows across the curved walls so that the room became a kaleidoscope of moving colour.

Both Joseph and Luke were staring up at the dome when the inner doors to the palace opened and a servant ushered them down a hall and into the audience chamber.

Joseph, unlike his son, had been in this room many times before. Huge frescoes covered every inch of its walls, telling the story of the life of Alexander in vivid colour. The room was rectangular and a narrow carpet ran the length of the marble floor to a dais, on which stood an ornate throne beneath a canopy bearing the Mamonas crest.

On the throne, dressed in a magnificent tunic of red brushed silk and surrounded by his Varangian Guards, sat the Archon. And while Joseph's fellow Guardsmen looked uncomfortable, Pavlos Mamonas just looked thunderous.

That his son wasn't dead seemed to Pavlos Mamonas a miracle. After the calamity, the Archon had ridden quickly to the stud with the family physician, who'd spent hours binding the boy's broken legs into splints while Zoe tried to distract him from the pain.

Pavlos's mood had darkened further when he'd returned to Monemvasia to find a messenger with the news that Mistra had not been taken. To his dismay he'd learnt that the city had, in fact, been saved by what seemed like the capricious whim of the Prince Suleyman, a man the Archon had thought he could trust.

Now before him stood someone he could vent his anger on. He looked at the boy and thought it inconceivable that he could not have prevented what had happened. And anyway, why had this Varangian been allowed to remain unscathed when his son lay in twisted agony upstairs?

'Your name?' he asked, as if he didn't know it well enough.

'Luke Magoris, lord,' he answered, looking his Archon straight in the eye.

I cannot be blamed for this.

Luke felt his father stiffen behind him, as if he'd read his thoughts. He looked at the three Varangians with their great axes sloped on their shoulders. None of them returned his glance.

52

'Luke Magoris,' went on the Archon, 'do you understand why you're here?'

Luke didn't reply.

The Archon looked beyond him to his father. 'Is the boy stupid, Magoris?' he asked.

'Lord . . .' began Joseph, but the Archon held up his hand.

'Please don't go on. I know he's not stupid. Otherwise he wouldn't be allowed near our horses. No, it seems he's just insolent.' Pavlos Mamonas rose from his chair and slowly walked down the steps to stand directly in front of him, his hands behind his back.

Luke returned his stare.

'Yes, insolent. Insolent and more concerned for his own skin than that of my son, who, it might be supposed, he was there to protect.' The Archon walked slowly around Luke, who stood rigidly still. 'My daughter Zoe,' he continued, 'tells me that, having provoked the horse to charge, you then threw my son in front of you to take the consequences. Is that true?'

Luke was stupefied, but forced himself to stay calm. 'No, lord. That's not what happened.'

The Archon stopped. 'You dare to call my daughter a liar?' His face was almost touching Luke's. 'After all you've done, will you now accuse my daughter of lying?'

Luke's mind was racing.

This is insane. Why is she doing this?

Mamonas's next words were barely audible to anyone but Luke and his father. 'Is my daughter a liar?' he whispered.

Luke didn't answer. The fear that had grown in him since entering the room was beginning to turn into anger. Then he felt a stinging pain. The Archon had slapped him hard across his cheek.

He heard a growl of protest behind him.

Mamonas turned on Joseph, challenge in his eyes. 'Magoris, don't make things worse for the boy.' Then he turned away, mounting the dais again and sitting on his throne in a hiss of silk. 'Send in my daughter.'

There was silence as the girl was found, a silence in which Luke looked directly into the eyes of the Archon. His body was trembling.

I must not lose my temper. I cannot win this. I must take what is given or my father will suffer too.

Then the door opened and Zoe walked in. She glanced at Luke and then went to stand beside her father, her hand resting on the back of the throne. If she felt either guilt or discomfort, she didn't show it.

'Daughter,' said the Archon, turning in his seat to address her, 'is it true that this boy, Luke Magoris, caused a young stallion to charge and trample your brother Damian?'

Zoe looked directly into Luke's eyes.

'Yes, Father. We arrived at the stud to see the new stallion but Arsenius cautioned us about approaching him. Luke told Damian that he would be safe if he stayed close to him. They climbed into the arena and Luke shouted at the horse when it wouldn't come to him.'

She paused. Then she said softly, 'The horse charged and Luke threw himself behind Damian, pushing him forward to take the horse's hooves.' She stopped. Her voice was low, halting. 'It was horrible.'

Luke could stand it no longer. *'That's not true!'* he shouted. 'I went into the ring alone. I told Damian not to follow me! She knows that's what happened!'

54

The Archon turned on him, spitting with rage. 'And Arsenius? Does he lie as well?'

'Arsenius wasn't there!'

'Silence!' roared Mamonas.

And silence fell, an awkward silence in which several people strove to control themselves, Luke more than any. He was bewildered and very angry. The three Varangians remained motionless, staring directly ahead of them.

Then Luke heard the Archon address him, his tone suddenly formal. A sentence was being passed.

'Luke Magoris, we find you guilty of the grossest neglect of your duty towards ourself and our children.'

Guilty? Guilty of what?

'We find that you recklessly allowed my son to come into contact with an animal likely to do him harm and then deliberately sought to protect yourself from the consequences by exposing him to further danger.'

What am I hearing?

'Your punishment will be as follows. It has always been the tradition that son follow father into my Varangian Guard, with all the privilege and status that goes with it. So it has been for generations. You, however, will not be permitted to do so. Neither I nor my son who, by the grace of God, will follow me, can count on your commitment to protect our persons.'

Luke's world crumbled around him. He felt faint. He heard his father gasp.

But the Archon was not finished. 'However, in view of your undoubted skill with horses, you will be permitted to continue as a groom in our household. Never again, though, will you ride out with any member of my family.' The Archon picked up some papers resting on the table beside him and began to read. 'You may go,' he said.

But Luke couldn't move. He felt his father prod him from behind. The Archon looked up.

'Leave!'

Luke found his voice, forcing himself to keep it steady. 'What about the horse?'

'The horse? What do I care about the horse? It almost killed my son!' shouted Mamonas.

'It was frightened. It cannot be blamed.'

His father took his arm. 'Enough, Luke,' he said quietly. 'This will not help.'

'It is the best horse you will ever own,' Luke went on, turning to face the Archon as his father tried to guide him from the room. 'And I can tame it.'

'You,' hissed the Archon, 'will leave now, unless you wish to be whipped. Magoris, take him away.'

Joseph felt the tension in Luke's arm. 'Luke . . .' he whispered.

Luke was still glaring at the Archon, rigid with fury. Then he blinked twice, glanced at Zoe and turned. His father led him from the room.

Pavlos Mamonas watched the door close behind them. Then he turned to the other Varangians. 'You may all leave!' he barked. 'And not just the room, leave the palace! I can't bear to have you all sulking around me. The boy deserved his fate.'

When they had gone, he looked up at Zoe, who was standing apart, watching him. 'Was that what really happened?' he asked eventually.

'More or less,' she murmured. 'Anyway, you've done the right thing.'

The Archon was silent for a while, wondering whether there was perhaps more to this. He knew his daughter better than himself. She *was* himself. Like him, she wanted everything in the world, especially those things she couldn't have. She'd grown up with Luke yet now she'd condemned him. Was there something more to this?

'Will you mind him no longer riding out with you?' he asked quietly.

'No, Father,' she replied. 'He was becoming tiresome. You did right to punish him.'

Pavlos studied his daughter. He knew that her fierce ambition had found its outlet in reckless promiscuity and a refusal to submit in marriage to any man. What a pity she would not inherit the Mamonas empire.

'What about the horse?' he asked.

She paused. 'He's probably right about that at least,' she replied. 'It's a magnificent beast and will fetch a high price. You should let him tame it. It's worth nothing to us dead.'

Her father nodded absently. 'They both need taming. Perhaps one will tame the other.'

Zoe laughed shortly. 'Yes,' she said. 'He should be tamed.' She paused and looked down at her hands. 'And Damian? He'll not be able to travel now.'

Damian was due to set off on a year of visits to the far-flung business interests of the Mamonas family. Now he couldn't walk.

Her father eyed her speculatively. 'What would you suggest, Zoe?'

'Send me. I'm more than competent.'

Pavlos Mamonas nodded slowly, the thinnest smile on his

lips. 'Yes. I'd thought of that. And knew you would have too. We will discuss it over dinner.'

Later, when they'd eaten and talked of business, they had a visitor. There was disturbance outside the room and the doors flew open. The Archon was so astonished by the sight of the man who entered that he forgot to bow.

It was the heir to the Ottoman throne.

Zoe had not even considered bowing. She wanted an uninterrupted view of this man she'd heard so much about. It was not the first time that he'd visited the palace but it was the first time that she'd set eyes on him.

The eyes that looked back into hers contained a mockery that men found disconcerting and Zoe intriguing. There was something depraved in the way they raked her body, lingering on her breasts for a period that would have insulted most women. Then a smile spread across his lips as she held his gaze. His skin was dark and unmarked, his nose hooked and prominent and his short black beard oiled to a perfect point beneath his chin. He was more attractive than any man Zoe had ever seen.

'Well, well,' he murmured as he walked towards her. 'Pavlos, you never told me your riches extended to such a beautiful daughter.' He bowed extravagantly, sweeping his cloak over his shoulder and kissing Zoe's hand, his tongue darting out to make secret contact with her skin. Zoe felt a shock run through her.

'Prince Suleyman, you are welcome,' her father said, bowing. 'My daughter Zoe.'

'Zoe, how charming,' said the Prince, his eyes not leaving her face. 'Are you married?'

'No, lord. Not even matched,' she replied. 'And you, sir, are you married or are all your pleasures to be found only in the harem?'

Suleyman smiled and turned to her father. 'What a girl! The second minx I've encountered in as many days! What on earth do you Greeks feed your daughters?'

The Archon raised an eyebrow. 'Second, lord?' he enquired.

Suleyman laughed. 'I'll explain everything, but first I need some of your delicious wine, Pavlos. My accursed religion prevents me from drinking with the army, so I must make up for lost time with you. Bring me some wine.'

Suleyman walked on to the dais and slumped into the Archon's throne, throwing his leg over an arm, taking the wine offered him. He drank it in one gulp and stretched out his arm for more.

He wiped his mouth with the back of his arm and glanced at Zoe. 'Does she—?' he began before the Archon cut him off.

'My family has no secrets, lord,' said the Archon smoothly. 'You may speak freely.'

'Ah, good. Well, you may know that Mistra was not taken?'

'I had heard as much,' said the Archon, with no trace of emotion in his voice.

'Yes, well, I know we had an agreement, but we may have to approach things differently.'

'Differently, lord?' enquired the Archon.

'Yes, differently, Pavlos. You understand what differently means?' Irritation was creeping into Suleyman's voice. 'It means that situations change and we must change our plans to suit them.'

'What has changed, lord?' asked Mamonas evenly.

'Well, for one thing, their citadel is impregnable,' the Prince said shortly. 'And for another, they have cannon.'

Now it was the Archon's turn to laugh. 'Cannon, my lord? Who told you that?'

'The daughter of the Protostrator. I captured her outside the city. Her name is Anna Laskaris.'

The Archon seemed to consider this. He had to be careful. 'They have no cannon, lord,' he said. 'They barely have enough arrows to shoot a dozen volleys at your army. The girl lied to you.'

Suleyman jumped to his feet, his glass shattering on the marble floor. He grabbed the Archon by his tunic. His face was red with rage. 'Mamonas, you go too far,' he breathed through clenched teeth. 'If my judgement tells me we cannot take Mistra then who are you to question it?'

Zoe stepped forward. She placed her hand on the Prince's sleeve and he turned to look at her. She was very calm. 'No one questions your judgement, lord,' she said quietly, looking directly into his eyes.

The Archon cleared his throat. 'And when *do* you intend to take the city, lord?'

The Prince turned back. 'We will take Mistra, Pavlos, when we are ready to take Mistra. It may be news to you, but my father's plans for conquest do not rest on the convenience of the Mamonas family.'

The two men looked straight at each other. The silence lengthened.

Then Zoe spoke. 'There is, however, an agreement.'

Suleyman glanced at her, a small smile parting his mouth. His teeth were very white. 'You seem to know a great deal.'

'I know that you are about to change our agreement and I'm interested to know in what way.'

Suleyman was too surprised to answer immediately. Then his smile broadened. He began to walk up and down.

'Yes, well, I know you've given us money, Pavlos, and we will honour our side of the bargain when the time is right. Make no mistake, you will eventually rule Mistra in our father's name, but you'll have to wait just a little longer. This was a raid to weaken them and show them our power. If Mistra had surrendered, as you assured us it would, then we would have occupied it and given it to you. But it didn't surrender and I was persuaded that it might be difficult to take . . . especially since they have cannon.'

He stopped and looked askance at the Archon, the challenge there. There was no reply and he went on: 'Our plans have changed, Pavlos. We intend to take Constantinople first. Our ships will leave soon to form a blockade.'

He paused, letting the news sink in.

'So we cannot afford to lose men on the hill of Mistra just now. We are grateful for the money and everything else . . . but we need something more. We need cannon. Can you get us cannon?'

The Archon was thinking hard. 'Cannon, lord?'

'Yes, cannon, Pavlos,' the Prince continued. 'Cannon for our ships. And another thing. We need you to stop any of the Emperor's navy going to Constantinople until we've got the cannon. Can you do that for us?'

'You ask a lot, lord,' Pavlos Mamonas said gruffly.

Zoe had been watching the exchange with her head tilted to one side. She was beginning to like this prince. 'Father, as the Prince knows, the Empire's navy is here at Monemvasia and we could find reasons to keep it here. Venice makes cannon and we are friends of Venice. Would you like me to look into it? I am, after all, to visit there.'

61

'Excellent!' laughed Suleyman, looking from father to daughter. 'I knew we could depend on you.'

He clapped his hand on the Archon's shoulder. 'One more thing, Pavlos. You'll only be able to stop the fleet sailing if the Despot trusts you. Can you think of a way of getting him to trust you?'

Unconsciously, the Prince had turned to Zoe. He saw that she was watching him; there was something unreadable in her eyes.

She turned to her father. 'I have an idea for how we might arrange that, Father,' she said softly.

Suleyman laughed again. 'Archon, this daughter of yours should rule the world! Now, I must get back to my army. Is there a discreet exit somewhere? And might your daughter be persuaded to show me the way to it?'

Zoe looked directly at her father. She gave the slightest of nods.

'Of course, lord. Zoe, please show Prince Suleyman out.'

Zoe led Suleyman through corridors in the basement of the palace. She was heading for a door that led on to a small alleyway that ran by the side of the building, a door that she knew would be unguarded.

As they walked, Suleyman watched the gentle sway of her bottom beneath the rich folds of silk that accentuated its shape as she moved. He felt himself harden against the silks of his caftan. He quickened his pace.

'So you are going to Venice?' he asked as he drew level.

'I am going everywhere my father does business, prince.'

'But you have a brother. I heard he was hurt.' He paused. 'Such a misfortune.'

Zoe glanced at him. He seemed to be serious. She remained silent.

'So you will go in his place. Is he like you?'

Zoe said nothing.

'He is not like you,' the Prince said quietly. 'And that, I suspect, is the problem.'

She stopped and looked directly into Suleyman's face. 'And you also have brothers,' she said. 'We have that in common.'

The Prince laughed. She saw there was a bead of sweat on his forehead and that his face had new colour. He looked up and down the corridor. It was dark.

'This is assuredly a great palace,' he said softly. 'What part are we in now?'

'These are the storerooms, lord,' she answered, adding unnecessarily, 'where we keep food.'

'And would they be occupied at this time?'

Zoe tilted her head and smiled as she stopped beside a door. 'I have no idea, lord. Shall we look?'

Zoe opened the door behind her and led Suleyman into a narrow room with a low, vaulted stone ceiling and a smell of damp. In the centre of the room stood a table.

She leant against the end of the table, her arms spread to hold its edges. Her breasts felt tight against the constraints of her tunic. She opened her mouth slightly to allow her breathing to come more evenly.

Suleyman quietly closed the door and turned the key in its lock. Then he walked over to the table and began, very slowly, to unbutton the front of her tunic, his eyes never leaving hers. She did nothing to stop him.

At the fifth button, just below Zoe's navel, Suleyman stopped and parted the tunic to reveal a white cotton chemise, also buttoned at the front. This time, using both hands, he tore it open. Only now did Suleyman's eyes travel down and his mouth curved into a smile of untrammelled lust.

He took each breast in a hand and bent down to kiss them.

Then Suleyman dropped to his knees and began to lift the bottom of her tunic, gathering the folds as it rose to her thighs.

As his tongue made contact, Zoe let out a low moan and, taking a handful of his hair, pushed his face into her groin, thrusting her hips up to meet him. Waves of pleasure rolled up her body and her other hand came up to caress her breast.

Suleyman rose to his feet. He began to lift his caftan and, as it rose to his waist, Zoe grasped him with her hand.

'You've done this before, I think,' said Suleyman thickly.

Zoe was guiding him between her thighs, stroking him as she did so.

Then he was inside her and the hard edge of the table was digging into her back as his rhythm became more urgent. His arms were either side of her head and she could see the fine knots of muscle in his upper arms, feel their tension in every part of the body above her.

She opened her legs wider, gathering him deeper, deeper, feeling him move inside against her bottom as it rose to meet him.

As the surge swept over her, she felt his body go rigid and he arced away from her, his bearded chin rising as if in summons. He grunted once, twice, then let out a long, long sigh as his body came to rest against hers.

For a while, neither of them spoke.

Then he rose, letting his caftan fall. He made a little bow.

'Zoe Mamonas, I think we will be friends.'

CHAPTER FOUR

MISTRA, SPRING 1394

Anna sat on the balcony of her home in Mistra with an untouched meal on the table beside her. It was her favourite: *garon*, a fish soup, followed by Cretan cheese and pancakes with honey.

But Anna wasn't hungry. She was too miserable to eat.

Her brother Alexis sat on the other side, staring hard at the floor and tracing the delicate curve of the tesserae with his left shoe.

Neither of them spoke. It had all been said.

It wasn't that Anna had expected to escape marriage. She'd always known that it would be required of her one day, and very likely that it would be to someone she'd never set eyes on. But was she really ready to take on the duties of matrimony?

What those duties entailed had been revealed to her by her mother over the weeks following the dreadful announcement. And although she'd known most of it, having spent much of her youth in the company of her brother's friends, it still came as a shock that she was now so close to realising it.

It was two years since her encounter with Suleyman and the time had been spent in a mood of wild exhilaration at having escaped death so closely. She'd even thrown herself into her lessons with an enthusiasm that had unnerved the monks.

And now this. In a week's time she was to be married to Damian Mamonas, a boy a year her senior whom she'd never met and had heard only bad things about. Even now, her father would be riding by his side, accompanying him to Mistra.

To take her away.

Forever.

What made it worse was that it was one of those spring days in Mistra when she felt that she lived in the most glorious place on God's earth. The sky was an unblemished blue and the mid-morning sun shone down upon the hill and its people as if it was their own, lending all the individual colours of house, square and garden a brightness that Anna hoped would stay in her memory forever.

My God, I love this place.

Even the people seemed intoxicated by the day. Since the siege, they'd seen Anna as something of a patron saint to the city, which embarrassed her and the Metropolitan of St Demetrius Cathedral in equal degree. And if half of them were sad to lose their icon, the other half were filled with pride that her illustrious match would make their despotate safer. At any rate, not one of them wanted to miss the entry into their city of the Mamonas heir and they chattered excitedly to one another as they gathered flowers to shower upon the bridegroom.

Anna had already made her peace with St Demetrius that morning. Before first light, when the streets were deserted, she'd walked down to the cathedral and sat alone in the front pew to watch the bright frescoes of the Blessed Family and saints reveal themselves in the tiptoed light of the rising sun. Every child of Mistra knew the story of St Demetrius, how he'd

66

been cast into a dungeon in Thessaloniki by the Romans and speared to death for refusing to abjure his faith. She'd never much liked the saint but she found herself beseeching him to grant the same protection to her as he did to her city.

Now she sat with her brother, awaiting her future husband and wondering what she should say to him when they first met.

Alexis looked up. 'Sister, you look beautiful,' he said, taking Anna's hand in his.

Indeed she did. Anna was dressed in a long red dress of finest Cypriot silk damask, tight-fitted at the bosom, with a deep neckline fastened at the front with cross-laces of gold thread. The long, triangular sleeves were decorated at the edges with an elaborate floral design and the effect of the red and gold against her fair skin was dramatic. On her head was a simple diadem of cream silk cord and her luxuriant hair had been braided into a single strand at the back, with two further plaits framing her face. From her ears hung crescent-shaped earrings of silver decorated with the monogram of the Palaiologoi, a gift to her from the Despoena.

She was lovelier than her brother had ever seen her and now, as he looked into those green, green eyes, he realised how much he was going to miss her.

'You look beautiful,' he said again, this time in a whisper, and squeezed her hand.

Anna looked into his clear, kind eyes and felt herself on the edge of tears. She bit her lip.

Then, mercifully, there was distraction.

Commotion came from the town below. The two of them moved to look over the balcony and saw people flocking through the streets to the city gate where the flag of the Palaiologoi flew. A ragged cheer went up from the crowd but they could see little beyond the houses around them. Anna's heart quickened as she realised that the man whom she was to marry was fast approaching the house.

Her mother appeared at the door to the balcony.

Maria Laskaris was a woman of legendary poise but the events of the past weeks had tested her to the limits. Her daughter was so young – but Maria herself had been far younger when she'd married and hadn't she been happy? And she knew about duty. When she and Simon Laskaris had wed, it was to seal a peace agreement between her father, a powerful Norman lord with extensive lands in the north, and the then Despot Manuel. Now her dead father's lands were part of the despotate.

She looked at her daughter and marvelled again at what had happened to her over the past two years. She had grown up, not just in body, but in mind as well. She was still impulsive and stubborn, but there was also a wisdom that her mother found reassuring given what might lie ahead. She'd not heard good things about her future son-in-law.

'Come, Anna,' she said. 'We'd better go down to the courtyard to wait for them.'

She took her daughter's arm and led her through the triclinium, down the stone steps and into the large courtyard with its imposing gateway on to the square. A tall cedar stood in the middle.

Outside the gate, they could hear the procession drawing nearer, the cheers and laughter of the crowd giving way to the sound of hoof on stone. And then Simon Laskaris was there, riding under the arch in his rich tunic and tall hat, with an uncertain smile pinned to his face.

Beside him rode Damian Mamonas, whose own face was set

fast in a smile of no warmth and whose dark eyes immediately sought Anna out as they accustomed themselves to the shade of the cedar tree. Whether what he saw pleased him, Anna couldn't tell, for his expression remained fixed. She felt sick.

He looked less than impressive. While handsome, he had a livid scar down one cheek and a pallor that suggested long hours indoors. His long black hair, which fell almost to his waist, seemed too heavy for his head and he rode awkwardly.

Damian dismounted in front of her and stumbled, waving away the arm of a servant. He fixed his gaze on Anna and she smiled back. Then he walked towards her, his limp causing one side of his body to dip low with every step. Anna looked hard into his face and still she smiled. She extended a hand.

'My lord, you are most welcome.'

Damian did not reply. He merely took her hand and bowed to kiss it. His lips were cold.

There was an awkward silence in which Anna looked at her father and then her brother who was now by his side. Alexis gave the merest hint of a shrug.

Then her father said: 'Anna, Damian has had a long ride. Why don't you take him inside where we can sit?'

Damian turned to him. 'Sir, the ride was not hard. I ride further than that daily. I'm just hot.'

The Protostrator gestured towards the stone steps leading up to the door to the house. 'Of course, of course. Please do me the honour of entering my house.'

But Damian didn't move. He was staring at the steep steps.

Anna stepped forward. 'Sir, I fear the heat is affecting me also. Would you help me in climbing these steps?'

Then she took his arm and began, slowly, to mount the steps.

Inside the triclinium, laid out on a long table that ran the length of the room, was a spread of cold game birds, fish, cheeses, fruit and sweetmeats all displayed on plate of gold and silver. At intervals stood jugs of cool Cypriot wine surrounded by bunches of grapes and twisted vines. Servants, dressed in the Laskaris livery, stood against the walls.

Damian was shown to his chair by Anna, who then sat down beside him. She poured him wine.

'Was your ride pleasant, lord?' she ventured.

But Damian was looking around him curiously, searching the faces of the guests who had started to arrive. 'I don't see the Despot.'

Anna wondered what she should say. It would be inconceivable for the royal couple to attend. Surely Damian must know this?

She decided to lie. 'I believe the Despoena is unwell, sir.'

It was not quite a lie. Bartolomea had confessed to Anna the day previously that her courses that month were severe. Damian shrugged. He drank some wine and leant forward to fork a quail on to his plate. As he ate, he nodded absently at arriving guests who bowed to him as they came into the room.

'How many rooms does this house have?' he asked at last.

Anna was taken aback. She'd never counted them. 'I don't know. Twenty?'

Damian considered this, looking through the large windows either side of the room at the two other wings of the house. 'I think not,' he said. Then he added, 'You will find our palace very spacious, and cool inside.' He drew a cloth from his sleeve and began to mop his brow.

Anna had never met anyone so rude. Was this the man with whom she was to spend the rest of her life?

'I look forward to counting its rooms,' she said. 'I'll bring my abacus.'

Damian looked up quickly. A small spot of colour had appeared in each cheek. But Anna had turned away.

There was laughter in the room and she could see Alexis's fair head rising and falling as he made his way towards them, stopping to greet friends. His charm washed before him like water over pebbles.

'Sister, will you introduce me?' Alexis was standing over them, his hand extended and a smile of untinctured friendship on his face.

Damian didn't get up. He only slowly put out his hand and said, 'I hear you've met the Prince Suleyman.'

Alexis grinned. He took the seat next to Anna. 'Yes, out on the plain. He seemed quite taken by Anna. Perhaps you should watch him.' He laughed, unaware of the cold look that Damian was giving him. and added, 'I hear you have some extraordinary horses at your stud. Now that you're to be married to Anna, I wondered . . .'

But Alexis didn't finish his sentence because the look that Damian was giving him was full of such venom that even he couldn't fail to notice it. What on earth had he said wrong?

But Anna had realised. 'Alexis, Damian has a twin sister famed for her beauty and as yet unmatched. I'm surprised you've not yet found room for her in the conversation.'

Alexis looked back at Damian. He seemed to remember something and reddened. 'I shall be honoured to meet her,' he said quietly. 'I hope the four of us will be friends.'

If the prospect of this friendship seemed attractive to Damian, he hid it well. He merely beckoned to a servant for more wine. Then he yawned. 'I find myself more tired than I thought.

Perhaps I might be found one of your . . . twenty . . . rooms in which to rest for a bit before the inevitable speeches?'

With some effort Anna controlled herself. 'Of course.'

As Damian limped away behind a servant, brother and sister turned to look at each other.

'Perhaps it's just tiredness,' said Alexis lamely. 'I get like that sometimes.'

'You? Never.' Anna was staring at the back of the man she was to marry. 'He's just unpleasant. How can I live with *that*?'

'I'm only fifty miles away,' Alexis said softly. 'I can be there whenever you need me.'

Anna looked into those good, brave eyes, eyes that wanted so badly to see equal good in the world. How did she deserve such a brother? She leant forward to whisper in his ear: 'It doesn't matter what he's like. With you in my life, I can always know love.'

The following morning was as bright as its predecessor and a gentle breeze stroked Anna's hair as she rode through the gates of Mistra on the first part of her journey to her new home.

The cheers of the crowds were still ringing in her ears as she steered the pretty palfrey that Damian had presented her with that morning down the hill towards the plain. If truth be told, she'd have preferred to ride her own horse but she could hardly refuse such a gift, and anyway the Mamonas horses were famous throughout Christendom. She patted the speckled roan on its neck and it whinnied in reply.

By her side rode Damian, looking bored and hungover from the revels of the previous night; Simon Laskaris had not stinted on either the quality or quantity of his wine. Damian had shown himself even less congenial drunk than when sober. This morning, he had yet to speak.

Anna refused to be affected by his mood, having resolved, on waking, to make the best of her situation. She'd also decided not to make all of the conversational running, having exhausted so many avenues the evening before.

Instead she talked to Alexis, who rode at her other side, and considered the countryside around her, so green and buxom in these first weeks of spring. The Vale of Sparta had recovered quickly from the ravages visited on it by the Turks and bounty was everywhere. New fields of wheat and corn were beginning their rise into the gold of harvest and fat oxen pulled blades through the rich soil.

Soon they met a caravan making its way towards Mistra and Anna remembered that the Spring Fair was to take place later in the week in the open ground before the city. The mules appeared to be laden with small jars of different coloured ointments packed into crates that swayed with the movement of the beasts. The last was ridden by a cheerful fat man who waved at their passing. Anna guessed him to be quack who would proclaim the miracles of his virility potions from a box while the wives of Mistra giggled like virgins. She'd enjoyed the spectacle before.

She was so lost in her thoughts that it took a moment for her to realise that Damian was finally speaking to her.

'I'm sorry. What did you say?'

'I merely remarked that you ride well.'

This was the first compliment Damian had paid her and she coloured with pleasure. 'Thank you,' she said simply. 'As do you.'

Damian nodded. 'Of course,' he continued, gesturing at

Anna's palfrey, 'not to ride such a horse well would be difficult. It's one of our best.'

Anna snorted. She looked around her. Behind were four boys of about her age, all big and blond. One had his head thrown back in laughter.

'Are all these horses bred by your family?'

Damian followed her gaze, turning in his saddle. 'Yes, and they are all fine, obedient horses, well trained. Except that one.'

Anna looked in the direction of his pointing figure and saw a magnificent horse of some size, which looked temperamental but seemed to be well controlled. Her gaze rested for a moment on the rider. He was the one that had been laughing. He was fair, blue-eyed and strikingly handsome. For a moment, their eyes met. He smiled.

'That was the horse that nearly killed me,' Damian was saying with feeling. 'I'd like to see it dead but my father judges it will fetch a high price one day.'

'Dead?' said Alexis. 'But it's beautiful!'

Damian reined in his horse. He was staring darkly at Alexis. 'Laskaris, do you think you've come far enough? Might you not be needed in Mistra for something?'

The river where they were to part was over a mile away.

Alexis began to reply but stopped when Anna shot him a glance. She looked back at Damian.

'Alexis was to accompany me to the river, lord. However, you're right. He might find better entertainment in Mistra.'

Damian scowled and turned his horse. He nodded at Alexis and rode on.

Brother and sister looked at each other. Anna pressed her lips together. She would not cry. 'Goodbye, Alexis.'

'Anna, I can continue . . .'

'No. Just go. I'll be fine. I'll see you at the wedding.'

She moved her horse to stand against his. She leant forward and kissed him on the forehead. He felt a tear on his cheek.

'Goodbye, Alexis.'

Luke was enjoying the ride. He'd never visited Mistra before, nor the great castle at Geraki where they'd broken their outward journey and were to sleep again that night.

Most of all, though, he was overjoyed to be riding Eskalon, as he'd named the stallion.

When he'd heard that the horse was to be spared, Luke had ridden out to the stud see him. On arrival, he'd banged on Arsenius's door.

'Luke . . . she made me say it!'

Luke was bewildered. 'No, Arsenius. I'm not here about that. The stallion. You've not done anything to him, have you?'

The man shook his head, too relieved to speak.

'Good! Where is he?'

And Luke had found the stallion and thought about little else since.

Over the next few weeks, an extraordinary bond had developed between horse and boy, one that in all his years Arsenius had never witnessed, even with Luke. Released from his Varangian training, Luke had spent every available day with the stallion, talking to it, cajoling it, teaching it, so that in time it seemed that they thought as one. And as the days turned into weeks, and the weeks into months, his admiration for the horse turned into something like love.

Now Luke was worried. Damian had only emerged from his sick bed six months previously, first learning how to walk again, then ride. And it was out riding that Luke had first seen him.

It had been on the road from Sikia to Monemvasia and Luke was enjoying the power of Eskalon as he galloped past the vineyards. Up ahead he could see two riders coming towards him, moving slowly. Only when it was too late to turn back, did Luke realise that one of them was Damian.

Luke remembered the look of pure hatred that he'd thrown at him as he'd passed.

Now he'd seen that look again when Damian had turned to point Eskalon out to his new bride.

As the evening shadows began to lengthen around the great walls of the castle of Geraki, the little party wound their way up the path to the fortress. The track was narrow and fell away steeply to their left, and the horses had to pick their way around small rockfalls.

Luke and his three friends had moved to the front of the convoy to ensure that the path was firm ahead, and Anna rode directly behind, leaning slightly forward on her horse to ease its climb.

They had just rounded a corner and Luke was bent over Eskalon's neck, studying what looked like some loose earth in the road, when he heard the cry behind him.

He spun round in his saddle to see a long flash of gold and red slither behind a boulder and Anna's palfrey rear, its eyes rolling in terror.

Had the snake bitten it?

Then there was no doubt. In the next instant, the horse veered off the path and hurtled down the slope, snorting in pain, its haunches scattering scree and bush as it fell. Anna was hanging on to its neck for dear life.

Luke reacted instantly. He spurred Eskalon after her, throwing his weight backwards to balance the load. He heard shouts of alarm from behind him.

Ahead, Anna had reached the bottom of the slope still clinging to her horse and was now galloping across the plain in the direction of a steep gulley. He could see her desperately trying to rein in the palfrey but the horse was not slowing.

Reaching the flat, Luke now dug his heels into Eskalon's sides and the horse bounded forward. He leant forward to whisper into his ear and felt the horse move faster. The gap between the horses was narrowing but the gulley was approaching fast and Luke feared how the young palfrey would react to it.

How am I to stop you?

They were now ten paces behind and Luke slid his whole body on to Eskalon's side, his arm wrapped around his neck.

Anna's hair was in front of him, vivid against the yellow grass of the plain.

'*Lean back!*' he shouted as Eskalon drew alongside her horse.

Closer. Closer.

Then he jumped.

Throwing himself at the palfrey's neck, he used his weight and the friction of his heels ploughing through the ground to slow the horse.

The gulley was no more than twenty paces ahead and closing fast but the palfrey wouldn't stop.

But Eskalon knew what to do. The big stallion, free of Luke's weight, put on one last burst of speed, pushing its nose in front of the palfrey and then veering suddenly to the right. The smaller horse banked sharply and then ground to a halt, falling to its knees in the movement.

Anna rolled off the horse and fell to the ground. Her horse picked itself up, whinnying in pain, and began to limp away.

Luke stood there, covered in dust and horse sweat, his heart hammering. He was bleeding slightly from one of his arms. Collecting himself, he walked over to Anna and knelt beside her, unsure how best to comfort her.

For Anna, a dam seemed to break. All of the worry and tension of the last weeks broke over her like a wall of water and she threw herself into Luke's arms. 'Thank you,' she managed between breaths. 'I think you saved my life.'

Luke didn't know how to reply. Her tears were wet against his shoulder. He just held her.

She drew back, tears smudging the dust on her face. 'What's your name?'

'Luke,' answered Luke. 'Luke Magoris.'

Anna looked into a face that had strength and honesty etched into its bones, a face so different from her betrothed's. She smiled.

'Thank you, Luke Magoris. I won't forget this.'

They both got to their feet, Anna patting the dust from her riding habit. Luke went over to the palfrey, which was placidly pulling clumps of grass from the ground. He knelt beside it, picked up a leg and tested it, talking gently to the animal as he did so.

'I fear it's lame, lady,' he said over his shoulder, replacing the leg on the ground and patting the horse's neck. 'Whether from the snake-bite or forcing it to stop is hard to tell.'

Anna nodded. She was watching Luke in fascination. The horse seemed to understand what he said. She had never seen anyone do what he'd done. She heard a shout and looked up to see Damian cantering towards her. Two guards rode behind him.

'Are you all right?' he asked.

'Yes,' said Anna. 'Luke here saved my life.'

Damian looked thunderous. 'Saved your life?' he snapped. 'He could have got you killed!'

Anna didn't understand. 'But surely you saw what happened? He endangered his life . . .'

But Damian was in no mood for listening. 'What I saw', he hissed, swinging round to face Luke, 'was yet another reckless, stupid act from someone who seems intent upon causing damage to our property. Look at that horse!' He pointed towards the palfrey, which was limping its way over to a new patch of grass. 'That horse is worth thousands! Look at it now!'

Anna felt her anger rising. 'I had thought, sir, that the palfrey was your gift to me? It would seem that you place greater value on the welfare of your horses than your intended wife.'

Damian glared at her, momentarily lost for words.

'It was not Luke's fault,' she said, seizing the advantage. 'If the horse is lame, it happened when it collided with the stallion and he wasn't even on its back.'

An unpleasant look had entered Damian's eyes. 'Yes, indeed,' he said. 'It was the horse's fault. As I've always maintained, the horse is dangerous and should be destroyed.'

He turned to a guard. 'See to it,' he said.

Luke stepped in front of Eskalon. 'If you want to kill this horse,' he said quietly, 'you'll have to kill me first.'

Anna walked over to stand next to him. She looked Damian straight in the eye. 'And if you kill this man, you will have to explain to your father and mine, not to mention the Despot, why you allowed the fate of a horse to rupture an alliance so painstakingly negotiated between our two families.'

79

Damian looked wildly from one to the other. He knew it was over. He was trapped.

He turned to the guards. 'Take him back to Monemvasia,' he said, pointing at Luke. 'And find the lady a new mount!' Then he wheeled his horse and cantered back towards the castle.

CHAPTER FIVE

MONEMVASIA, SPRING 1394

On the following evening, Luke was surprised to find himself amongst the liveried grooms standing at the gates to Monemvasia, awaiting the arrival of the Mamonas heir and his bethrothed.

The sun was making its slow descent to meet the hills above Gefira and shining directly into his eyes, making it difficult for him to see much beyond the first bend of the road that wound its way up from the port to the city gate.

Next to him stood his father, dressed in full Varangian garb. He looked at the corselet of gilded scales, the red tunic, the dark blue *chlamys*, clasped on the right shoulder and at the great two-handed axe that rested against his father's side and he wished he'd never ridden out to the stud that day. But then, would he have found Eskalon?

In front sat Zoe on a white palfrey whose caparison embroidered with black castles shifted against its rump as it moved. He hadn't seen her since the Archon had passed sentence on him. He'd heard she'd been abroad, visiting the Mamonas businesses. Damian, still an invalid, had been left behind.

Luke thought of the previous evening when he'd come to

the palace between two guards, neither of whom was quite certain what to do with him.

They'd asked at the entrance for Pavlos Mamonas, only to be told that he was discussing the forthcoming wedding with the Metropolitan who had just arrived from the capital. Instead, Zoe had appeared.

She'd changed. The voluptuousness that had always seemed imminent had now settled on her like a rich mantle. How dramatically different, thought Luke, to Anna's fair loveliness. They were as night and day and they were to live together under the same roof.

Zoe had dismissed the guards and they'd walked together into the palace. She'd given him wine and he'd been so surprised that he'd not heard her first words.

'I asked you how the ride back was, Luke,' Zoe was saying. 'Hardly original, I know, but one has to start a conversation somewhere, especially when it's been so long since the last one.'

Luke didn't answer. However long ago the last meeting, he still remembered the part Zoe had played in it.

Then she smiled again. 'It seems my family is getting practised at doing you wrong, Luke,' she said. 'First there was the business with the stallion and now this.'

Luke was watching her closely. Was this the real Zoe?

'From what I've heard,' she went on, 'it would appear that my brother's intended bride owes you her life.'

She paused. 'I suppose you must hate me, Luke, after the lies I told my father.'

Luke remained silent.

'Do you know why I lied?' She turned away from him to look out of a window. 'If you hadn't been blamed for what happened, my brother would have fallen even further in my father's estimation. Pavlos Mamonas may love his son but he thinks little of his judgement. And judgement in business is all, Luke, especially if you are to run it.'

Luke had known this girl since birth, known her capacity to lie. 'I don't think so,' he said quietly to her back. 'You lied because you didn't want the truth to get out. You encouraged Damian to enter that ring because you knew he might be hurt.'

She spun around, new colour in her cheeks. 'You'd dare to suggest I would deliberately put my brother in harm's way! Why would I do that?'

Luke studied her for several moments. 'You know why. And it worked.'

That had been last night. Now, ahead of them on the road, the flags of the Laskaris and Mamonas families had emerged from the bend, borne aloft by two mounted men-at-arms. Behind them rode a third soldier carrying the flag of the Palaiologoi. Then Luke saw Anna riding beside Damian, her expression a mask of self-control. Damian had his eyes fixed on Luke and he looked murderous.

Zoe stepped forward to greet Anna, but before she could do so, Damian kicked his horse and stopped in front of his sister. He leant forward in his saddle. 'What is *he* doing here?' he hissed, pointing at Luke.

Zoe ignored the question. 'Welcome, brother. Our father wishes to see you at the palace. Immediately.'

Damian looked thunderstruck.

'Immediately,' repeated Zoe quietly.

There was a moment's pause; then, with a grunt, Damian kicked his horse and rode under the gate of the city.

Zoe looked around at the staring faces and smiled. She stepped forward to help Anna dismount while Luke took her horse's reins.

When Anna was on the ground, she embraced her. 'Anna, welcome. I have been so excited to meet you.'

Anna was unprepared for such a greeting. She leant forward to receive a kiss on each cheek. Then Zoe stepped back, still holding Anna's hands.

'You're far more beautiful than the portrait they sent us,' she smiled. 'Mind you, that was six months ago and I dare say we all change so fast at our age.'

Then she put her arm through Anna's, turned and took her into Monemvasia.

Later, in the throne room, Pavlos Mamonas was sitting and glaring at his son. His expression was grim. Next to him stood Zoe, her hand on the back of the throne.

'Can you explain to me,' he said at last, 'what persuaded you to behave like a spoilt schoolboy on the plain before Geraki?'

'Father—'

'Don't!' snapped the Archon, raising his hand. He rose and began to pace up and down on the veined marble that surrounded the dais, his leather shoes squeaking as he turned.

He stopped in front of Damian. 'Let me explain to you, as simply as I am able, what this alliance means to our family.' He thought for a moment. 'Not long ago, this Sultan's father won a great victory at Kosovo against the Serbians.' The Archon resumed his pacing. 'Why was that important?' he asked. 'Because it meant that our empire was finally surrounded and that it was only a matter of time before it fell to the Turk. It may happen next year or in ten years, but fall it will.'

Mamonas paused again and looked at his son. Damian's leg had begun to ache and he wanted to sit down.

'When I die, Damian, you will inherit a trading empire that stretches across the world, one that I have nurtured by knowing whom to back. And right now, if we want to go on selling wine to the English, silk to the Italians and arms to the Turks, we would be foolish not to back Suleyman, who will be the next sultan. So whatever he wants us to do, we will do.' Mamonas took a pace towards his son. 'And what he wants very much at the moment, Damian, is for you to marry Anna Laskaris.'

'But why is that so vital to his plans?' Damian asked.

'Because,' said his father with some exasperation because they'd had this conversation before, 'Suleyman wishes to take Constantinople. To do that, he will need to know that no help will come from the rest of the Empire. And the rest of the Empire these days, Damian, is the Despotate of Mistra and the fleet that resides in our ports here in Monemvasia. Suleyman wants new trust between the cities of Mistra and Monemvasia. This marriage will achieve that.'

Damian was silent. He glanced at a nearby chair and wondered if he dare sit in it. He looked at Zoe, poised at the right hand of their father. 'I am well enough to travel,' he said. 'You should send me abroad as you did Zoe. I need to learn things.'

Pavlos Mamonas sighed. He walked over to his son. 'Perhaps, Damian. But for now, just go and be nice to your wife.'

Damian limped out, leaving silence behind him. Something important had been said and Pavlos Mamonas and his daughter both knew it.

It was Pavlos who spoke first. 'You always knew it would be thus,' he said quietly. 'Damian is my son. He must inherit.'

85

Zoe said, 'So why did you bother to send me away if you always intended to give it all to him?'

Her father didn't answer at first. Then he said, 'He is my son. He must inherit.'

'But I am better qualified.'

He knew it to be true. It had always been true.

'I'm sorry,' he said.

Some time later, Zoe stood on the terrace of the Mamonas Palace. A perfect orange orb had risen in the west and the stars were beginning to take their place in the darkening sky. The sea was all around, black and huge, its power deep beneath the shaft of restless red and gold that shivered beneath the moon. She breathed deeply and looked out at this vast desert, a desert across which her family's floating caravans travelled to places she would not visit again. Never again.

Think. Don't let anger cloud your judgement. There is another way.

Yes, there was another way, another empire to rule. An empire far, far larger.

Zoe lifted her head to the moon, fuller than crescent, and smiled.

Suleyman. I have his attention. Now I need his trust.

Three nights later, and at a later hour, Anna was lying in Damian's bed.

She was alone and nervous and she kept looking at a small vial of herb essences that the Despoena had given her earlier. They were intended to heighten desire in a young bride.

Should she take it? What if Bartolomea had bought it from that charlatan they'd met on the road?

She felt nothing but cold trepidation. Was she frigid? No, she'd admired Alexis's handsome friends and more than once had thought how nice it would be to lie with one. The problem, she had to recognize, lay with the man to whom she was now married, whose arrival she expected at any moment. It wasn't that he was ugly, or had bad teeth, or smelt; it was simply that he was the coldest person she'd ever met. And while she was, of course, a virgin and had no experience of how to pleasure a man, she didn't believe that she could evoke any passion in him.

Perhaps it would help if she distracted herself. There were certainly other things to think about. There was the meeting with the Archon, who had been kind and welcoming. Then there was the visit to the Head Cook, who'd taken her through the fifteen courses that would be served at her wedding feast and had made her sample the wines so that she was quite tipsy by the time Zoe had come to collect her to look at the wedding gifts. And finally, she'd met Joseph. She'd known he was Luke's father the instant she'd seen him. It was not just his height but his eyes, which matched Luke's and spoke of honour and goodness.

Then had come the wedding.

In the early hours, Anna had risen and been dressed in a long, sweeping dress of white crushed silk, embroidered at the sleeves and neckline in gold fleur-de-lis. On her head had been pinned a tiara, encrusted with tiny jewels, at the front of which sat an enamel castle in miniature.

The wedding itself had passed in a blur. So many people, so much music and incense. And flowers, flowers everywhere. Anna had been stifled by the heat and the attention, her dress too heavy and her shoes too tight. She'd begun to feel the panic that she'd known in the hole and had silently cursed the aged Metropolitan as he stumbled through the service with all the forgetfulness of old age.

87

Then it was over and she and Damian had walked back down the aisle of the Panagia Hodegetria past the Despot, past her parents and Alexis, past a thousand nods and smiles and out into the brilliant sunshine of the square where giggling girls had showered them with flowers from the balcony above. They'd walked up to the rocks behind and there, in the bay below, had sat the Byzantine fleet bedecked with bunting, the decks lined with cheering sailors. Anna had looked across at her husband and wondered how much gold had been spent to arrange such a show.

The wedding feast had been held in the gardens of the palace, where long tables, groaning with food, had sat within open-sided tents and musicians with viols and tambours played beneath fruit trees. Luke, Matthew, Nikolas and Arcadius had been summoned to wait at the tables and were standing with trays of drinks when Anna arrived on the arm of her new husband. When she'd seen Luke, she'd released Damian's arm and gone over to take a cup from his tray.

'Your talents are endless, Luke Magoris,' she'd smiled. 'Horse taming to the serving of refreshment. I am glad to see you here.'

'And I to see you, lady,' Luke had replied, bowing. 'On this happiest of days.'

She'd looked at him then, looked for the sarcasm but seen only goodwill. For a moment she'd allowed herself to study the broad forehead above eyes of piercing blue, the long mane of golden hair, the firm line of his jaw. Then she'd turned away.

In the middle of the lawns had stood a large pavilion of magnificent coloured silks that rustled gently in the breeze, its ropes threaded with gold and its poles garlanded with flowers. Anna had never seen anything so splendid and was admiring it when a dark figure arose from within it and came out into the sunshine.

Suleyman.

The heir to the Ottoman throne was smiling and his arms were spread in greeting. 'This tent is my gift to you both,' he'd said in perfect Greek as he bowed. 'And, lady,' he'd said, taking Anna's hand, 'should you ever find yourself wandering lost outside a city's walls again, perhaps it might afford you some small shelter.'

Anna had taken her hand away

'I am surprised to see you here, highness. I had thought we were at war. Your gift is not welcome.'

Damian had gripped her arm and begun to speak, but Suleyman had raised his hand. He was watching her with interest.

'It is a tent,' he'd said with a shrug. 'Give it to a servant if it pleases you.'

The wedding feast had not been a happy affair. The Despot had been unaware of Suleyman's invitation and struggled to maintain his composure when the two were presented to each other. After all, it was widely supposed that Bayezid's galleys were, even then, on their way to blockade his brother the Emperor Manuel's capital, Constantinople.

Shortly after the main course had been served, Theodore had risen. 'My lord Mamonas, sadly I must leave earlier than expected. A matter has arisen at Mistra that requires my return.'

No one had believed it. The Despot had signalled to his retinue and they'd left.

And Anna hadn't even said goodbye to Alexis.

Now, lying in this vast bed, hung with silk curtains and

spread with herb-scented lawn sheets, she looked up at the Mamonas arms emblazoned on its silk tester and felt utterly alone. Then a new dread entered her soul. She looked again at Bartolomea's potion. Was now the time to take it? Would she even need it? After all, Damian had appeared quite drunk by the end of the banquet, slurring his words and leering at a servant girl who'd bent too low to serve him wine. But then she'd watched Zoe take him by the hand and walk him slowly over to the long shadow of a tree where they could barely be seen. She'd seen her bend close to him, so that their foreheads touched, and they'd talked for a long time.

Then Zoe had taken his head in her hands and kissed him on the lips.

Anna was remembering her shock at seeing this when she heard the creak of the bedroom door. Damian was standing there in a red velvet nightgown.

Too late to take the potion now.

From the candles burning around the room, she could see that he looked nervous. And he was very drunk.

She leant across the bed and drew the covers back, then patted the sheet beneath them. 'Will you come to bed, sir?' she asked.

Damian swayed and then steadied himself against the door. He looked around the room. 'Why are all these candles lit?'

'I thought you might like to see your new bride,' she said.

He seemed to consider this possibility. Then he staggered over to the corner of the bed and sat down heavily, facing away from her. He was breathing quickly.

'Come here,' he said. She began to move across the counterpane.

'No!' he barked. 'Come *here*!' He was jabbing his finger at the floor in front of him.

Anna climbed off the bed and walked round it to stand in front of him.

'Take it off,' said Damian.

'Sir?'

'The dress, shift, whatever it is. Take it off!'

Anna began to unlace the cords threaded through her bodice, her hands moving with the quick rise and fall of her breasts. Once they were undone, she unhooked it from her shoulders and let it fall to the ground. Quickly she drew her arms up to shield herself.

'Take them away,' whispered Damian. One of his hands, released from a sleeve, had begun to move up and down beneath his nightgown. Sweat was gathering at his temples. His breaths were coming in rasps.

Anna was transfixed with horror. It wasn't meant to be like this.

'Take them away,' barked Damian, the movement at his groin more urgent. 'Take your hands away *now*!'

Anna did what she was told and stood there, naked, her skin aglow in the light of the candles. She looked down with appalled fascination at the hunched figure before her who was now using his free hand to feel her breasts, pulling and twisting her nipples and running his palm across their tips. Then the hand moved down to her groin.

'Open them!'

Anna opened her legs. She felt a shock of pain as Damian thrust his fingers inside her, invading, probing, wounding her. Going deeper and deeper. She pulled his hand away.

Damian looked up at her, his eyes unfocused, his mouth

91

slack with lust. A sliver of sweat ran down the scar on his cheek. He pulled himself to his feet, using the bedpost. Anna stepped forward, attempting a smile.

'Why don't you remove your nightgown, Damian, and come to bed?'

A stinging pain exploded across her cheek as Damian slapped her. 'You bitch!' he shouted.

'But . . . ?'

What had she done wrong?

'You'd like that, wouldn't you? To pity me! Do you think I didn't know what you were doing at the steps of the Laskaris House? How dare you pity me!'

He'd stopped rubbing himself and with both hands threw her across the bed. Then he fell on top of her, pulling his gown up at the front. He grabbed her hand. 'You do it.'

Miserably, Anna began to move her hand up and down.

'Faster!' he urged, his breath hot against her ear. His hand was at her throat.

She rubbed faster, closing her eyes, wanting to finish this as quickly as possible.

Damian went rigid and his fingers dug into her neck so that, for a moment, she couldn't breathe. Then he rolled away

Anna felt a wave of burning shame. She could bear the pain in her neck and on her breasts, but this humiliation was more agonising by far. She wondered what she could say to make him understand that, whatever his hurt, he could not treat her like that ever again.

She turned to him, but he was lying on his side and away from her. He was fast asleep.

Outside, standing in shadow in the corridor, was Zoe. She'd

heard very little of what had happened in the bridal chamber but she could guess.

She will still be a virgin after tonight.

But why did it matter? Why indeed was she there, listening to the muffled agonies of two people beyond the door?

She knew the answer to this. She'd seen the way that Suleyman had looked at Anna at the wedding. He'd not looked at her like that.

She needed to win Suleyman's trust. But perhaps she needed to win Anna's first.

CHAPTER SIX

MISTRA, SUMMER 1394

The Despot was not a man often moved to anger, but when he was, it was impressive.

Certainly, that was the opinion of Nikolaos Eudaemis, Kephale of Monemvasia and the Despot's representative in that city. In theory he had the same powers as the Archon; in practice he was not even close.

Eudaemis had been summoned back to Mistra to explain why, after three months, some important elements of the marriage agreement, such as the handing back of Geraki Castle, had not taken place. Geraki was of particular significance since it was critical to the defence of the Vale of Sparta and its rich farmland.

Theodore was beside himself. 'How dare he?' he shouted, stabbing the papers on the table in front of him with his finger. 'Is it not written there in the contract in black and white? Or perhaps the monks of St Sophia drank too much of their altar wine and couldn't spell Geraki? Tell me, Nikolaos, which part of the contract does the Archon not understand?'

'I don't know, Majesty. He's always too busy to see me,' said the man wretchedly.

'Too busy? Too busy to see the appointed representative of the Despot?' yelled Theodore, his face purple with rage.

Simon Laskaris stepped forward. 'Majesty—' he began, but the Despot rounded on him.

'Don't, for once in your life, Simon, tell me to be reasonable! I'm sick of being reasonable! I've been reasonable for three months, written letter after letter and nothing has happened! Reasonable does not work!' Theodore stopped suddenly and eyed Eudaemis malevolently. 'Is he bribing you as well?' he asked, his voice more even.

'Majesty!' cried the Kephale in shock.

'Well, it wouldn't surprise me. He seems to bribe everyone else,' said the Despot moodily.

Simon Laskaris coughed, judging this change in tone to be a good time to intervene. 'Sire,' he said, 'why don't we allow Nikolaos to go and rest after his long ride and we can talk to him later when we've had more time to consider things. You'd like a rest wouldn't you, Nikolaos?'

The Kephale looked at him with gratitude. He glanced at his sovereign, who was still watching him darkly. Then Theodore nodded. Eudaemis bowed his way backwards from the room, leaving the Despot alone with his Protostrator.

'He's taking bribes, isn't he?' said Theodore, looking at the door through which the Kephale had left.

'Oh yes, lord,' said Simon Laskaris cheerfully. 'Do you imagine he could afford that Goulas mansion on the salary we give him?'

Theodore groaned. 'Whom can I trust beyond you, Simon?' He took his old friend by his arms. 'I'm sorry for shouting at you.'

'It's nothing, lord.' The Protostrator smiled. 'And there are plenty of people you can trust. Alexis, for one. He's outside waiting to give his report to you.'

'Good, good,' said the Despot, tiredly. He went over to the table and poured three goblets of wine. 'Show him in.'

Alexis had been sent by his father to Monemvasia a week previously to check on reports that the fleet had yet to set sail to the support of Constantinople. He had travelled alone and incognito. Now he was walking through the door, his clothes and face grimed with the dust of a long ride.

'Alexis!' beamed the Despot, all signs of tiredness vanished. He walked over to embrace his godson and thrust the goblet into his hand. 'How were the roads?'

'Free of bandits, my lord. The country seems at peace since the Turkish raid, and the people are happy.'

'That's good, that's good. And much praise must go to you and your men for keeping it so.'

Alexis bowed and turned to his father. 'I'm afraid I heard no word of Anna, Father. They say she keeps to the palace and barely takes a step outside.'

Laskaris shook his head. It was unlike his daughter not to be curious about her new home. And what of the many letters he'd sent her, none of which she'd answered?

Theodore glanced at his friend. 'I dare say she's busy coming to terms with her new life, Simon. It must all be very strange to her.'

Simon was not convinced. He walked over to the table where the papers were laid out. 'Lord, we have here a list of the Empire's warships that have been resupplying in the deep-water ports around Monemvasia. Now, Alexis, are you able to tell us how many have left for Constantinople?'

'None, Father.'

'*None?*' exclaimed the Despot. 'But only last week we were told that eight were ready to sail!'

'I know, lord,' said Alexis. 'But the Archon has ordered further repairs to them so they are to stay at the docks.'

'He can't do that!' Theodore's voice was beginning to rise again. 'He knows how badly they're needed at Constantinople!'

'Alas, he can, lord,' said Laskaris. 'You will recall that in one part of our recent agreement, as reward for returning Geraki and giving us funds to rebuild the wall at Corinth, he was to take control of the provisioning of the fleet at Monemvasia. It seemed sensible given his experience.'

'Why on earth did he want that?' asked the Despot.

'We assumed, lord, so that he could rake off some profit. It seemed a small price to pay for the extra efficiencies to the fleet. After all, he controls all the ports around there anyway.'

Theodore thought for a moment. He took another draught of wine. 'So what do we do, Simon?' he asked at last.

'We take control of events, sire,' replied the Protostrator. 'We send a force to take control of Geraki in your name. And we do it without delay.'

'And then?'

'Then, lord, having shown that we are in earnest, you and I go to Monemvasia and demand that he release the fleet. He will have no choice but to comply.'

Theodore considered this. 'And whom should we send?' he asked eventually.

Laskaris looked at his son. 'Alexis, are you ready to ride to Geraki?'

Alexis was not happy with the men riding behind him. They

were Albanian mercenaries and he didn't entirely trust them. But his men of the Guard had been away on exercise, so he'd taken what he could get.

There were only twenty of them, which Alexis judged to be a prudent number. Any more, and the garrison of Geraki would see it as an attack, and Alexis knew it would require thousands to take one of the strongest fortresses in Greece. No, for this mission to succeed he needed guile: guile and the authority of the Despot.

They had not left until midday but had covered the ground quickly and it was late afternoon when he saw the great bulk of the castle on a distant hill, its walls and towers dominating the plain around it. It was still flying the flag of the Mamonas.

Alexis wondered when the garrison would first see their approach. He spurred his horse faster and turned in the saddle to signal for his companions to do the same. It was vital that they gave the garrison commander as little time to think as possible.

The fortress was getting closer now and Alexis looked up at its battlements, shielding his eyes from the sun. Then he saw a puff of white smoke balloon into the sky and, a second later, a crack like thunder echoed like a shockwave across the plain. It was difficult to see across the distance but Alexis was certain that he'd seen the flash of sun on metal.

Cannon.

Was that why the Mamonases were so reluctant to give up their castle? Was it because they wanted to test their cannon there? And if they did, why did the Despot not know anything about it?

Who are the cannon for?

On the walls of the Castle of Geraki, Richard Mamonas narrowed his eyes to better see the small party of horsemen racing across the plain as if the very devil was behind them.

'Is there a flag?' he asked an officer by his side.

'No, sir, and they're riding too low in the saddle to see their hauberks. But they're coming from the direction of Mistra. Would you like us to intercept them? I could send a party, but we'll have to move quickly. They're almost at our gates.'

'Send forty mounted crossbowmen with someone you trust,' ordered Mamonas. 'Whoever they are, I don't want them in the castle. Understood?'

Minutes later, the forty crossbowmen were assembled in the square of the castle and were ready to ride. The huge doors were slowly being winched open and more archers were mounting the battlements around the castle gate to provide support if needed.

The captain of the party was about to issue orders when there was a shout from the direction of the keep. Richard Mamonas was striding across the square, buckling on his sword as he came.

'You may stand down, Julius. I will lead this one myself.'

Out on the plain, Alexis had just signalled the order for his men to sit up in their saddles, and twenty Palaiologian crests, the two-headed eagle of Byzantium, came into the view of the garrison watching them from the battlements.

Up ahead, he could see the castle doors slowly rolling open and the first of a troop of horsemen canter out to meet them. Except for the man in front, all were carrying crossbows.

How many of them were there? Alexis counted thirty, then forty riders. They were outnumbered two to one.

The lead rider reined in his horse as he approached Alexis and, at a signal, his troop fanned out to form a crescent around the Albanians. Then they stopped and lifted their crossbows into the aim. Forty catches were unlocked.

Alexis recognised the man in front of him from the wedding. He knew him to be a Mamonas and racked his memory for a name.

'Richard Mamonas at your service,' said the man helpfully, bowing from the saddle. 'And you are Alexis Laskaris. I believe we met at my cousin's wedding to your sister.'

'Of course. It is a pleasure to meet you again. I come on the orders of our Despot.' Alexis paused and looked around him, smiling carefully. 'The wedding you most graciously remember me from was, I was led to understand, the mark of a new friend-ship between our two cities. Was the news perhaps not passed on to your men?'

Richard Mamonas patted the air beside him and forty cross-bows were lowered. But they remained unlocked.

'Excellent!' beamed Alexis. 'Now perhaps we might discuss this business of the Despot's inside the castle? It's hot out on this plain and I am croaking for some wine.'

But Mamonas didn't move and nor did any of his troop. Alexis heard muttering from the men behind him and he held up his hand. Then he moved his horse closer to Richard's. He leant forward in his saddle and spoke softly, the smile still on his face.

'Mamonas, I mean to enter this castle. I am doing so on the orders of the Despot . . . *your* despot, in case you'd forgotten. Now please move aside.'

But Richard Mamonas didn't. 'I'm sorry but I cannot allow that to happen. I have very clear orders from the Archon.'

100

Alexis looked surprised. 'And who rules the Despotate of Mistra, Richard, your archon or our despot?'

There was silence. The two men locked gazes, and there was no compromise in their eyes. Alexis tried another tack. He kept his voice low.

'Is it the soldiers?' he asked. 'If it's my escort that's troubling you then I can leave them outside.'

Still no response.

Alexis cocked his head on one side as if he were considering something. Then he threw back his head and laughed.

'Of course!' he said, slapping his thigh. 'Of course! It's the cannon! But the Despot will be delighted when I tell him. They'll be so useful against the Turk. I assume that's what they're for, aren't they?'

For the first time, Richard Mamonas looked uncomfortable. Someone said something behind him. The garrison soldiers had assumed that the cannon were to be used against the Turks and it came as a surprise to learn that the Despot knew nothing about them.

Alexis decided to press home the advantage. He backed his horse away from Mamonas and addressed the garrison soldiers directly.

'All of you know that, by the terms of the recent treaty drawn up between the Despot and Archon, this castle is to be handed over to the Despot's command. You know this because the terms were displayed in your city's square. I am here to take that command.'

He looked slowly along the line of the men, all of whose eyes were fixed on his. 'I know that you are soldiers of the Archon, but your first loyalty is to your emperor in Constantinople and to his brother who rules here in this despotate. Our common enemy is the Turk. And if we want to remain Christian and to stop our families from being sold into slavery, then we can no longer fight between ourselves. We must unite behind our despot.'

Richard Mamonas looked at his soldiers. Some had lowered their crossbows and all were listening intently.

But Alexis wasn't finished. 'I am now going to ride my horse through that gate. And when I'm inside, I will order the lowering of the Mamonas flag and the raising of that of the rightful ruler of this castle: the Despot.'

His eyes swept over the men again. 'If any of you wants to stop me, you have only to pull a trigger. But if you pull that trigger, then our land will be plunged into another civil war and the Turks will rejoice. The choice is yours.'

There was complete silence. Even the Albanians, most of whom spoke no Greek, knew that something important was about to happen.

Alexis kicked his horse and rode slowly past Richard Mamonas, who moved sideways to let him pass. He began to ride towards the gate.

Then Mamonas looked up at the battlements and gave an imperceptible nod.

There was the sound of released bowstring and the blur of an arrow in flight. Alexis Laskaris fell from his horse to the ground.

In an instant, Richard Mamonas had leapt from his horse and had run to where Alexis was lying. It was an expert shot and the arrow was embedded deep in his lower neck, above the rim of his cuirass. Blood was oozing from either side of the shaft. He knelt beside him. He looked up. 'Who fired that shot?' he shouted. 'Bring me the man who fired that shot!'

Alexis was white with agony and had rivulets of sweat coursing down his cheeks. His breathing was laboured but he was trying to say something.

'Don't speak,' said Mamonas gently. 'The arrow is deep. But I dare not move it lest you die from the shock. We must get you to a surgeon.'

He stood up at the sound of approaching footsteps to see an archer being dragged forward between two guards. 'Did you fire that shot?'

The archer looked confused. 'Yes, lord, but—'

He never finished the sentence because Mamonas stepped forward, drew his dagger and plunged it into the man's heart.

'Take the body away and bury it,' he said.

Thirty miles away, Anna was sitting in her bedroom at the palace, trying to read. She had a headache.

She seemed always to be getting headaches these days, which was strange since she'd rarely had them before. She supposed that it might be because she was taking so little exercise. She was used to riding out daily but here, whenever she'd asked, some excuse had been found as to why she couldn't.

At least she hadn't had to meet her husband again. After that terrible night, she'd been moved to a different room. She hadn't seen Damian for months.

There was a knock on her door. Anna hurried to open it.

It was Zoe and she was alone. She looked up and down the corridor before coming in. She walked over to the bed and sat on it. She leant forward and took Anna's hands. 'Something has happened,' she said. 'It's Alexis. He's been hurt.'

Anna felt faint and her knees nearly gave way. She uttered a little groan. 'Hurt?' she asked weakly. 'How hurt?'

'Badly,' said Zoe. 'He was shot by an arrow.'

The room seemed to spin around her and Anna had to hold on to the bedpost to stop from falling. 'What . . . what happened?'

'I'm not certain. It seems there's been some sort of action at Geraki Castle. My father and brother were hearing of it from a messenger. The door was open.' She paused, taking hold of Anna's shoulders and drawing her to her breast. But Anna pulled away.

'Where is he, Zoe? I must go to him. Will you help me?'

'Of course,' replied Zoe. 'I am your friend. Geraki is a two-hour ride if you go fast. But you must leave quickly. My father won't want this news to get out.'

Zoe helped Anna change into clothes suitable for riding, opened the door carefully and led her down the corridor to a small side door at the end. 'This is a staircase the servants use,' she whispered. 'It leads down to the kitchens and you can leave by the rubbish door. There are no guards on it. Then you must make your way down to the stables. The rest is up to you.'

The stables were dark when Anna reached them and seemed unguarded. She couldn't believe her luck. Perhaps the soldiers had sneaked off to some tavern in the nearby Cretan quarter.

She lifted the heavy latch of the big oak doors and pulled them open. Their noise startled some of the horses and Anna hushed them. The moon outside gave her enough light to see a row of stalls in each of which stood a horse, looking at her. Her eyes travelled along them until she saw her palfrey. She'd heard that it had recovered from the accident. She'd take the palfrey.

Finding a saddle leaning against the wall, and a bridle

hanging above it, she moved quietly down the aisle until she was at the stall. A minute later she was leading the horse back towards the open doors, silently cursing the ring of its hooves on the stone. Then she heard a snort to her right, one she recognised. She walked over to Eskalon and pressed her cheek to the felt of his nose.

'Wish us luck,' she whispered.

The moon disappeared.

Someone was silhouetted in the doorway and whoever it was had armour and a sword. The figure was swaying. Anna could smell the beer from where she was standing.

'Who's in there?'

Anna decided to bluff. 'How dare you speak to me like that!' she hissed from the darkness. 'I suppose you can't see who I am?'

She strode forward, still leading the horse, waving him out of her way as she passed into the moonlight. The man staggered back and stared stupidly.

Anna dropped the palfrey's reins and walked up to the man, who towered over her. She sniffed. 'I believe you are drunk,' she said, looking up at him. 'I wonder what the Archon will do when I tell him. What do you think he'll do?'

The man scratched his beard.

'What do you think he'll do?' she asked again.

There was a long pause while the man thought and Anna's spirits began to rise.

This is working.

'I think we both know what he'll do,' said Anna softly. 'So I suggest you let me ride out of here and we'll forget what has happened.'

Then the man found his voice. With an effort, he straightened himself and adjusted the sword at his side. He cleared his throat noisily and a sly look entered his eyes. 'Lady, I know the Archon will punish me for abandoning my post. But he would do worse if he found that I'd let you ride out.'

Anna bit her lip. So she was indeed a prisoner. She decided to take a different tack. 'Soldier, do you have a brother?'

The man looked bewildered. 'I have three brothers, lady.'

'And do you love them?'

'I love them enough,' he answered.

'Well,' said Anna, 'my brother . . . my only brother, is lying at Geraki Castle and is badly wounded. He may die. I have to be with him.'

The soldier looked unpersuaded.

'If you let me go to him,' she went on, 'I promise that you will take a rich reward from the Despot.'

The soldier said nothing and Anna felt her temper rising. 'What must I do for you to let me go?' she asked.

There was a long pause.

'Well, lady . . .' the soldier said slowly. The sly look had returned to his eyes. '. . . you're a pretty thing and—'

He got no further.

There was a deep thud as something heavy connected with the back of his head. He pitched forward and lay senseless on the ground.

'I didn't want to hear the rest of that sentence,' said Luke as he stepped forward into the moonlight. He looked with disgust at the body beneath him.

'Have you killed him?'

'I'm afraid not, lady, but he'll have a sore head for some days. Come, help me to bind him. The guard is due to change in less than an hour.'

As they pulled the body away, Luke said, 'That was a pretty speech. I almost thought you would win him over.'

'I think I did, didn't I?'

Luke smiled and stripped some linen from a hanging cloth to stuff in the man's mouth. He took his sword and tucked it into his belt. Then he tied his hands. In the moonlight his own seemed oversized. Anna put her hand on his and saw how small it was in comparison. It was trembling.

'Will you ride with me to Geraki, Luke?'

An hour later, the two of them were riding hard across open country. The moon was almost full and clouds straddled its face like worn curtains. The land was mostly scrub and rock for they were steering clear of the road. The landscape came and went around them, one moment a ghostly apparition, the next a mass of shadow.

The noise of the night had long since given way to the pounding of their horses' hooves on the earth. But its smell was everywhere, and Luke filled his lungs with the aroma of flower, herb, vine and salt that was Mistra. He felt more alive than he had for months and thrilled to the feel of the air rushing past his temples, lifting his hair behind.

Beside him, Anna's smaller horse was trying hard to keep up with Eskalon. Luke looked across and saw the dread in her eyes and he thought about the courage of this girl who'd been so badly used by those meant to protect her. Then he thought about what had happened at Geraki. Anna had told him what she knew as they'd ridden. But why would a Mamonas garrison want to hurt the son of the Protostrator so soon after their alliance had been sealed in marriage? It didn't make sense.

Anna's thoughts were only of her brother. She had no idea how badly wounded he was or who was tending to him but she knew that being with him, now, was the most important thing she had ever wished for.

He cannot die.

They crested a hill and Luke pulled Eskalon up to get his bearings. The road was beneath them, snaking dimly into the distance, and he could just see the hill of Geraki on the horizon. He thought they should probably return to the road since he knew that they were close to the deep gulley and he wasn't sure exactly where it was.

Anna had stopped next to him, but before she could kick her palfrey into the descent, he held up his hand to stop her. He was leaning forward in his saddle, listening hard.

'Did you hear something?' she whispered.

'The sound of a horse, maybe more than one. On the road ahead.'

She could hear it now. There was more than one.

Luke said, 'We'll have to let them go by. We can't risk keeping from the road any more. Let's hope they pass quickly.'

They turned their horses back down the lee of the hill and rode back to some trees where they dismounted and tethered them. Then they walked back to the crest and fell to their bellies to watch the travellers pass. The moon was behind a thick cloud and there was no sign of the approaching riders except the snort of horses and the jangle of bridles. They didn't seem to be travelling at more than a walk. Then they heard something else: the squeak of wheels turning and the movement of heavier harness.

'They've got a cart,' whispered Luke. A horrifying thought was beginning to form in his mind.

Anna had had it too. 'They couldn't be *moving* him!' she whispered in disbelief. She began to crawl forward.

Luke put his hand on her shoulder. 'It might not be them. It could be anyone.'

'Out here, at dead of night, with no lights?' asked Anna. 'I think it's them.'

Just then the moon reappeared. Below them were four mounted soldiers, all with the unmistakable crest of the Mamonas on their hauberks, and a man driving a low cart. There was a dark shape in the back of the cart.

Anna gave a little cry and lifted her hand to her mouth, her eyes wide with horror. She tried to stand but Luke took her arm. He forced her gently to the ground and began to crawl back down the slope in the direction of the horses.

Luke had no plan. He had no idea what they would do when they got to the cart but he knew Anna had to be there and that every second counted. When they were clear of the crest, they got to their feet and ran back to their mounts. In seconds, they were spurring their horses back up the hill, Anna in front.

Suddenly she stopped and wheeled round to face Luke. 'You can't come with me. If they see you they'll know you hit the guard and helped me to escape. You cannot come.'

Luke ignored her and kicked Eskalon to pass. She grabbed his bridle and pulled hard so that Eskalon was forced to turn his head and stop beside her. She held it tight and looked directly into Luke's eyes.

'Luke, you've done enough,' she said. 'He's *my* brother.'

'And it's *my* empire,' said Luke quietly. 'I'm a Varangian, Anna.' He leant forward. 'If Alexis was shot, he was shot for a reason. I want to know why.'

He turned Eskalon and crested the hill, Anna behind him.

*　　　*　　　*

Richard Mamonas heard them before he saw them. He was talking to the wagon-driver when he heard a cry and the sound of hooves approaching fast from the hill to his left.

He pulled his horse to a halt and drew his sword. He could see two shapes galloping towards him, both with long hair strung out in the moonlight. One was a woman.

'Why are you moving him?' the woman screamed.

Mamonas cursed. She was supposed to be imprisoned in the palace. He didn't recognise the man that rode beside her.

Anna had reined in her horse. 'Why have you moved my brother from Geraki?'

'We are taking him to Monemvasia,' Mamonas said. 'To a surgeon.'

'But you'll *kill* him!' Anna spurred her horse over to the wagon and leapt to the ground. She ran to the back of the cart and climbed, as gently as she could, into it, kneeling in the straw beside her brother and taking his head in her hands with infinite care.

Richard Mamonas made a move to follow her but found himself looking at the tip of Luke's sword.

'Who did it?'

Mamonas glanced around. His men were too far away to intervene. He shook his head. 'It was an accident,' he said. 'A simple mistake.'

'Not so simple,' said Luke.

He backed over to the wagon, his sword raking the air to left and right. He looked over its side.

Anna was sitting with Alexis's head in her lap. The moon had re-emerged to bathe everything in a wash of grey and Alexis's skin was as candle wax. Anna bent forward to kiss his cold brow. 'What have they done to you?' she murmured, tears rolling down her cheeks as she smoothed the hair at his temple. 'My darling, what have they done to you?'

Alexis could hear her, but only just. The arrow was still in his neck and the sway of the cart had caused such searing agony that he had slipped in and out of consciousness until he no longer knew where he was.

But he knew that voice.

'Anna . . .' he murmured. 'Can you . . . get me some . . . water?'

Anna looked up and found Luke. He swung his sword round to the wagon driver.

'Water this instant or I'll put this through you.'

The man hurried to find his pigskin sack. Luke passed it to Anna. She pulled out the stopper and brought it to Alexis's lips, tilting his head forward to help him drink. She looked down into the face she loved more than anything on earth.

Alexis was drenched in sweat, his face shining in the moonlight. There were dark shadows around his eyes and he was feverish, his body shaking in spasms. His breathing was coming in rasps. Anna saw a clumsy bandage wrapped around his neck, its cotton black with congealed blood. She dared not remove it, yet she feared infection would set in if she didn't.

'Luke, we need a surgeon.'

Luke nodded. He turned to the wagon-driver. 'Tell your officer to come here. Now!'

A moment later, Richard Mamonas was standing next to the cart.

'We can't move him any further. It's killing him,' Luke said. 'Is there anywhere nearby that we can take him?'

Richard Mamonas thought quickly. This was unexpected and the man looked as if he knew how to use his sword.

'I believe there is a barn where they store hay up ahead, perhaps half a mile,' he said.

'Good,' said Luke. 'We'll take him there.' He turned to Anna. 'I know of a surgeon. I'll ride back and get him.'

For a moment Richard Mamonas thought about stopping him, but Luke lifted his sword. There was an unmistakable challenge in his eyes.

'I *will* go,' he said quietly.

Mamonas stepped aside.

Then Anna reached over the side of the cart and took his arm. 'Ride fast, Luke.'

An hour later, Anna lay on straw next to her brother with her head on his chest. Her eyes were screwed shut to prevent her tears from washing down her cheeks and on to his body. She was holding her breath so she could hear every pulse of the precious heart that beat beneath her.

They were alone in a barn that had holes in its roof through which the stars winked. There were stalls in shadow at one end, the single candle casting a very local light. The scene might have been one of nativity were it not for the blood.

Alexis had not spoken since they'd laid him there. He was deep within an ocean of sleep, and when he rose to its surface, his mouth would open and he'd cry out. His blood was all around him, pooled between the islands of straw. It was still oozing from the sides of the soldier's shirt from which Anna had fashioned a bandage. The arrow was still inside him and she dared not remove it.

When will the surgeon come?

She heard a groan and lifted her face to his. His breath was hot and his tongue quivered between open lips. His eyes were open but unseeing.

'Water.'

The flask was already in her hand and she brought it to his mouth, gently tilting it so that the water washed against his tongue. A trickle escaped and ran through the stubble of his chin.

How long has that been there? You are barely a man.

The groan again and an intake of breath. Alexis's head moved. Was he trying to speak?

Anna raised herself to kneel beside him. She put her palm to his brow. 'Alexis, what do you want to tell me?'

His head moved again and his face widened into grimace as his shoulder moved. He was looking at the arrow.

'The surgeon is coming,' Anna whispered. 'He's on his way. Luke went for him.'

He doesn't know who Luke is.

'Do you want to speak?'

'Cannon,' he said.

'Cannon?'

'They have . . . cannon. At Geraki.'

'Don't speak. Let me speak. Just move your head to reply.' She frowned. Why was this important? Unless . . . 'Are they for the Turk?'

It was a meagre movement, a fractional move of the head. Then he was asleep again.

Anna watched him for a long time, watched the sheen of life evaporating from his brow, watched the uneven, stuttered breathing that seemed to be slowing to a standstill. She moved with infinite care to lie beside him again. This time the heart-beat seemed fainter.

When will the surgeon come?

*   *   *

Three hours later, as the first hint of dawn began to creep over the horizon, he was there and Anna was praying.

Please God, don't let him die.

She heard a cock crow somewhere in the distance and her stomach gave a lurch. She prayed with greater urgency.

Lord, he has ever been your good and obedient servant. If you wish for some reflection of your goodness here on earth, let him live.

But Alexis was so still. The only sign of life within him was the feeble rise of his chest and the rattle that had arrived in his throat. Was this the sound of death?

She looked at the surgeon kneeling at her side, washing the blood from his hands in a little bowl. Luke was sitting in the shadows and hadn't spoken since he'd arrived with the man. They were the only ones in the barn.

'Will he live?' she asked, dreading the answer.

The surgeon was an Arab in his forties with kind eyes and the same long white hair as her father. She could see he was good at what he did and had tried his best. He didn't answer but studied his hands as he rubbed them dry on the towel.

Anna looked at her brother. He was lying on a linen sheet that had once been white but was now drenched in his blood. Around him had been placed new candles so that he looked like a sacrifice. His head rested on a pillow and his mouth was slightly open, revealing teeth broken when he'd clenched them as the arrow was withdrawn. A clean white bandage was now wrapped around his neck and shoulder. His fever seemed to have subsided and, with his eyes closed, he looked almost at peace.

'Will he live?' repeated Anna.

'Lady . . .' he began.

'Please, be honest.'

'Lady,' he began again, 'you should know that the arrow has done great damage. Not only is his lung pierced but it has severed the cord at his spine. If he does live, it will not be for long. And it will not be a life.'

Anna rocked back on her haunches as his meaning tore through her mind. Her brother, who lived for the adventure of living, unable to move.

She heard movement behind her and Luke knelt down beside her. For one so tall, he made little noise.

But the surgeon hadn't finished. 'Some believe it is better to die than to live in such a state.'

Anna turned on him, sick with horror at what he was saying. '*No!*' she whispered. 'I will not kill my brother!'

There was a slight movement below them and they all looked down at Alexis. He had turned his head a fraction in her direction. His eyes were open and tears glistened on his pale cheeks. There was love in his eyes, love and entreaty.

'Please.' His voice was barely audible.

Anna gazed down at him through a film of tears. 'I can't,' she whispered. '*I won't.*'

'Please, Anna,' he pleaded, his voice a croak. 'I want . . . to die.'

Anna leant forward to move aside the candles down one side of his body. Then she lay down gently beside him and stroked his cheek. 'I love you more than anyone in the world, Alexis. I cannot kill you.'

There was a gentle cough above her and the surgeon spoke. 'Lady, it is not for you. It is for him.'

She glanced up at him, his face a blur through her tears, before looking back at Alexis, who had closed his eyes again, his face resigned. He had fallen back into unconsciousness. She stared at him for a long, long time. Then she raised herself to her knees and pressed her lips together.

Luke was watching her intently. Then, without thinking, he put his arm around her shoulder and drew her towards him so that her head was resting on his shoulder. His strength passed through her body.

'How would you do it?' she whispered.

'I have a potion,' said the Arab. 'It will be quick and it will be painless. I promise you.'

Anna looked down at the body of her brother. She stared into his face, smoothing back his hair. Then she leant forward and kissed him on his forehead.

'Goodbye, Alexis,' she said.

CHAPTER SEVEN

MONEMVASIA, SUMMER 1394

Anna awoke from her nightmare drenched in sweat and curled like a fetus on the stone floor. In the light of the oil lamp she could see that her bed was a mass of twisted sheets, some as damp as her nightdress. In her dream, she'd been in the hole again; whatever it was that was trying to get to her through the roots had come terrifyingly close this time. She realised that every time it was getting closer. And these days the dream came to her every night. She got to her feet unsteadily.

She heard the key turn in the lock and a guard stood in the doorway.

'I heard a cry, lady. Are you hurt?'

It was taking Anna a moment to remember where she was. She looked around the room that had once been a cistern and vaguely wondered whether the shadows of its arched ceiling were part of her dream. The room was cold and the lamp only served to darken the room beyond its reach. She looked at the guard. He was an older man with short grey hair and a beard, her father's age perhaps. He had kind eyes.

'Can I have more light? It's very dark in here. I have only one lantern.'

The soldier looked uncomfortable. He felt sorry for this strange, silent girl but he had his orders. 'I'll see what I can do, lady,' he said. 'Shall I empty your pot?'

Anna was embarrassed but too weak to really care. 'Yes, please,' she said and stepped aside to let him pass. The guard walked over to it and then stopped, looking bewildered.

'There's nothing in here, lady.'

'Oh, I thought . . . thank you anyway.' She sat down on the bed, suddenly exhausted.

'I'll go now, lady, if there's nothing else.'

'No . . . no,' she replied. She heard the door lock.

What she wanted to dream about was Alexis.

Alexis.

In that final, searching look into his face, she'd tried to stitch every thread of his young beauty into the fabric of her memory. She wanted to dress her soul in its precious cloth, holding it in there forever. And she wanted to tear off little bits nightly to wrap around her dreams. But all she could remember was the look of fear in those eyes when he knew he was going to die. And when this horror arose before her, she knew that her heart was broken and would never be whole again.

I killed him. I killed Alexis.

She closed her eyes, forcing them shut so that her neck strained with the effort. She rocked back and forth on the bed, her shoulders hunched, hugging herself. Hating herself. She wanted to be somewhere else, anywhere else. With Alexis.

How can I die?

She hadn't eaten for days, the time she'd been in this room. Could she starve herself to death? She looked down at her emaciated body and saw that she'd drawn blood above her elbows with her fingernails. What if she never ate again?

How long does it take to die?

She lifted the nightdress and looked at her legs. She still had scratches from the straw of the barn and she was filthy. It wasn't that she'd been denied a bath; she'd refused it. In fact she'd been denied very little. The food had looked good and there'd been wine. She had books and they'd even provided a rug for the floor. Her bed had sheets and her clothes were neatly arranged in a cupboard. She was imprisoned, but not with any hardship.

At least the headaches had gone. They'd disappeared when she'd stopped eating.

In her moments of lucidity, she worried about Luke. Had he been punished for helping her to escape? And what of her parents? Did they yet know of their son's death? If they did, they would need her with them. They'd need her there now, to see in her some pale reflection of his goodness, of his greatness.

Alexis.

In the city of Mistra, her parents had just received the body of their son and her mother's hair had, overnight, turned the same shade as her husband's.

The Laskaris family had enjoyed a life so far unblemished by tragedy. Now, Alexis was dead and it was too much for Maria to bear. Her agony had echoed through the city every second of the night and had continued through the morning. She had refused to leave her room and her husband had excused himself from all official duties to be with her.

The body had been brought to them by the Kephale Nikolaos Eudamis, who had explained the dreadful accident at Geraki. But from the moment that Alexis had been laid out on the table, the terrible wound still open at his neck, they hadn't really been listening. What did it matter how it had happened? What mattered was that their only son would never again breathe the air of Mistra. So the Kephale had quickly left for the Despot's palace to repeat the story and assure his prince that the Archon would allow no further delay to the departure of the fleet and to present him with the keys of Geraki Castle. Then he'd left with as much speed as court protocol allowed.

In Monemvasia, the Archon was sitting at a long table with his son and daughter. None of the three was speaking; the only sound came from the hiss and spit of a candle on the table before them. Damian was staring into its flame while Zoe watched the wax congeal down its sides. Damian stole occasional glances at the man at the head of the table.

Their father was staring directly ahead. They'd never seen him like this before. He'd always been a man of decision but now he looked as if events were out-pacing him.

'I should have gone.'

Zoe looked at him. 'Father?'

'I should never have entrusted such an important mission to that fool Eudamis. I was a coward. I should have gone to speak to Laskaris myself, father to father.' The candle flared slightly and it was enough to break the Archon's vacant gaze. He looked from one to other of his children and leant forward, bringing his hands together beneath his chin. 'What happened out there? Was it really an accident?'

Damian shrugged his shoulders. 'It seems so,' he said gloomily. 'But we'll never know for sure since our idiot cousin killed the archer who fired the shot.'

'But isn't that in itself suspicious?' went on the Archon.

'Well,' answered Damian, 'Richard says that he'd met Laskaris

120

at my wedding and they'd become friends. He acted impulsively.'

Zoe said, 'I can't see why it would suit Richard any more than the rest of us to go to war with the Despot. He just panicked, that is all.'

His father nodded as he considered this. She went on.

'Father, you were right not to go to Mistra. Your presence there might've enflamed things and you'd have had some difficult questions to answer about Anna.' She glanced at Damian. 'I'm not sure things are quite as bad as you think. We've given them back Geraki, and the cannon were removed as soon as Richard knew they'd been discovered. They are on their way to Suleyman so the fleet can sail now. And remember, it was an accident. Some stupid, over-eager archer with too much sweat on his thumb. It won't be the first time it's happened.'

'But what about the cannon?' he asked, looking anxiously at his daughter, who seemed entirely collected. 'When they take possession of the castle, they'll get their Albanians back. They'll learn about the cannon.'

'So bribe the Albanians. Give them money to disappear.'

That might work. He turned to his son. 'Where's your wife?'

Damian smirked. 'I have her held in an empty cistern downstairs with no window. She won't escape again.'

His father looked up sharply. 'See that she doesn't, Damian. We don't know what Alexis might have told her before he died.' He paused. 'How did she *get* to Geraki?'

'I don't know how she got out of the palace, Father,' said Damian, 'but I think I know how she got to Geraki. That stallion that you allowed Luke Magoris to keep? It had been ridden hard when we saw it the following morning.'

'By Luke?' asked Zoe, a little too quickly.

Damian nodded. 'He's the only one who can ride it. And Richard said that there was a man with her.'

'Perhaps it's time for the horse to go,' she said.

His father frowned. 'Killed?'

'No, sold. It will fetch a good price from the Turk. They need destriers.'

Damian smiled. 'He'll not like that.'

'Nor will she,' said Zoe quietly, and she rose to leave.

A little later, in the basement of the palace, the guard sitting outside Anna's room saw Zoe approach. She was holding a tray with food and had clean sheets over one arm.

'Open the door.'

The guard took the key from his belt and turned it in the lock. Zoe walked in and stared at the girl on the bed. She put down the tray and sat down next to Anna. She seemed shocked.

'What have they done to you?' she whispered. 'What in mercy's name have they done to you?'

Anna looked surprised. 'Why, nothing, Zoe. They care for me well. See for yourself the food on your tray.'

'But you're not eating it. Look at you!' She took Anna in her arms, stroking her filthy hair. 'And you smell,' she said gently, drawing back and looking into Anna's eyes. 'When did you last have a bath?'

Anna was embarrassed. 'I . . .'

'Well, you'll have one now.' She let go of Anna, walked to the door and banged on it.

When the guard appeared, Zoe asked for a copper bath to be brought, filled with hot water, and soap and towels. Then she busied herself remaking Anna's bed.

The bath arrived and the door was locked behind it. Zoe

asked Anna to lift her arms so that she could take off her night-dress. She tried hard not to look at the body that emerged. Anna's ribcage protruded from her sides and her hip bones shone like pale cheese in the light of the oil lamp. Zoe helped her gently to stand in the bath and began to soap her body. Steam rose around them.

'Am I very thin?' asked Anna.

Zoe stopped soaping and wiped her eyes with the back of her hands. She tucked a stray hair behind her ear and got to her feet. 'Yes, you are very thin.' She paused. 'I heard about Alexis. I'm sorry.'

Anna looked away. In spite of the steam, she shivered. 'I miss him. I dream.'

'Dream? Dream of what?'

'Of a hole. A grave. It frightens me,' she said softly.

'You are scared of being buried?'

'Something like that.'

Zoe took this in. Then she said, 'It was an accident.'

'Was it?' asked Anna, turning back. 'Perhaps the arrow, but not the journey back in the wagon. That's what killed him. Who was Richard Mamonas obeying?'

Zoe looked down at her hands. 'Nobody,' she said quietly. 'My father is as distressed by this as anyone.'

'And the cannon?' asked Anna. 'Might this have anything to do with the cannon my brother saw at Geraki? The cannon that the Despot doesn't know about?'

Zoe was silent. Anna had stepped from the bath and covered herself with the towel. She was watching Zoe carefully.

'Your family are still helping our enemies, Zoe,' Anna said evenly. 'What I don't know is how much you are helping them too. Suleyman was at the wedding. I saw you talking to him.'

Zoe stared at her. She seemed to be considering something. Then she turned away. 'I hate Suleyman,' she said softly.

'Why?'

When Zoe turned back, her eyes were wet. 'Can't you guess?'

Anna could guess. She looked down at her hands.

'So we are allies, of a sort,' continued Zoe. She paused. 'If I helped you escape, would you trust me then?'

'Where would I go?'

Zoe pretended to consider this. She needed Luke in Mistra where he might lead her to something she very much wanted. And she needed this girl's trust. 'Luke Magoris. That's whom you should go to. After all, he saved your life.'

'And you'd take me to him?'

'Not take you, no. But I can get you past the guard and out of the palace. And I can tell you where he lives.' She smiled. 'Then perhaps you might trust me.'

Two hours later, Luke was sitting at a table on which his dinner lay untouched beside him and his wine undrunk. Next to him, with her arm around him, was his mother.

Luke had returned a short while ago from the Mamonas stable where he went every evening to bid Eskalon goodnight. Except this time his stall had been empty. He'd guessed immediately what had happened and run to the nearest guard.

'Where is he?' he'd shouted at the soldier, grabbing the neck of his aventail. 'Where is my horse?'

And the man had told him. Damian himself had come to the stable to oversee the removal of Eskalon. The stallion had not wanted to leave without Luke and it had taken four men to drag it through the stable door and on to a waiting cart.

And Damian had watched all this with a grin on his face and a whip in his hand.

Luke shook his head in bewilderment. He loved Eskalon. He'd talked to him every day for the past two years and had gone to sleep every night with that giant head, those intelligent eyes, in his thoughts. The prospect of a world without him was unthinkable.

'Luke,' Rachel said, taking his face. 'Look at me.'

Luke turned.

'What was always going to happen to that horse?' she asked softly. 'What happens to every horse from the Mamonas stud? What is the *point* of that stud, Luke?'

Luke said nothing.

His father sat down beside him and put his hand on his shoulder. 'I plan to ask the Archon to reinstate you as a Varangian,' he said. 'His mood is changed these days.'

His son looked at him in disbelief. '*A Varangian?*' he said in a tone that Joseph had never heard before. 'Do you think, Father, that with all that's happened I could ever serve that family?'

His father looked as if he'd been hit. He took a step backwards.

'Who do you think was there when they took Eskalon away?' Luke continued, hitting the table with his fist. 'Who do you think was there with a whip in his hand?' He was breathing hard and his voice had risen to a shout. '*It was Damian, Father!* Don't you see that he hates every nerve in my body for what happened to him? How *could* I serve him?'

There was silence as father and son stared at each other. Luke looked at his mother. She looked stricken.

'Oh God, what have I said?' Luke groaned.

His father was shaking his head slowly, his great beard

swaying above his tunic, a look of inexpressible sadness in his old eyes.

'Luke, we are Varangians—' he was beginning when Luke cut him short, something he'd never done before.

'And I will *be* a Varangian, just not one that serves this archon. Our empire, that same Empire that made the Varangian Guard, is in its death throes. And our archon is giving the knife to its *assassin*! Father, haven't you been listening to what I've told you about the cannon?'

'That was Alexis Laskaris's word—'

'Word? Alexis Laskaris died because of those cannon!' shouted Luke. But he'd gone too far. His father slapped him hard across his face.

There was a knock on the door.

All three of them froze. No one ever visited at this time of night. The knock came again, more urgently.

Luke went over to the door and opened it.

Anna was standing in the doorway wearing a dark hooded cloak that Luke recognised as Zoe's. She was breathing hard and her shoulders were rising and falling beneath the cloak. There was a sheen of sweat on her brow and her eyes were dull and had dark rings around them. Her eyelids were flickering, either from illness or fatigue.

'Anna!' he gasped. 'What . . . ?'

But before he could finish the question, she had pitched forward into the room, landing on her knees. Rachel rushed to her side and gently lifted her up. Then she took her cloak and guided her to a chair.

'I'm sorry,' said Anna, sitting down. 'I heard voices and didn't think I'd found the right house, so I waited in the alleyway.' She looked bewildered, turning to Luke. 'Then I recognised

Luke's voice. So I knocked.' She stopped, still looking at Luke. 'I'm sorry,' she said again. 'But I have nowhere else to go.'

Then Luke found his voice. 'Anna . . . you're so thin, your arms . . . What have they done to you?'

'They locked me in a room in the basement. They had to. I know about the cannon.'

Luke went over to the chair. He knelt and took her hand. 'Anna, how did you get like this? Have they been starving you?'

'No . . . no. It's not like that. I haven't wanted to eat.' Her eyes filled with tears and she buried her head in his shoulder. '*I miss him so much!*' she whispered.

'Hush,' said Luke softly, stroking her hair. He looked up at Rachel. 'Mother, can you pour some wine?' When it had been passed to him, he gently lifted Anna's head and guided the cup to her lips. 'Drink this,' he said. 'It will help. How did you get away?'

Anna sipped the wine. 'It was Zoe. It's the second time she's helped me to escape. I owe her a lot.'

Luke got to his feet and took the chair opposite her across the table. 'Why would she do that?' he asked, almost to himself.

Anna shrugged. It was half a shiver. The wine was doing some good. 'She told me once that she wanted to make amends. For things she'd done to you.'

Luke shook his head, unconvinced. 'Well, it hardly matters now. We've got to get you away from here, back to Mistra. I will help you, of course – but my father can't.' He glanced at Joseph who was watching them, confusion in every part of his face. 'He is sworn to the Archon.' He took Anna's hand, searching the thin face before him. Was she even hearing him? 'So we have to leave. I don't know where we'll go, but we'll find

127

somewhere. And we have to go now. This is the first place they'll search.'

He got up and picked up her cloak from the back of a chair. She stood unsteadily to put it on. Then he guided her to the door.

'Luke,' said Joseph from behind him.

Luke turned. Joseph took his son in his arms and hugged him fiercely.

'Listen to me,' said Joseph. 'You're right – you must leave, but only because they *will* come here to search.'

Luke nodded.

'So,' said Joseph, 'find your three friends and take her somewhere you can all look after her until it's safe to leave. I will tell you where to go.'

By now the hour was late, Monemvasia was abed and only the cats prowled the streets. Both dressed in dark cloaks, Luke and Anna hurried through the maze of alleyways until they reached Matthew's house. Luke put two fingers to his mouth and gave a low whistle.

Once Matthew was dressed and had climbed through his window and from there to the ground, he set off with Luke and Anna to the next house. The moon was on the wane and they needed the flickering lights of the street lamps to guide their way.

Fifteen minutes later, the five of them were sitting in the pews of the little church of St Andreas, hard by the city's sea walls. They could hear the sound of the waves on the rocks outside. Anna was sitting a little apart, looking up at a mural painted on the ceiling above the altar. From the lights of two suspended lamps, she could see an angel of the Last Judgement

128

reading from a lectern, while all around were the damned in torment. Serpents were writhing through the limbs of sinners waiting to be pitched into hellfire while far above floated the saved, smugly processing across the ceiling to join God the Father enthroned. Anna found herself looking for the face of her brother amongst them.

Alexis.

'Anna, have you heard anything we've said?'

'No . . . I'm sorry . . .'

'We're going to take you to a cave we know of on the other side of the Goulas,' said Luke. 'It's a climb up the rock but you can make it with our help. It's hidden from view by bushes and you'll be safe there.'

Anna nodded.

'But it means getting you through the city gate,' said Matthew. 'So one of us will stay behind and you'll wear his cloak. The guards are used to seeing four of us leave together.'

In a moment Anna was wearing Nikolas's cloak. It smelt of sea and fish.

Nikolas grinned. 'They'll know it's me from the smell. Just keep the hood up.'

CHAPTER EIGHT

MONEMVASIA, SUMMER 1394

The cave was bigger than Anna imagined it would be, and much lighter. Both were a great relief.

It had been a difficult climb and the five of them had waited in the church until dawn before attempting it. Now, it was her fourth dawn there and Anna sat at its entrance, wrapped in a blanket against the early morning chill, staring out across the bay of Monemvasia. The mountains skirting its edge were slowly taking shape beneath a changing sky and a low mist hung over the sea. Around her, hundreds of birds had begun their noisy tribute to the new day and Anna could hear the screams of cats, far below, as they fought over scraps washed on to the rocks overnight.

The shore on this north side of the Goulas was almost non-existent. The cliff walls rose straight from the sea and the rocks at its base were jagged and lashed by waves in all weathers so that it was impossible for boats to put in. Even if they had, they'd not have seen the mouth of the cave since it was covered by the branches of a laurel bush that grew out of the rock. It was the perfect hiding place.

Anna wondered who'd lived here in the past. There were

letters etched into the walls and she felt the presence of past habitation. She'd heard of hermits escaping the world to live in caves and wondered if that meant God remained in the place after they'd gone. She thought that God *was* perhaps in this cave with her, for she felt happier than she had in weeks.

She'd even managed to stop thinking about Alexis.

Anna looked out of the cave. The sun had crested the horizon behind her and stretched out across the waves like a ladder to heaven. The sky was becoming lighter and birds rose from the rocks around to warm their wings and chase away the last of the night.

Then Anna heard something unexpected below her, the neigh of a horse. It was coming from the direction of the port of Gefira, hidden from view to her left. But the port was too far away for the sound to have come from there. The animal must be on the rocks below. Or out at sea.

She strained her eyes to see into the mist. She heard the neigh again, closer she thought, and definitely coming from the sea. How was that possible?

A moment later, she understood. Coming around the edge of the rock, and quite far out, was a small merchantman lying low in the water flying the Mamonas flag. On its deck, tethered to the mast and moving with the roll of the ship, stood a horse.

Eskalon.

Anna's mind raced. If Eskalon was on a ship then he was leaving to be sold. He was leaving Luke. If Eskalon was being sold, it could only be Damian's work. Could he have found out about Luke's part in her ride to find Alexis? Was this Luke's punishment?

Anna pressed her head against the laurel, pushing aside the leaves to get a better view. It was undoubtedly Eskalon and he looked frightened. He was leaving to be sold to some Norman knight to brutalise into submission. And if he didn't submit, as Anna feared he would not, then he would be killed. She felt sick at the thought.

Anna looked around at the contents of her cave, at everything Luke had brought for her. She had blankets, a pillow, food, water, towels and an oil lamp with enough spare oil to keep it burning. All she could need, in fact, except company. Then she looked at the last object, a small crossbow that Joseph had given Luke to shoot squirrels with. She remembered how Luke had knelt behind her in the cave, his hands on hers, as he'd shown her how to use it.

Another memory came to her. They'd been at the gate on the night of her escape, four of them in cloaks and hers smelling of fish. She remembered how Luke had stopped to face her in the dark and then gently lifted the hood to cover her head. She remembered how he'd put his arm around her shoulders, shouting to the guards that Nikolas was sick and in need of the old Jew's remedy. She remembered how he'd squeezed her shoulder to reassure her that it would work. And she'd known that it would; that he was strong enough to protect her.

Later, Anna was asleep when she heard a rockfall outside. She rose to her knees and moved the laurel to look down. Someone was climbing up to the cave. She was surprised at how much she wanted it to be Luke.

It was Luke.

She saw his hair, the colour of straw, moving with his shoulders as he climbed, and the fair down that shivered on his forearms as he reached out for a handhold. A brown hessian sack was slung from his shoulders. He paused and glanced up to the cave.

'Help me up,' he panted as his head drew level with the cave's entrance. Anna took his hand and leant back with all her weight to help him in. Then he was there, sitting on the floor in front of her and lifting the sack from his shoulders.

'I have food and more oil and another blanket. I thought it might be cold at night. And I brought you a book.'

Anna's heart lifted. A book was a luxury.

'Where did you get it?'

'Zoe gave it to me to give to you. It's written by Anna Komnene about the reign of her father the Emperor Alexios. She said you'd find it interesting.'

'Anna Komnene?' Anna smiled. 'I was named for her. But where did you see Zoe?'

'I met her in the *mesi odos*, buying something. She was anxious to know where you were. I told her only that you were safe. Then she gave me the book.'

'She's kind,' said Anna.

Luke considered this. 'It wasn't always so. Anyway she's suggested you leave by sea since the bridge is heavily guarded. It would seem to make sense.'

'But surely we just need to wait for the Archon and Damian to leave?' asked Anna.

Luke shook his head. 'The Archon will only leave when he has to. He's worried that his estates will be confiscated if he goes.'

'Is the Despot marching on Monemvasia then?'

Luke nodded. 'I managed to get a message to Mistra about the cannon. It seems the Despot means to punish Pavlos Mamonas.'

133

'And Damian.'

Damian. They hadn't talked about the man who was still her husband. He'd been away, permitted finally to engage in the business of the Mamonas fortune.

'And Damian. He's leading the search for you.'

Luke began to unpack the sack, taking out the rug and a knotted napkin, which he untied to reveal some bread, onions, cream cheese and a *sphoungal,* a baked egg dish that Anna had said she liked. A smaller napkin held figs stuffed with chestnuts.

'These are my favourite,' said Luke. 'My mother made them for you.'

'Your favourite? Then you must join me. I can't eat all this on my own.'

They began to eat, comfortable in the silence of food shared. At last Luke wiped the breadcrumbs from his mouth.

'I think I have a plan to get us away.'

'Us? Are you coming with me?'

'You'd never make it on your own. Anyway, I need to go to Mistra.'

Anna put her head on one side. 'And leave your friends, your family? Why must you go to Mistra, Luke, except to take me there?'

Luke didn't answer.

Anna leant forward. She picked up the book and trailed her fingers across the leather. 'Anna Komnene writes about Varangians,' she said quietly. 'And my father told me that their treasure is buried somewhere on the hill of Mistra.' She paused. 'Is that why you must go there?'

Luke took the book and opened it. She knew he would say nothing more. She watched him turn the pages. She put her hand on the open page. 'Can you read, Luke?'

He looked up. 'A little.'

'Would you like me to read to you? About the Varangians?'

Luke smiled and handed the book to her. 'I'd like that very much.'

Much later, when the lamp had been lit and Anna's eyes were straining to read, she closed the book. It was evening.

Luke had hardly moved a muscle for six hours. He'd barely breathed.

'They were brave,' she said. 'Like you.'

He held her eye for a moment and then began to gather his things. 'I must go. I need to be in the house in case they search it.'

Anna nodded, surprised at her disappointment. 'Of course. Tell me, how is Joseph?'

Luke's face darkened. 'We argued the night you came,' he said. 'It's never happened before, not like that. I fear I'm not the son he should have.'

Anna thought of Joseph, thought of his eyes. It was inconceivable that he'd not be proud of Luke.

Luke got up. 'Anyway, it's not important next to what you have to do.'

Anna rose and went to the cave entrance. She turned to face him. 'I know about Eskalon, Luke. I'm sorry.'

'I loved him, Anna,' he said simply.

Anna stepped forward and hugged him hard. 'I know,' she said.

When Luke had gone, Anna sat on the ground and thought. So much had happened in the last few months, so much that was bad. One by one, the good things of her existence had fallen away and her future seemed saddled with guilt and uncertainty. A week ago, she'd feared for her sanity.

Then had come Luke. Yet again, when she'd needed him most, he'd been there. And his only intention seemed to be to do what was right.

From almost her first consciousness, Anna had known about intention, other people's intentions. With the Despot childless, she'd always known that her hand in marriage was the most important in the despotate and that it would only be given away for the highest of prices. Now she was married to Damian, a marriage that, with luck, might be annulled. After all, it had hardly been consummated. But that didn't mean that she'd then be free to place her heart where she wanted. No, it would then be her duty to make another expedient marriage, for her family, for her despot.

For Mistra.

Anna decided she must cast Luke from her mind. They could never be together so there was no point in thinking about him. Instead she picked up Zoe's book and began to read from where she'd stopped with Luke. And it was only when the weak flame of the lamp was the only light left in the cave that she put the book down.

She lay down on the blanket and looked up at the pitted roof of the cave, its shadows moving in the light. She would ask Luke to give her a second lamp. She didn't like the dark. A sudden gust of wind caused the flame to leap and then nearly go out and she moved her body quickly to shield the lamp. She shuddered at the thought of a night with no light.

When will you be back?

* * *

Two nights later, at the Mamonas Palace, Zoe was standing naked in front of the open window of her bedroom, looking out into the gathering night. The sun had just set and giant black clouds were scudding across the sky. The first spits of rain touched her cheek and she shivered, hugging her arms and lifting her head to feel the caress of wind on her forehead.

'There's going to be a storm,' she said.

There was no answer from the man lying on the bed. He was admiring the curve of her back and the swell of her buttocks and remembering them above him moments ago, moving in urgent rhythm to the rise and fall of his hips. That was certainly the best ride he'd had with any woman, including the most expensive whores in Constantinople, and he wondered whether his reward extended to another one. Probably not, he concluded.

Richard Mamonas had always desired his young cousin but had never allowed it to develop into anything more. He didn't believe that love was part of her repertoire of feelings. Nevertheless her ruthless determination intrigued and excited him in equal measure and he was glad that he'd finally earned his way into her bed.

'Have you ever loved anyone, cousin?' he asked her back.

Zoe turned around and eyed him warily. 'Why is that important to you?' she asked.

'It's not particularly.' He yawned. 'I just wondered, that's all.'

'What if I told you there was someone I wanted, someone who rejected me?'

Mamonas laughed. 'I wouldn't believe you.'

'Well, there was.' she said quietly.

Zoe moved to a chair where a silk gown lay sprawled. 'I think you should go,' she said, putting on the gown and tying its sash. 'And be careful when you leave.'

Without waiting for an answer, she walked back through the window and on to the balcony. Another gust of wind pressed the silk against her breasts and she gathered the material around her, tightening the sash. She shivered again.

Someone who rejected me.

Far below, beyond the sea wall of the lower town, she saw the same sight she'd seen for the past four nights. The three friends of Luke's were loading a small boat to go fishing. One was holding a lantern above his head while the other two were lifting a large crate into the vessel.

Zoe smiled.

Clever. Very clever.

In the cave, Anna was starting to worry. The wind was definitely rising outside and great gusts were breaking through the laurel bush, scattering the flame of her lamp. She had tried to use the blanket as a screen, huddling over the light beneath it, but the oil fumes had made her choke. Now she did the best she could to shield it with her body and prayed that it wouldn't go out.

If only Luke was here.

No. That way lay pain. Instead, she considered Anna Komnene's descriptions of the Varangians. Luke had told her of Siward Godwinson and his five hundred followers who'd formed the first English Varangians. Like their lost treasure, Anna had always thought it myth but here, in this book, was the story of the first battle they'd fought for Alexios at Dyrrachium.

She'd described how the Byzantines had used Greek fire against the Normans, something else the Empire seemed to have lost. She described it as made of sulphur and shot through tubes of reed, falling 'like a fiery whirlwind on the faces of the enemies'. It was said to burn on water. But where was it now? The secret of how to make it had gone, disappeared into the fog of time.

Greek fire, Varangians, gold. Three things the Empire needed.

Anna thought of Luke and his refusal to answer the question of why he needed to go to Mistra. She knew it wasn't the gold, it was the duty. The duty of every Varangian, since the time of Siward, to fight for his emperor.

Something that Luke cannot do in Monemvasia.

Lost in this thought, Anna hadn't noticed that the screech of the wind outside had risen and that the gusts entering the cave were getting stronger and more frequent. She shivered as a savage blast tore through the laurel bush and spilled over her back. The oil lamp spluttered.

Then it went out.

It was suddenly very dark in the cave, and colder, and the sounds of the wind and rain seemed much nearer. Anna felt the first clutch of fear enter her soul. She stretched out her arm to find the wall but felt nothing. She inched to the side until her hand touched the rock. She sank to the ground, feeling for the blanket to wrap herself in. Instead, her hand knocked over the pitcher of water and she felt cold liquid against her knee. Where was the book? The water must not reach the book he'd brought her.

She spread both hands out across the earth, only finding the lamp, which scalded her. Her hands met the crossbow and then, *thank God*, the book, and she clutched it to her breast like a relic. Eventually she found the blanket and wrapped it around her shoulders. She sat there, with book and crossbow, willing herself to endure.

Fear was all around her now, and it was growing.

Luke.

What was that? She'd heard a scratching noise from the laurel bush, outside the cave, but close. It came again. Was it the bush moving against the rock? No, this was a different sound, not a natural one. Anna froze in terror.

Go away!

The sound came again, closer, just the other side of the laurel.

Please, I will be good. Not lie to my mother.

Anna was paralysed with fear, her body rigid and hunched, her eyes raking the darkness for the first sign of what was coming for her. She found some movement in her hands and gripped the crossbow with one while the other felt along its top. The bolt groove was empty.

Then it came. She heard the laurel branches roughly parted and a sudden rush of wind enter the cave, flattening the blanket against her legs and letting fly the pages of the book. She closed her eyes and screamed.

'Anna!'

Luke.

It was Luke. There. In the cave. Luke. But she couldn't move.

'Anna, help me in!'

The wash of relief had swept past her now and her mind was clearing, her limbs beginning to respond. She put down the crossbow and book and moved towards the voice. She could just make out the black mass of a body half inside the cave. She reached out her hand.

'Take it. There!'

Luke's hands were in hers. She rocked backwards to help him climb in. Then he was there, somewhere, in front of her, his breathing filling the cave. She felt for him, and then threw herself into his embarce, sobbing with relief.

'Whoa!' said Luke from the darkness. 'You'll have me out of the cave again!'

Still she held him, her face buried in his chest, her tears coursing down his tunic and her breath hot against his shoulder. She held him tighter than she had that first day on the plain below Geraki. She held him so closely that, in the suspension of his breath, she could feel the pounding of his heart against hers.

'*You've come,*' she whispered into his shoulder, feeling his hair against her cheek and looking up to where she thought his face to be.

'Of course I came,' said Luke softly. 'The storm. I thought your lamp might go out. I thought that you'd be afraid.'

Anna lifted her fingers to his face, feeling for his lips. Then she raised her head and kissed him, a brush of a kiss at first and then deeper, more urgent.

She lay back on the floor of the cave, pulling Luke to her. She covered his lips, cheeks, hair with kisses as she held his head in her hands, lifting her chin when his own moved to her neck. All thoughts of the future had left the cave as Luke had entered it and Anna felt nothing but the urgency of *now*. In this world of storm and terror, here was a living thing she could trust, she could depend on, she could hold on to.

Then Luke gently pulled away from her, holding her shoulders in his hands, searching for her face in the blackness.

'Anna . . . what is this?' he said, his voice full of wonder. 'Should we light the lamp?'

'No,' she answered. 'Just hold me. Please.'

Much later, they lay in the darkness listening to the storm die outside the cave, both deep in their thoughts. They lay on one blanket and another covered their bodies, Anna's back pressed against the comfort of Luke's chest, one leg curled around his like a mooring rope. His arm held her close to him, his hand resting on the curve of her breast and his face lost in the mass of her hair, breathing in its scent of salt and musk.

Luke didn't know if Anna was asleep for she hadn't spoken for a long time and the rhythm of her breathing was soft and even. He hoped that she was, that whatever demons had been with her in the cave had been chased away. She deserved peace.

He knew that he was in love with her, that he'd loved her from the moment he'd seen her on the journey from Mistra. He knew, too, that it was a love without a future. Anna was daughter to the most important man in the despotate, save the Despot himself, and he was the son of a Varangian Guard. Whatever had happened in this cave, however right it had been, it would never, could never, happen again. It would remain locked in his heart as the most beautiful of memories.

But he would not sleep now. No, he would stretch this moment of pure happiness for as long as it would stretch, and when Anna awoke to tell him that they could never be together, he would smile, would understand, would leave.

But Anna was not asleep. Anna was lying as still as she could, keeping her breathing even, because she wanted Luke to think her asleep. She wanted him to know that the joy he'd given her had been so complete that its only consequence could be the peace of sleep.

But she also wanted to think.

In one way, things were much clearer now. She had no doubt that she loved Luke and that, whatever it took, she would find a way to be with him. She supposed that if they managed to escape to Mistra, Luke would make a new home there. Perhaps he would find his treasure and be rich. But what if he didn't? Surely he could be found some employment with the Despot or her father and they could remain lovers, secret lovers but lovers nonetheless? She felt suddenly light-headed.

Anna very slowly turned to face Luke, bringing her hands up to feel his face. His eyes were open and she could feel the stretch of his smile as she ran her fingers through the light stubble of his jawline.

'Do you love me, Luke?' she whispered.

'Yes,' he answered. 'I have loved you from the moment I saw you.'

'More than Eskalon?'

'More than Eskalon.'

'And what if I could not be with you? Like Eskalon?'

'Then I will love you from afar. I will love you wherever you are and wherever I am.'

Anna was silent for a while, gently stroking his face. The first light of the new day was eking its way into the cave and the wind had dropped. Anna wanted the dawn to come, for the sun to rise quickly above the rim of the eastern sea so that she could properly see this man who had given her so much.

'Will you light the lamp now?'

Luke rolled over to find the flint that he'd brought with him. He lit the lamp and placed it on the blanket between them. The little shadows cast by the dancing flame made their features sharper, their eyes brighter but also moved to the beat of a happiness in the air between them.

At last Luke spoke. 'We will have to get off the island soon. Perhaps tomorrow.'

'Good,' said Anna. 'I want to go. But why tomorrow?'

'Because Damian has searched the city and found nothing. His men are searching the outer town now and I fear they'll come here. The Despot's army is marching on Monemvasia and the Archon is getting ready to leave . . . They seem determined not to leave without you.'

'I see. So how will we get away?'

'We'll do as Zoe suggested, leave by sea. Matthew and the others have gone fishing at dusk for the past week, leaving from the jetty at the sea wall. They always take a box full of nets and bait. Tomorrow you'll be in that box.'

'Will that work?' asked Anna, shuddering at the thought.

'Yes. The guards have got used to seeing them and will suspect nothing.'

Anna thought about this. A small, dark place. She breathed deeply. She didn't like it but could think of no alternative. And he would be with her.

'All right, Luke,' she said softly. 'I'll do whatever you want.' She reached out her arms to him and smiled. 'But only if you kiss me again.'

CHAPTER NINE

MONEMVASIA, SUMMER 1394

Late the following afternoon Luke was upstairs at the Magoris home, surveying the wreckage of his bed. The soldiers had come on the previous evening to search the house and, in their enthusiasm, had broken one of its sides. With luck he wouldn't need it again.

For the hundredth time that day, he smiled.

His parents hadn't asked him where he had passed the night but his look needed little explanation. He'd spent the day going about his everyday business, helping his mother and visiting the stables to check on the horses. But it had all been done in a mood of such blissful abstraction that Rachel had twice had to repeat herself to be understood.

It was as if time had stopped during the hours he'd spent with Anna in the cave. He could think of nothing else. He'd never experienced such happiness and it still suffused every fibre of his being. For the first time in his life, anything seemed possible and he had one single purpose to his life: to take Anna away from Monemvasia that night. What the future would bring afterwards, God only knew.

Now he was getting ready for the task ahead. He'd dressed

himself in tough leather breeches and a woollen smock since the wind was rising again and the sea might be rough. He'd packed a small bundle of extra clothes and taken from beneath his mattress what little money he'd saved over the years. He would have to ask his mother for food.

That was going to be the hardest part. He assumed that his parents had no idea of his plans but they would have to be told now. He could hardly bear to think of how they would take the news.

'Luke?' It was his mother's voice from downstairs. It sounded unsteady.

It had to be done now.

Luke descended the staircase and found both his parents waiting for him.

Luke tried: 'Mother, Father, I should tell you—' he began, but his father cut him short.

'Luke,' said Joseph quietly. 'We know where you're going.'

Luke looked at these two people who'd given him all of their love and asked for so little in return. These people whose love he was repaying by running away. They suddenly looked old and vulnerable.

'Do you love her, Luke?' Rachel asked.

He looked into those brown eyes searching his face to understand. 'Yes, I love her.'

'But she's . . .'

'Yes, Mother, I know who she is. But she's also someone who needs my help. If she stays here, she will be taken to the Turks. I have to help her.'

His mother nodded slowly, knowing that, whatever she said, he would go. She went over to the table and began to wrap some food in a napkin, a tear staining a fold in the white cloth.

Joseph watched his wife for a moment, then cleared his throat and came over to stand in front of his son, putting his hands on Luke's shoulders.

'There are some things I need to say to you, Luke,' he said quietly. 'First of all, you will need money and I'll give you what I have.'

Luke began to protest. 'I—'

'No,' his father interrupted. 'You will take it. If not for you, then for her.' Joseph went over to the table and picked up a small leather bag of coins, which he put into Luke's bundle. Then he led Luke over to the box against the wall and unlocked it. He brought out the sword.

'I was to give this to you on your sixteenth birthday, but you gave it to yourself instead and I took it back. I want you to take it now. Through the years I've done my best to teach you how to use it and you've learnt well. Now you must use it to defend yourself. And Anna.'

Luke took the sword. He walked over to the candle and lifted the dragon-head pommel to its light. There was no object in the world he thought more precious than this sword. It had been Siward's, given to him by the Emperor Alexios, and had been all that he'd taken when he'd fled the burning city of Constantinople.

He turned. 'Thank you, Father. I . . .'

Joseph shook his head. 'We don't have much time, Luke. Let me talk. You are taking Anna back to Mistra. That is good. I was going to take you there one day, to find something.'

'The treasure?'

Joseph dipped his head.

'So it wasn't myth.'

'No, and it may not be treasure, it may be something else. I don't know.' He paused again. 'There are things I haven't told you, things I was going to tell you when you were older.'

Luke waited, watching his father closely. The sadness that was never far from his eyes was deeper now, his brows creased beneath its weight.

'Your grandfather, my father, was called Siward, as were all Akolouthoi before him. Have you never wondered why I don't bear that name? Or you?'

Luke had wondered. Now he would know. He'd stopped breathing.

'Have you never wondered how he died?'

'You told me. He died from the plague.'

'He didn't. Your grandfather left Monemvasia just after you were born. It was said that he went to Mistra, took the treasure and went abroad.'

Luke felt numb. 'He stole it?'

Joseph nodded. 'So it is said.'

'And that's why you changed your name?'

Joseph sat down. 'I was forced to by the others. It was the agreement. We'd not talk of the past if I erased it from my name. I did it for you, so that you could grow up without the shame.' He paused. 'That's why the treasure became myth.'

Luke was slowly nodding his head. A veil had been lifted. Now he understood the sadness that never left his father's eyes, the things that were said and unsaid between the older Varangians.

'I believed the myth.'

'And you were right to.'

'So you think it's still in Mistra?'

Joseph nodded. 'Possibly. Or he may have taken it somewhere else. For safekeeping.'

'Why are you so sure?'

'Because he would never have stolen it, Luke. I knew him.'

'But why did he leave then?'

Joseph shrugged. 'I don't know. All I know is that he left behind the sword that you now have. He did that for a reason.'

They were both silent for a while and the only sound in the room was the wind outside. Then Joseph rose.

'Now you must go. Take the sword and go to Mistra with Anna. We'll join you there when this Archon has fled and I'm released from my oath.'

Luke moved forward to hug the big man, the sword still in his hand. Rachel joined them and for many minutes father, mother and son stood in the little room, locked in silent embrace.

At last Joseph pulled away. 'You must go, Luke,' he said again, picking up the bundle to give to him. But Rachel clung on for a moment longer, pressing herself to her son's chest and warming his smock with her tears. At last she let him go.

'Take care, Luke,' she said, and kissed him.

When Luke finally left the house with his sword and bundle, Nikolas was already waiting for him in the street outside. There were still a few hours of light left in the day but they couldn't waste any more time; they hurried to the city gate.

Once there, they realised that time was even scarcer, for there was a long queue of people waiting to go to their homes outside the city. Everybody was being stopped and there was a company of soldiers marching down the *mesi odos* to continue the search of houses beyond the city walls.

Luke cursed and looked at the head of the line. Luckily, he knew one of the soldiers. They walked to the front of the queue, ignoring the grumblings behind them.

'Michael,' Luke shouted loudly at the guard, 'you were here the other night when I had to take Nikolas to the old Jew? Well, he's got it worse this time. Let us through.'

The people at the front of the line backed away and the guard hurriedly waved them on. Then they were out of the city and the road to the bridge stretched away down the hill, the houses of the Jewish quarter climbing to their right. Luke gave his sword and bundle to Nikolas while his friend handed him his cloak.

'He gave you his sword,' said Nikolas with a low whistle.

'Yes,' said Luke. 'I hope I don't have to use it tonight.'

When Nikolas had left, Luke set off down the main road, past the cemetery and the warehouses to the Monastery of St Lazarus at the bottom of the hill. He turned right and skirted its wall until he reached the rocky ground beneath the Goulas. Looking around to check that he wasn't being followed, he picked his way over the rocks, hugging the bottom of the cliff, until he came to the cave. He gave a low whistle and looked up to see Anna parting the laurel bush above.

'Ready?' he called, as quietly as he could.

The next moment Anna had thrown a small bundle down to him and climbed out of the cave. Her toes had barely touched the ground before she was in Luke's arms.

He looked down at her uncertainly. 'Are you angry with me?'

She kissed him hard on his lips. 'No,' she whispered. 'I'm not angry with you. I love you.'

Luke lifted her chin so that they could see each other's eyes.

'Anna, last night was enough. When we get to Mistra, you'll never have to see me again.'

She began to say something but he put a finger to her lips. 'Shhh. Later. Now, take this.'

Luke gave her Nikolas's cloak and she put it over her shoulders, fastening the clasp at her neck. They set off across the rocks, Luke holding her hand.

'Where's Nikolas?' she asked. The smell of fish was all around her.

'I sent him to the Jew Barnabus,' replied Luke. 'He'll give you something for seasickness. The wind's getting up again.'

Anna looked up at the sky. The wind was rising and the sky was darkening, with black clouds blowing in from the mainland. Two dogs appeared in front of them, scavenging on the rocks, and began to bark. Luke threw a stone, hitting one, and with a yelp it skulked away. Far out at sea Anna could see a fishing boat, its sail billowing as it was hauled down. The boat's lantern came and went behind the waves.

'Is it safe to go out in this weather?'

Luke stopped and looked out to sea. Then he turned to her and squeezed her hand. 'It's a strong boat, Anna,' he said. 'Besides, we don't have any choice. They're searching the whole island tonight.'

'But why go back into the town? Can't we take a boat from somewhere outside?'

Luke shook his head. 'There's nowhere else to launch it; the island is all rocks. It's either the jetty at the sea gate or the wharves at the bridge to the mainland and we daren't go there. They're crawling with Mamonas men. The portello is the only way off the island.'

They moved on and soon reached the monastery wall and

then the road. Anna pulled the hood over her head as they began the walk up to the city. The way was busy since it was the hour when people finished work, and no one paid any attention to the tall figure and his smaller companion who held their cloaks close to them against the wind.

At the cemetery gates, Nikolas was waiting for them and grinned when he saw Anna. 'Does it smell too badly?' he asked, peering into the hood.

'Just don't expect to marry, Nikolas,' she replied.

The three of them crept behind the wall and knelt around the two bundles.

'We need to make just one bundle,' said Luke. He brought out the little crossbow. 'You can't take this, Anna.'

'No, I must take it,' said Anna quietly. 'You gave it to me. Now, show me how to use it again.'

Luke looked at her for a moment and then smiled. He showed her how to load it using the single stirrup. He was about to remove the bolt when she stopped him.

'Leave it in.' She slipped it beneath her cloak.

Nikolas stood. 'See you both later,' he said, 'at the church.'

Luke and Anna moved off towards the gate, pulling the cloaks around them and looking for a group to fall in with. As predicted, people entering the city were being waved through and Luke saw that they were given barely a glance. Then, when they were nearly at the city gate, and too late to turn back, Luke nearly collided with an officer who was leading his men out.

'Watch where you're going, oaf,' shouted the man.

Damian.

Luke's hood was almost entirely covering his face. Anna had walked on, head down, and was passing the troop of soldiers Damian had been leading through the gate. Luke saw one of them laugh and nudge his companion as the smell of fish reached their nostrils.

He dared not turn around.

He could feel Damian's presence behind him, could sense that he'd stopped and was watching him. His heart was beating to a tempo that made him giddy and the hand that was keeping his sword rigid beneath the cloak was suddenly clammy with sweat. He moved it from pommel to hilt, ready to draw.

But there was no shout, no restraining hand on his arm. Luke walked on, every footstep a marathon, and eventually caught up with Anna. The soldiers had left the city.

He smiled at her. 'That was close.'

They moved off together along the *mesi odos*, turning down a narrow side street that wound its way to the church where they'd agreed to meet the others. When they got there, Matthew was standing at the door and he ushered them in quickly. Arcadius and Nikolas grinned when they saw them. Beside them stood a large box with its lid removed. Inside was a tangle of nets.

'When do you usually leave?' Luke asked his friends.

Arcadius looked out though a church window. Two saints stood either side of it, their garments holed where the fresco's paint had fallen away. The church was in need of a patron.

'We could let it get darker, and it'll help if the rain comes back,' he answered. 'We should leave within the hour.'

Luke went over to Anna. 'I'm going out to check our route. I want you to stay here and keep these fools quiet.' Then he looked round his friends. 'You'd better hide the box for now and do some praying. That's what churches are for.'

Outside the church, he looked around the little square. It

was true that he wanted to check their route to the portello but he also wanted to make sure that they hadn't been followed. The encounter with Damian was still fresh in his mind.

And there was something else as well. He wanted to see the city for what might be the last time. Something deep inside told him that he might not return to Monemvasia.

As he wandered through the darkening maze of cobbled alleys, he thought that this was as much a city of sounds as of buildings. The voices of life – the cry of a baby born, the cry as another was made – rolled through these narrow, chamfered streets like a gentle wind, insinuating itself through window and chimney and connecting all these people one to another. He loved this island city for all its smells and petty squabbles, for all its grudges and long, long vendettas. He loved its walls, its jumble of houses, its churches and squares, all echoing to the vast and limitless rhythm of the encircling sea.

The street in front of him was suddenly dark and Luke looked up at the sky to see a cloud bully its way in front of the crescent moon and the first spit of rain hit his brow. They could wait no longer. He turned and ran back through the streets to the church where Nikolas was keeping watch. Inside, the other three were seated in a pew, whispering.

'We should leave now,' said Luke.

At the portello, huddled under its arch against the rain, two guards watched Luke round the corner of the steps, followed by Matthew and Nikolas who were carrying the usual box.

'Going with them tonight, Luke?' grinned one of the soldiers as they got up to let him pass. 'You must be mad. It's blowing a gale out there and it's getting worse!'

'Nikko here says it's the best time to fish,' laughed Luke as he walked between them, looking behind to make sure that his two friends had enough room to get through. He glanced through the gate.

'On second thoughts, you might be right.' He turned. 'Nikolas, have you seen what it's like out there?'

The sea was much bigger than Luke had expected it to be, the waves driving up the rocks as if to sweep the city away and the boats moored either side of the long jetty dancing up and down like puppets. Luke looked out to sea to see whether any other craft were out there.

It was empty.

One of the guards had left the gate to stand next to Luke while Matthew and Nikolas hurried down the stone gangway to the jetty.

'I don't like the look of that,' muttered the guard. 'I should leave it tonight, Luke. Go tomorrow.'

Luke pretended to consider this.

'Well, let me talk to the others,' said Luke. 'I'll see how keen they are. You'd better get back under that arch.'

The soldier nodded and turned away. Luke watched him disappear through the gate and then hurried down the gangway. He was grinning. This was going to work.

His two friends were waiting for him at the end of the jetty but they hadn't yet put the box into the boat.

Why weren't they moving?

Luke called to them but they weren't looking at him. They were looking behind him and horror was etched on to their faces. Then one of them pointed.

Luke stopped and looked around.

Coming towards him down the jetty were ten soldiers,

Mamonas men. They were holding long halberds pointed before them.

Above them, sitting on a rock, was Damian.

Damian.

For a moment, Luke stood there, stunned and disbelieving, his mind racing. He turned and ran to his friends, then wrenched open the lid of the box and pulled out his sword. Anna was looking up at him, pale and questioning.

'Damian's here. But we can still get away.'

He turned to his two friends. Nikolas had grabbed a boathook while Matthew held a fending pole and one of the nets. They looked like gladiators.

'This is not your fight!' Luke shouted through the rain, looking from one to the other. 'Give yourselves up! They won't harm you!'

Neither of them moved.

'Luke, we're Varangians,' said Matthew. 'We don't surrender, you should know that. We'll hold them off while you get away.'

Flanked by Matthew and Nikolas, Luke waited for the soldiers who were moving quickly towards them down the jetty. It was only wide enough for them to advance three abreast but the guards wore long hauberks of mail, with helmets and aventails, and all of them had swords at their sides. The boys wore woollen smocks and only Luke held a sword. It was an uneven match.

The soldier in their middle, facing Luke, seemed to be in charge and was mumbling something to his companions on either side, who were nodding. Luke didn't like this. Why were they holding halberds when they had swords? It didn't make sense.

Then it did.

When the guards were ten paces away, their leader gave a

shout and the soldiers either side of him rushed forward, pointing their halberds straight at Luke. Luke stepped back to parry the lunge while Matthew and Nikolas turned to defend him, ready to chop at the long weapons from the sides. But at the last moment, the guards swung the pikes away from Luke, hitting the Varangians in their midriffs and sending them plunging into the sea.

Luke was alone. It was ten against one.

Now the men in front of him dropped their halberds and drew their swords, the sound of steel harsh above the patter of rain on wood. Luke looked at the three blades in the first rank and wondered whether the years of training had readied him for so unequal a fight.

Behind the soldiers, Damian had risen from his rock.

'Give yourself up, Luke,' he shouted. 'You can't beat these odds. Just give me back my wife.'

'Let me go to him.' Anna was standing beside the box behind him and had the little crossbow tucked in her belt. She stepped forward.

'No. Get back. We're going to leave this place as I said we would.'

Then, as Anna stepped away, the charge came. With a roar, the three guards ran at him, their swords thrust forward like spears, and Luke skipped backward and to the side, parrying one attack and ducking low to avoid another. As the third soldier swung towards him, Luke lifted his blade and the two swords locked for a minute until he threw his weight to one side and kicked the man's back to send him into the sea.

Luke knew he would have to rely on speed and agility with these odds and, above all, not lose his sword.

A fourth guard now sprang forward, his sword raised above

his head, and Luke just had time to parry the blow, inches from his head, when, from the corner of his eye, he saw his first attacker charge from his left. He thrust his sword hilt into the face of the man to his front and brought his knee up to his groin, pushing him into the path of the other as he doubled up in pain. Then he kicked out savagely so that one man crashed into the other and, arms flailing, they both toppled off the jetty.

Three down. This was good, but the odds were still bad.

He swung back to face the remaining soldiers. They seemed reluctant to charge and Luke welcomed the respite. He was breathing hard and needed to judge how best to resist the next attack. He rocked slowly from side to side on the balls of his feet, testing his balance against the slippery surface of the jetty and raking the line of his adversaries with the tip of his sword.

Come on, you bastards!

Then his heart stopped. In the second rank, one of the soldiers had sheathed his sword and was raising a crossbow to rest on the shoulder of the man in front. The man was taking aim.

There was a roar from the portello.

Standing there, lit by the rain-spattered flames of the torches either side of the gate, was the giant figure of Joseph. He was dressed in full Varangian armour and was holding his huge two-handed axe. A dead soldier lay at his feet.

Luke saw his chance. He flung himself forward towards the man with the crossbow.

But too late. The bolt slammed into him and he was lifted off his feet by the force. He felt searing pain in his shoulder as he fell on to the jetty, his sword spinning through the air to land, miraculously, by his side.

Luke looked down at the bolt. It was buried deep but hadn't hit any bone. He reached up and, with a grunt, wrenched it free. Blood pumped from the open wound, matting his hair and running between the wooden slats below.

Anna tore the cloth belt from her waist, the little crossbow clattering to the jetty beside her, and crushed the cotton into a ball to hold to the wound.

Damian was on his feet. 'Kill him and get back to the portello!'

In front of them, the soldier was reloading his weapon as his companions hurried past him down the jetty.

Joseph was holding his axe in both hands and swinging it in great circles in front of him. No one could get near him and two more soldiers lay at his feet. Above him, Luke could see guards on the battlements, watching.

Helped by Anna, he struggled to his feet, one hand holding the cloth in place, the other his sword. His head was spinning and he felt weak. He looked up to where his father had felled the last guard and was now taking great strides down the gangway to get to the jetty. The crossbowman had stopped halfway down and seemed uncertain what to do.

I must keep Damian talking.

'How did you know?' he shouted.

'How did I know? I followed you!'

Anna now stepped in front of Luke. She was still wearing her cloak and its sodden folds were clinging to her like a second skin. Her hood was drawn back and her wet hair glistened in the light of the torches.

'Damian, it's me you want, not him,' she said. 'Let him get away and I promise to come quietly.'

'Not entirely right, Anna,' said Damian. 'I want both of you.'

159

Then there was another roar and, looking up through the wind and the rain, Luke saw what he'd dreaded to see.

"NO!"

Joseph had fallen to his knees, a crossbow bolt sunk in his back.

He'd been shot from the city walls behind. He took off his helmet and shook his great head, his hair spraying rain across the wood beneath him. Then, with another roar, he got slowly to his feet and began staggering towards the men in front of him, dragging his axe behind him.

'Kill him!' Damian screamed. But no one moved. *'Kill him, or I'll kill you!'*

This time the man with the crossbow raised the weapon and took aim.

Luke didn't hear the bolt released but he saw his father drop the axe, his body rigid and his head thrown back. The Varangian let out a howl of pain and rage, his arms flailing as he tried to get hold of the bolt. But it was in too deep.

Joseph pitched forward on to the jetty and lay still.

'No!' screamed Anna and ran towards him. Damian grabbed her. He wrenched the crossbow from her and aimed it at Luke.

'He wasn't meant to die!' he shouted. 'Why did the old fool have to interfere?' He glanced behind him. Two guards were running towards them down the jetty.

Luke was not listening. He was numb with shock. He stared beyond Damian and Anna to the crumpled heap of his father.

The soldiers had reached Damian and he threw Anna at them. *'Get her away from here!'*

They began to drag her down the jetty, one with his hand clamped to her mouth.

Then there was someone beside Luke.

Matthew had climbed back on to the jetty, his body dripping. 'Take the boat!' he shouted. 'Take it and go. You can't do anything for her.'

Luke stared at his father. He couldn't move.

'Go!' screamed Matthew.

Still he stood there.

Mathew pushed.

Luke toppled back into the boat, grunting as his shoulder hit the wood. A moment later, his sword and bundle had been thrown in beside him. Then came the rope.

'*Go!*'

Immediately, Luke felt the powerful current lift the craft and begin to bear it away. He wrapped his good arm over the side and struggled to his knees, wiping the salt from his eyes. He could just make out a small figure being dragged up the gangway.

'Anna!' he yelled, but the wind carried off his voice. He looked around him. The heaving sea was a mountain range with snow-capped peaks, an invisible hand tearing white from their tops. A jagged bolt of lightning ignited the horizon and, seconds later, a blast of thunder shook him to his core.

He was sailing into a gigantic storm.

PART TWO

CHIOS

CHAPTER TEN

THE MEDITERRANEAN, SUMMER 1394

It was the squeal of pigs that eventually dragged Luke from unconsciousness.

At first all was black around him. But then, as his eyes grew accustomed to the dark, he began to make out curves: of the hull sweeping away, of the deep shadows of bulkheads, of the enormous backside of a speckled pig.

As the squeal came again, he turned his head painfully to the right and saw animals in pens. There seemed to be pigs, chickens and at least one pair of goats. Above him, he could see the outline of a hatch with a sliver of sunlight around it, rising and falling with the swell of the sea. Motes of dust danced in the beams like cinders, shuddering as waves hit the ship's side.

Any surprise that Luke felt on seeing the pigs was soon replaced by astonishment that he seemed to be alive. He had a scattered memory of towering seas silhouetted against continuous lightning and a thunder so deafening that the very planks of his little boat had seemed to come apart. He could remember cold rain driving against his back like a beating as he cowered under the rowing bench, holding on to his shoulder, which pulsed with the pain of salt in an open wound. And he could remember the sudden sense of weightless dread as a huge wave lifted his flimsy craft clean into the air, turning and turning as it fell, so that Luke knew for certain that he was going to die.

And, last of all, he remembered the fleeting sense that he didn't much care if he did. His father was dead, Anna taken and he had no idea of the fate of his friends who'd stood with him on the jetty. What was there to live for?

Anna.

Anna was there to live for.

And here he was, alive and somewhat mended. Although his shoulder still throbbed, it appeared to have a bandage around it and he was wearing fresh clothes. He'd even been washed. What he hadn't been, though, was fed and he felt hungrier than he'd ever felt in his life. Even the stench coming from the animal pens couldn't remove the deep, gnawing pang that he felt in his stomach. He looked around to see if any food had been left for him but couldn't see a plate. He wondered whether hens could lay at sea.

Luke took a deep breath and rocked his way up to lean on his good elbow. He peered into the gloom of the hold and saw, at one end, wine casks stacked on top of each other from floor to ceiling. Each barrel-end had the Mamonas castle stamped on to its wood and the word 'Malvasia' written beneath it.

So at least I know whose boat I'm on.

In front of the casks lay pile upon pile of animal hides – goatskins, sheepskins and cowhides – and Luke recognised the smell of decayed shit, lime and urine that meant they were fresh from the tanner's yard. It looked as if something else might be stacked beneath them.

166

On his other side, and much closer, were the animal pens, with wooden hurdles between and steaming straw covering their floors. Given the curve of the hull, the animals spent much of their time in collision as the boat moved with the swell. And each was followed by a shriek of fear.

Luke shook his head slowly to try to clear the dots of light that were clouding his vision and groaned as he realised that his head throbbed every bit as much as his arm. And he had a raging thirst as well. He got to his knees and began to shuffle his way over to the animal hides. Perhaps there might be some crates of fruit underneath.

He began to lift the hides off one by one to see if they were covering another cargo. It was slow and painful work since they were heavy and their stench almost overwhelming. At last he saw the outline of a crate. He managed to pull it free so that it clattered to the floor.

Luke paused to see if the noise had been heard above. He looked around for something to open it with. In the gloom he made out a loose iron hoop hanging from a barrel and, ripping it free, straightened it with his knee and inserted one end into the gap between the lid and the crate. Putting all his weight on it, he heard the crack of splintering wood as the lid came free. Inside, neatly packed and with their mechanisms glistening with oil, were six crossbows.

Luke lifted one out to examine it, turning it towards what little light there was. It was made in Venice and of the very latest design.

He put the weapon back in the box and felt his way along the other crates, all of which appeared to be identical. Then, deep in the shadow of the bulkhead, his hands suddenly moved from wood to metal, the curved, heavy metal of a bronze barrel, rough and pitted to the touch, with thick hoops of iron surrounding it at intervals.

Cannon.

These must be the cannon at Geraki Alexis had told Anna of. Were they on their way to Constantinople? Presumably so.

Luke's mind raced. Judging by the movement of the boat, they were at anchor, which meant that they would be close to land. But with his shoulder wound he wouldn't be able to swim far, if at all. Perhaps, if the boat was on its way to Constantinople, Luke could find a way to enter the city's walls and get warning to the garrison. But first he needed to know where they were.

He felt his way back up the line of crates and then moved to the stairs leading up to the hatch. By climbing two of the steps and pushing hard, he was able to extend the opening to a sliver of the world outside. And what he saw gave him a surge of hope.

Climbing above the deck rail outside was the towering mass of the Goulas.

They must have been driven back by the storm. Perhaps he could somehow get to the mainland and from there to Mistra. Then the Despot and Anna's father could be told everything.

Luke stepped back down into the hull, replaced the lid on the crate and jostled it back into place. He picked up the broken hoop and began banging it against the underside of the hatch. He heard shouts, running feet and the squeak of bolts being released. The hatch was lifted and Luke found himself blinking into the late-afternoon sun and, framed against it, the bearded faces of four seamen.

There was a loud shout behind them and the men moved quickly away to be replaced by a man of florid complexion with costume to match. He was clearly someone of means since his doublet was slashed at the sleeves to reveal extravagant silks while the sword at his hip had a richly jewelled pommel. On his head sat a hat the size of a turkey plate, which supported a ruby the size of a vegetable. Luke guessed him to be about forty years of age.

The man's face creased into an enormous smile and he bowed as deep as a Florentine dancing master. Then he extended a hand through the opening to help Luke on to the deck. Once there, Luke found himself encircled by sailors, most of them bare-chested, who seemed to be staring at him with awe.

The captain beamed at Luke as a father might to a favourite son. He took him in his arms and planted a kiss on both cheeks before turning to his men and issuing a torrent of Italian. He finished with a dramatic sweep of the arm and a cheer went up from the company.

There was silence.

'I'm afraid that I don't speak your language,' said Luke. 'You see, I'm from . . .' He had raised his hand to gesture to the Goulas, except that he suddenly realised that it wasn't the Goulas after all. The boat was anchored in the lee of a vast black escarpment that rose vertically from the sea and which ran into the distance as far as the eye could see. Perched at its top were a cluster of white houses interspersed with blue-domed churches, steep, stepped streets and balconies with hanging flowers. The lower houses seemed to be built partially into the rock. There was a faint smell of sulphur in the air and a gentle steam rose from the sea all around.

Where on earth am I?

'Santorini!' came a voice from the sterncastle as if the answer had materialised on deck.

Luke looked up towards the rear of the ship to see an extraordinary figure leaning against the upper rail staring up at the cliff face. He was a man in his middle years, of medium height and generous waist. His hair and beard were long, luxuriant and greying, obscuring much of his face, although a prominent nose could be seen pointed up at the rock and wrinkling with the smell around it.

'Sulphur!' said the man in Greek. 'We are in what the poet Dante Alighieri might have referred to as a "circle of hell", or a "*basso loco*". We are in the middle of a volcano and what you see around you are the sides of its crater. Quite extraordinary.'

Luke looked at the man in amazement. He was dressed from head to toe in a garment that was part tunic and part toga and had sandals on his feet. The toga was of a startling whiteness that dazzled the eye even under an afternoon sun. He looked like a veteran angel.

Luke opened his mouth to speak but the Greek wasn't finished.

'In his *Critias* dialogue, Plato suggests that the civilisation of Atlantis existed here thousands of years ago and was swept under the sea by the force of the volcano's eruption. Anyway, this is all that's left of the island – this big caldera and a persistent smell of fart.'

The man paused, dipped his beard to his chest and began to hum in a distracted sort of way, moving his lips in concentration. Then he stopped as if he'd suddenly remembered something important and turned to face Luke.

'I'm sorry, my manners. Georgius Gemistus Plethon, citizen of Adrianopolis, at your service.' The voice was deep and rich, the words almost music. This was a man who liked to be heard. 'You may call me Plethon.'

'Luke Magoris, citizen of Monemvasia, at yours,' replied Luke with a small bow. The sailors were still staring at him open-mouthed and the captain appeared anxious for him to say more.

'Do you speak Italian, by any chance?' Luke enquired.

The older man tilted his head to one side and stroked his beard. Then he leant over the rail towards Luke and lowered his voice to a whisper. 'Ah, well, that depends. To you, I may speak fluently in Greek, Latin, French, English, Arabic and Italian. To the dogs that surround you I prefer to pretend that I know only the rudiments of Italian. To do otherwise would be to invite conversation at a level I am unlikely to find con-genial. For they are Venetian bandits to a man.'

Luke looked at the man in astonishment.

'However,' he went on, 'you will doubtless be keen to know what they are saying to you. The captain, who is a scoundrel without parallel in Christendom, says that he thanks God that he has been the instrument of your salvation from the terrible storm that blew you both all the way to Santorini. They found you adrift on some log and believe that your rescue was a manifestation of God's infinite mercy.'

Luke turned back to the captain. He stepped forward and put out his hand. 'Thank you . . . *grazie* for rescuing me,' he said, smiling into the face before him and shaking the man's hand vigorously. Then he pointed at himself. 'My name is Luke Magoris. Luke.'

The captain bent into another deep bow, his hat sweeping dust from the deck. When he'd straightened and smoothed the front of his doublet and curled a moustache, he turned to his crew and dismissed them with a wave of the hand. Then he said something to Plethon and beckoned to him. The Greek sighed loudly, grumbled something in a language that Luke didn't understand and descended the steps to join them on the deck.

The captain put one slashed arm around each of their shoulders and began to walk them in circles around the deck. He spoke with deliberate slowness.

'He wants to know,' Plethon said, translating, 'how you came to be out in such seas. Oh, and his name is Rufio.'

Luke thought quickly. He needed to be careful. He decided that simplicity might be best.

'Please tell Signor Rufio that I was fishing too far out from my home in Monemvasia and didn't see the force of the wind until it was too late.'

Plethon looked at him quizzically across the chest of the other man and then shrugged. He spoke for some time in halting Italian before being interrupted by Rufio, who stopped walking and looked in amazement first at the Greek and then at Luke.

'He wonders,' explained Plethon, 'how anyone could be such a cunt.'

'Did he say that?' queried Luke. 'I don't think he said that.'

'Well,' said Plethon, 'what the man says and what he means are very rarely the same. He is, after all, Venetian. In a moment he will tell you that he is bound for Constantinople and will be delighted to take you there. What he means is that he doesn't believe a word you've told him and will therefore sell you to the first slave trader he meets.'

Luke looked at the captain, whose smile was still one of untarnished goodwill.

Plethon walked to the side of the ship and looked in apparent fascination at the huge rock above them. He had started to hum again.

The captain had reopened the conversation, this time with Plethon at the rail. He was gesturing at Luke. The Greek was nodding impatiently as he listened and making small grunting noises in between his humming.

'Yes. As predicted, that was the offer to take you to Constantinople. I have said yes on your behalf since your alternatives appear limited.'

Luke considered this and then bowed in thanks to the Italian. He had no idea which of these men to trust but he needed time to think. Then Plethon spoke again to the captain.

'What are you saying?' asked Luke.

'I am telling him that, despite appearances, I believe you to be a young man of some means and that you should be treated accordingly. He might believe this since you were found on your log clutching a fine sword. He has agreed to give you the spare cabin. I should accept it.'

'Please thank him for his generosity,' Luke said, 'and ask him whether my sword might be returned to me.'

Following the translation, there was a pause. Then the captain, still smiling, shrugged and went over to a chest on the deck, took out Luke's sword and handed it to him. Bowing again, he walked over to the door of the cabin beneath the sterncastle and opened it, gesturing Luke to enter.

The cabin was small but reasonably light, with two portholes above a narrow, suspended cot and a tiny writing table next to it. The desk had two stout candles on it with congealed wax ribbed against their sides. The cabin had been used recently.

Luke sat down to think and realised that both his headache

173

and the severe throb in his shoulder had largely disappeared. There was a knock on the door and a crewman entered with a plate of cold chicken, bread and a paste of olives. With it came a flask of water and another of wine. Luke had never in his life tasted anything so good and he ate and drank too fast. He lay down on the cot.

Think. I must think.

He had no idea where Santorini was or whether it belonged to the Empire, Venice or Genoa. In any event, he was too weak to swim the distance to the rock and it had looked difficult to climb. He knew that Constantinople was five days' sail from Monemvasia and, if they'd been blown off course, might be a week from Santorini. A childhood of running around the port of Gefira told him that this was a square-masted *querina* whose crew would have to work hard to make it sail more than sluggishly. These were the workhorses of the Venetian merchant fleet and were turned out in their hundreds by the Venice Arsenale. Normally they would sail in great caravans of merchantmen, but this one was on its own and carrying interesting cargo.

But what of the extraordinary Greek? He was clearly a man of considerable learning and he'd said that he was a citizen of Adrianopolis. But hadn't Adrianopolis been lost to the Turks some thirty years past? Wasn't it now renamed Edirne as their capital? Why was a Greek scholar living in comfort with the Turks? Why did he so hate the Venetians? And, most importantly, why did he appear to want to help Luke?

As he turned these thoughts over in his mind, Luke felt a sudden weariness envelop his body and he closed his eyes. In moments he'd fallen asleep.

*   *   *

It was nearly dawn when Luke awoke and the first thing he realised was that the boat was moving. He could hear the ripple of a calm sea passing along the side of the ship and the crack of the canvas sail above. Looking through a porthole, he could see the dim outline of the horizon, a black mass rising and falling against something less black, and the wink of stars as they moved in and out of his vision.

He put his hand to his shoulder and lifted the corner of the bandage, probing the surface of the wound with his fingers. It was almost closed, the skin at its edges puffy and raw, and Luke realised that the bolt had done far less damage than he'd thought. He tensed the muscles around it and swung his arm to test the extent of movement. He might even be able to swim a short distance.

Then Luke heard a familiar humming above him coming from the sterncastle deck. The Greek must be awake. Luke rolled off the cot and felt his way towards the door, opening it carefully, not wanting to wake the captain. He crept his way to the steps leading to the upper deck and climbed them on tiptoe. The humming was coming from the ship's side.

Plethon was leaning on the rail looking up at the sky where the first glimmer of light was beginning to give dimension to the world. Luke went over to lean next to him. The older man went on humming with total absorption. Then he cleared his throat.

'Kervan Kiran.'

'I'm sorry?' asked Luke.

'Kervan Kiran. It's what the Turks call Venus, the morning star,' said Plethon, pointing to a twinkle low in the eastern sky. He began to hum again.

'What does it mean?'

'It means,' said Plethon, for some reason now whispering, '"caravan breaking".'

Luke pondered the significance of this. Perhaps there wasn't any.

'You see, their caravans move across the desert at night.'

Luke nodded, unclear as to whose caravans he meant.

'For Muslims,' continued his neighbour, 'the dread hour is not at night but at noon when the devil takes the world in his horns and prepares to make off with it. And the only thing that stops him is the cry of *Allahu Akbar* from the minarets at midday. Quite extraordinary.'

Luke looked up at the star and thought of camels being tethered in the last dune-shadows of the night, of tents being erected in the sand against the fierce sun to come, of a people that moved with the calm movement of the moon. And he thought of this boat also moving with the night – and going where?

He needed some answers.

'May I ask, sir,' began Luke, 'where you yourself are travelling to?'

'Me?' answered Plethon. 'Well, assuming I escape slavery at the hands of these vermin, I shall be returning to my home in Adrianopolis. I have come from Methoni and from the tedium of a discussion with the Roman Bishop there about the possibility of union between our two Churches.' He paused. 'Methoni,' he explained helpfully, 'is a Venetian stronghold on the west coast of our glorious Peloponnese.'

Luke knew this but kept quiet. He wanted to know more about this strange man. 'Why do you dislike the Venetians so much?'

Plethon looked at him in astonishment. 'Why? Why?' he cried. 'Do you know nothing of our history? Do you not know

176

that it was their own Doge Dandolo, a man blinded by age and evil, who was first over the walls when the Franks took Constantinople two hundred years ago? Had you not heard that the dogs put a whore on to the Patriarch's throne in the great church of Sophia and danced around her nakedness? Or perhaps it had escaped you that the wealth and learning of our empire, so carefully amassed since the time of Constantine, now resides in Venice?'

Plethon's hum now resumed at a higher pitch while his fingers drummed the rail like rain. His discovery that Venetian perfidy was unknown to his fellow passenger caused him to fix a gaze of horror past Luke as if a pack of duplicitous Doges might be climbing over the sides of the ship. But he wasn't quite finished.

'Dislike is too soft a word,' he whispered. 'I loathe and despise every Venetian on the face of this Earth and wish them all consigned to whichever of Dante's circles of hell is most uncomfortable.'

'And the Turks?' asked Luke cautiously. 'Should we not be saving our hatred for them?'

The older man seemed to consider this carefully. 'I have lived among the Turks for thirty years now and find little to hate beyond their dogs. For some reason they love their dogs, while we Greeks prefer our cats. Every one of their cities is infested with flea-bitten mongrels. Even jackals scavenge in Adrianopolis by night and keep the citizens awake with their howling. But the Turks seem to like them, and at least they turn the city's rubbish into shit for the tanners' men.'

Plethon paused and returned to his humming. 'Yes, that's interesting,' he murmured after a while. 'Why do we Greeks prefer the indifference of cats? I'll have to think about that.'

177

Luke said, 'So if they're not fighting us for our cats, what are they fighting us for?'

Plethon straightened himself and stretched, his long beard lifting clear of his chest in a movement of some grace. 'The Turks fight for Islam and that is a strange and contradictory religion. To understand the Turks you have to first understand Islam,' he said at last. 'Consider this. While we in the west taunt and kick the mad of our society, in Damascus they put them in institutions with fountains and music to ease their pain. Yet they have a regiment amongst their irregulars called the *deli*, which is full of the insane and fills moats with their dead.

'In most things that matter, like mathematics, astronomy and medicine, they are far advanced of us and yet their religion, which drives all their actions, closed its doors to new interpretation five hundred years ago.'

Luke thought of the man on the donkey with his potions on the road to Mistra. He thought of the mad of Monemvasia sitting amongst the cats in the streets. He looked at the morning star and saw it flickering like the last, guttering flame of a faraway candle and he looked at the new glow behind the sea's horizon, the passage from the still of a Muslim night to the movement of a Christian day.

'Islam is not so bad,' Plethon continued. 'At least they don't have fornicating priests to sell them salvation. The Turks carry it on their backs as their camels carry their silks. Five times a day they unravel their mats, face to the east and pray to their God, wherever they are, and they don't need illiterate priests to help them.' He paused again. 'Even their heaven is better. Wouldn't you rather lie with virgins than endure the eternal choir practice we're offered? And is our God so very dependable? Who created the earthquake forty years ago that allowed the Turk to cross over into Christendom?'

Luke had never heard such fabulous heresy. This man's knowledge seemed as limitless as the dark sea around them. 'Will they take over the world?' he asked.

'Their genius,' Plethon replied, 'is in their tolerance. Certainly they've won some battles, but the truth is that the common people *prefer* to be ruled by them. No one forces them to convert to Islam and they have to work a day a month for their new landlords instead of the three days a week under our system. And they feel safer. Someone at last protects them. So, yes, perhaps they will take over the world.'

'And you think we should welcome them?'

'No, no, *no!*' cried Plethon. 'A thousand times no! The Turks are nomads. They like to live in tents. They know nothing of building, of art, of culture or learning or creating the foundations for progress. Believe me when I tell you that they will build a great empire, and we may be part of it, but it will decay. Why? Because Islam hates change. The world cannot be ruled by people who don't want to change!'

Luke felt in part reassured. However admirable, the Turks had to be resisted. 'So what should we do?' he asked. 'How do we stop them?'

Plethon sighed deeply and looked down at his hands as if some answer might be found in the dark pattern of veins on their back. He shook his head slowly, his thick eyebrows creased in concentration. 'It was as the fool Bishop said,' he answered. 'We have to unify the two Christian Churches of East and West. We have to stop rubbing the pebbles of our theological differences smooth with endless debate. We have to stop arguing about papal primacy, purgatory and the procession of the Holy

Spirit. We have to stop worrying about how to properly make the sign of the cross. We have to unify these Churches which have been at war for three centuries so that the Pope in Rome can call the powers of Christendom to one final crusade against the Turks. It's our only chance.'

Luke was silent, listening to the humming of his companion above the sounds of the ship as it ploughed its course through a sea whose shifting surface was catching the first glimmers of dawn. He'd heard the case for union and knew that the Emperor Manuel favoured it as a means of gaining help from the West.

'And then there's the Varangians, of course.'

Luke looked up sharply. 'Varangians?'

'Yes, surely you've heard of them. The Emperor's Guard? Four of them were said to have taken a treasure from Constantinople when it fell to the Franks and brought it to Mistra. The myth has it that the treasure can save the Empire. It must be a lot of gold.' He looked at Luke. 'Didn't you say that you were from Monemvasia?'

Luke nodded. 'And am descended from one of those Varangians.'

Plethon stared at him in astonishment. 'So you know of this treasure?'

'Only that it's been lost,' replied Luke, shaking his head. 'No one knows what or where it is.'

The older man stared at him for a long time. Then he shrugged and returned to the view. The humming resumed.

Luke suddenly felt cold and hugged his shoulders as he stared out to sea. A memory was creeping up on him. He saw his father, his axe an arc of silver above his head. He saw it frozen mid-air as a bolt found its mark. He shivered.

What had he died for?

'So what do you believe in then, if neither our faith or theirs?'

Plethon turned to him and frowned. 'I believe in reason,' he said quietly. 'And I believe our teacher should be Plato, since Plato equates good not with some God, but with reason. There is a new dawn of reason rising in the west, among the city states of Italy. Bayezid must be stopped because he will put out its light.'

Luke's head was pleasurably lost in this labyrinth of new ideas and he wanted to listen to this man forever. But the first, blinding rays of the sun reminded him that he might be in imminent danger.

'Sir,' he asked, 'may I perhaps come with you to Edirne? If you were to put me under your protection, would the captain dare move against me?'

Plethon put his hand on Luke's good shoulder. He was shaking his head. He looked around the deck to check that they were still alone.

'Luke,' he said softly, 'you clearly have little experience of Venetian greed. Look at you. You are tall, strong, blond and handsome. You will fetch a good price for them in the slave market and nothing that I say will stop them from trying to get it. No, your only hope is escape.'

But how?

'The captain,' the Greek went on, 'speaks freely to the crew in my presence, believing that I cannot understand much of what he's saying. Yesterday he told them that we would be putting into the island of Chios two nights from now. That will give you the best chance to escape. Chios is owned by Genoa.'

'Why would he want to put into Chios? I thought the Venetians hated the Genoese?' asked Luke.

'Because,' whispered Plethon, 'it is only three miles from the Turkish mainland. So my hunch would be that they plan to meet the Turks there to do some transaction. And you might be included in the merchandise.'

Luke thought of the crossbows and cannon below. 'They will give them cannon. Cannon to take to the siege of Constantinople. I saw them. In the hold.'

Plethon looked up sharply. 'Cannon? Are you sure?'

'Very sure.'

'That is bad,' Plethon said gloomily. 'Well, we'll know if I am right by the smell. You can smell a Turkish galley two miles away – the stench of slaves chained to their oars.'

'I'll need to escape. Can you help me?'

Plethon nodded slowly. He was suddenly very serious. 'Yes, Varangian, you do. I will do what I can.'

By now the sun was clear of the horizon and Luke lifted his face to enjoy its soft warmth. He thought of the freedom to do this every morning of his life. What would it be like to awake slumped over an oar?

A shout in Italian behind him brought him back to the present. Captain Rufio was striding across the deck towards them, wearing a new doublet of shiny black leather and long riding boots that almost covered his multi-coloured hose. He seemed more delighted than ever to see Luke, pinching one of his cheeks and ruffling his hair.

Plethon began walking away. 'That's what they do to slaves,' he said over his shoulder. 'I should look to that fine sword of yours.'

Two nights later, Luke was lying awake in his cot, fully dressed, his unsheathed sword beside him beneath the bedclothes and wine on his breath. He had been well supped and irrigated by the captain, who had entertained both Plethon and him with a dinner of partridge cooked in apple, eggplants and *katsouni* washed down with sweet *vinsanto* wine from Santorini. And Rufio had offered toast after toast, refilling every glass in between. Luke had done his best to drink slowly, to add water when he could and even to empty it through a porthole when Rufio had left the cabin. But he was unused to wine and it had had an effect.

Now he tried to focus on the beam above his cot, lit by the full moon outside. It seemed to have a name scratched into it that he couldn't read. The ship rose and fell with the gentle swell and the moon appeared and disappeared from the port-hole like a mime show. All was quiet outside his cabin but there was a new, putrid smell in the air and Luke thought of what Plethon had told him of Turkish galleys.

He knew that they were at anchor in a tiny lagoon whose shores were no more than a hundred paces from the ship's sides. He could swim that distance. There were whispers outside and the squeal of bolts pulled back from the hatch over the hold. A cargo was being brought up to the deck. He heard the splash of oars and felt the bump of a smaller craft come along-side. There were grunts and low curses as heavy objects were lowered over the sides and the occasional thump as something metal hit wood.

There were more whispers and Luke guessed that if he was to be taken, it would be now. The door would open and he'd be rushed, tied up and thrown into the boat alongside the cannon. On the other side of his door he could hear the heavy breathing of men who'd recently exerted themselves. Luke tensed his body and gripped the hilt of his sword, moving his other hand to hold the edge of his bedclothes, ready to tear them off when the time came. He shook his head to try to clear it of the fog of wine, sucking deep breaths of air through his teeth.

Then it happened, but not as he'd expected.

He heard the handle turn slowly and the creak of the door as it inched open. Through half-open eyelids he saw a man silhouetted and two more behind, one of whom seemed to be carrying a coiled rope. The man sniffed; the smell of the Turkish galley was stronger now. It must be close.

Luke let out a drunken snore and heard a stifled laugh from one of the men. He turned on to his side, grunting and smacking his lips, offering his back to them. He heard the men move forward with greater confidence, greater carelessness.

Now!

Luke leapt from the cot, sword in hand, and lunged. The man in front let out a screech of pain as the sword tip ripped open the skin of his upper arm, blood quickly spreading across his shirt like a tide. He pitched backwards on to his companions, who fell out on to the deck, dropping the rope and clubs they were holding. Luke leapt through the door and slammed his sword hilt into the face of a man who doubled up in agony; Luke brought his pommel down on the back of his head, sending him crashing to the deck. He looked up to see the third man rush at him from the side, a spar in his hand, and Luke lifted his sword to parry the blow while rocking back on his heels to let his attacker overreach himself. Then he spun around as the man passed, kicking the back of his legs and sending him sprawling against the rail. He leapt forward and brought the side of his sword down sharply on his back. The man fell heavily to the deck.

There was a shout to Luke's left and he spun round to see Rufio advancing on him, sword in one hand, dagger in the other and no hint of a smile on his lips. Behind him were two other sailors with swords, one also carrying a net. Luke glanced quickly at the rail and wondered if he had time to get to it. He looked back at Rufio, who was only feet away and shaking his head. With a roar, the Italian raised his broadsword and charged.

Luke was surprised at how fast the man could move and only just had time to duck Rufio's swing, feeling the rush of wind on his hair as the blade passed an inch above his head. He stepped back and parried as the next stroke came with terrifying speed. This man was an expert swordsman.

Luckily, Rufio's two companions seemed happy to let him fight alone and Luke could turn his full attention to how to use his youth and extra height to gain some advantage. One thing he had on his side, he realised, was the likelihood that Rufio did not want to kill him, for a dead slave wouldn't command any price at all. He could afford to take chances.

With this in mind, Luke went on to the attack, bounding forward and using his sword as a spear, jabbing it at the Italian's face and neck with short stabbing thrusts. The captain parried them with his broadsword but the weapon was heavy and his arm slowed with the effort. He fell back towards the mast and then, with his back against it and his sword locked at the hilt with Luke's, he let fly a vicious kick which caught Luke in the stomach, winding him and sending him flying back towards the rail. In an instant, the Italian had sprung forward with a cry of triumph, gesturing to the man with the net to follow him.

Luke felt weak and dizzy and knew he was unlikely to be

able to resist them both. He gripped his sword and prepared to do his best.

Then something unexpected happened.

'Basta!'

From the deck behind him came a shout followed by a torrent of perfect Italian. Plethon was standing there, dressed only in the white toga, with his arm raised as if he were addressing the Senate. Rufio was so astonished that for an instant he forgot his adversary, and that instant was enough for Luke to climb on to the ship rail and dive into the sea, sword still in hand.

It was a twenty-foot drop and Luke landed badly, his wounded shoulder taking much of the impact. Nevertheless, he turned on to his front and kicked for the shore, paddling with his strong arm. He could see commotion on the ship's deck and Rufio leaning over the side jabbing his finger in his direction. Then a crossbow bolt plunged into the sea beside him and Luke ducked underwater. Further bolts hit the sea and dived deeper, his shoulder protesting all the way.

Holding his breath, Luke swam as fast as he could towards what he thought was the shore, clutching his sword to his front. At last, with his lungs bursting and spots of light exploding before his eyes, he broke the surface and was relieved to see that he was almost at the rocks. No more bolts were being fired at him and he guessed that he was far enough away from the ship to be nearly invisible.

He pulled himself up to his knees and looked around him. At the end of the bay there seemed to be a deep beach of sand leading on to grass that climbed inland in a series of overlapping hills. He could see some dim figures grouped together on the sand with a boat beached in front of them. Were these the Turks? Above him was scrub, knee-high and interspersed with jagged rock that would make running difficult. While he remained low, he would be shadowed against the hill so he decided to keep to the shallows and try to make his way along the edge of the lagoon via the shoreline. He could see the ship's boat silently gliding towards the shore, its oars muffled with hessian. On it would be the cargo of crossbows and cannon. He saw the outline of a cloaked figure standing in the bow and guessed that this was Rufio. Could he have given up?

Luke considered this as he stumbled through the shallows. Rufio might worry that he'd tell the Genoans what he'd seen and from them it would reach the Emperor Manuel. But then again, what had he actually seen? As far as Rufio knew, Luke had no idea of the cargo in the hold.

Luke decided to strike inland. Crawling up the hill, he found what looked like a sheep-path in the moonlight and set off in the direction of the hills. Every now and then he stopped and stood in silence to listen for any sound of pursuit. Nothing. The Venetians had either given up or were quieter than ghosts.

The path was gentle to begin with and then began to climb steeply, the stream beside it losing itself in a gully that turned into a ravine. There were stepped terraces either side in which stood strange, twisted trees, planted in rows, that Luke had never seen before. They were smaller than olive trees and their smooth trunks shone dimly in the light of the moon. Whatever they were, they were giving off a scent very different from the Turkish galley. It was sweet and aromatic and Luke wondered if the trees had some medicinal use.

The going now was easy and Luke hurried on, determined to put as much distance as possible between him and the Venetians and hoping to come across some village where he could persuade the Greek inhabitants to take him to their Genoese masters. But the landscape was deserted except for row upon row of these strange trees.

At last, towards dawn, he crested the hill and looked out over a broad valley of groves and orchards to what looked like a cluster of houses at its end. There were no lights to be seen amongst the buildings, which Luke thought strange. It was nearly daybreak and most farmworkers would be preparing to leave for the fields by now. He wiped his brow on his sleeve and strained to hear any sounds of animals.

Luke broke into a slow run, breathing evenly against the pain of the wound rubbing against the rough fabric of his tunic. As he reached the plain, he lengthened his stride and saw that he'd misjudged the distance to the village and that the first houses were already taking shape. He heard a dog bark and then another. Dogs usually meant people.

The village was indeed inhabited but not by anyone who wanted to meet him. As he walked up the dirt track between the houses, the low moon casting his shadow long across the ground, he heard the sound of a slammed shutter and the growl of a dog behind a door. He held his sword in one hand and his eyes raked every shadow for movement, his senses alert and his body tensed.

He stopped and cleared his throat.

'I am a friend,' he shouted. 'I'm a Greek, like you, and I flee the Turks. You have no need for fear.'

Silence. Another dog growled.

'I need to speak to someone.'

More silence, and then the sound of a bolt released from its lock and the squeak of protesting hinges as a door was inched open. '*Here!*' hissed a man's voice to his left. 'Here, where I can see you!'

188

Luke lowered his sword and walked slowly towards the voice, keeping his head turned in the direction of the moon and hoping that his fair hair was clearly visible in its light. He stopped in front of the door and waited.

'Where are the Turks?' whispered the man. He was old and bent and the moon made the thin strands of white hair on his wrinkled head shine like gossamer. Luke heard a low growl beside him and glanced down to see a large dog leashed by his side, its teeth locked in a snarl.

'They'll be at sea by now,' answered Luke. 'I left them some hours ago in a small bay beyond those hills.' He turned and pointed in the direction he'd come. 'They were collecting some cargo from a Venetian round ship.'

'They were at Fana Bay,' said the man. 'What was the cargo?'

'Cannon,' said Luke. 'For the Turks.'

The man spat into the earth at Luke's feet. 'Venetian pigs,' he mumbled. 'They'd sell their own mothers.'

Luke very slowly laid his sword on the ground in front of him. Both man and dog watched his every move. Then he felt a hand on his shoulder and spun around, his heart racing. Backing away from him was a younger man, with a single, dented cuirass strapped to his chest. A sword was slung at his side and he was holding his hands in the air. He bent down to pick up Luke's sword and offered it to him, nodding slowly as he did so.

'The Turkish galleys are too fast for the Genoans to catch them,' said the man. 'But I can give you my horse and you can go and tell them what you've seen. You should go to the big castle at Chora and ask for Marchese Longo. He is the leader of the Genoese.' The man paused and looked up and down the little street. 'I am Dimitri. We've been raided many times by Turkish pirates, and children have been taken into slavery.'

'Give me your horse, Dimitri,' Luke said.

By midday, Luke was standing in the entrance hall of the Giustiniani Palace inside the great castle of Chora.

Chora was more a fortified town than a castle since there were as many houses and churches inside the walls as out. Most of the island's Greek nobles lived there while their Genoan overlords lived on their estates outside the city in the rich plain of the Kambos to the south. The castle had been built by the Byzantines two hundred years before and was enormous. It had strong walls, one overlooking the sea and three land walls surrounded by a wide moat.

It had taken Luke three hours to ride there from the village on a thin, asthmatic horse that preferred the grass of the verge to the thrill of the open road. He'd passed through a rich, hilly country in the south with steep valleys latticed by terraces of olive groves and row upon row of the strange shrunken trees. He had ridden through villages with fields of cattle and pigs at their edges and vegetable plots beyond. This was a prosperous land that seemed blessed with good soil and plentiful water and yet the people were reserved and fearful, watching him with suspicion as he urged his wretched horse towards their capital.

Coming out of the hills, he had ridden on to the plain of the Kambos, which was a place of even greater bounty, with orchards of orange, lime and tangerine next to fields of wheat and vineyards heavy with purple grapes. Here there was an earth so rich that its dark ochre colour seemed to overwhelm its produce. The land was criss-crossed with canals and narrow, high-walled lanes whose verges rippled with wild tulips. Every now and again a gated arch would announce another estate and he'd see the tops of mansions and tall cypress trees to shield them from the fierce meltemi winds of summer.

Luke was overwhelmed by the prosperity of the place, a prosperity even greater than that he'd seen on the Goulas of Monemvasia. He was fascinated by the churches with their square, pillared bell towers; by the gaudy, puffed doublets and feathered hats of the men he passed on horseback. This was indeed a place to prosper in.

But the wheezing of his horse soon jolted him back to reality and before long he was riding under the emblazoned arch of the Porta Maggiore and handing his reins to a servant at the base of a steep flight of steps that led up to the entrance to the Giustiniani Palace.

If Marchese Longo was surprised at the tall, fair figure in filthy rags and bandages that required his extraction from his meeting, he was far too well bred to show it. Dressed in a black doublet of marbled silk and a shouldered cloak cut in the French style, he strode into the entrance hall with two black hunting hounds in tow. His clothes and hounds seemed designed to complement the white squares of the floor so that the three of them might have been part of a game of chess.

'Signor Magoris, I am so sorry for keeping you waiting,' said Longo in almost accentless Greek, his hand stretched out in greeting. 'The twelve of us in the Mahona meet only once a month and, as you will imagine, there is much to discuss.'

Luke had no idea who the twelve might be or what the Mahona was. He held out his hand and felt this dark man's gaze settle upon him as his many-ringed hand made contact with his own. Longo was of middle years and middle height, with streaks of grey in his beard, but there was a tautness in his bearing that suggested energy.

Longo turned from Luke and issued a low whistle and the two dogs came instantly to his side and sat each on a white square, looking up at him with tongues adrift and true love in their eyes.

'I am told that you have news of importance,' said Longo, smiling and feeling the velvet of an ear between thumb and forefinger. 'You have seen Turks in the south of our island? Would it be convenient for you to take wine in my office and tell me about it?'

Luke was about to answer when a rumble came from beneath his shirt.

'And food!' said Longo. 'Of course. You cannot have eaten for hours. May I ask my cook to prepare something for you? Some cold chicken?'

Luke felt faint with hunger and gratitude. 'Thank you.'

Longo and his dogs led him through into a sumptuous dining room of rosewood-panelled walls hung with Flemish tapestries and a long oak table stretching the length of the room. He clapped his hands and issued instructions. He held a chair back for Luke to sit on and went to a side table where a pitcher of wine and goblets stood.

'I should add some water to it,' said Longo, handing him the cup. 'Chian wine is strong and yours is an empty stomach. Not a good combination for the telling of a tale.'

Luke was adding water to his wine when the food arrived. There was cold chicken and quail, bread, cheese, figs and olive paste and Luke ate as slowly as his hunger allowed. Longo watched him, making no attempt to hurry him into his story.

At last, as Luke was washing the grease from his fingers, he spoke.

'How have you found yourself in Chios, Signor Magoris?' he asked. 'I would say from your clothes that you did not expect to come here; indeed I would say that you've been recently engaged in some fighting, probably on board a ship, and escaped by swimming to the shore. What I'd like to know, though, is what this has to do with the Turkish galley that has been seen in our waters these past few days?'

Luke gathered his thoughts. He had rehearsed a version of events but now found himself telling this man much, much more.

Longo only interrupted twice; once to scowl and mutter something when told of the cannon at Geraki, and once when Luke described his encounter with Plethon. Then Longo smiled, his eyes filling with delight.

'Plethon!' he exclaimed. 'I have not seen him in years. Now that had been a rare treat if he'd come with you to our island!'

Luke said, 'I believe he saved my life. If he hadn't appeared when he did, I'm sure the captain would have killed me.'

'Signore,' laughed Longo, 'talking and dressing up have never been hardships to Plethon. And however lunatic his pronouncements, each one is a gem. He rarely comes to Chios, but when he does, I will follow him as my dogs do me, not wasting a moment of that mind!'

Longo became serious again. 'But you'll want to know how we can stop the Turks. Sadly, we could not possibly intercept the galley even if we wanted to. It is a fast ship and we in Chios are not minded to declare war on the Sultan just yet.'

Luke listened to this, knowing that he'd discharged his duty in reporting the cannon and that events were now beyond his control. Suddenly, a wave of exhaustion broke over his body so that he nearly swooned under its weight. He stifled a yawn.

'You must be very tired,' said Longo. 'We can talk more about this tomorrow.'

Luke awoke the next morning to a choir. Every bird in Chios seemed to have gathered at his window, determined to display its individual repertoire. He'd slept deeper than he thought possible and had been untroubled by any wound of shoulder or memory. For a long while, he lay looking straight up at the white ceiling above his bed, its colour mirroring the emptiness of his mind. He wondered idly what time of the day it was and, were he to rise, what clothes he should put on.

This question was answered by closer inspection of the room. Draped over the back of a chair was a suit of clothes with leather boots and his sword propped neatly against them. They looked much too grand for him.

There was a knock on the door and a servant entered. He bowed from the waist. 'The lord Longo begs your company downstairs when you feel sufficiently rested,' said the man. 'May I help you to dress, sir?'

'What hour is it?' asked Luke.

'It is still early, sir, and the weather on the Kambos is fine,' replied the servant and, as if to prove it, drew back the heavy curtains to reveal a sun shining straight into the room. Luke blinked and shielded his eyes from the glare. Then he swung a leg over the edge of the bed and walked over to the pail.

Ten minutes later, he was looking at himself in a long mirror and thinking he quite liked what he saw. Luke was not vain, but the tall, elegant figure in its smart leather doublet and riding breeches looked as impressive as it did unfamiliar.

And that was exactly what Marchese Longo thought when, five minutes later, Luke presented himself for breakfast on the pillared veranda.

'Now, that's much better,' he said with a smile as he rose to greet Luke, looking him up and down with satisfaction. 'I hope you slept well?' Longo walked over to a side table on which there were plates piled with fruit and a jug standing in a bowl filled with ice. 'Will you honour me by eating some fruit and cream from the estate?'

Luke sat down to eat amidst a pile of papers, a peacock quill stuck into an inkstand and an up-ended blotter. He noticed that Longo's fingers were stained indigo as were the two tips of the melon slice that he'd half eaten. Luke helped himself to melon, plums and cherries and pulled off a chunk of the rye bread sitting on the table before him. As he ate, he looked into the courtyard below where palm trees ringed tulip-beds surrounding a wide, circular area of coloured cobbles. Two saddled horses were standing side by side in the shade of a tree.

'I have to leave for my estate at Sklavia after breakfast and I was hoping you might accompany me,' said Longo, following his gaze. 'It's a morning's ride. It will give me a chance to show you something of our island.'

Luke was used to a world where kindness was shown for a reason. Marchese Longo was being more generous than the situation warranted and was a shrewd man of business. Without any unease, he wondered what his purpose might be.

'I should be delighted,' he replied.

Longo was silent for the first part of the journey and Luke was able to enjoy the bustle and colour of the outer town. Every race imaginable seemed collected there, from tonsured monks to shaven-headed Moors, from skullcapped Jews to plaited Scandinavians, and the harbour was a forest of masts and rigging. Cargoes were in constant transit, from cart to quay, from quay to hold, and the shouts of warning, the curses of contact, were hurled between ships, barrels and people like rotten fruit. And the smells! Luke lifted his nose like a hunting hound and breathed in the scents of cinnamon, cloves, liquorice and nutmeg that spoke of distant trade.

Coming into the bay was a huge galley, its oars unscrolling from the water to stand erect as combs and the silk canopy of its aft-deck winking its fringe in the early sun. Above its mast flew pennants emblazoned with the calligraphy of Allah and Luke turned to Longo with a question on his lips.

'No, not the same one,' said the Italian. 'Yours was a war galley; this one is a trader. See: no ram at its front and much less smell. The cargo will see to that.'

'What will it be carrying?' enquired Luke.

'Oh, some spices, I would wager, for us to take on to Genoa.' Longo paused. 'But see that big round ship coming in behind it?'

Luke capped his eyes with his hand and squinted into the light. The ship was big and riding low in the water, its steering paddles nearly horizontal.

'Now that's a valuable cargo,' Longo said. 'That ship is carrying alum.'

'Alum?'

'Yes. We take it from the Phocaean mines beside Smyrna, which we run under license from the Turk. Then we transport it to our port at Foca further up the coast and bring it here before shipping it on to Florence. We took two hundred thousand pounds' weight there last year. For the Arte della Lana. It's used by the dyers for fixing their colours.'

'But why do they stop here?' asked Luke. 'Why not go straight to Italy from Foca?'

'Because we have something even better for them to take back,' replied Longo with something like pride in his voice. 'When you rode across the island, you must have seen rows of small trees, hardly bigger than bushes? Trees giving off a strange smell?'

Luke nodded, drawing his horse closer to Longo's to hear above the noise of the harbour.

'Those are mastic trees and they are one reason we Genoese are here on this island. On Chios, there exists a sweet combination of climate and soil that means that this is the only place on earth where this kind of mastic can be grown.'

'But what is mastic?' asked Luke.

'Mastic is the juice that we take from the trunks of those trees and turn into a sweet that the Sultan's harem cannot get enough of. The women love it to chew because it sweetens the breath. The harem alone takes a week's crop!'

The two men rode on in silence. By now they had reached the outskirts of the town and the broad sweep of the Kambos stretched out in front of them.

'When did you Genoese come to Chios?' asked Luke, as they passed an arch crowned with the emblem of a sphinx holding a bunch of grapes.

'Fifty years ago,' replied Longo. 'At that time, twelve nobles of Genoa, of which my father Tommaso Longo was one, formed a *campagna,* or society, which they named the Mahona Giustiniani. Each family added their surname to that of Giustiniani so as to underline our loyalty to the Byzantine Empire, which, after all, owns the island, Justinian being the greatest of their emperors. All newcomers to the campagna are obliged to do likewise when they buy into it. The society was given a thirty-year lease by the Emperor John Palaiologos to exploit the island and, so successful has been the enterprise, we've extended it.'

The Italian pointed up at the sphinx emblem. 'Originally we came to make wine and that emblem can be seen above the gates of many estates of the Kambos. But then the Turks discovered a liking for the mastic and everything changed. For the better and worse.'

Longo paused as he doffed his hat in greeting to a passing rider. 'Better,' he went on, 'because the mastic has made use of the southern part of the island where it proved impossible to cultivate the grape. Worse, because we have had to move families there to grow it and these have become the target for Turkish slave traders. Now many of them have lost children and wish to move back to the north. They feel safer there – and who can blame them?'

Longo turned in his saddle to look squarely at Luke. 'But that is not the real problem. The real problem is that the Greeks don't trust us to protect them. They see the Genoese almost as much as an enemy as the Turks. They have hated us ever since we came here. What we need is someone down there who they will trust.'

Luke began to understand why Longo might want to befriend him. A man trained in the Varangian tradition of fighting, and Greek to boot, might prove useful. But what of his plans.

Luke looked down at his sword, at the dragon head that moved with the rhythm of the horse. What had his father said about Siward?

He left behind the sword that you now have. He did that for a reason.

But the reason was in Mistra, not Chios. He was on this island by a quirk of fate. Should he let fate play its hand a little longer?

198

As the sun climbed to its zenith in the sky, the hour of the devil's horns that Plethon had talked of, and the horses began to hang their heads low and their riders to yearn for the cool shade of stone, the two men began the long climb out of the plain and up to Sklavia. As the slope got steeper, the path wound its way through ever-narrower terraces of vines, olives and citrus groves with water channels bubbling cool water to feed conduits in between. Looking back over his shoulder, Luke could see the Kambos laid out like a rich patchwork quilt as it stretched its way to the sea beyond. No wonder Longo chose to live here.

They entered an avenue of tall cypress trees casting small stabs of shadow in the noonday sun like dragon's teeth and providing no shade for the riders. At the far end, Luke could see a magnificent arch and beyond it, just visible between its pillars, the shimmer of water. Soon they were riding into gardens of exquisite colour and proportion. Pools sparkled amongst lawns full of wandering peacocks. Exotic flowers tumbled over low hedges and on to paths of coloured pebbles, and ranks of cypresses lined the perimeters, standing guard over the giddy chaos within.

Luke rode in wonder through garden after garden until they reached two high pillars on which sat the sphinx and its grapes, carved in the same vermilion stone. Through them was a court-yard containing a wide stone staircase that led up to a three-storeyed building with white marble pillars running the length of its veranda. At the other end of the courtyard was a large cistern, adjacent to which stood a vertical wheel of oak. Nearby, a donkey munched placidly into a nosebag.

'That is a *manganos*,' said Longo, pointing at the wheel. 'We use it to draw water from the well.'

Two grooms appeared from the space beneath the steps and took the horses' reins while the men dismounted. Longo took Luke's arm and they climbed the staircase together.

'Marchese!' came a voice from above.

And looking up, Luke saw the greatest wonder in this day of wonders.

Standing there was, quite simply, the most beautiful creature he had ever seen.

CHAPTER ELEVEN

THE CITY OF SERRES, RUMELIA, WINTER 1394

The snow lay thick upon the ground and the air was colder than brass. Anna's horse picked its way through the uneven cobbles of the street leading to the city gate, the ballooning fog from its nostrils shifting the scene of misery on every side. It was eleven years since the Turks had taken Serres from the Empire and the contradiction of rape and renewal lay all around. The carcasses of churches stood next to gleaming new minarets while sparse stalls of fruit and vegetables raised some colour amidst the ruins. In between the stalls stood braziers around which the transactions of survival took place in hand-rubbed exchange.

Anna was dressed in quilted felt, her head veiled and haloed by ermine. She wore thick rabbit-skin gloves and layered leather boots, also lined with fur. She was, to all intent and purposes, Turkish, from her stirruped toes to the crown of her padded head. And, as her retinue had left from the harem's Gate of Felicity, the citizens of Serres jostled to gawp (and discreetly spit) at the small party as it rode past.

The riders approached the city gate and a platoon of janissaries paused to bow deeply, their tall white hats tapping the

201

ground like fingers. As the men straightened, fourteen hands rose to curl fourteen moustaches and fourteen eyebrows arched in appreciation of the sight before them.

As was proper, Anna ignored the courtesy and kept her gaze firmly on the street ahead.

The janissary commander made himself useful by clearing a path before them, swirling his baton to left and right with unnecessary vigour while waving them forward with his free hand. Anna's companions closed up to assist the process, reaching out to hold on to one another as their horses whinnied and stamped.

Then they were through the gate and finding balance amidst the frozen ruts of the road that ran south. The janissaries saluted and turned back and Anna kicked her horse forward in the direction of a hill where stood the forest of tents and banners that made up the field headquarters of the Sultan Bayezid.

The road was busy with traffic going in and out of the city. Shawled families, sitting astride their roped possessions, exchanged uneasy glances with swarthy *akinci,* the gazi tribesmen bribed to bring their lives west to settle this new land and pave the way to the next conquest. The cold, dense air muffled the sound of movement and the shouts of encouragement or warning drifted quickly away above the mist of animal breath that hung over everything.

Anna had arrived at Serres in the early autumn with the Mamonas family, following a rushed departure from Monemvasia. The family had fled aboard a Venetian galley under cover of darkness and had landed at Thessaloniki further up the coast. From there, they'd taken the road to join the Sultan at Serres, passing Ottoman messengers rushing east to carry their ruler's firman summoning all fighters to the planting of the Horsehairs.

And now the huge lance was there before her. It was surrounded by a guard of janissaries and several fur-clad eunuchs armed with pens, there to record the first arrivals to join Yildirim in further conquest within the Dar ul-Harb, the Abode of War.

It was planted in the centre of a large plateau and a breeze splayed and twisted the hairs while little eddies of snow curled around its base. At the other end of the field, groups of sipahi cavalry, dressed in the skins of wild beasts, charged in turn at a suspended brass ball, shooting arrows from the saddle as they went.

Anna walked her horse around the edge of the field in the direction of the tents. She assumed that her companions would know which belonged to Devlet Hatun, wife of Bayezid, to whom she had been summoned. She guessed it would be splendid, as befitted the mother of the Sultan's second son, and as quiet and well ordered as the harem itself.

In the three months she had been at Serres, Anna had been imprisoned within a corner of the old Byzantine palace that had been given over to the women of the Sultan. She had not seen Damian or his father or Zoe and her only contact with the outside world had been the whispers and giggles of the beauties gathered for the Sultan's unpredictable pleasure. She had retreated into herself, turning over and over in her mind the events at Monemvasia, events that increasingly centred on the golden figure of Luke. And she found herself praying, day and night, that he'd somehow survived the storm.

Then, just when she thought she might drown herself of boredom in one of the scented pools, a summons had reached her. Devlet Hatun wanted to see her. But not within the whispering corridors of the harem. She was to meet her outside the city amongst the tents and flags of the army gathering to march on Constantinople.

Now she watched as two vastly turbanned officials rode out to meet them, their long black robes brushing the snow either side of their horses. They bowed from the saddle, then turned and led her through the maze of silk, canvas and rope to a large tent of exquisite greens.

Anna dismounted and waited while murmurs announced her coming. Then the silks were parted and she entered a world of shadow and shimmering heat. There were braziers of latticed gold around the walls, the glow from their coal hearts beating warmth into the tent. Thick carpets of intricate weave overlapped each other while cushions the size of galleys were piled around poles garlanded with vines. On the cushions rested girls of every age, some clothed and some naked, some talking, some sleeping, while others glided between the groups bearing trays of delicacies and bowls of sherbet. A tiny orchestra sat back to back playing instruments whose strings merged with their tumbling hair.

And no one looked at Anna as she stood there, blinking.

The light in the tent seemed to come from roundels of candles suspended from the tops of the tent poles. To begin with Anna could see little beyond the shapes immediately in front of her. Then, as her eyes grew accustomed to the shadows, she saw that there was a low, canopied dais in the centre with two thrones side by side on which sat a woman and a boy.

Only they seemed to notice her.

Bowing low to the couple, Anna unbuttoned her coat and laid it gently on the ground. Then she walked between the bodies until she stood in front of the dais, her heart beating like a drum.

No one spoke and Anna felt beads of sweat collect on her brow and between her breasts. The woman in front of her was perhaps twenty years her senior, quite small and tending to plumpness beneath the swathes of silk that covered her from head to foot. Dark eyes, not unkind, scrutinised her from above an embroidered veil that clung to the contours of her face like a gauze.

The boy beside her was on the cusp of manhood, well made and possessing an intelligent gaze. Suddenly he smiled and a row of perfect white teeth appeared.

Anna's heartbeat slowed.

The woman moved to unhook the side of her veil and Anna saw that she was smiling too, but with teeth less white. She held up a hand and a tray appeared at Anna's side. The boy spoke.

'It is hot wine, since my mother, assumes you to be cold after your ride,' said the boy in flawless Greek. 'But if you prefer sherbet, it can be brought.'

Anna glanced at the woman whose expression had not changed. 'Please thank your mother, Prince Mehmed, and tell her that the wine will revive me,' she replied, taking the cup.

'Would it please you to sit?' asked the boy, indicating a chair that had materialised behind her.

An extraordinary silence followed, extraordinary because the conversation of the surrounding groups didn't cease and yet no sound came from them. The tiny orchestra, too, kept playing but no notes could be heard. The perfect choreography of movement around them permitted total discretion and was a thing both wondrous and beautiful to Anna, who was already feeling the effects of the wine steal up her limbs like immersion in a warm bath.

The boy looked at his mother and then at Anna. 'Do you know why you're here?' he asked.

'In Serres, lord?' replied Anna. 'I suppose because my husband is here.'

'And yet you have not seen him.'

Anna felt her heart begin to beat quickly again. She stared at the boy.

Mehmed joined his hands in his lap and looked down at them. 'Why did the Mamonases bring you here? Would it not have been easier to leave you in Monemvasia? Surely the Despot would have been happy to find you there?'

'I am here as a hostage, lord,' said Anna.

'I think not,' said Prince Mehmed, looking up and frowning. Anna saw that the eyebrows were high-arched like his mother's. 'I think you are here because my brother, the Prince Suleyman, desires that you be here. And my brother, Allah willing, will be the next sultan.'

Anna felt sick.

'I think,' continued the Prince, 'and my mother thinks, that you will be part of the bargain struck with the Mamonas clan.'

Anna said nothing. She just sat staring at the boy. New drops of sweat had gathered at her temples that owed nothing to the heat of the tent. She looked away towards the musicians as if the logic of soundless music might help her think.

Bargain? What bargain?

The Prince leant forward and dropped his voice to something barely above a whisper. 'We are natural allies, you and I,' he said softly, 'and our alliance springs from shared danger. My brother and I are very different. He looks to cities and courts for his pleasure. He looks to the West as the Dar ul-Harb and to Constantinople as his capital in years to come. I, on the other hand, have gazi blood in my veins. My mother is of the Germiyan tribe, sister to its leader Prince Yakub. I like tents, not cities. And I prefer the East.'

He drew even closer. 'My father and brother are not close. My brother has been tasked to take Constantinople, a city that has never fallen except to the Franks. My father believes he will fail. But if he succeeds, then my brother will challenge Bayezid, who is not the man he was. You and I will both suffer if my brother becomes sultan. You, with your honour, and I, most assuredly, with my life. We are natural allies.'

'But how can I help you, lord?' Anna asked slowly. 'I am a seventeen-year-old girl married to a Greek merchant.'

Mehmed smiled. 'No, you are much more than that, Anna. You are the daughter of Simon Laskaris, Protostrator of Mistra. He has influence with the Emperor Manuel, who will either choose to defend Constantinople or surrender it. My brother has been entrusted with the siege and if he succeeds, he will become sultan and the West will become the Dar ul-Harb.' He paused. 'And I shall succumb to the bowstring.'

'And if he fails?'

'If he fails?' said the boy softly. 'Who knows? Perhaps someone other than him will become sultan. Someone who will lead his gazis eastwards. Someone who might be a friend to your empire.'

Anna and the boy looked at each other in silence.

'So what would you have me do?'

'A discussion will take place this afternoon,' said the Prince. 'There is a side passage to my father's audience tent which leads to a women's room with a grille from which you can see and hear the proceedings. My mother will take you there. I want you to listen.'

Anna considered this.

'And then?' she asked.

The Prince picked an invisible speck from his silken sleeve. Anna suddenly remembered how young he was.

'There are people who have come to this camp whom you know.'

'Who has come, lord?' asked Anna.

'The Emperor, the Despot . . . and your father, Simon Laskaris.'

Anna's heart jumped.

'Why have they chosen to come?'

'They haven't. The emperor has been vassal to the sultan for some time. Manuel has to obey a summons or face war.'

'But he faces war already.'

'Not yet. There may yet be a chance to keep the peace. He had no choice but to come. None of them did.'

'Are they in danger?'

Mehmed looked up into her eyes. 'Yes, they are in danger. They must escape this place tonight.'

Anna hadn't realised that the tent of Devlet Hatun was connected to that of Bayezid. It was as if the entire palace in Serres had been reconstructed out of silk on this hilltop, the echo of stone exchanged for the whisper of fabric.

Anna was waiting in a small anteroom and a low table had been set before her made of sandalwood and inlaid with mother of pearl. On it was laid fruit and wine and flowers of the summer somehow preserved to show colour in winter.

Eventually, she heard sounds of conversation and the wall opened to reveal the small figure of Devlet Hatun and a tall woman by her side. The woman was unveiled and dressed in a cowled cloak of velvet thrown back from her shoulders. Her fair hair fell well below her shoulders to contour small breasts and brush the first curve of her hips. Her face was proud and angular, with a straight nose above wide nostrils and full, decisive lips. She regarded Anna with no expression of pleasure or enquiry.

She was, emphatically, of royal blood.

Then there was a further rustle and Zoe Mamonas stepped into the room. Anna gave a little cry and stood up. 'How . . . ?'

Zoe walked towards her. She looked tired and drawn. 'How do I dare come before you after what happened to Luke?' she suggested, stooping to sit cross-legged before her with the grace of a courtesan. 'Because, Anna, I had nothing to do with it. It was Damian who recognized Luke when you came through the gate. And it was he who guessed that you would try to make your escape that night. He followed you.'

Anna studied the wide, guileless eyes between dark eyelashes laced with kohl. She looked at the earnest intent in that pale face and the hands now drawn to the mouth in what looked like entreaty. In a day of uncertainties, this was an uncertainty too difficult to fathom.

'I don't know,' she said after a time. 'I don't know what to believe any more.'

Zoe placed her hands, palms down, on the table. It was as if she had delivered an offering but had nothing more to give. 'You don't have to believe me. Just believe these women when they say that you are in danger. Why would they lie?'

In the silence that followed, the tall woman stepped forward, lifting her cloak in one hand, to occupy the chair from which Anna had risen.

'I am the Princess Olivera Despina,' she said. The voice was surprisingly deep. 'I am the fifth wife of Bayezid and the daughter of King Lazar of Serbia. My father was executed by the Sultan at the field of Kosovo five years ago, since when I have been the executioner's wife.' She paused and studied a ring on her left forefinger. 'After that battle, the Sultan used three battalions of dead Serbs as his banqueting table.'

She looked up at Anna. 'My brother, Stefan Lazarević,' she went on, 'is now vassal to the Sultan. He too has been summoned here.'

She looked at the other two women and smiled. Then she returned her gaze to Anna. 'We all represent different causes. You, your honour and the Empire; me, a murdered father; the Princess Devlet, her son's future. Quite enough, one might think, to establish common interest.'

Anna looked across at Zoe. 'And you, Zoe, what is your interest?'

Zoe Mamonas looked down at her feet and, for the first time, Anna saw discomfort in her poise.

'My argument' – her voice was soft – 'is with Prince Suleyman.'

The silence that followed this statement was complete. A dog barked beyond the tents and a janissary's cauldron clanked somewhere nearer.

Then the woman who had not thus far uttered a word spoke. 'We must go,' said the Princess Devlet Hatun. In Greek.

At the centre of every storm there is an eye of calm. And so it was in the court of the Sultan Bayezid.

While his messengers dashed to every corner of the Ottoman Empire to call his subjects to arms, while roads were repaired to ease the progress of his armies, while provisions in prodigious quantities were amassed at every stopping point along the way, the inner sanctum of the court was an ocean of peace and tranquillity.

Like the palaces of Bursa and Edirne, the camp contained a series of tented courtyards, with carpets and fountains and orange trees in tubs within, their poles hung with painted lanterns and their walls lined with living statues that never spoke above a whisper. There were three courts here. The first conducted the business of the palace and city. The second contained the offices of state, the archives and the divan rooms where the Sultan's viziers met. The inner sanctum, where the Sultan held audience, was a place of absolute quiet unless the Lord of the Two Horizons chose to break it.

Here, on this winter day of snow and approaching dusk, the braziers glowed with fresh and scented coals and three huge dogs slept at the feet of the Sultan Bayezid. He was, at this time, around forty years of age and the dash of his youth had largely departed, leaving behind a bloated husk of rouged and temperamental decadence. His appetite for female companionship had largely disappeared as had large numbers of his teeth, but his appetite for wanton cruelty remained stolidly intact.

He was still a formidable and dangerous man and his sons, vassals and courtiers feared every hair in his luxuriant beard. The rise of a tapered eyebrow in displeasure was still enough to cause men to tremble, and the slow lift of a pudgy finger enough to send them to the bowstring.

He was magnificent, all-powerful and capricious.

Now, he lounged across several large cushions and tickled the flank of a dog with his toe. He was dressed in a tunic of damask studded with pearls buttoned over straining silken pyjamas. A jewelled turban of intricate layers sat above a face ruined by excess; heavy lids shielded eyes that darted to left and right in a parody of his former verve. With one hand he stroked the flaxen hair of a pageboy of teenage years and perfect skin, a gift from the Emperor of Trebizond. In the other he balanced a silver goblet of wine between two fat fingers. On a table beside him sat a dish piled high with sugar.

The Sultan's tongue was stabbing the inside of his cheek. He had toothache again and nothing his doctors did could alleviate the pain. So he drank instead.

Anna was watching him closely from the other side of the grille. Beside her sat Devlet Hatun and Olivera Despina who was whispering into her ear.

'The one next to the Sultan, the one with the heron's plume, that is the Grand Vizier Kara Halil Candarli. He is wise but devious.' She paused. 'He served the Sultan's father, Murad, before him.'

Anna looked at the other people present. There was Prince Suleyman, Prince Mehmed and, beside him, a younger boy. Despina followed her gaze.

'That is Prince Musa, third son to Bayezid. He shares the same mother as Suleyman but the brothers hate each other. Musa is only ten years of age but is very serious. He reads the Koran every moment of the day and seeks only the company of learned men. He despises the excesses of his eldest brother.'

Anna looked at the pale-skinned boy with large, uncertain eyes and a hooked nose. He looked nothing like Suleyman.

'Who are those two, standing behind the Princes?' whispered Anna, pointing slowly at two well-made men standing together.

'The taller one is Evrenos Bey,' answered Olivera Despina. 'He is the Sultan's best general and has been with him at every victory. He is fanatically loyal to Bayezid and would die for him. He is of Byzantine descent but a convert to Islam.'

'And the other?'

'The other is the brother of the Princess Devlet. He is Yakub Bey, Emir of Germiyan and one of the most powerful gazi princes in Anatolia. He became vassal to the Sultan three years ago.'

Anna studied Yakub closely, something about him inviting further enquiry. He was a man of medium height but powerful build and wore a long, quilted coat trimmed with the furs of different animals. His face was lined and weather-beaten and his nose flat, interrupting a scar that ran from eye to lip.

'What is a gazi?' she asked.

'They're the men of the steppe, the tribes that Bayezid and every other Ottoman Turk are descended from. There are many tribes, and the Germiyans are one of the largest. Each tribal land is called a *beylik*.'

Then someone spoke.

'Grand Vizier,' said the Sultan, dismissing the boy from Trebizond and putting his goblet down on to the table, 'we have summoned our subjects and vassals here to Serres to decide where will be our next Dar ul-Harb.' He paused and ran his tongue between his lips, wincing. 'There are those, like my son the Prince Suleyman, who believe that our destiny is to the west. There are others' – here Bayezid nodded at Yakub – 'not least the beyliks of our tribal homelands, who believe that we should confront the Khanates of the Black and White Sheep who threaten our eastern frontiers. Our Christian vassals await our pleasure outside but first we of the Faith should talk between ourselves.'

Bayezid turned to Candarli. 'Tell us your view, Grand Vizier.'

213

Candarli bowed low to the Sultan. 'Majesty, we are fortunate to be ruled by a sultan who can rightly call himself Lord of the Two Horizons. But what do we have on each of these horizons? In the east there are the Khanates and the remaining beyliks who have yet to see the glory of your rule as our friend Yakub of the Germiyans has. But these are not our enemy.'

Anna looked at Yakub, who was looking at his feet. She saw that Bayezid was watching him closely.

'Meanwhile,' Candarli went on, 'we have both opportunity and threat before us in the kingdoms of Christendom. What remains of the Roman Empire is weak and the lands of Thrace and Macedonia are empty of people and we can settle the akincis of Anatolia there at will. But the Christian kings are jealous of your success and, even now, Sigismund of Hungary and Mircea of Wallachia are entreating the Pope to bless another crusade against us. The lord Evrenos Bey can talk further on this subject.'

Evrenos Bey stepped forward to stand directly before his sultan. He bowed. 'The Grand Vizier is right, Majesty,' he said. 'Duke Philip of Burgundy has raised seven hundred thousand gold ducats to spend on such a crusade. There has been a long war between the English and French, which is in truce at this time, so there are many knights eager to join it. The new Pope Boniface is urging all the Kings of Christendom to act.'

'And how would our armies fare against such a crusade?' asked the Sultan. His tooth was throbbing ever harder.

'Majesty, our armies have been everywhere victorious. There is no army in the world that can beat us.'

The Sultan smiled and nodded. 'Indeed. We are everywhere victorious except where our eldest son sees fit to show mercy on a Greek city. Prince Suleyman, what is your view?'

Anna saw Suleyman's face colour. He bowed stiffly to his father and looked around the faces in the room. 'Father, Evrenos Bey and I decided *jointly*' – here he glanced at the general – 'not to risk an assault on Mistra because we wished to preserve our army for the attack on Constantinople. And we must secure Constantinople before making further advances into Christendom.'

'Ah,' said Bayezid, 'Constantinople. The Red Apple. Why do you think we call it that, Prince Suleyman?'

'Because, Majesty,' replied Suleyman, 'it is the sweetest fruit. Constantinople is still the greatest city on Earth and you cannot truly call yourself Lord of the Two Horizons until you have conquered it.'

Bayezid flushed and his hand moved to his beard. He looked hard at his eldest son. Then he laughed. It was a rasping sound without humour. 'And perhaps the Prince Suleyman will be the one to do it? Or would the charms of the city's female citizens again be enough to deter him?'

Suleyman was holding himself in check. Just. Anna could see that his fists were clenched.

The Sultan turned to look at his second son. 'I believe that the Prince Mehmed and Yakub Bey take a different view?'

Mehmed didn't reply immediately. He glanced at Yakub beside him. Then he spoke.

'Father, the Emir is chief amongst the leaders of the gazi tribes and it is they that form the heart of our empire. These men sense threat from the East, not the West. From the Emir Temur, whom some call Tamerlane, whose horde is moving westwards and may ally itself with the Khanates to attack us. Prince Yakub believes, as I do, that we should make peace with the Kings of Christendom and move east to secure our frontiers against the greater threat of Temur.'

The Sultan Bayezid was slowly shaking his head. 'You speak with great wisdom, Prince Mehmed. And it may be that we need to confront Temur before long. But our spies tell us that he will be employed for some time in the north fighting his cousin Tokhtamish of the Golden Horde and afterwards is more likely to attack the Ming Empire of China than move west. Yakub Bey?'

The gazi chief spoke slowly in a voice little above a growl. 'It is well known that the Mongol Temur claims sovereignty over the Turkmen tribes of Anatolia and is angered by your annexation of the beyliks. Temur is your enemy.'

Bayezid ground his teeth and one of them exploded in pain. He lost his temper. 'Temur?' he roared, thumping the cushion to his side and leaning forward so that his beard brushed his knees. Muscles had appeared in the walls of his neck. 'Temur?' he shouted again, and Anna, behind her grille, felt the shock wave of his anger. 'Who is this Temur? Who is Temur?'

There was complete silence around him and even the dogs seemed to have stopped breathing.

Bayezid had risen to his feet and was standing directly in front of Yakub, staring down into his eyes. 'I have no fear of turning my back on Temur or Tamerlane or whatever he calls himself,' he hissed through shaking beard. 'Tamerlane is an illiterate barbarian who delights in massacre. I am Bayezid, Sultan of Rum and Sword of Islam. I have never lost a battle and have sworn that I will see my horses watered at the altar of St Peter's in Rome.'

He paused. 'Believe me, emir, when I tell you that I will see that happen. And so will you. By my side.'

He glared at Yakub for a while longer before turning to look at the others, each in turn. 'So my will is this: we will take

216

Constantinople quickly – if, that is, we do not manage to persuade the Emperor Manuel to surrender the remnants of his eunuch empire beforehand. And we will do nothing to dissuade the armies of Christendom from marching against us. And when they do, we will defeat them in such a way that they will never march again.'

He looked around again at the assembly, breathing hard and challenging any dissent. None came. He sat heavily back on his cushions. 'Then we will deal with this Tamerlane.'

Anna sat with her face very close to the grille, its thin material rising and falling with the tiny pulse of her breathing. There was utter silence around the Sultan now and Devlet Hatun leant forward and gently touched Anna's shoulder, indicating that she should draw back lest the movement be seen. Anna turned in the semi-darkness and saw that she and Olivera Despina were holding hands. The fear that radiated around Bayezid had reached beyond the tent walls to envelop them like smoke. Anna sat back in her chair and reached out to place a hand on theirs. She thought suddenly of how it must be to live every hour of every day with this fear, to watch it wind its ugly coils around the people you love.

Bayezid had ordered more wine to be brought and sat staring darkly into the contents of his goblet. Then he rose slowly and walked over to warm his hands at a brazier. 'Prince Suleyman,' he said without looking around, 'tell us how we are to take Constantinople.'

Suleyman exchanged glances with the Vizier. Anna saw that a small dagger, its hilt heavy with jewels, was held to the Vizier's belly by the folds of his sash.

Suleyman said, 'The sea walls are the city's weakest point and it was these the Venetians breached two centuries ago

217

when they finally prevailed. But we will need command of the sea to achieve that.'

'Which is why we have built Anadolu Hisar,' said Bayezid. 'You told me that the castle would prevent any Genoese ships from coming to the city's aid from the north.'

'And so it will, Father,' said the Prince. 'Especially when it is equipped with cannon. But there remains some threat from the south. The Byzantines still have some warships that they've prudently kept beyond our reach at Monemvasia. These we have managed to delay from setting sail until our own ships have cannon on them.'

'And they have cannon now?'

'I have arranged it so, Father. The ships have cannon and the city of Constantinople is sealed. The blockade is intact.'

Bayezid looked sulkily at his eldest son. 'That may keep the Byzantine fleet away, but how do we get through the walls?'

'Bigger cannon, Father,' said Suleyman. 'And ships. So that we can destroy the walls and starve the city.'

'And where do we get those?'

'Venice. The Venetians make the best ships and cannon in the world.'

But Bayezid was already shaking his head. 'I won't talk to those dogs.'

Suleyman stepped forward. 'Father, you don't have to. Outside awaits the Archon of Monemvasia, Pavlos Mamonas. It was he who ensured that the Byzantine fleet has sailed too late to prevent our blockade of their capital. But the Archon has done more for us. He has also got us cannon, Venetian cannon.'

Suleyman paused. 'Father, the fleet from Monemvasia is sailing into a trap. With the cannons, we will blow it out of the water.'

218

Bayezid looked warily at his son. 'And you trust these Mamonases? They are not of the Faith.' The Sultan pulled slowly at his beard. Anna looked round at the other men who were all regarding Suleyman with interest, some friendlier than others. She wondered what deeper connection Suleyman had with the family she had married into.

'Very well,' said the Sultan eventually. 'Bring them in.'

In the time it took the Sultan Bayezid to drink two goblets of wine and hurl another at a hound, the Mamonas father and son had been fetched from some outer courtyard. Both men had snow on the shoulders of heavy woollen cloaks that shook itself to the floor when they made their bows.

Bayezid studied them before speaking. 'Archon, you and your son are welcome at our camp. It seems we have made you await our pleasure outside in the cold.' He stole a questioning look at his Grand Vizier. 'Remove your coats if you so desire.'

The two men did so and bowed again more extravagantly in the new freedom of movement. They were dressed in long tunics of plain damask. Their heavy boots, still clotted with snow, emerged from their skirts like furred animals. Damian looked at the exquisite rug below him now wet with snow.

Bayezid was staring hard at Damian with a mix of curiosity and calculation. His eyes roamed upwards from his offending boots to the long hair that clung like jet curtains to either side of his pale face.

'Give no thought to the carpets,' he said. 'They are removed nightly so that our imperial feet may delight in fresh texture each morning. It is of no consequence.' He turned to Pavlos. 'We are given to understand that it is you that we have to thank

219

for this excellent wine. But it is dangerous both to my girth and reputation. We may ask you to make it weaker.'

Pavlos Mamonas bowed again but said nothing.

The Sultan continued: 'We also understand that you have provided us with cannon, and for this we are grateful.' He paused. 'We are curious to know why it is you wish to help us.'

Pavlos Mamonas said, 'Monemvasia is a city long famed for its independence. We are a place of merchants who feel allegiance to no cause beyond that of peaceful trade.' He parted his hands as if the gift of reason were laid out on the carpet before him. 'You, lord,' he went on, 'are Yildirim, a thunderbolt sent from heaven to be the Sword of Islam. We believe that, in time, you will conquer the world. And you will need the profits of commerce to pay for such conquest. We stand ready to provide you with such profits.'

Bayezid threw back his head in a gurgle of laughter that made his beard quiver like a breezed treetop. 'Well said, Greek!' he said. 'I will send you to the dog Temur to pour Greek honey into his barbarian ear!'

'Lord, I speak only the truth. My family has long traded with your court. The wine you enjoy comes from our vineyards; much of the fruit you eat comes from our orchards. Now we bring you the cannon you need to sink the fleet we have delayed from coming to the aid of Constantinople. We hope that we have so far proved consistent in serving your interests.'

The Sultan nodded absently.

'Majesty, the Venetians may be your friends or your enemies. They fear your advance into Christendom and may yet send a fleet to break your blockade of Constantinople. And the Venetian fleet is powerful.'

Bayezid scowled at Pavlos Mamonas.

220

'But, lord,' he went on hurriedly, 'they are also bitter rivals of the Genoese and will seek any opportunity to gain some advantage over them. We ourselves are friendly with the Doge and know that the Serenissima has long coveted the monopoly of the trade in alum from the great mines at Phocaea that you currently bestow on the Genoese. The trade has made the Genoese of Chios, from where it is shipped, rich beyond avarice.'

Bayezid had begun to fidget. The business of commerce was beneath his imperial gaze and he was beginning to find himself bored. The Grand Vizier stepped forward.

'His Majesty does not want to hear the sordid details of Italian trade squabbles, Mamonas. Please speak to the theme.'

Pavlos Mamonas took a deep breath. 'Lord, I can deliver to you Venetian cannon, ships and neutrality in your war against Constantinople. In exchange, I would ask you to consider granting the monopoly in the trade of alum, and licence to manage it from the island of Chios, to the Republic of Venice once you have assumed control of the Byzantine Empire.'

'But do they not already have the monopoly of alum from Trebizond?'

'They do, lord, taken from the Genoese some time past. Therefore I would ask, in addition, that Venetian ships be allowed past Constantinople so that the markets in the west can continue to receive alum.'

'At considerable profit to the Serenissima,' murmured the Sultan. 'You ask a lot, Mamonas.'

Bayezid looked at his Grand Vizier and Candarli looked at Prince Suleyman. Then the Vizier spoke.

'And what advantage does the Mamonas family derive from such an arrangement?' he asked quietly.

221

'The Mamonas family wishes to expand its wine production beyond the shores of the Peloponnese,' answered Pavlos Mamonas simply. 'There is plenty of land on Chios and the soil is well suited to our grape. There is also a port to facilitate its distribution.'

'And that is all? You just want land on Chios?'

'That, Lord, and the Despotate of Mistra which we would rule as your vassals.'

There was a period of silence in the tent broken only by the noisy yawn of a dog and the rustle of the Sultan's sleeve as he reached for more wine. He rubbed one eye and then the other, closing them briefly before arching an eyebrow at his vizier.

'But, Lord Candarli, do we not have an alliance with the Genoese over Chios?'

'Yes, Majesty. The Genoese control the trading outpost of Pera across the Golden Horn from Constantinople. We deemed it wise to gain their favour given their control of the Black Sea.'

Suleyman said, 'Father, the Archon understands fully that we cannot risk antagonising the Genoese. But what if the island became ungovernable for them? What if its Greek population were to rise up and cast them out? I am told that the island is frequently raided by pirates from the mainland who abduct Greek children and take them into slavery. The Greeks no longer trust the Genoese to defend them and are planning to take matters into their own hands. What if the island became *available*?'

Sultan and Grand Vizier exchanged glances, one more amused than the other.

'It seems you know a lot about these raids, Prince Suleyman,' said Bayezid between the tight lips of a smile, 'and it seems their timing is most convenient to your cause.'

Suleyman said nothing and his face betrayed no emotion. Bayezid was watching him closely, weighing a question in his mind, focusing hard despite the wine. He turned suddenly to Damian Mamonas.

'I hear, my young lord Mamonas,' he said quietly, 'that you have a most delightful new wife?'

Anna's heart stopped. She did not want to be any part of this conversation. She felt the hand of Devlet Hatun squeeze her fingers.

'Yes, lord,' replied Damian.

'And your wife was the one my son spared before the walls of Mistra?'

'Yes, lord, although it happened before my betrothal to her.'

'Yes, yes, of course,' murmured Bayezid, smiling fondly at the young Greek. 'And what part does your wife play in this bargain you have struck with the Prince Suleyman?'

Anna felt two sets of fingers dig into her arms, holding her on her seat to stop her from falling forward against the grille. Nausea rose in her gorge and she knew she would be sick unless she did something. She didn't want, or need, to hear Damian's answer. She needed to escape.

CHAPTER TWELVE

SERRES, RUMELIA, WINTER 1394

The wine had been warmed and probably strengthened and it slid down Anna's throat with the softness of newly drawn milk. She sat in the tent of Devlet Hatun and looked up at the two women who'd brought her there and saw her future in their slave eyes. She was even dressed as one of them.

Then she thought of Luke and what they'd so nearly made happen and a shiver of sorrow crept up her spine like the trace of a frozen finger. She lowered her head and looked into the depths of her goblet; pieces of cinnamon bumped against the rim in lazy circles. She was stronger for the drink.

It was an hour since she'd come from Bayezid and she'd spent it in silent and horrified contemplation of her future.

I am to be part of the bargain.

At last Olivera Despina spoke. 'Your father, the Emperor and the Despot are before the Sultan now, as is my brother Prince Stefan.' She paused and took Anna's arms in her hands. She looked hard into her eyes. 'The Sultan is becoming drunk and unpredictable. I fear for their lives.'

'Then we must act,' said Anna.

The flap to the tent opened and Mehmed appeared. He was

224

frowning and walked quickly towards them. 'The last part was short,' he said, glancing over his shoulder. 'My father has given the Emperor an ultimatum and he wants an answer tomorrow. Surrender Constantinople or watch every citizen of the city killed or enslaved.'

Anna gasped. 'He cannot mean that. Why would he want a capital with no population?'

It was Olivera Despina who answered. 'We would do well to remember that he took six thousand slaves when Thessaloniki fell. And now he has Temur to compete with. He can certainly mean it.'

'There's worse,' Mehmed continued. 'My father made a boast when his vassals had left the tent.' He paused and looked at Anna. 'The Emperor, the Despot and your father must escape. Tonight.'

Princess Despina's tent was smaller than Devlet Hatun's and it housed no naked odalisques or miniature orchestra. But then she was not of nomadic stock and had no taste or feel for the steppe. The carpets on the ground were Persian and less deep than the Sultan's and the silks of the tent walls were partially hidden by Flemish tapestries. A bed stood between two wood burners, which scented the air with rose. Anna's head was clearing quickly from the fog of wine.

Olivera Despina was brisk and purposeful and Anna liked her better every moment.

'Quickly, change into these.' She pointed to some clothes that lay on the bed. 'They're my maid's and include a veil which you would do well to arrange with care. Your hair is not of Turcoman origin.'

While Anna changed, the Princess spoke.

'Your father, the Emperor and the Despot are in my brother's tent. I will be permitted to enter, and with me goes my maid whom God has blessed with the same height and shape as yourself. And she is always veiled.'

'Why will your brother be with them?' asked Anna, stepping forward to allow the Princess to hook her veil into place.

'Because my brother, although a Christian, is still a sworn vassal of the Sultan. If anyone can persuade Manuel to relinquish his empire, it will be the man who lost his on the field of Kosovo.'

'Manuel will not surrender his empire,' said Anna with more conviction than she felt.

'No?' replied Olivera Despina. 'Not even with the prospect of his subjects being slaughtered by the Turk as he looks on? If he cannot escape this place, he will surrender.'

She stepped back to look at Anna. 'You are ready to go. Say nothing from now on and especially in my brother's tent, whatever the temptation. Recognising you will make it harder for your father to leave.'

She lifted the folds of the entrance and both of them stepped into the biting cold of the evening and a semicircle of unexpected soldiers.

'Majesty,' said a muffled voice, 'we are here to escort you.'

The voice came through the mail of an aventail so that it seemed as if two eyes had spoken.

'Who sent you?' asked Olivera Despina, recovering her poise. 'I asked for no escort.'

The question was unnecessary. The light from the torches, held aloft by every other of the dozen men, illuminated the gold mail of the Sultan's personal bodyguard.

The captain of the guard signalled to his men to form two

lines either side of the women. Then he bowed to the Princess and made the gesture to depart.

Walking behind her, Anna could see fear stiffening her every movement and prayed it was only visible to her.

They heard Prince Stefan Lazarević's tent before they saw it. The men's voices were audible in the still night air and they were all talking at the same time. The Emperor's Varangian Guard, all bearing axes, stood outside the tent, stamping their feet and blowing on their hands. There were six of them.

Inside the tent, Manuel and his brother faced each other across a table with two guttering candles at its centre. They stopped talking and looked up as Olivera Despina entered. A much younger man stood behind them.

'Sister!' he cried. 'They did not tell me you were at the camp!'

Brother and sister embraced and stood holding each other's faces, searching each other's eyes for signs of hope, or even the comfort of a father's memory.

Anna looked at her own father and saw a man she had not seen before.

Simon Laskaris had aged by twenty years. His face was gaunt and lined with misery. Behind Anna's veil, tears were falling and they were a river and warm to the taste and she couldn't stop their flow. She willed herself not to move, not to run over to take in her arms this shrunken man with disordered hair and wild eyes.

What has happened to you?

Why did she even need to ask that question? Here was a man who had lost a son and a daughter and any will to live. Here was the one man in the tent for whom death would be a release.

'Princess, we are pleased to see you.' The Emperor of the

227

Byzantines raised his hands in greeting. 'Have you further news for us? Are we to leave this place alive?'

The Princess looked at her brother and raised her finger to her lips. Then she moved to the table, taking Prince Stefan's arm as she did so. Everyone, except Anna, moved to surround the candlelit surface as if to bear witness to a sacrifice.

But before Olivera Despina could speak, there was a loud sniff and they turned to see a nose appear between the entrance folds of the tent. Then came a second. The Sultan's dogs trotted over to the table and began to explore the clothes of those gathered at its edges.

Then the page from Trebizond stepped into the tent, smiling. His face glowed with an unnatural light and Anna wondered whether some concoction of oils was at work to create this miracle. He was perhaps twelve years old and Anna wanted very much to touch him. She turned to see him better and it was then that she saw the dagger in the sash at his waist. Its jewelled pommel had caught the light of a candle and was sending stars to the roof of the tent.

It was the Grand Vizier's.

Assassin.

Her movement had been seen by the boy, who turned to her, still smiling.

'Girl,' he said in musical Greek, 'there is wine outside. Bring it.'

Anna hesitated. Should she understand Greek? Should she leave a tent that contained her father and an angel with a dagger?

The boy looked at her curiously. Then he repeated the command in Turkish and Anna found herself bowing. Outside, she was met by a servant holding a tray on which stood four silver

228

goblets. She took the tray and went back inside, putting it down on a table beside the entrance.

The boy had moved further into the tent and was still smiling.

'My lords, I am the Prince Caspar, nephew to the Basileus in Trebizond and page to the Sultan Bayezid. My master has sent with me some hot wine to assist your discussions. He wishes these only to be held between his vassals and asks, therefore, if you, Protostrator, would wait in another tent?'

The boy looked with innocence at Simon Laskaris, who seemed uninterested in the proposal. Anna's eyes, bright above the veil, bored into Theodore's back.

Do not let my father leave with that boy.

But the Emperor smiled at the young prince from Trebizond.

'I know your uncle the Emperor well, Prince Caspar,' he said. 'Certainly the Protostrator can retire.'

The boy bowed and turned to Anna. 'Please serve the wine. The Emperor first.'

Anna was thinking fast. How could she prevent her father leaving? The tray she was holding was warm which meant that the wine in the goblets must be very hot.

She walked towards the Emperor but there was a dog in the way. It was circling the carpet, its long head down, looking for a place to settle.

Anna tripped.

The dog reacted as Anna had hoped. The head spun round towards her, its teeth bared. Anna let out a cry and fell against her father. The goblets fell to the floor, one releasing its contents over Simon Laskaris's hand.

The old man grunted in pain. His hand was scalded and he

held it to his chest. Then Olivera Despina was at his side examining the burn.

'Quick,' she said, 'we must take it outside to the snow.' She turned to Anna. 'Help me.'

The women led Simon Laskaris out into the snow, Anna holding the hand as gently as she was able. Outside, she knelt next to her father and pressed snow on to it. Around them stood the six Varangians and, beyond them, the soldiers of the Sultan's bodyguard. There was a moon.

Anna looked hard at her father. He seemed oblivious to the pain and there was still no recognition of Anna in his vacant eyes. She fought back her tears.

Olivera Despina glanced at her. She whispered. 'We will leave him out here until I can take him away myself.'

When they re-entered the tent, the boy had changed. The gold had dulled, the halo had faded and there was no smile on the face that turned to look at them. He looked petulant and his hand was resting on the dagger at his waist. Behind him, the three princes were huddled together, talking in whispers. The dog was standing above the fallen goblets and licking the remains of the wine from the carpet.

'Lord Laskaris's hand needs attention,' Olivera Despina told the boy. 'I will take him to my tent where my women can see to him.'

The boy glanced down at the dog, which had brushed against his leg. His expression was a mix of irritation and something Anna thought might be fear.

'The Sultan's women will see to the wound,' he said, looking up. 'He must come with me.'

'I am a woman of the Sultan,' replied the Princess quietly.

'Or is the pleasure you give to our lord such that he no longer knows who his wives are?'

The boy's gold turned to crimson and he bit his lower lip. Anna wondered if he might cry. There was a long pause and the three men behind stopped their conversation to watch. The dog let out a long sigh.

Then there was a command and the sound of weapons raised in salute. A mailed arm swept open the tent flap. A cold blast of air nearly extinguished the candles and bumps arose on Anna's bare arms. Prince Mehmed walked in, followed by his mother and the masked captain of the Sultan's bodyguard. He was holding Simon Laskaris by the arm.

Mehmed drew the boy to one side and asked him something. Then Mehmed turned to Simon Laskaris and took his hand, inspecting the damaged flesh.

He addressed Theodore: 'If my father's page has orders to remove the Protostrator, then he will go with him. The burn is of no consequence.'

Anna opened her mouth to shout to the Despot that it was a trap, that her father was to be murdered.

'Control yourself, girl,' hissed Olivera Despina, spinning around.

By now, Simon Laskaris was being bustled out of the tent by the guard captain, Prince Mehmed and the boy following.

Anna, released from the Princess's grip, fell to her knees. Her hands were covering her eyes and through her fingers she could see the dog on the carpet lying very still. Too still.

She looked up. Others were looking at the dog as well. The dog that had licked the wine from the carpet.

The dog that was now dead.

The Princess knelt down beside her. 'You knew?' she asked.

'No!' whispered Anna. She paused and looked across at her through a film of tears. 'Why did you stop me from helping my father?'

'Because you would have betrayed us,' she replied, getting up. 'Your father is safe.' She looked down at the dog. 'I didn't think it would be poison.'

Anna unhooked her veil.

Theodore had been staring at the Serbian princess's maid for some minutes, shaking his head slowly in amazement. Now he smiled.

'*Anna.*'

Anna went over to him. 'Majesty, I am glad to see you. But this is a place of death. You must take my father away.'

There was commotion outside. A heavy weight fell against the side of the tent.

The tent flap opened and the captain of the guard stepped in, his sword drawn. The plume on his helmet was stiff with cold and there was ice on the aventail covering his face. He looked around the room, then turned and wiped each side of his blade on the tent door before sheathing it in a single movement. Anna looked hard into his eyes. They were unblinking and fixed on her and a flash of memory came to her. Then he lifted a hand and unhooked the aventail, letting it fall to his shoulders.

Yakub.

'Your father is safe, for now,' he said. He turned to the Emperor Manuel. 'Majesty, the boy is returned to his tent. The Sultan sleeps and his bodyguard is tied up and gagged. My men are outside. But we don't have much time and you must leave now. Lord Laskaris is waiting with the horses.'

The Emperor was composed. 'And my guard, Prince Yakub?' he asked. 'What of them?'

232

'One of the Varangians is dead, lord. They barred our entry. It was necessary.'

Manuel frowned but then nodded. He put on his cloak and walked over to Prince Stefan. 'I fear that next time we meet will be on the field of battle and on opposite sides. God go with you.'

The Despot had put on a cloak and pulled the hood over his head. Yakub drew him to one side and spoke to him in a whisper.

Theodore walked over to Anna and placed his hands on her arms. 'You cannot come with us, Anna,' he said softly. 'Yakub has told me why you're here. We cannot provoke Suleyman into sending another army to Mistra.'

Anna nodded dumbly, willing herself not to run from the tent into the arms of her father.

'We owe you our lives.' He bent down to kiss Anna on the forehead.

Anna said nothing and felt the hand of Devlet Hatun on her shoulder. Then she remembered something.

'Wait!' she said. 'The Turkish fleet at Constantinople. It has cannon, supplied by the Mamonas. Our fleet is sailing into a trap.'

Theodore's face darkened. 'You're sure of this?' he asked.

'It is true,' said Olivera Despina. 'I heard it myself.'

The Despot nodded and then looked at Anna. 'We shall take care of your father, I promise.'

CHAPTER THIRTEEN

CHIOS, SUMMER 1395

The consensus amongst the twelve Genoese families that ruled Chios was that the Longo estate at Sklavia was not only the finest on the island but also the closest to paradise it was possible to find on this earth.

It was further generally agreed, amongst the men in particular, that Marchese Longo was a lucky dog to have married Fiorenza Komnene, niece to the Emperor of Trebizond and certainly the most beautiful woman on Chios, if not in the world. And everyone agreed that it was the combination of these two felicities that rendered him a man of such amiable disposition.

When Luke had first set eyes on Fiorenza at the top of the steps to Longo's villa, his breath had left him like a bellows. He'd stared at her in silence before remembering to bow and had been rewarded with two perfect dimples that bracketed a smile of pure warmth.

'May I introduce my wife, Fiorenza?' had come a voice from behind him.

Fiorenza descended the stone steps like a zephyr, placing each slippered toe in front of the other with grace, to stop two above Luke where she had the advantage of equal height. She looked him straight in the eye, her head slightly tilted, and lifted her hand to be kissed, dimpled smile intact.

Fiorenza was thirty years of age and, like the day around her, at the late pinnacle of her loveliness. Her hair, yellow as buttercups, fell in tendrils over her cheeks and, rippling back from her forehead, was caught in a fall of intricate and tight-plaited loops, all threaded with ribbons. Her eyes were a pellucid blue beneath arched brows and her skin was fair and untouched by the sun.

Luke's tongue had become lead.

'Luke Magoris,' he said in a whisper and straightened to see kind amusement in her face. Her hands dropped to the side of a simple dress of cream silk, its bodice lightly embroidered, from which her bosom rose and fell without hurry. She was studying him with some interest.

'Luke is from Monemvasia,' continued Longo, joining Luke on his step and kissing his wife's hand. 'He has made a fortunate escape from Venetian slave traders and will be our guest.'

'Then you must be tired and in need of something cool to drink,' she said, turning to Luke and taking his hand. She led him to the top of the steps and on to a broad veranda where two servants waited with trays.

That had been six months ago when Luke was still raw with grief and a blank tapestry on which Fiorenza might weave. Her interest at that first meeting on the steps had been that of a keen intellect confronted by something different. Fiorenza was clever, adored by her husband and bored to distraction by island gossip. And since God had yet to bless their marriage of ten years with children, she was in need of a hobby.

And here was a young man of eighteen in need of rest,

friendship and, above all, education. From the first day of their aquaintance, Luke showered her with questions; about the island, about its people, its trade, about her. And through it all, she discerned an unspoken sadness, a sadness that sought some diversion in learning.

Fiorenza quickly saw that there was something about their guest that was beyond the ordinary. He was certainly imbued with physical advantage, as evidenced by the giggling servant girls. But he also seemed to have a capacity to absorb and retain information that was truly remarkable.

Then there were the horses.

From the start, Luke had displayed his skill with horses. There was a stud at Sklavia where a Berber stallion from the Maghreb had recently been put to Persian mares, the experiment so far showing disappointing results. The blood-mix had proved volatile and the offspring was unworkable.

But Luke had stepped calmly into its paddock, Marchese and Fiorenza holding their breathe from the fence where they watched, and begun to talk to the animal. And little by little, day by day, they'd seen the horse change so that, within a week, Luke had a saddle on its back and, within two, was riding it across the fields of the estate.

A week after this, Luke had made a request.

'I want to learn. Will you teach me, Fiorenza?'

She had been in the garden, picking flowers.

'What do you want to learn, Luke?' she'd asked.

'Everything you know.'

So Fiorenza had begun the task of giving Luke the education of a Princess of Trebizond. She had concentrated on those bits of learning most expected in a cultured man: languages, mathematics, history, astronomy and literature, with some Latin to provide mortar between the bricks. Led by Fiorenza, Luke's mind had roamed across continents, lingering with the Venetian Marco Polo in the palaces of Kublai Khan before riding on the backs of Greek Gods through Ptolemy's heavens to sit among the seven hills of Rome listening to the love calls of Catullus.

Fiorenza used the whole island as her laboratory – its landscapes and skies, its legends and memories – to bind the strands of human knowledge to her purpose. She told Luke the story of the birth of the island, of how the God Dionysus had first taught the islanders to cultivate wine, having rescued his wife Ariadne from the clutches of Theseus and the trauma of the Minotaur; of how her wedding diadem had been set in the heavens as the constellation of Corona; of how their son Oenipion had been its first king and his daughter Chiona had given the island its name.

They would ride to the village of Vrontados to sit on the rock where Homer read his *Iliad* and visit the forests of the Voreiochora to rest in pine groves on the slopes of Mount Pelinaios, needles deep as fleece beneath their feet. They would shiver beneath stalactites in the caves of Ayios Galas and welcome the warm bounty of spring as they galloped through clouds of lavender and meadows of poppies.

Book upon book was laid as a tantalising feast before Luke and he gorged himself, falling asleep to dreams of shapes and numbers and words and music. At night, he sometimes thought of Plethon and of his yearning for fusion between the cultures of East and West, a fusion that would bring reason and logic and peace. He thought that Fiorenza might be the perfect symbol of that fusion, being all that was most elegant and mystical about the East yet having transplanted so well into the rich, commercial soil of Genoese Chios.

He also thought about Mistra. Somewhere in that city might lie the clue that would connect his dragon sword to the Varangian treasure. But Mistra was hundreds of miles away and he had no means of getting there.

But most of all he thought about Anna and the gulf between them. The more Luke learned of the world, of its grim logic, the greater the chasm yawned. He was the son of a soldier. She was the daughter of the second man in the despotate. It had all been an impossible dream.

Part of his learning would be to forget Anna.

And now, on a still summer evening, Fiorenza sat at one end of a table set out under a vine-woven trellis in the gardens of Sklavia. The lamplight shone on the latticework of her sleeves and the exact and regular folds that defined the bones of her body. A woman fingered a lute somewhere in the shadows and frogs pulsed in the trees and scented undergrowth of the borders. And far above them the arc of Corona was clear and curved and bright in the heavens and Luke looked at it and felt the ancient voice of the island breathing all around him.

Around the table sat the twelve families of Chios, or at least their signori, and their wives. Here were the Campi, the Arangio, the Adorno, the Banca and the other families which, fifty years ago, had formed this remarkable experiment in collective, joint-stock money making on an island they called Scio and for which they paid the nugatory annual rent of five hundred hyperpera to the Emperor in Constantinople. At their head sat the remarkable Marchese Longo, handsome, astute, good and married to the miracle of Fiorenza, Princess of Trebizond, and together they ruled, first among equals, in justice, wealth and splendour.

Apart from Luke, there were two others present not of the

twelve families. One was Benedo Barbi, engineer to kings, emirs and two popes. He had been born in Genoa but had come to the island from Alexandria. He had been here for over a year now to build new defences for the port of Foca and the castle at Chora, and advise on irrigation systems for the vineyards of the Kambos.

The other was a man from Cyprus who was telling them about sugar. 'It is the best thing the Arabs have given us,' he was saying. 'The very best. The West has a sweet tooth that cannot be fed by us in Cyprus alone. Even the Sultan eats a bowl of sugar every day. You came here to Chios fifty years past and we took Famagusta twenty years ago. Your wine,' and here he raised his cup in salute, 'has prospered but our sugar has prospered more. You have room to grow sugar cane here, especially in the south, and we think you should try it.'

'But we're building up our mastic business there,' said the elderly Gabriele Adorno, shaking his head, 'and we believe that the Turk will take more and more of it as the taste for it spreads beyond the harem. Besides, it's what we know how to do.'

'Indeed,' joined in Giovanni Campi, 'and as for wine, we are experimenting with a Grechetto grape which we believe will blend well with the Malvasia variety. We'll need more room for that.'

Luke watched a lizard hang from the fluted sides of a pillar and thought about sugar cane and the mills and refineries and factories that would be required. Benedo Barbi had provided a practical and commercial edge to Fiorenza's teaching and with it had come the confidence to offer his opinion.

'Would the money not be better deployed building up the defences of the island?' he said. 'The Turkish pirates are growing more daring in their raids on the south and you will lose your

239

workforce down there if you don't do something to protect them.'

Heads greyer than his nodded around the table and a moth the size of a small bird landed in front of Luke, spreading its wings as if delivering something.

Benedo Barbi spoke. 'Luke is right. The system of small forts we are planning in the south will eat up a lot of capital. Sugar is an expensive business; I have seen the factories in Syria and they are sophisticated.'

'Yes, yes,' replied the man from Cyprus, 'but growing sugar can be its own defence. The Turk will not take an island if the tribute he gets from sugar grown with our efficiency is more than he would get doing it badly himself. But wine? Apart from the Sultan, none of them drink it.'

'But what of our mastic, which they so crave?' asked Zacco Banca. 'We give them tribute from that. The Turk knows nothing of growing mastic.'

'They could learn,' said the man. 'And from what I've heard, your Greeks down there might feel safer under Turkish protection. How close are they to rebellion, do you think?'

There was silence around the table and Luke looked at Fiorenza, who'd said nothing but had watched the conversation closely through her bright, intelligent eyes. The moon had risen behind her like a halo and a bat or skittish bird had fluttered across it. Pastilles had been lit to ward off the mosquitoes and their scent lingered the length of the table. The sound of the cicadas was unbroken and comforting in its uproar. She smiled.

'Well,' she said, glancing at her husband, 'we have a plan for that.' She looked around the table and settled her gaze on Benedo Barbi. 'Signor Barbi and Luke will travel tomorrow to the south and agree the location of the forts. Luke is Greek and well placed to reassure the villagers of our intent to protect them.'

Later on, when the pastilles had burnt out and the wine run low and the smells of this perfumed isle had drifted in with the night, Luke listened half-heartedly to the subject that any gathering of Genoese with time on their hands would revert to: the Venetians.

It was more than twenty years since Genoese and Venetian guests had lit the fuse of war by brawling at the coronation of young Peter de Lusignan of Cyprus, and fifteen years since the Genoese had taken, then lost, the island of Choggia on the edge of the Venetian lagoon. The hatred felt by the rival cities was now firmly centred in the eastern Mediterranean and in particular on the islands of Cyprus and Chios, where fortunes were to be made and exchanged in the businesses of alum, wine and sugar.

By this time, Fiorenza and the other women had retired to their beds inside the house, along with some of the older gentlemen.

The man from Cyprus refilled his glass and said, 'The Venetians want your alum and your wine and they want your island. What if they find common purpose with the Turk? I hear rumours that the Serenissima's envoy is well received at Edirne. Not by the Sultan, but by his son Prince Suleyman.'

Luke felt drowsy and a little befuddled but he knew the answer to this. 'If you can get the people of Chios on your side then this island can be defended against anyone,' he said. 'Currently, the Venetians can exploit the divisions between Greek and Italian. Who's to say they're not behind these pirate attacks?'

241

Marchese Longo nodded in agreement. He turned to the engineer. 'Benedo, how quickly can we get forts built in the south?'

'Quickly enough. Perhaps a year, lord,' replied the engineer. 'But I am working on something else as well. Luke knows about it.'

'Something else?' asked Longo.

'Greek fire, lord.'

'Greek fire? But, Benedo, the secret's been lost!'

'To the Greeks, perhaps. But its ingredients are known to chemists in Alexandria: naphtha, quicklime, sulphur and nitre. It's just a question of getting the mixture right. I am experimenting.'

'I heard it was a state secret,' said Zacco Banca. 'They say that its operators only knew of one component each, that only a handful understood how to put it all together. What does it do?'

'It burns on water,' said Barbi. 'Perhaps it is even ignited by water. Certainly the reaction between quicklime and water is explosive. It can sink a pirate fleet.'

'Well,' Longo said, 'you must continue to experiment, Barbi, and whatever you need will be given to you. But for now, we must think of these forts. How will we find the garrisons to man them?'

Luke said, 'Why not simply make each village into a fort? It would be a lot cheaper.'

'But what if they rebel?' asked Banca. 'Won't that just *encourage* them to rebel?'

'Not if you do something else as well,' replied Luke. 'I think, signori, you might consider allowing the villagers some share in the profit from the mastic. Why not make their interests align with yours? It would be cheaper in the long run.'

At this, there was an uncomfortable silence and glances were exchanged around the table. The Genoese were not famous for sharing profits. Wine washed into glasses and the cicadas argued more loudly.

'Luke is right. And my wife agrees with him,' said Longo carefully. 'The Greeks will fight to defend a just government.'

As he spoke Luke smelt something unexpected. There was sulphur in the air and the sweet, acrid smell of burning citrus. The others had smelt it too and Longo lifted his head and pointed his nose to left and right.

'Is that burning I smell?' he asked. 'Can anyone else smell burning?'

There was a shout in the distance and the sound of feet running fast across grass. Luke could see a glow in the sky behind the garden beyond.

In the direction of the house.

'Lord!' came a voice from the darkness. A body emerged from the shadows, dishevelled and flushed from running. 'The orchards around the house are ablaze! The fire is spreading towards the house!'

Longo came to his feet. 'Are the women within?'

'I don't know, lord,' panted the man. 'The servants . . .'

Before the sentence was out, Longo was running fast across the lawn and the other men were following, their doublets left on the backs of their chairs.

As they jumped the borders and ripped their hose on thorned roses, the smell grew stronger and the glow brighter. This was no small fire, but one that spread across a wide field of lemon trees and its flames could now be seen dancing in jagged

243

abandon against the night sky. The house, when it came into view, was wreathed in swirls of smoke but didn't seem to be alight. Its towers and castellations were black and vivid in silhouette and the Giustiniani flag stood stark and unmoving on its pole. Luke whistled softly.

At least there's no wind.

A mass of people surrounded the house, some with buckets, some with rakes. They had cowls lifted to protect their noses and mouths. Nearly everyone was shouting.

Luke looked around, searching every face. None was Fiorenza. He saw Longo look at him quickly, alarm etched into every feature. They ran towards the arch leading into the front courtyard, nearly colliding with their guests, all in their nightgowns and holding garments to their faces. Fiorenza was not among them. Luke stepped aside to let them pass and then ran into the house, Longo beside him.

Longo stopped. 'I can see to my wife. This fire didn't start by itself. Take some men and see if you can find the people who did this.'

Luke nearly said something, but then he turned and ran back across the courtyard to where the Genoese were standing in a huddle, husbands comforting wives.

'My lords,' he said, 'this fire was lit by men who may still be here. We must find them. Will you help me?'

Swords were drawn to solid nods and the toss of heads casting off the effects of the wine. There were now lines of men feeding water to the fire and its spread to the buildings seemed checked. The trees in the orchard were throwing off sparks of exhausted flames and the grass beneath was black and smoking. Luke led the party into the field, signalling for the men to spread out, and each ran with his blade ahead of him, ready for the rush from the shadows.

Deep into the orchard, Luke saw something. A shadow amongst shadows. A running figure, hunched, darting between the ruin of the trees. Luke launched himself into a sprint, his boots smoking, his shirt wet with sweat and smudged with falling cinders. He could see little in front of him but heard the break of wood and the rasp of desperate breath. Then the figure was ahead of him and moving fast and a spent torch was in his hand until he flung it away. He was weaving between the skeletons of trees and Luke could see the rough smock and breeches of a Greek peasant.

Luke was gaining on him and the man knew it. He looked over his shoulder. Luke recognised him. He was the man from the village, the man who'd given him his horse. Luke threw himself forward and brought him to the ground. He rolled him over, his sword at his throat.

'Say nothing!' hissed Luke. 'There are men here who would kill you for the sport. Say nothing and lie still. We need to talk.'

The man lay rigid; he didn't struggle and didn't open his mouth. Around them were the sounds of search and the crackle of fading flame. Luke lowered his sword slowly, keeping his eyes fixed on the man.

'Come with me,' he said, and got to his feet, holding the man by the scruff of his neck. He crouched into a run, pushing him ahead, keeping a hand on his head to keep him low. He looked behind and was relieved to see no one. The two of them stumbled forward, knees hitting their chests, until they reached a narrow hut with wooden slats that were warm and flaked by the fire. They stopped, put their backs to its wall and looked at each other with suspicion.

'Why?' asked Luke. His sword was still in his hand but slack by his side. He rubbed soot from his cheek and swept his hair back from his eyes.

The man didn't answer.

Luke laid his sword on the ground. 'Why?' he asked again.

The man looked around, back at Luke and then beyond him, out into the night. His shoulders slumped and he slid his back down the wall, the slats rucking his shirt up and his arms coming to rest in his lap. He put a hand to his temples and closed his eyes. He rubbed his eyelids and shook his head slowly from side to side.

Luke brought himself down to the man's level and Dimitri turned his head.

'And why you?' he asked quietly. 'You are Greek yet you dine with the Genoese. We have seen you riding with the Byzantine princess, dressed as they are and planning your enrichment at our expense. Have you no pride?'

Pride. Did he have pride? Luke had thought of everything in these past months except perhaps that.

He said, 'You could have killed people.'

Dimitri shook his head. 'No wind. It was intended to frighten, not kill.'

'So why?'

Dimitri let his head fall back against the wood. 'We want protection. Protection from the pirates and, if we can't get that, then the means to defend ourselves.'

At that moment, there was movement in some bushes to their left and they both looked towards it. There was a glint of metal. Luke picked up his sword and thought about using Dimitri as a shield, then discarded the idea. Instead the man beside him spoke.

'Don't shoot, Marko,' he said tiredly, his hand stretching to lower Luke's sword. 'We won't win by killing Greeks. Come out here. He wants to talk.'

A man rose slowly from the bushes. He was wearing a loose leather jerkin with a belt at its waist and a knife in the belt. He was holding a crossbow. He walked over to them, checking to left and right.

Luke was staring at the crossbow. He got to his feet. 'Where did you get that?' he asked.

Marko didn't reply. He was holding the weapon in a way that suggested he was unpractised in its use.

'I want to help you,' said Luke, turning to Dimitri. 'But I need to know how you got that weapon. I've seen it before.'

There was a long pause.

'We found it on the beach,' said Dimitri at last. 'Five cases of them, all brand new. We assumed they were intended for the garrison.' He paused. 'Perhaps they were shipwrecked.'

'Was it the beach at Fani?' asked Luke. He stretched out his hand to take the weapon and Marko glanced at Dimitri, who nodded. The bolt was removed and Luke took the weapon. He studied it carefully: it was identical to those he'd seen on the ship.

'This weapon was left for you to find,' said Luke quietly. 'By the Venetians. They want you to rebel against the Genoese so that they can take over the island.' Luke looked from one man to the other. 'They'll be worse masters than the Genoese, I promise you.'

The men exchanged glances. Luke returned the weapon to Marko. There was a dog's bark in the distance, then another.

'Look,' he said to Dimitri, 'you shouldn't stay here. Get back to your village and take the rest of your men with you. I'll ride out to you tomorrow and we can talk then.'

Dimitri nodded once and turned away. 'Until tomorrow, then,' he said.

CHAPTER FOURTEEN

CHIOS, SUMMER 1395

The next morning broke fair but smudged with the residue of burning. The west walls of the villa were black with soot but otherwise untouched. The orchard was a charnel house of sodden, still-smoking branches in various contortions. It looked like a battlefield.

Luke rose early and found Longo kneeling amidst the carnage. He was wearing a white cotton shirt and leather breeches with no hose. He looked tired and his hair clung to his head like seaweed. He looked up when he heard Luke approach.

'They could have done much worse,' he said, looking around him. 'I wonder what held them back.'

Luke knelt beside the older man. He scraped away the ash on the ground with his fingers. 'Isn't it good for the soil, lord?' he asked.

Longo raised his eyebrows, surprised. 'Fire? Yes,' he replied carefully. 'After all, it's all the same.' Then he looked at Luke, this time with speculation. 'It is a pity that we caught no one last night. It would be useful to know why they didn't go any further.'

Luke continued to dig at the ground, lifting earth in his

hands and smelling it before letting it run through his fingers.

'Luke, did you see anyone?'

The two men looked at each other. Then Luke smiled and nodded. Barely a nod.

He said, 'My lord, I have to ride south today to meet the men who did this. Not to punish them but to talk to them. Can you trust me?'

Longo whistled quietly through his teeth.'I should have guessed. Who are they?'

'I can't tell you that, lord,' he said. 'I think you know that.'

Longo sighed. 'Yes. Of course.' He turned towards the house and, taking Luke's arm, began to walk. Luke looked up at the balcony and saw Fiorenza standing there. She was watching them.

'You may go,' said Longo, 'but I want you to take Fiorenza with you. She is Greek, Luke. Like you.'

Luke saw there were two horses tethered below the balcony. This had been decided long ago.

'We should leave immediately,' he said.

They did not speak on the ride south. The land was flattened and baked by a remorseless sun that annihilated colour and created stark contrasts of form. The well-ordered fields of the Sklavia estate soon gave way to rolling hills of scrub and grass and yellow broom which fell into valleys of olive and carob groves and the strange, stunted trees that Luke now knew to be mastic. The rivers were dry, their beds cracked and scattered with rocks and birds that stood on one leg, erect and motionless. The air was filled with the scent of aridity and stagnation and past abundance.

Luke was absorbed by the rise and fall of the parted mane of his horse and the pimples of rough grey skin between. He thought vaguely of his Greek and Genoan loyalties and of the woman riding beside him who represented some version of both. And when he'd finished considering that, he thought of Anna and of a ride through the night, so long ago, when he'd felt nothing more complicated than the urge to protect.

At one point they stopped to rest the horses and eat a meal of cold partridge, cheese and bread with good wine from a flask that had kept it cold. They ate and watched the horses crop the grass and nuzzle each other and toss flies from their noses.

A week ago they would have talked. Or Fiorenza would have talked and Luke listened and enjoyed the rich cadence of her voice. Now there was comfort in silence.

They rode on through the afternoon and its weight fell heavy on their shoulders and on the beaded necks of their horses. Fiorenza seemed unperturbed by the heat and sat upright and alert as if expecting a summons. Beneath a turban pinned with a wisp of jewel-set osprey, she wore a thin half-veil across her nose and mouth. Her belted tunic was of plain, unadorned cotton, which she wore loose so that she pass for either a woman or a boy.

When the village came into view, they reined in their horses and watched the movement of people below. The villagers had seen them and were pointing them out to each other. In the low evening sun, the shadows of the scattered houses stretched long across the wide central street and divided a gathering procession into patches of separate movement. All were carrying something, a basket with food or a flask, and the air was full of excitement. A festival.

'It's the start of the *kendos*, the harvesting of the mastic. It goes on for the next six months,' said Fiorenza. 'They begin it with a night of drinking and love among the trees under the moon.'

Luke looked at her. 'Drinking mastic?'

Fiorenza laughed. 'You've not tasted it? It's a medicine, not a recreation.'

Beneath them a flask of wine was being passed along the line, its wicker sides catching the last sunlight. There was a call and someone looked up at them and raised it in salute. A burst of laughter followed and a dog rose and darted between the shadows. Luke saw a figure detach itself from the mass and shield its eyes, looking up. It was Dimitri and he waved.

'Come, let's join them,' called Luke over his shoulder as he kicked his horse forward. 'And, lady,' he went on, 'let me talk. It was I they allowed to live last night.'

Fiorenza took up her reins and followed him down the winding track, adjusting her veil against the dust and evening insects. A thin smell came to them of lime and rotting vegetables among the poppied fields. A clutch of swifts and warblers darted up, startling the horses; a chaffinch rose as a blur and then flapped into yellow motion.

The procession had begun to wind its way out of the village, down the hill towards the groves and orchards, but Dimitri walked forward to meet them. Beside him came the brawn of Marko and neither wore a smile of welcome.

'It is an honour to greet you, magnificent lady,' said Dimitri, bowing stiffly towards Fiorenza, his voice measured and without enthusiasm. 'We didn't expect such an honour.'

Luke dismounted and led his horse to stand in front of Dimitri. 'Dimitri, greetings,' said Luke. 'Princess Fiorenza is here because she understands this island better than anyone. Her counsel will be invaluable.'

He looked back towards Fiorenza. 'If the Princess wishes to dismount, then it would be my pleasure to present you to her.'

In one graceful sweep of the leg, Fiorenza dismounted and walked towards the two men, her unveiled smile as dazzling as on the day Luke had met her. The dimples punctured her cheeks like buttons and she proffered a hand at an angle of tact, to be kissed or shaken as custom dictated.

Dimitri chose to kiss it as Luke thought he might. He said: 'You are welcome, lady.' He looked back to Luke. 'Is the Princess to join us in our conversations?'

'Of course,' replied Luke. 'She knows the minds of the Genoese. Her husband leads them.'

Dimitri glanced at Fiorenza and nodded shortly. 'Most assuredly.'

Fiorenza stepped forward. She was radiant and entirely at her ease. 'Can we join the procession?' she asked brightly. 'Where do we go?'

'To the sea, lady,' replied Dimitri. 'Or at least we go to the mastic groves closest to the sea to celebrate the kendos. By all means come with us. What better place to talk than amongst the trees that are the cause of our problems?'

An hour later, Luke and Fiorenza were walking their horses down amongst olive and carob trees and between hills which opened like pages on to a sea of dark amber. They had just born witness to the birth of a full moon from its water bed and the disc hung washed-grey in a night of small colour. As it grew in strength, and as they drew nearer, a white scimitar of sand appeared with the sea blunting its edge as it slid over rocks to the salt flats above the beach. The cicadas were less busy here and an ass brayed above the plodding clink of a bell which sounded somewhere on the hill.

Dimitri walked silently by their side. Luke studied this strange man who had education beyond that of a mastic-grower and anger beyond that called for by piracy. He wanted to know more of him but knew it was not yet the moment to ask.

Someone close by lit a torch and the world beyond its glare vanished to be replaced with a closer scene of low, shrub-like trees with wrinkled scales for bark. Around the base of each had been cleared a circle of white earth, luminous and ghostly. The smell of soil and salt grew stronger as the shapes around them took form, carried perhaps by the clusters of night insects that ebbed and flowed around the light. More torches were winking ahead of them and the murmur of conversation carried up to them on the wash of the waves as they neared the sea.

Then they were surrounded by people who emerged from the shadows like wraiths in their thin clothes, their children at their knees staring up at the strangers from gaunt faces. A smell of wine tempered the tang of salt and sweat and cedar and everywhere small amphorae lay on their sides beside half-finished meals and discarded shawls, their red pitted sides catching the flicker of flames. The noise had died and the air was dense with unease.

Fiorenza passed the reins of her horse to Luke and turned to unstrap a saddlebag. She took from it a large bundle, which she laid on the ground, and then reached back to pull free a rug of coarse wool rolled up with cord. She picked up the bundle and carried both to a nearby tree, unrolling the rug to cover the white earth at its base. Kneeling on the rug, and with her back to the children, she very slowly began to untie the bundle, deliberately shielding its contents from the strained necks behind.

Then she stopped and, in the silence, emitted a gasp of theatrical wonder. She drew back her head so that eyes, bright as crystals, emerged from the shadows.

Then she did something Luke, Dimitri and every other adult least expected.

She winked.

It was not the wink of a princess or of anyone of quality. It was the wink of the theatre and its effect was sudden and electric. A child giggled and another laughed. Then a third stepped forward to see what the wonder might be, and a fourth pushed past her brother to get a better look.

The night was suddenly filled with the happy gurgle of merriment and Fiorenza was at its centre, handing out sweetmeats and treats to children who'd never believed the world contained such things. They came forward and received and skipped away, their mouths crammed with delicious food whose juices ran down their chins and smocks and pitted the dry earth like rain. Their joy was contagious and swept across the gathering like a genial plague so that a time of apprehension turned, as it was meant to, into a time of celebration.

Dimitri stood apart and said nothing.

Luke was watching her but made no move. He could see the unfolding of a plan, pre-set by an intelligence greater than his, and he would not interfere with its execution. He watched the donation of the last sweet, the dispatching of the child to a parent then spoken to with kindness in their own tongue, the kneeling to inspect a foot damaged by some thorn. He watched it all as one watches the slow distribution of paint across a canvas and he marvelled that he'd ever supposed there might not be a plan.

Eventually, Fiorenza returned to them, laughing.

'There will be some sore heads tomorrow. Tell me, Dimitri, will they dance tonight?'

'Those who've drunk *souma* will dance the dance of the fig,' the Greek replied, 'which is not a pretty sight . . . unlike your performance tonight.'

Fiorenza ignored the barb and instead knelt to inspect the circle of earth beneath the nearest tree. 'Is this clay?' she asked, raking her palm gently across the surface.

'It is.' Dimitri knelt by her side. 'When the trees weep the tears of St Isidore, it falls on to this clay where it can be seen and separated.'

'St Isidore, the patron saint of this island?'

'The same,' replied Dimitri. 'Later, you will see the effigy of the Roman Noumericanos, who gave him his martyrdom, burnt upon the water. It is said that the first tree wept its mastic the night Isidore died.'

Luke had seen Judas burnt at Easter and knew the frenzy of song and dance that would precede the execution. The blur between the Christian and the pagan was at its vaguest on nights like these and Dionysus, born of Zeus's thigh, protector of Chios and God of both wine and madness, embodied it to sodden perfection.

'And these mastic tears,' said Fiorenza, moving to sit with her back to the tree, 'is it true that they grow solid the minute they emerge from the bark?'

'They do. And it's only in the south of this island that this miracle occurs,' replied Dimitri. 'That's why these trees are so valuable. This is the only place on earth with the climate and soil for this alchemy. This is the only place from which the Turk can receive the gum or aphrodisiac for his harem, where the cure for snakebite can be found, where the agent for embalming the dead exists. It is contained, lady, within the bark you lean against . . . and your husband will not give protection to the alchemists.'

Silence fell between the three of them.

It was not shared by the villagers down on the beach, who'd begun to form circles for the dance. Somewhere a drum began to beat and a wind instrument sent its first, wheezing notes into the night. The torches were now either spent or extinguished and the moon had resumed control, tipping the revelry closer to the unseen and perhaps profane.

Dimitri had taken sesame bread, curds and some prickly pears from a basket by his feet and put them on the ground between them. He lifted out a flask and poured wine into a small, earthenware cup and offered it to Fiorenza. She was studying him with the same interest she'd bestowed on Luke all those months ago.

'You are not of these parts,' she observed. 'What is your story, Dimitri?'

By now the benevolence of shared food was having a softening effect. Dimitri smiled guardedly. 'You guessed?' he asked.

'It wasn't hard,' she replied, smiling back. 'Your accent is not of this island and your conversation betrays you. What brings you to Chios, Dimitri?'

The man was probably about the same age as Fiorenza but he looked, at that moment, much, much older. He sighed and chewed off a part of the loaf, spitting out the seeds with a delicate precision. 'I don't know how much I can trust you,' he said. 'Either of you.'

'You can't,' said Fiorenza, taking a small sip of the wine and looking over the rim of the cup at the man. 'But you can trust the Venetians less. Luke was right last night when he said that they made the gift of the crossbows to you.'

It was said simply but both men looked up sharply.

'You were there?' asked Luke.

'It doesn't matter who was there,' she replied. 'What matters is that they're using you and perhaps we're using you less.'

Luke stared at her. This was a Fiorenza he hadn't seen.

Dimitri laughed shortly. 'Your family have held Trebizond for nearly two hundred years, against all odds. I think I can understand how.' He reached for the flask. 'My story is long and complicated and too much for this night. Yes, I am educated. I learnt all that the son of a competent doctor should know. I was born in the city of Manisa on the mainland and lived there until the Sultan took it five years ago. I wanted to be a doctor like my father but my teaching was cut short when an Ottoman dagger opened his throat because he wouldn't leave the side of a dying child.' He paused and drank from the flask. 'The child was my sister.

'I fled Manisa and took work at the alum quarries further up the coast. There I met a woman who was Genoese and the daughter of the man who ran things. We married in secret because she was already intended for another. Her father discovered the match and we fought and I killed him.'

He looked up at Fiorenza. 'So then I took ship to Cyprus, thinking the Franks might make better masters. But I was wrong, and now I am here.'

No one spoke for some time and the rhythm of the drum kept time for dancers on a beach in a different world.

'Then we have something in common,' said Luke eventually.

'I, too, am a fugitive and have someone I love far away. In Monemvasia.'

'Not so far away,' Dimitri said. 'Bianca is dead. Killed by her father. That's why I killed him.'

Fiorenza hugged her knees, resting her chin on them so that the exquisite line of her face was in profile to Luke. He thought he saw the shine of a tear in her eye.

Luke said, 'But you have stayed here. You, an educated man, have chosen to live amongst uneducated people. Why?'

'Because I know something that can make me rich.' He said it without emphasis.

Luke waited. Something had persuaded this man to trust them thus far with his story.

The noise below them had receded, the festival having moved towards the water where the effigy of the Roman admiral stood in the boat that would be his pyre. There was laughter under a tree nearby and the pale movement of a body in submission. Everywhere lay the dim, moon-struck shapes of amphorae and the earth was stained with spilt wine. Dimitri was looking at Luke and there was challenge in his eyes.

'Last night,' he said. 'Last night, I asked you why *you* had chosen the Genoese way and you gave no answer.'

Luke had, in fact, considered his answer to the question for much of the night. 'At first I was merely grateful to be safe and fed. I wanted to leave at the first chance. Then,' and now he smiled at Fiorenza, 'I was given an education.'

'Not even duty?' asked Dimitri. 'Shouldn't the son of a Varangian be thinking about his duty to the Empire?'

Luke nodded. 'Dimitri, I think of little else. But where would I go? And might I not better serve the Empire with some education? I will go when I know where I can be of most use.'

A man appeared from the darkness with the moon on his hair and a new flask of wine in his hand. He put it down and disappeared.

Luke said, 'Now, you were telling us how you will become rich.'

Dimitri picked up the flask and poured himself more wine. 'Not just me. I want these people to be rich too because I know, as you should' – he looked from Luke to Fiorenza – 'that I won't become rich from this miracle of mastic unless I can guarantee the safety of the workers who bring it to life.'

Luke leant forwards, a new light in his eyes. 'That's why we've come here, Dimitri, to find how we can make this happen!'

Slowly Dimitri nodded.

He turned his head towards the beach and for a long while seemed lost in whatever was progressing on the sands of the little bay. There was now fire on the water and the silhouette of Noumericanos was engulfed in flames.

Fiorenza lifted her cup. 'To St Isidore, patron of Chios and sailors!'

Luke was beginning to feel drowsy after the long ride and yawned. A dog walked into their circle and studied each of them before lying down to sleep.

Dimitri suddenly got up and walked away, not towards the sea but into the trees. The night gathered him up like a blanket and they heard the crack of a branch not far away. There were voices.

Fiorenza looked at Luke and there was a question in her eyes.

Then Dimitri reappeared and with him was a girl, carrying a candle. She was in her late twenties and looked Greek. She had lustrous black hair that fell beyond her shoulders and shone in the pallid flame. She had a small face and what beauty she had resided in her eyes, which were large and unblinking. She was frightened and the slight body beneath a chemise of coarse wool was trembling at the shoulders. Dimitri was leading the girl towards them by the hand.

'This is Lara,' he said. 'Lara came with me from Cyprus.'

The girl was staring at Fiorenza in fascination. The Princess from Trebizond, who missed nothing, extended her hand, beckoning for Lara to sit by her side.

The girl sat and her body uncurled in the warmth of the other woman's smile. Dimitri sat at her other side.

'Do you know what probably decides the fates of millions of people as much as the Sultan's skill on the battlefield?' he asked Luke quietly, stroking the back of Lara's hand and tilting his head slightly as if the question might be a joke, or a riddle.

'No,' answered Luke.

'The Sultan's toothache,' said Dimitri. 'The Sultan eats sugar and there are more holes in his teeth than in a Cretan cheese. The man who will decide the fate of you and me is in constant pain.'

Fiorenza spoke. 'I have heard this,' she said. 'Bayezid's rages can be timed according to the pain he feels in his mouth. His doctors give him medicine but he still eats sugar.'

'His doctors are fools, lady,' said Dimitri with feeling. 'Bayezid needs more than opiates to cure his toothache. Lara worked in the sugar fields in Cyprus. She has probably tasted more sugar than all the kings of Christendom combined. When I met her, she could hardly eat or talk from the pain in her teeth. Now she has no holes and talks more than you would imagine.'

Dimitri reached behind him and pulled forward a satchel of worn leather. It was stained and frayed and well travelled. He opened it and brought out two small pouches, tied at their tops, and a blunt candle with wax congealed on its sides. He used Lara's candle to light it, placed it on the ground and carefully opened the pouches so that their contents were visible to everyone in the circle.

In one was a pile of hard, translucent resin, grey-brown in colour, each piece the size of a misshapen coin. In the other was white powder.

'Mastic and alum,' said Dimitri. 'One from this island of Chios and nowhere else, and one from Phocaea, no more than ten miles from here, where the best alum in the world can be found. And both places still belong to the Genoese.' He turned to the girl. 'Lara,' he said softly, 'can you open your mouth?'

The girl parted her lips to reveal a row of crooked teeth and leant forward into the sphere of light around the candle. Dimitri gently lifted her chin and turned the girl's face so that both Luke and the Princess could see inside her mouth. He used his forefinger to direct their gaze to Lara's teeth.

'You see these grey bits? These used to be holes but I have filled them with a substance that sticks to the tooth and is not disturbed when she eats. The substance moulds itself, when soft, to the walls of the tooth and so fits perfectly when it hardens. The substance is a mix of alum and mastic.'

Luke whistled softly. 'What would the Sultan pay for this!' he whispered.

'Not just the Sultan, but everyone who eats sugar, and there are more of them every year. Think of the market, now and in the future. It's enormous!'

They all stared at the piles that had been transformed into things of value. It was as if gold had been laid before them. Only Lara seemed unaffected by the excitement and instead gazed at Dimitri with pride and, thought Luke, a good deal of love. He wondered, without urgency, how the two of them had met.

'So this is what we now have to protect,' continued Dimitri, 'a future market which will make us all rich.'

'Do the villagers know of this?' asked Fiorenza.

'Yes, great lady, they know. They may not eat sugar but the mastic also damages their teeth. They, too, have *fillings*, as I've chosen to term these little bits of magic. They are very aware of the potential market.'

'But why attack Sklavia?' she asked. 'What good was that going to do?'

Dimitri smiled. 'It brought you here, didn't it? Would you have come here otherwise?'

Fiorenza was nodding slowly, absorbed by the cleverness of the strategy. He must have known, somehow, of Luke and Benedo's planned trip to the south. The timing of the attack was perfect.

'So,' said Luke carefully, 'we come once again to the main issue. How do we protect you?'

'Ah,' replied Dimitri, 'now that is *your* issue. How indeed do you achieve that? Not, I can tell you, with the corrupt and cowardly garrison at Apolichnon.'

'No,' agreed Luke, 'not with that. You have to be able to protect *yourselves*. We will need to build walls around the villages and put garrisons inside them.'

'Inside the villages? To live amongst us?' asked Dimitri with incredulity. 'There would be revolution!'

'Of course Dimitri's right,' said Fiorenza. A noise from the beach made them turn. The boat was now a heap of glowing embers and was sinking. Its reflection in the water was a livid tongue within the pathway of silver that stretched to the horizon, growing smaller as the boat went down. On the beach, the dance was over and part of it had become a brawl with laughter at its fringes; people were returning to the trees to sleep. Mothers held the hands of children who sagged with exhaustion and looked for a circle of white on which to unroll their rugs.

Fiorenza sighed and stood up. 'We should sleep,' she said. 'Tomorrow we have work to do.'

'You will sleep *here*, lady?' asked Dimitri.

'Of course. Where else?' She smiled and bent to kiss Lara, and then walked back in the direction of the horses.

'Tomorrow we will find a solution,' said Luke and he rose to follow Fiorenza into the darkness.

In the same darkness, much later on, it was impossible for Luke not to be aware of the woman's presence. Her scent, always discreet, was in the air around him, and her breath was a soft echo of the waves caressing the beach.

Luke was lying on his back as he had been for some hours. The stars, scattered above him between the branches of the tree, were so plentiful as to be able to discard a few towards a sleeping world.

Despite his best intentions, he was thinking of Anna.

They were in the cave and the lamp had been relit to cast a spray of light across their bodies as they lay side by side, numb with the exchange of pleasure. He thought of her small breasts and of how they trembled under the fingers of wind that reached through the branches at the cave entrance. He thought of the space between and beneath her breasts, of the fragility of a ribcage that was too prominent.

And he thought of holding her and holding her and holding

her and of two heartbeats pressed together and of a deep, deep longing that had never really left him.

Anna.

Then he dreamt. He was back in Monemvasia and it was night and he was running and something evil was behind him. He could hear its low, guttural breathing and the noise was quite distinct because there was no other sound in the city; none of people talking or cooking or children preparing for bed; none of dogs or cats; none of the sea breaking on the rocks beyond the sea walls. He was alone in a city of dead.

Now the beast was behind him and gaining on him but he had one clear thought: that he knew this city and whatever was behind him didn't. He knew its infinite and tiny streets, its dead-ends and circularities. And he knew that, if he could just put distance between him and the monster, he could hide.

Then there was a cry and he looked in its direction and Anna was there at the end of a street, beckoning and beckoning and he couldn't move because his feet were stuck and wouldn't move.

He screamed.

But it wasn't Anna who was holding him beneath a canopy of branches that moved with the wind he felt on his cheek. It wasn't Anna who stroked the sweat from his forehead and murmured comfort in his ear. It wasn't Anna who kissed him on the mouth and then again on the nose, and back to the mouth with the softness of goose-down.

Fiorenza.

But Fiorenza couldn't hold him against the pull of the dream that was rising up again around him. He was slipping from her, slipping from her, and he tried so hard to cling on but couldn't and the black walls rose up on all sides.

And the beast was still there.

This time there was darkness. Not the darkness of a night with no moon but one that was complete and forever. This was a darkness whose dense fabric had evil woven into its very core. This, he knew, was the darkness of the labyrinth.

The beast was still here, with him, and its stench was all around him and its faeces were sticky beneath his feet. But he didn't know this place and the monster did and its black bull's head would be turning left and right on its muscular neck, sniffing and sniffing and *knowing*.

There was no sound. Nothing, except the laboured breathing of a mutant man-bull that had no goodness in its being, no reason even, only an insatiable appetite for human flesh.

A movement to his left. A movement of stealth and bull-cunning. Then the beast was upon him and the weight of its neck fell on to his shoulders and threw him to the ground. The head bit and bit in the darkness, searching for the ecstasy of living food. Luke drove his sword upwards into the monster's belly, feeling the coarse, matted hair of the chest meet his hilt. The neck above him stiffened and arched high in a scream of anger and agony. And as he pulled the sword free, he shouted something.

Anna. Anna. Anna!

'Anna! Anna! Anna! An—'

He smelt the familiar scent first. Then his eyes opened and it was almost day and a face of great beauty was looking down at him. He was soaked in sweat and he tasted wine on his breath and his eyeballs felt too big and ached with a rhythm that made him close them again.

He remembered everything and knew that this had been both dream and revelation, sent from above or deep, deep below. And he remembered a kiss.

'Where have you been, Luke?'

Luke opened his eyes and looked at the woman who may have been part of the dream; there was no trace of anything beyond concern in her face and no part of her body touched his.

'I dreamt of a labyrinth.'

'What sort of labyrinth?' asked Fiorenza, frowning.

'A labyrinth in Knossos, or Monemvasia. It *means* something, Fiorenza.'

She smiled and nodded and got to her feet. 'Then you must have time to think about it, Luke,' she said quietly, and walked away.

But, this time, the scent didn't go with her. It stayed with him because it was on him. On his mouth, his nose, his chin. And there was no guilt or fear, but only relief and happiness.

CHAPTER FIFTEEN

CHIOS, SUMMER 1395

It was two weeks after the kendos that Luke saw Marchese Longo again. He had spent the intervening time with Benedo Barbi and they had built something of extraordinary beauty.

The translation of a dream into substance had been no easy task and had required Luke to summon forth scenes that he hoped never again to revisit. His part was the idea, a fantasy of breathtaking ingenuity. The practical elements had been supplied by the engineer and, to a lesser extent, Fiorenza, who'd watched and encouraged and never made mention of the night under the trees.

Now Luke, Dimitri and Benedo Barbi stood around a large table at the villa at Sklavia on which was presented the new village of Mesta, or perhaps a maze, or a labyrinth. And Marchese Longo, elegant in sleeveless pourpoint with a chain of gold spanning his broad shoulders, was looking at it in wonder and some shock.

Barbi had used compacted sand to create the height and contours of the little hill on which the village stood and the fields and orchards around it had been built using moss and fine red earth with twigs for trees. A track in white clay ran through the fields to the single entrance of the village, which had a solid wall, with towers at its four corners.

'This is the first innovation,' Barbi was saying, letting his fingertips drag lightly along the length of the wall, 'and I've seen it work well in the Kingdom of Sicily. You build the outer ring of houses such that their walls, without windows, form the wall of the village. The towers at the four corners are taller and curve outwards to provide the lookouts with views of all the perimeter.'

Longo peered over the maze and reached out to touch a tall, four-storey tower at its centre. 'What's this?' he asked.

'That,' said Luke, 'is not the point, lord. That is the last place of refuge when all else has failed. If I'm right about this plan, then it will never be used.' He brought his hands, templed, to his mouth. 'Imagine that you are a pirate. No, imagine that you are a band of pirates, perhaps fifty in number and all well armed.' Luke's hand hovered above the chalk that marked the track to the village. 'You have landed at Apothikas Bay and it is night and the road runs straight to Mesta, which you know to be a collection of mean houses with mastic in the storehouses, children in their beds and a garrison six miles away at Apolichnon, fat and lazy with your bribes.'

'Really?' asked Longo, looking up and frowning.

'Really,' said Fiorenza, who had come into the room, silent but scented.

Marchese frowned.

'So,' continued Luke, 'you have been to this village before. Then you took what you came to take with no resistance offered and now you are complacent. But then you see a new village, which has arisen in the place of the old one. And this one seems to have walls and only one gate to enter by. So you approach with caution.

'As you approach, the sky is suddenly lit with fire-arrows and you can be seen and the next arrows hit some of your men but you are not disheartened because a fiercer defence means more to defend. So you rush the single gate and manage, somehow, to force it open and, with shouts of triumph, you pour into the village.'

Luke looked across to Fiorenza, who was smiling slightly. 'Except it's not like any village you've ever seen. It's a village from hell. It's a labyrinth.'

Luke paused and walked around the table to stand next to Longo. He leant low over the model so that his head was just above the maze of tiny streets and houses. 'Now you're inside the village,' he said, his voice dropping almost to a whisper, 'but it seems deserted. So you assume everyone is hiding inside their houses which are, incidentally, much taller than when you were last here. Three storeys high, in fact.

'You break down a door, since there are no windows at ground level, but instead of people you find animals inside and only a trapdoor in the ceiling to get to the rest of the house; and the ladder has been pulled up.'

By now, Longo was stooped inches above the model too, peering with curiosity at the inside of a house, its roof removed by Benedo Barbi.

'Yes,' Luke was saying, 'in this village it's the animals that live on the ground floor and there is no staircase to the floors above, just a ladder. Each house has its landing on the first floor, which leads to the living areas. And on the second floor, every house is connected to the next by a walkway above the street. So the village, in essence, has two levels.'

270

'Ingenious,' said Longo softly.

'But there's better to come,' continued Luke. 'Remember, lord, that you are a simple pirate and by now a little confused. So you leave the animals alone and come back out into the street just in time to see a pair of heels disappear around a corner, and you give chase. But you are in a maze which has corners and dead-ends and some streets which end in tunnels and some which don't and some which seem to join to another street but in fact it's a painting and you run into a wall.'

Longo was shaking his head slowly from side to side.

'Then you notice, above you, a whole different world of interconnecting walkways which you cannot get to but which can certainly get to you. And you know this because the man beside you has been shot by an arrow released from an arch across the street and you've just heard the scream of another man, in the street next door, scalded by boiling water poured into a tunnel through a hole in its roof.

'So now you're getting enraged and a little scared and you think about burning it all down but everything seems to be built of stone, not wood, and anyway you don't know where all your companions are because your whole band of fellow pirates is hopelessly lost in this maze.'

Benedo Barbi was pointing out details of the model to Longo, removing bits from houses and whole arches from streets and spanning alleyways with tiny ladders which he lifted between two fingers.

'By now, lord,' said Luke, straightening and looking at the back of Longo's head which was bobbing up and down with the flow of information, 'by now, you might have given up.'

'Indeed, you might well.' Longo was laughing now.

'But let us say that you are an unusually tenacious band of pirates who don't give up and, despite everything, manage to get to the centre of the village. What, lord, will you find at the centre of this labyrinth?'

'Why, this tower,' replied Longo, pointing at it.

'Yes, you will. And' – Luke bowed slightly from the waist and smiled – 'it will be the final indignity heaped upon you! It will be your nemesis. Dimitri, pray tell Lord Longo of our tower.'

It was the first time that Dimitri had been asked to speak and, such was his surprise, he was silent for some moments.

'Well, lord,' he said at last, 'to begin with, this tower is much bigger than any we have had before; big enough, in fact, to hold every person in the village. Then you will see that it has no door at all on the ground floor and can only be entered at the first level, using a ladder that is then drawn up. It has a large cistern below and a tunnel that runs to a well outside the village, so it'll never run out of water. And there's room in the upper levels for a month's food and all the stored mastic. It is the last line of defence and impregnable.'

There was a long pause when nobody spoke and everyone looked at Longo, who was still bent over the model, lifting things and putting them back and then moving to look at them from a different angle.

'Ingenious,' he repeated at last, 'but expensive. Too expensive, I fear. We are protecting mastic, not gold.'

'But it *is* gold,' said Fiorenza. 'Listen, my lord, to what Dimitri will tell you of our mastic.'

Dimitri produced again his worn satchel with its two pouches, the contents of which he laid out in a field somewhere outside the village wall. He told of his invention and Longo's eyes shone with imagining.

'So you see, my lord,' said Fiorenza, moving to stand beside her husband, 'the villagers *will* have something to protect beyond the lives of their children. They will be protecting mastic because it will be *theirs*. Part of this plan involves giving the villagers a share of what they produce.'

'So where will the mastic belonging to the campagna be stored?' asked Longo.

'At the new port,' answered Benedo Barbi. 'It will be stored in warehouses at the new port we will build at Limenas, two miles north of Mesta. It will be stored in the place it is shipped from and this is where the full garrison will be stationed to protect it. It's logical.'

'A new port?' asked Longo with incredulity. 'A new port on top of a new village? How can we possibly afford that?'

'Not just one new village, lord,' said Luke, 'but many. This new industry will require new labour and we'll need to protect *all* the villages where our workers live. Next to be built will be the village of Pyrgi.'

Longo looked from Luke to Barbi to Dimitri and then to his wife. He was shaking his head. 'But the money,' he said. 'Where will we find the money?'

Fiorenza turned to face her husband and her fingers traced the length of the gold chain across his chest. 'We can borrow the money,' she said. 'The alum that we ship from Chora goes mainly to the city of Florence for the Arte della Lana. Their banker is a man called Medici. In exchange for alum and mastic at a discount, he will fund this venture.'

'You know this?' asked her husband.

'I've talked to his representative on the island,' she replied. She smiled up at him and her dimples had never looked more charming. 'He, too, has holes in his teeth.'

Marchese Longo looked at his wife in wonder, as did the others. It was the first that any of them had heard of this part of the plan. Then he leant forward and kissed her on the forehead.

'You are mysterious and extraordinary,' he whispered.

Longo drew apart and circled the table, once again taking in the brilliance of the idea before stopping to address them all. 'This is revolutionary and will take time to absorb. There are many issues to discuss with the other signori, not least how long we can expect to stay on this island. Remember there is only so much time left on our lease.' He spread his hands before him. 'But I thank you all from the bottom of my heart. I believe that, between you, you may have come up with something that will secure our future here and I'm grateful beyond measure. Now you must leave me to think.'

He turned to Luke. 'Luke, please do me the honour of talking further with me.'

Longo walked to the door and Luke followed him, giving Dimitri a wink as he passed. Once outside the room, he was led to an antechamber with deep chairs and portraits crowding the walls amidst rich hangings. Longo sat and gestured to Luke to do likewise while a servant set wine and olives on a low table between them.

'Luke,' said the older man when the man had left, 'how long do you plan to stay with us on Chios?'

Luke was taken aback. 'Lord, I mean to leave for Mistra soon,' he said carefully.

'You must know that Fiorenza and I have become fond of you. We have not been blessed with children and perhaps it is your misfortune that we see you almost as our son.'

Luke felt the blood rise in his face. He thought of a night

274

beneath mastic trees. 'You . . . you honour me, lord. I do not deserve it.'

'But you do,' went on Longo. 'Without you, this idea would never have happened. And it's brilliant.'

'Thank you, lord,' said Luke.

'Anyway, I wanted to say this to you.' Longo leant forward and lowered his voice. 'I want you to lead this venture and, if it works, I will make you part of the campagna. You will be rich, Luke.'

Luke stared at him. 'Lord, I am but eighteen!'

'Yes, but never did an eighteen-year-old have such a head on his shoulders,' said Longo. 'Will you do it?'

Luke's mind was racing. How could he tell this man, who had been so good to him, why he must go to Mistra? 'I will think about it, lord.'

Longo stood up. 'I cannot ask for more. Please do think about it and know that there is a home for you here on Chios if you want it. And as an added inducement, you will take the full profit on the first boatload of mastic to leave the new port of Limenas when it's completed. Build it fast, Luke.' He smiled. 'Now, there is someone who arrived on this island yesterday and wants very much to talk to you. Come.'

Marchese Longo led the way down the corridor towards an arch through which light spilt from the veranda. As they approached, Luke could hear the sound of voices, one of which was Fiorenza's.

Then he heard another and a wave of unexpected joy swept over him.

Standing on the terrace, white-bearded, white-togaed and gesticulating, was the unmistakable person of Plethon.

As Luke stepped into the sunshine, the philosopher turned and gesture became embrace.

'Luke!' he said, pulling away and looking up into a face he'd last seen diving from the side of a ship. 'I was overjoyed to hear that you'd found Longo. And Fiorenza tells me that you've found much more: Latin, Italian, mathematics . . . the list is endless. She tells me that you're a glutton for learning.'

'I have a gifted tutor,' he said. 'And now I have another. How long will you stay?'

Plethon didn't answer. Instead he made a little bow to Fiorenza and Marchese. 'You will forgive me if I steal Luke from you for a while?'

Fiorenza's head was on one side and one blameless eyebrow had risen in surprise. Then she smiled. 'Only if you speak in Latin.'

Plethon bowed again and drew Luke away. He led him over to a belvedere shaded by trellised vine and sat, arranging the folds of his toga on his lap. 'I am only here for today, Luke. I go to Monemvasia tomorrow and then on to Venice. I have come to Chios to talk to you.'

'To me? What about?'

Plethon smiled and lifted his hand to smooth his beard against his chest. 'I have been learning a lot about you, Luke,' he began. 'It turns out that you have talents—'

Luke interrupted. 'Sir, Fiorenza is—'

'I know, I know. She is herself remarkable. But I'm not talking about that. I'm referring to your escape from Monemvasia. You tried to bring a girl with you. The daughter of Laskaris, the Protostrator.'

Luke stared at the man. How did he know?

'You were friends?'

'Plethon, she is the daughter of the Protostrator.' He paused. 'Yes, we were friends.'

'Ah, I see,' said the philosopher. 'She's out of reach so you've schooled yourself not to think of her.'

Luke looked down at his hands.

'Well, you should cast aside this sense of inferiority, Luke. You are more than her match.'

'Because I can now speak Latin?'

Plethon placed a hand on Luke's shoulder. 'You lost your father, Luke. I'm sorry. What was his name?'

A memory: darkness and wind and sea; a big man lying still on a rain-lashed jetty. He closed his eyes. 'Joseph.'

'And his father?'

'Siward. Why is it important?'

Plethon ignored the question. 'Why did Siward leave Monemvasia?' he asked.

Luke chose not to answer.

Plethon removed his hand and rose. He swung a fold of toga over his shoulder and looked out over the view. 'I have been in Constantinople,' he said. 'The Emperor summoned me. He is interested in the Varangian treasure that is said to be buried somewhere and wants my help to find it.'

Again Luke made no comment.

'I began by going through the Varangian archives. A man called Siward, who'd come from the Peloponnese, turned up in Constantinople just after you were born. Would that be when your grandfather left Mistra?'

Luke said nothing.

Plethon continued. 'He wanted to join the Varangians but was too old. Then he was enrolled at the special request of the Emperor himself.'

The philosopher paused. He turned. 'Why would the Emperor do that? Was it, perhaps, because Siward brought something with him?'

Still no reply.

Plethon tried another tack. 'What did your father tell you of the treasure, Luke? That your grandfather stole it?'

'He didn't steal it.'

'No, I don't believe he did. And nor does the Emperor.'

'So why did he move it, then?'

Plethon shrugged. 'Because he thought it was unsafe where it was? I don't know. Did your father say what he thought the treasure might be?'

What had his father said?

If it is gold. It may be something else.

'He didn't know what it was,' he said quietly. 'But I don't think he thought it was gold.'

Plethon nodded slowly. 'No, quite possibly not. But he thought it lay still in Mistra?'

'Yes.'

Plethon continued to nod, his lips pursed. 'Or in Constantinople perhaps. After all, that's where he's buried. In the Church of the Varangians, where they say the treasure first came from. Perhaps he brought it back.'

Luke had no idea. Plethon was looking at him strangely.

'His tomb is magnificent,' he said quietly. 'Very ornate. As befits a prince.'

Luke looked at him in astonishment. 'What did you say?'

'Luke, your grandfather was the direct descendent of Siward Godwinson, Prince of Wessex, in a place called England. He was the first English Varangian.'

Luke continued to stare at him.

Plethon smiled. 'Which is why you've got to cast off this sense of inferiority, Luke. You have royal blood in your veins. You're more than her match.'

Luke said, 'But many Varangians were called Siward.'

'But they were not Akolouthoi, Luke.' He paused. 'Did your father not speak of this?'

Luke shook his head. 'He never mentioned my grandfather. Until the night I left.'

'No. He was ashamed. But I don't think he had any reason to be. Certainly the Emperor didn't think so, otherwise he'd hardly have let him rejoin the Guard.'

Luke leant back against the stone of the belvedere. There was so much to absorb, so much to understand. If what Plethon said was true, then everything had changed.

He felt suddenly light-headed. 'You said you were on your way to Venice. Why?'

'Because I believe that they're building cannon for the Turks. Bigger cannon to bring down walls. And Chios has something to do with it. The Venetians want the alum trade and it's their price for the cannon.'

'How do you know all this?'

Plethon tapped his nose with his finger. 'Because philosophers have friends in many places.'

'You're a spy?'

Plethon smiled. 'I am many things, Luke. I hope to persuade them not to build the cannon but I doubt I'll succeed. The Venetians only listen to money and that's the one thing the Empire of Byzantium doesn't have.'

Luke considered what he'd been told. 'You think the Venetians are behind these pirate raids, don't you?'

'Don't you?

'Yes, I do. I've thought so for some time. But we have plans.'

'So I've heard. Fiorenza tells me they are ingenious. They want you to stay, Luke. So do I.'

'Why? I want to go to Mistra.'

'You're more useful to the Empire here. Making sure that the Venetians don't succeed in getting hold of this island is very, very important. If I can't appeal to their better instincts in Venice, then the realisation that they won't succeed at Chios might just persuade them not to give the Turk the cannon.'

'Won't the Turks simply go somewhere else for their cannon?'

'Perhaps, but they would take much longer to arrive, by which time the Sultan may have been persuaded to change his plans. His court is divided about Constantinople anyway. There is a new threat rising in the east. Tamerlane.'

Fiorenza had told him of Temur the Lame, a man creating destruction on a scale unseen since Genghis. A man moving gradually west.

'Which is why I need you here. To delay things. Delay is our friend.'

'So I am to accept Longo's offer?'

'Yes.' Plethon paused. Then he said softly, 'Princes are sometimes not free to act as other men.'

He rose. 'I am to leave for Monemvasia tomorrow. Anna Laskaris has returned there with the Mamonases who have been reinstated under Turkish protection. Do you have a message for her?'

Luke smiled.

You are more than her match.

'That I'm alive.' He paused. 'And can speak Latin.'

280

CHAPTER SIXTEEN

MONEMVASIA, SUMMER 1395

The view from the roof of the Mamonas Palace, perched high on the Goulas of Monemvasia, was unrivalled. The only buildings higher were the church and the citadel, neither of which had a balconied terrace to provide Olympian scrutiny of the world below.

The terrace covered the entire area of the building and had a cool, marbled floor of complicated design that involved sea creatures paying court to a bearded Neptune standing in damp majesty astride a cockleshell. Its colours were expensively derived: Siennese for the yellow of fish and human skin; Parian for the whites of the waves; Carrera for the blue-grey of the sea and, most magnificently, Phrygian for the purple of the God's cloak.

At one end of the terrace was a formal rose garden in raised, battened beds with small pear and tangerine trees in bronze urns, speckled in verdigris, at each corner. At the other were more beds, this time filled with herbs: thyme, coriander and rosemary, with chamomile for tea and wild stevia for sweetening it. Above were vine-woven pergolas, heavy with bunched grapes and honeysuckle that in daytime would draw humming birds to feed. Against the balustrade were borders of spider orchids, cyclamen and tulips, entwined with clematis and passiflora that spilled through its arches to tumble down the palace like garlanded hair.

But now it was far into the night and there was only smell to distinguish one flower from another. The moon was three-quarters full and set within a clear sky pitted with stars and it cast a soft glaze over everything it touched. It was almost light enough to read by and certainly to play chess, which was convenient for the two naked players lying either side of a chessboard. A brace of cats, one tortoiseshell and the other a pale grey Persian, were curled asleep beside them, their seal-soft skin aglow and rippling in the light breeze from the mainland. There was no sound beyond the hush of the wide, open sea and the languid rustle of silk.

Suleyman had pitched his tent, as he always did, on the roof.

Strictly speaking, it was not his to pitch, being his wedding gift to Damian and Anna, but it was a thing of great beauty and he felt sure that Damian would not begrudge the comfort of his only sister.

Zoe knew this place well. It was where, as children, she and Damian had eaten their best food: huge flat species of fish with pink-white flesh steaming through silver skin, cooked on the outdoor grill and sprinkled with herbs from the garden. Their father had been the cook and had talked, as he turned the fish, of the Mamonas business, pointing out their ships in the sea lanes below and describing cargoes and exotic far-flung destinations. Zoe had listened while Damian had teased the cats.

Later, it was where she had brought her lovers, usually men from the palace guard or a groom from the stables, whose mix of old sweat and new fear had so excited her. And quite often, in the throes of urgent coupling, she'd wondered how the cats had got there to watch them with such indifference.

Zoe moved a chess piece now with equal indifference and yawned. The game was beginning to bore her and she wanted to feel air on her skin, still sticky with royal seed. She rose, stretched and walked over to the balcony, resting her elbows and breasts on a cushion of clematis with her long hair following its tumble over the edge. The city beneath was firmly asleep and entirely quiet. Indeed, the only movement she'd witnessed had come from Anna some hours before, adrift in the orchard below with the aimless gait of a sleepwalker. It was ironic, she thought, that Anna now had more freedom to move than she did.

It was half a year since the Mamonas family had returned from Serres, secure between the ranks of a regiment of janissaries. They had faced the sullen stare of a citizenry now implacably in the camp of the Despot, a citizenry saddened that his army had been unable to deny entry to the janissaries.

'Who are you now?'

Zoe continued to stare out into the night. They'd been playing a game.

'I am Queen Zenobia,' she murmured, 'and I am looking over the flames of burning Palmyra and awaiting the legions of Aurelian who I hope will ravish me, one by one.'

'Ah,' said Suleyman, 'now that would be something to watch.' He paused. 'I believe the House of Orhan claims some ancestry from Zenobia. We should certainly take Egypt from those Mamluk pederasts. As she did.'

They were both silent for a while, contemplating a desert kingdom dedicated to wealth and the worship of Baal.

'How did she die?' asked Zoe, turning back to the night.

'Zenobia? They say she was taken back to Rome in golden chains and given a villa at Tivoli where she entertained philosophers for the rest of her days.' Suleyman rolled on to his back on the soft hides of antelope covering the bed. He looked up at the silk ceiling of the tent, mysterious in the blur of sandalwood smoke that drifted up from a brazier. 'Is that what I should do with you?' he asked, smiling into his oiled and pointed beard.

Zoe turned her body so that the moon made sand dunes of her breasts, her nipples casting shadows across them. Her legs were apart and the tendrils of hair between them were stark against the white of the balustrade. 'Perhaps, but not philosophers. Come here.'

Prince Suleyman shook his head. 'No. I am spent and you are insatiable. We need to talk.'

Zoe closed her legs and turned back to the view. 'What do we need to talk about? Not Anna.'

Suleyman sat up. 'I want to talk about Anna.'

'You are obsessed,' said Zoe over her shoulder. 'She would never satisfy you. And she loves someone else.'

'Which makes her all the more appealing. She interests me.'

'Do you want to talk to her or fuck her?' asked Zoe.

'I don't know, both probably,' he said. 'I want her to come of her own volition.'

'Which she won't.'

'Not now, no. But she thinks of you as a friend. That's why I'm happy for her to be here with you rather than at Edirne. You can persuade her.'

Zoe considered this. Her body was very still. 'And if I refuse?'

'Then you can forget Zenobia,' came the reply. He studied

the back of his hands, turning each in the light to trace the contours of dark veins. 'What is it that you want, Zoe?' he asked, looking up at her.

She didn't answer.

Suleyman went on. 'Your father and brother want lordship of Mistra and a licence to print money on the island of Chios. But what do *you* want?.'

Zoe turned very slowly and without provocation. Her jet-black hair fell with natural gravity and her pale face was more serious than he'd yet seen it. She looked him straight in the eye and she did not blink. 'I can get you Anna' – her voice was soft – 'but my price is high.'

'Name it,' he said, equally softly.

'Luke.'

'And Luke is . . . ?' asked Suleyman, intrigued.

'Luke is . . . a friend.' She had never sounded like this before and it unnerved him.

'A friend?'

'Yes, to me and especially to Anna. I need you to find him.'

Suleyman thought about this. *A friend to Anna?* He smoothed the sheet with his hand.

'Where do I look?' he asked.

'Look for the unusual,' she said quietly. 'He will make himself known somewhere. He is . . . he is different.'

Suleyman looked at her for a long time and something deep inside him, which he didn't altogether recognize, stirred in its sleep.

'I will try,' he said at last.

Much later, after they'd made a softer love than before and the first chill of dawn had crept over their sleeping bodies, they both awoke and knew that a new and important pact had been made between them. And neither wished to discuss it quite yet.

Zoe turned her head to look at the man who would, one day, rule over the Ottoman Empire.

The man who would take Anna for his wife.

'Tell me how it goes at Constantinople,' she said.

'The siege is dull,' said Suleyman, putting his hands behind his head and stretching his body to reach cool in the sheet below. 'Sieges are always dull and the army hates them. The only excitement comes from your cannon.'

'And our fleet?' asked Zoe, turning her body to him and curling a strand of his hair around her forefinger.

Suleyman wondered which fleet she meant. He supposed the Greek one.

'It never arrived. It turned back before we ever caught sight of it. Someone must have told them of the cannon on board our ships.'

Zoe thought about Anna and the camp at Serres. Getting her for Suleyman would be difficult. Difficult, but not impossible. She rolled on to her back.

'Your father, is he pleased with how the siege goes?'

Suleyman laughed. 'He's pleased with everything these days,' he said. 'A man from Chios appeared one day with a way to fill the holes in his teeth, and it worked. He has no more pain and can eat as much sugar as he likes. I've never seen him so happy.'

Zoe raised herself to lean on her elbow, suddenly interested. 'From Chios? What man?'

'No one knows,' said Suleyman. 'He appeared, did his work, then left. He was a miracle.'

'And the treatment? How did he do it?'

Suleyman shrugged. 'He left before we could get the secret out of him. But my father now has a special affection for Chios.'

Zoe considered this. Later, she would consider it further. 'Well, I am glad he's no longer in pain,' she said quietly and reached to stroke her lover's cheek, which was dark and scaled with beard and divided by a ridge of high bone. She shivered and pulled up the sheet to cover them both.

'But he still has cares,' continued the Prince. 'There's another crusade gathering in the west to come to the aid of Constantinople. The Duke of Burgundy is emptying his purse to recruit knights and buy horses. Your father has probably sold him a few.'

'So will Bayezid lift the siege?' she asked.

Suleyman yawned. 'Perhaps.' He rolled on to his side, studying her. 'But enough about the siege, I am here to forget it. Last night we made a pact. Do you have a plan yet?'

Zoe looked back at him. 'Yes, I have a plan. And this is what I want you to do. Listen carefully and do not speak.'

Later that morning, Zoe was feeding peacocks in the Court of the Lions in a place where she confidently expected Anna to pass. She was dressed in a long caftan of white cotton and had a straw hat on her head.

The Court of Lions was a more or less accurate copy of the same at the Alhambra Palace in Al-Andalus, and had been built by her grandfather who'd sold horses to the Emir Yusuf. As might be expected, it had a fountain at its centre made up of an alabaster shell basin supported by twelve marble lions and a cloister round its sides whose horseshoe arches were supported by columns and muqarnas covered in fine calligraphy. The colonnade was paved in white marble and its walls were

covered in blue and yellow Iznik tiles with borders above and
below of enamelled gold. At one end, a pavilion had a map of
the world drawn in coloured marbles on its floor.

Zoe was admiring the iridescent blue-green train of a peacock, hoping that the peahen nearby would offer enough for
it to raise its tail. She admired the gaudy male of this species
as much as she despised the female.

'What do they eat?'

Zoe turned and looked up at the girl whose every feature
was the opposite of hers. She looked at her hair which today
was free of veil or flowers or ribbons and which fell to her
shoulders like coppered gold. Her gaze travelled down a body
whose curves gave shape to the simple tunic she wore. She
looked up into viridian eyes.

'What do *you* eat?' smiled Zoe, getting to her feet and taking
Anna's hand. 'I haven't seen you looking so well in all the time
I've known you.'

Anna coloured slightly and changed the subject. 'Are they
from India?' she asked, looking towards the now fanned tail
of the peacock which stood, ridiculously, facing them.

'I think so,' replied Zoe, following her gaze. 'I believe they
were a gift to my father from the Sultan Nasir who rules in
Delhi and has a fondness for our wine.'

Anna let go of Zoe's hand and walked over to a stone bench
sheltered by a pergola woven with jasmine. Zoe came and sat
by her side and they watched the peacocks which strutted and
barked like bankers on the Rialto.

Anna said what Zoe had been waiting for her to say: 'Prince
Suleyman is here.'

Zoe looked at her and saw the tension that had hardened
her mouth. 'Yes,' she said evenly. 'I believe he is.'

There was a silence which each wanted the other to end.

'What will you do?' asked Anna eventually.

'Apart from avoid him? Nothing much. What will *you* do?'

Anna looked back at Zoe and then beyond her to scan the courtyard behind. It was empty of anything but peacocks. 'I don't know,' she replied. 'I heard what was said at Serres. Do you think there is a pact?'

Zoe took her hand. 'I suppose it's possible. But it was only Bayezid that mentioned it. If Suleyman had anything to do with it, why would you be here rather than at Edirne?' She paused. 'Could it be, perhaps, that Prince Suleyman is trying to protect you?'

'From Bayezid?' Anna shook her head. Bayezid preferred princes from Trebizond.

'God knows,' Zoe said, with bitterness, 'I've no affection for Suleyman. But my father says that he's not forgotten the day at Mistra when he first saw you in the forest. Perhaps he just wishes to protect you. Perhaps that's why you're here.'

Anna was still shaking her head. 'I don't believe it.'

But then she thought of the long months at Serres and the impeccable politeness of a dark man with a pointed beard who could, at any stage, have ravished her.

'I don't believe it,' she said again.

'Well, you must believe what you like,' said Zoe. 'For myself, I would rather not think about Prince Suleyman at all. Was that what you wanted to talk to me about?'

'No, not that,' said Anna.

Zoe knew what Anna wanted to know. 'It is unlikely that he survived,' she said gently. 'The storm was terrible that night. One of our ships was driven as far as Santorini.'

The peacocks watched them, their heads erect.

289

'We've had no news of Luke. I'm sorry.'

'No. Well, it's unlikely that you would,' said Anna evenly, looking down into her lap and folding her hands. 'He's hardly a man of consequence.'

Anna thought of the scribbled message passed to her earlier. 'There's something else. I need to get off the Goulas, to go down to the lower town. Can you help me?'

Zoe nearly asked why but checked herself. 'It might be possible, I suppose. With an escort.'

'Can you get me one?'

While Zoe and Anna were sitting on their bench in the Court of Lions, Suleyman was lying on the bed in his tent high up on the roof, drinking sherbet and studying his toenails with no interest at all.

In front of him was a small man, on his knees, whose head was tucked between his shoulder blades and whose face was flat to the floor.

The Prince was irritated. 'I can't hear you properly. Stay on the floor but lift your head to me. Now say it again.'

The man's beard was long and had got caught in a silver chain hanging from his neck. He grimaced with pain as it came free. 'Majesty, I was saying that the Sultan your father is perhaps more exercised than he was about the new crusade from the west. As you know, the Voivode Mircea of Wallachia joined forces with King Sigismund of Hungary two years ago to take back their fortress of Nicopolis on the Danube frontier. It now seems the King has succeeded in finding common ground with more of his neighbours. Even Prince Vlad of Transylvania is wavering in his alliance with us.'

Suleyman flicked a fly from his sleeve and yawned. 'I don't

think we need be unduly concerned,' he said. 'The King of Hungary has difficulty enough keeping order between all those Magyars and Slovakians and whatever other rubbish he rules over before taking us on.'

The man said nothing and held his hands, which were trembling, between his chin and the carpet.

'What of the Prince Lazarević? Does my father trust him?'

'The loyalty of the Serbian Prince is unquestioned, Majesty. After all, your father is married to his sister.'

'It means nothing,' said Suleyman nastily. 'My father had the Prince's father killed along with most of his relatives. He is likely to remember it . . . So what is there new to report? Everything we have so far discussed I already know. Stand up.'

The man stood with some difficulty. He was not young and his joints were stiff. 'What is new, lord, is that a celebratory mass was held in the Cathedral of Saint-Denis in Paris last week at which the Duke of Burgundy's eldest son, the Count of Nevers, swore himself to lead the crusade and to dedicate his first feat of arms to the service of God.'

'But he's a child!'

'He will be the nominal commander, sire. It is the Marshal Boucicaut of France who will lead the army.'

'Ah,' said Suleyman, smiling. 'Now, that's better. Boucicaut is good.'

'And, lord, the alliance he commands is now impressive. Apart from Burgundy, France and Hungary, it includes Venice, Aragon, many of the German princes and the Hospitallers. And of course Byzantium. England will send money and some archers.'

Suleyman whistled softly. 'That *is* impressive,' he agreed. 'And what of the two Popes? Are the knights to get indulgences from both Rome *and* Avignon?'

'Indeed, Majesty,' said the man, quite seriously.

Suleyman stretched and stood up. He walked over to that part of the balcony where a buddleia, newly arrived from China, was attracting butterflies. The shrub's white, tubular flowers, full of nectar, were covered in insects with heart-shaped wings of brown silk, veined with chrome. 'Did you know,' he murmured as much to himself as anyone else, 'that the Ancient Greek word for butterfly was *psyche,* which is also the word for a man's soul?'

He seemed transfixed by the creature. 'And in the East,' he went on, 'they hold the superstition that if a butterfly chooses to perch on you, then the person you love is on their way to see you.'

Then Suleyman brought his other hand down on his arm so that the wet debris of the butterfly was scattered across his palm. 'I do not believe in superstition,' he said, lifting his palm and looking at it. He walked back to sit on the bed, wiping his hand on the sheet. A cat jumped up and licked what was left. 'Now, what else?'

The older man cautiously wiped the sweat from his hands on the back of his caftan. 'Some news from Chios, lord,' he said.

'Ah, Chios,' murmured the Prince, a thin smile stretching his lips, 'my father's latest lover.'

'The Sultan has forbidden any interference in the island's affairs.' The man hesitated, the next sentence caught somewhere near the top of his beard. Then he took courage. 'So . . . I wondered, Majesty, where such an injunction might leave your plans with the Venetians.'

Suleyman looked up sharply. 'Why should it change anything? Can I help it if these tiresome pirates insist on attacking the island? What could it possibly have to do with me?'

The man pretended to take this seriously. 'Quite so, lord,' he said, 'but the pirates are attacking the very villages which make the mastic which has filled the holes in your father's teeth. Or at least they were.'

'Were?' asked Suleyman. 'What do you mean, "were"?'

'Well, lord,' went on the man, 'the pirates were somewhat less successful in their last attack. It seems the villagers were better prepared for them. There is some talk of them building new villages with better defences And they're being led.'

Suleyman looked up. 'Led? By the Genoese?'

'No, Majesty, by someone other. A young Greek.'

'And do we know who this person is?'

'Our friend on the island tells me that his name is *Luca*. Or at least that is the Italian version, lord.'

'*Luca?*'

'Yes, lord. Luca.'

Prince Suleyman was sitting on the edge of the bed and, the man was relieved but mystified to see, smiling now with real pleasure.

'Luca,' he murmured. Then he rose and walked to the wall and clapped his hands. The buddleia exploded with butterflies of every colour and the Prince made no effort to harm any of them. He turned.

'I want you to bring this Luca to me as soon as humanly possible. I don't care how you do it but I want him brought, unharmed.'

'Yes, lord.'

'And you had better inform the Venetians that our raids must cease for a while.'

Later that evening, Anna was making her way to the steps to the lower town in the company of a huge giant janissary called Yusuf who apparently spoke no Greek and, judging by his silence, might not speak at all. Anna felt conspicuous in his presence, for he was startlingly ugly. Although the evening was warm, she wore a long, woollen cloak that fell to the ground and her head was covered by a hood pulled forward over her hair so that she looked like a monk.

Once through the gate of the Goulas, Yusuf bowed and turned back.

In the lower town, the lamps were beginning to be lit and all around was the clatter of preparation for the last meal of the day, cats assembling at doors for the promise of scraps. A donkey, chewing into a nosebag, was standing next to a cistern in a tiny square and its owner was filling amphorae while examining the catch of a fisherman who'd paused to open his bundle. The sea wall was close and the calls of late swimmers could be heard beyond its battlements. The scent of the sea was fresh and all around and moving in on a soft breeze to replace the hot, animal smells of the land.

She reached a small house at the end of a street with a low door in its wall and a window with a piece of coarse cloth hung for a curtain. Anna knocked on the door.

It was opened by Matthew, whose grin reached from ear to ear.

'Lady, you are welcome,' he said, and stepped back to let her pass. 'Please come in. This is my father, Patrick.'

He gestured to a bearded colossus behind him whom she

recognised. The man was standing, slightly stooped, in front of a table that ran the length of the room and around which sat the two other boys, Nikolas and Arcadius, and two older men, also lavishly bearded, who must be their fathers. On the table were the remnants of a meal. There were no women present and indeed little room for anyone else beyond the six gathered. A wooden staircase in one corner led to the room above.

Anna walked in and sat at the table. She looked from one to other of her friends. 'Nikolas, Arcadius . . . I'm happy to see you. Are you well?'

The boys smiled at Anna but didn't speak. Their fathers looked solemn. One of them spoke.

'I am Basil and the father of Arcadius, Anna,' said the man gravely. 'We are well but a little hungrier than when you last saw us. We work as fishermen now and eat too much garon.'

One of the boys laughed but it had not been meant as a joke. All of them looked thin and gaunt and Anna realised what it had meant for these men when the Mamonases had first fled Monemvasia. The long-standing connection of Archon to Varangian had been severed forever and in its place had come janissaries and hunger.

'Could you not have gone to Mistra?' she asked.

Basil nodded. 'We plan to go there. That is what we are here to discuss.'

Anna looked around at the faces all watching her. She smiled and placed her hands, folded, in front of her. 'Your message said that there was someone who wanted to meet me.'

'There is.'

It was a voice from heaven. Two sandals, then ankles, appeared at the top of the stairs. Everyone looked up and was rewarded by the sight of a descending philosopher clad from shoulder to shin in a toga of the purest white.

'Georgius Gemistus Plethon, evacuee of Constantinople, at your service,' said the man as he arrived on earth and, within the tiny space available, performed an awkward bow in Anna's direction. He gathered an armful of toga and threw it carelessly over a shoulder before sitting down heavily on the last available chair. Then he lifted his beard, which was the longest in a room of long beards, and placed it delicately on the table in front of him, patting it down to the wood. 'I have long wanted to meet you, Anna. We have a friend in common.'

'We do?' asked Anna in surprise.

'Why yes, yes indeed. One Luke Magoris. Is he not a friend?'

Anna felt the room shift beneath her. 'Luke? You've seen him?'

'Seen him, conversed with him,' replied Plethon brightly. 'Indeed, it was only last week that I sat with him and debated the possibility that the world may be round. In Latin.'

'Luke Magoris? Latin?' She looked at Matthew, who sat halfway down the table and was regarding the angel, or prophet, as if he was mad.

'Yes, Latin,' replied Plethon testily. 'The script we were discussing was written in Latin so it seemed prudent to interrogate it in the same tongue.'

The three boys and Anna exchanged glances.

'Ah,' went on Plethon, his voluminous eyebrows raised in new understanding, 'yes, I see. You share the common conviction that the world is flat and stable. Well, we shall see. The Portuguese King Henry sends his ships further and further south each year and none have yet dropped off.'

There was silence around the table as each considered what

296

they had heard. Then Anna spoke. 'We do not know any Luke Magoris who speaks Latin,' she said carefully.

'No? Well he's learnt. And more. I believe he's competent in Italian as well. After all, on Chios he's surrounded by the brutes. He has to be.'

For the first time, Anna was daring to fill her senses with the giddy taste of hope. She felt tipsy with its fumes and a feeling such as she'd not felt in months rose within her as this man's words sank in. 'He's learnt? Luke is alive and has learnt Latin? And you are his friend?'

Plethon nodded impatiently. 'I consider myself to be thus, yes.' Then he looked quizzically at Anna. 'But he said you were clever. You don't sound very clever. He said that you had taught him things in a cave.'

Anna threw back her head and laughed. 'Luke!' she cried. 'You're alive and you speak Latin!'

Then she rose from her chair and, to the astonishment of all present, walked, or rather danced, over to Plethon and kissed him on his forehead.

'I'm sorry,' she said bringing her fingers to her lips as Plethon blushed and put a hand to his brow. 'I hardly know you. But you know Luke and he's alive and I will always love you for telling me that.'

Then Anna remembered where she was and why she was there. She turned, wiping tears from her cheeks. 'I'm sorry,' she said again, this time to her embarrassed audience. 'It was a surprise. I'm sorry.'

But Plethon was far from embarrassed. He was quietly chuckling to himself and staring with approval at Anna. She was every bit as lovely as Luke had described.

Then a throat was cleared. 'The news is good,' said Patrick, 'and we must thank God for Luke's deliverance. But time is short and we need to discuss other things. Plethon, I think you want to say something?'

'I do, indeed I do,' said the man, still looking at Anna, who was wiping tears of happiness from her cheeks.'I believe you to be Varangians, yes? Descended directly from those who fled to Mistra from the desecration of our beloved capital by the Franks two centuries past?'

Three beards nodded slowly.

'Good. Well, I'm speaking to the right men then.' Plethon paused and stroked the long train of his own. 'What is it that you believe they brought with them when they fled?'

The Varangians exchanged glances. None spoke.

Plethon waited a while for an answer. Then he asked simply, 'If Luke has put his faith in me, would it not be reasonable for you, too, to trust me? I suppose not.'

Plethon sighed and a hand disappeared inside the folds at the front of his toga. When it re-emerged, it was holding a ring: large, gold and embossed with a double-headed eagle. It was pitted with age and glowed in the light of the candle.

'This is the ring of Manuel, our emperor,' he said. 'It was given to me by the same five weeks ago when he bade me farewell from the sea gate of the Blachernae Palace. I passed through the Sultan's blockade in a Genoese round ship from Pera which carried me on to Chios.'

Patrick leant forward and carefully lifted the ring from the open palm. He turned it into the light of the candle, examining it from every side. Then he passed it to David, Nikolas's father.

'You may know,' Plethon went on, 'that a great army is assembling in the west to march to our aid. They say that the flower of Christian chivalry is polishing its armour and that the force will be large enough to crush the Turk once and for all.'

Plethon paused and leant forward.

'Perhaps they *will* defeat the Turk and I can go back to my beloved home and it will be called Adrianopolis again. Perhaps. But what then?' He looked around at seven people waiting for the answer. 'Well, what happened the last time that a great crusade came to the aid of Constantinople?'

Patrick began to nod slowly, his thumb and finger at work on his moustache.

'It's why you are *here*, Varangians!' said Plethon with some feeling. His palm came down hard on the table. 'They can't help themselves! Last time they sacked our city and raped our nuns when there were a million people inside its walls. This time the citizens number fewer than fifty thousand and most of them are armed with pitchforks.' He paused. 'And why did the Franks do it? Because we couldn't pay them what they wanted.'

Now all three of the older men were nodding, as Plethon, philosopher and orator, used the weapon of silence. Basil was holding the ring and he placed it deliberately on the table before the man in the toga.

'So the Emperor needs the Varangian gold to pay them off?'

Plethon nodded. 'Quite possibly. If it is gold.'

'What did Luke tell you?' asked Patrick.

'He told me that he didn't know anything about the treasure beyond legend. He told me that he would have learnt more from his father but his father is dead.' He paused, scraping off a vein of wax from the candle in front of him with his finger-nail. 'Tell me, Patrick, why is Luke called Luke? And why is Joseph called Joseph? Why are they both not called Siward?'

The Varangian exchanged glances with his companions.

'It's not such an odd question,' Plethon continued. 'After all, the Akolouthos was always called Siward. Father to son, always Siward. And the family name was Godwinson.'

'I will tell you what we know,' Patrick said. 'Luke's grandfather Siward and our fathers quarrelled. Siward left with the treasure. It's no longer at Mistra.'

'He stole it?'

Patrick didn't answer. Matthew, Nikolas and Arcadius stared at him. They'd not known this.

'Well, I think I can help,' Plethon said. 'There was a Siward who rejoined the Palace Guard in Constantinople a few months after Luke's grandfather left Monemvasia. He spent the rest of his life there and was buried with honour in the Varangian church. I think it was the same man.'

'Rejoined the Guard? But he would have been fifty!' said David.

'It seemed the Emperor intervened.'

'But he was a traitor!'

'Was he? Are you sure that he took the treasure? Why would a rich man rejoin the Varangian Guard?' He lowered his voice. 'Why do you imagine they quarrelled, David?'

There was no answer. Three Varangians were considering the possibility that it had been *their* fathers, all now dead, that had wanted to take the treasure.

Anna held her breath, watching Matthew, Nikolas and Arcadius watch their fathers.

'No one knows what or where the treasure is,' Plethon continued softly. 'But I believe that it wasn't gold that was removed from Constantinople that night. I think something much, much more important was taken, something so important that it had to remain hidden where no one could find it. I think Siward moved it to make sure that remained the case and that a grateful Emperor rewarded him.'

Patrick was shaking his head, the frown driven deep into his forehead. 'So you think that he simply gave the treasure to the Emperor?'

Plethon shook his head. 'No, I think he hid it somewhere else.'

'But where? In Mistra or Constantinople?'

Plethon looked down at the piece of wax, held between his fingers, which he had moulded into a ball. 'That's what I'm here to find out,' he said simply.

Outside the room, the sounds of a little city poised between land and sea were fading as the first noises of the night crept in. A church bell sounded across the red-tiled roofs and some laughter came and went, shut away with the closing of doors and the bolting of windows. Quite soon, the soldiers at the three gates of the lower town would be ushering through the last travellers and, much to the annoyance of the citizenry, the muezzin would call his small, military flock to prayer.

'I am afraid we will disappoint you,' Patrick said eventually. 'The secret of the treasure is lost to us.'

'Siward left no clue?'

'He left nothing but his sword,' said Basil. 'Which Luke now has. Or had.'

Plethon sat there, twisting the wax round and round between his fingers, staring at the candle.

His sword.

There was sound from the street, of footsteps and of conversation approaching and then stopping. He frowned and looked at the window. Matthew got up and opened the door. There was nothing there.

Plethon stood. He turned to Matthew. 'There is one more thing. The Emperor has need of his Varangians. There are only a few of you left now, here and in Constantinople. He wants you to join this crusade.'

Basil grunted. 'Well, we're no longer sworn to the Archon, it's true. But how would we leave? The Turks guard every gate.'

Plethon went over to Basil and put his hand on his shoulder. 'I didn't mean you,' he said gently. 'You may not be sworn to the Archon any more, but you're still sworn to guard a treasure that might yet be here somewhere. I meant your sons.'

Matthew asked, 'but what about Anna? And Rachel? We can't leave them here.'

'So take them with you,' said Plethon. 'Find a way to escape. Go to Chios, leave Anna and Rachel there and take ship to Venice.'

Nikolas had risen. There was excitement in his voice. 'So how do we do it?'

The silence was broken by Anna. 'I think I may know of a way.'

'You have a plan?'

'Yes,' she said. 'And something better. I have someone who might help us.'

Yusuf was standing in front of Zoe in her bedroom within the palace. His hands were behind his back and he was trembling. She, fully clothed but prepared to be otherwise, was tracing the contour of a pectoral muscle at exactly eye-level and her breathing was quicker than normal.

Yusuf was ugly but, for Zoe, ugly was new.

'Where are you from, Yusuf?' she asked, allowing her hand to drop from his breast and travel slowly down the valley that led to his groin.

'Edirne, lady,' replied Yusuf in perfect Greek. The statement ended in a gasp as Zoe's finger brushed the tip of his penis, prominent beneath the soft folds of his janissary pantaloons.

'The Devshirme?' she murmured, her fingernails moving very slowly down its length to rest somewhere beneath.

Yusuf nodded. His face was red and a contortion of vein and perspiration. Zoe turned the hand and slowly pushed it forward between his legs and then up, so that her open palm was suspended fractionally beneath his balls. She lifted a middle finger and began to rub it gently in the place where, had he been a woman, his vagina would have been, getting closer, with each stroke, to a puckered hole behind.

'And the man she met was also from Edirne . . . Plethon, wasn't it? Did you know of him?'

Zoe pressed the hole and discovered that she'd been right. A small convulsion, definitely of pleasure, ran through the man's great body. He gasped and his hands, still behind him, were clasped and shaking.

'I knew of him, lady,' he said dully, fighting for vowels. 'He . . . he used to speak in the forum. Of learned things.'

'And *you* understood him? A great big ugly brute like you understood him? A great *big* . . .' Zoe moved her hand up to grasp the object so apparent between them and began to stroke up and down slowly. 'What did he talk about?'

'He talked about . . . our Greek forefathers. I was a child, lady . . .'

'A child, yes. Not so big . . . then,' she said, squeezing harder, the rhythm quickening. 'And what did he talk about with the girl tonight, Yusuf?' she asked, rising on tiptoe to get closer to his ear. 'What did they talk about?'

'It was hard to hear, lady . . . something about a treasure. Oh.'

Zoe had stopped the movement and held him, poised, her thumb idly caressing the tip.

'Treasure? Varangian treasure?' she asked sharply.

'Yes, lady . . . please . . .'

'Only if you are very clear, Yusuf. Did they say where it was?'

'They talked of a sword.'

A sword. Luke's sword.

Yusuf had screwed his eyes in the effort of containment and Zoe, still on tiptoe, was smiling up at him and one hand resumed the movement while the other began to unbutton her tunic.

'Open your eyes, Yusuf,' she whispered. 'You can look, if you want.'

He looked down and saw one breast, then two as Zoe drew the tunic apart. They were the colour of satinwood and without flaw and the nipples were darker than mahogany.

'Would you like to touch, Yusuf?' she murmured, her tongue at the base of his neck. 'Would you like to touch them?' Her hand moved behind him and grasped one huge buttock and a finger found the hole again.

But this was too much.

With a groan, the giant bent forward and the hands left his back and grasped Zoe's hand as, with one deft and final movement, she pulled him into heaven. His shoulders rose and fell as if in laughter but the sound that came from his mouth was not laughter. He fell to his knees, grappling with the front of his pantaloons, trying to stem the flow, his whole body in unwanted spasm.

304

'I'm sorry, lady . . . please,' he moaned, not daring to look up.

But Zoe was not looking at him. She had walked to the other end of the room, buttoning her tunic as she went, to where a towel was folded beside a low bathing pool. 'Get up,' she said, dipping her hand in the water and wiping it dry. She threw the towel at Yusuf.

'Here, clean yourself,' she said, 'and then tell me the rest. With accuracy, if you want to live.'

Yusuf, now standing, was feverishly wiping the front of his trousers, his big head bobbing up and down with the effort. 'He had come from Chios, lady. He spoke of someone there called Luke. The lady was glad of the news. She had thought him dead.'

Zoe clapped her hands together. 'Hah! I *knew* it. So he's alive. What is he doing on Chios?'

'He has learnt Latin,' said Yusuf, knowing it wasn't enough. 'And Italian . . . from the Genoese.'

'And how to fill men's teeth, I don't doubt,' murmured Zoe. She turned to the man. 'Anything else?'

'The girl means to escape, taking the woman Rachel with her. With the help of a friend.'

'Ah, a friend. Yes.' Zoe smiled. 'You may go. Find Prince Suleyman and ask him to join me.'

Yusuf, still clutching the folds of his pantaloons to cover the stain, bowed in relief and turned to go.

'And Yusuf?' said Zoe over her shoulder as she walked towards the balcony. 'One word of what has happened in this room tonight and you will never talk again.'

It was much later when Rachel was awakened by a freshly

changed Yusuf who signalled to her to dress for travel and brought her, in some bewilderment, to Anna's bedroom. Anna was already wearing breeches and a thick, woollen smock so as to be ready for either sea-borne or mounted escape.

Rachel seemed more frail than when she'd last seen her, but her frailty was bolstered by a new joy that had been born the moment that Anna had told her that Luke was alive. She felt exultant, ready for anything: in particular ready to join her son on Chios as soon as humanly possible.

Now Anna sat opposite Rachel in a room that was almost dark and they held hands and told stories for comfort and to pass the time. A single lamp stood on the table between them with its wick almost burnt through. It was smoking slightly and its light made monsters on the walls. The palace outside was silent and asleep.

'Speaking Latin!' whispered Rachel. 'He must have been educated.'

'Was he always clever?' asked Anna.

'Well, he shared a few lessons with the twins long ago but they stopped it for some reason. Perhaps Damian was jealous.'

Anna wanted to imagine Luke as a young boy, running barefoot, knees scratched, or riding bareback, his arms clinging to the neck of an animal he already understood better than other people.

'Were they close once, the three of them?' she asked.

'Close? They were inseparable! They shared everything from their toys to the bath. The servants had to be sent down from the palace to bring them home. I loved those twins like my own.'

Rachel was laughing softly at the memory, her hands steepled in her lap.

306

'I used to take them with me to gather kermes outside the city. I would put them on a donkey, one, two, three, with the baskets behind, and they would laugh and laugh at its ears and the silly noise it made when they pulled them.' She paused, eyes faraway. 'Yes, they were very close.'

'So what happened?' asked Anna gently.

'They grew up, I suppose. But something else as well.'

Anna was still, allowing Rachel to decide whether or not to find comfort in disclosure.

'She was always a difficult girl,' said Rachel, looking up. 'She had everything she wanted but only wanted the things she couldn't have.'

Anna felt the very first pricking of a new fear deep, deep inside her stomach. It was a fear without name or, for now, explanation. But it was there.

'Luke?'

Rachel nodded slowly. 'Luke, money, power. It was difficult to tell which was more important to her.' She paused. 'Probably money and power. She was always a clever girl.'

Anna didn't have time to think further because there was a muffled knock on the door and Yusuf arrived to take them somewhere else. He stood in the doorway and nodded to Anna, who helped Rachel to her feet. Then they walked out into the dark of the corridor and along it until they reached the top of a curving staircase that swept down to the hall below.

The hall was lit by torches held in sconces on the walls that were beginning to splutter. Standing in the centre of the space was Zoe, alone. The janissary guards were either asleep or had been persuaded to absent themselves.

Holding Rachel's hand, Anna tiptoed down the staircase, stopping every third step to listen to the palace around them. When they reached the bottom, Zoe put a finger to her lips and beckoned for them to follow her. Anna glanced behind and found that Yusuf had left them. They crept into the lobby where, centuries ago, Luke had stood with Joseph to learn his sentence.

The first glimmer of dawn was framed in the opening at the top of the dome and it cast everything in a spectral glow. Waiting there were Matthew, Nikolas and Arcadius, armed but not armoured; each stepped forward silently to kiss Rachel. One of them gave her a hooded cloak and helped her to tie it at the throat.

Zoe took Anna to one side. 'You know the way to the cellars below?' she whispered. 'You know the door through the kitchens into the street? Go there. It's unguarded and once outside you can make your way to the gate to the lower town. How you get through that is your business.'

Anna nodded and walked past the three young Varangians who'd formed a little circle around Rachel, and into the deep shadows of the corridor that led to the staircase. Her heart was beating a rhythm of increasing hope. She wanted to run to the stairs but knew that any noise would be fatal.

Then she heard a noise.

Behind her: a command and the drawing of steel. Her stomach lurched and she turned back to see the three Varangians, swords before them, staring up at the balcony. Zoe was standing next to them looking aghast. She glanced in the direction of Anna and her eyes bore into her.

Stay where you are.

Anna put her back to the wall of the corridor and edged along its shadow to see into the lobby. Lining the balcony were at least a dozen janissaries, each with an armed crossbow pointing below.

With them was Suleyman. And Yusuf.

Yusuf. Do you work for Zoe or Suleyman? Who has betrayed us?

Suleyman's hands were clasped, his forearms resting on the balustrade.

But this was no thunderbolt. He was unsteady on his feet. He seemed unlikely to wield the sword of Islam to much effect. Perhaps this Burgundian crusade would succeed after all.

He glanced at Suleyman. Surely, thought Luke . . .

His hands were clasped and his forearms resting on the ledge. He was leaning over and he was smiling. Anna watched, appalled, as he began to walk slowly down the stairs, his black eyes moving around the hall in search of something, someone. He went up to Zoe and walked around her once before stopping beside her, his mouth level with her ear.

'Someone, I think, is missing, lady,' he whispered. 'Where is she?'

Zoe turned so that her face was very close to his and facing Anna. 'I regret that she's flown, lord,' she whispered, quite loudly. 'She's flown to somewhere you won't find her. Somewhere safe.'

'Safe from me?' he said, drawing back a little. 'You know it's my father she should fear, not me. I am trying to help her. Have you told her *that*? I imagine not.'

Suleyman and Zoe locked stares; then he laughed softly and walked backwards to the bottom of the stairs, still holding her gaze. 'Yusuf!' he called without turning. 'Bring me your sword!'

The giant came down the stairs and handed an unsheathed scimitar to his master. Suleyman, his eyes still fixed on Zoe, put his thumb to its blade and felt its sharpness. Then he pointed at Arcadius. 'Kneel,' he commanded.

Arcadius stood still, his big body frozen in indecision. Suleyman walked over to him.

'*Kneel!*'

Matthew came to stand by his side, Nikolas beside him.

'If he is to die, then we all die,' he said.

'Yes,' said Suleyman agreeably. 'You will if you don't tell me where Anna is. If she is in the town, she will be found – probably by my father's men who are already here. Would you want that for her? Now kneel. All of you, or I'll ask Yusuf to make you.'

It was Zoe who spoke next. 'I'm sure they will tell you what they know, Prince Suleyman. They will tell you that Anna has escaped to a place they have no knowledge of. That is what they will tell you, one by one, as you kill them.'

There was the sound of a footfall and Anna stepped out of the shadows. 'I am here.'

Suleyman turned and saw her. The light from the dome was stronger now and it turned her hair into fire. Anna was upright and uncowed and there was challenge in her voice.

'If it is me that you want, then take me,' she said. 'But Rachel and the Varangians go free.'

Suleyman raised an eyebrow. 'Lady, these men cannot go free.'

Anna walked up to him. 'If you want me to come with you, prince, they will go free.'

Suleyman pretended to weigh all this in the delicate and capricious scales of his mind, as if this sequence of events had not been rehearsed some time beforehand. He stroked his beard to its oiled and tapered point and looked at Anna with questioning eyes.

'So, lord,' said Anna, looking up at him with her head tilted in query, 'am I to come with you or not?'

CHAPTER SEVENTEEN

CHIOS, SUMMER 1396

'Come out, Lara!'

It was as if the kendos was happening again. Behind the door to Lara's house in the new village of Mesta, there was a good deal of shouting, some giggling and much singing, all of it female. And Dimitri, waiting outside, felt like joining in.

But then that wasn't the custom. The custom had it that, on the morning of his wedding day, the groom would arrive at the house of his bride with his family and she would come out, in all her finery, and they would process to the church. Dimitri, however, had no family and Lara, who'd been living with him in flagrant sin for the past two years, no house. So the village had improvised and Dimitri had vacated his house a week beforehand and gone to live with Luke and now he was back, with Luke, Fiorenza, Marchese Longo, Benedo Barbi and most of the village, to collect her.

It was the first day of May and therefore another excuse for celebration on the island. The unmarried girls of the village had risen early and had poured in a giggling torrent into the fields to collect garlands of wild flowers to lay on their door-steps. That night the young men would roar like bulls through the streets, stealing them from doorstep and balcony to present to the girl they most admired. Lara's garland, pinned to her door, was a twisted riot of poppies, butterfly orchids and hyacinths tied together with the woody stem of fennel.

Prometheus had brought fire with a torch of fennel. Dimitri had brought his love.

He was standing with a small plate of candied almonds, *koufeta,* in his hand and wondering what they'd done with his goats. Like all of the new village houses, his front door usually opened on to the cosy domestic arrangements of a goat couple that greeted visitors with even more noise than today. It was all part of the revolutionary plan for this new kind of village. But all plans had to make way for a wedding.

Beside Dimitri stood Luke dressed in his best doublet of flowered silk, belted above a hose striped yellow and red which, Fiorenza had insisted, was the latest thing in Siena. Fiorenza herself was dressed less colourfully, restricting herself to a long coat of pale saffron damask above pointed slippers of Moroccan leather. Her perfumes were discreet and her golden hair was gathered in a jewelled coif with a peacock's feather behind.

Marchese Longo and Benedo Barbi were both wearing black silk, in pourpoint and hose, and boots that reached high up their calves. The four of them, as planned, exuded an air of prosperity and optimism.

'Lara, come out!' called Dimitri again, laughing and shaking the garland with his banging.

There were squeals from within and someone started a song that rang through the door like a challenge.

'The church will be dust by the time I get you there!' He turned to Fiorenza, his arms open and palms to the heavens.

'Try rattling your plate,' she suggested.

312

But he didn't have to, for then the door opened and a hand-maiden appeared bearing a tray on which sat two wedding crowns, decorated in flowers, and an empty dish. Nudged by Luke, Dimitri stepped forward and emptied his koufeta on to it and then stepped back to await the coming of his bride.

Lara stepped forward into the sun dressed in a pure white chemise of silk that fell to her ankles. Her black hair would have been blacker had it not been tinged with henna and it hung in flowered waves to her shoulders.

'God bless you this morning, Dimitri,' she said, taking the empty plate from his hand and rising on tiptoe to kiss him on both cheeks.

'God bless you, Lara.'

And that was the signal.

The crowd erupted into bawdy cheering and formed itself into some sort of procession, led by the girl carrying the koufeta with candle-bearers at either side. A group of musicians played bagpipes and ouds and drums and children skipped by their side, barefoot and clapping. The villagers danced and sang and shouted greetings to each other as two brawny men picked Dimitri up and put him on their shoulders where he rocked back and forth to the tempo of the drum.

'Shall we join them?' said Fiorenza to the only three men in the village not moving. She laughed. 'You look like dummies at the tilting range! Take off your doublets or Genoan pride will be on its back by noon.'

The way to the church was short and strewn with flowers. On either side were the first three-storeyed houses of the new Mesta, built to Luke's dream and Barbi's design, and they were indeed extraordinary. Barbi had spoken of the *carrugi*, the narrow streets of his native Genoa, when he'd heard of Luke's labyrinth, and he'd understood immediately the system of vaults, arches and bridges that would allow the villagers to go to any part of their village without their feet ever touching the ground.

The first part of the village to be built had been the tower, which would be the storehouse of the community as well as its place of final refuge. Next had come the church and the laying out of a small central piazza with shops and taverns. Then this, the first of many streets, had been built at the same time as work had begun on the outer, unbroken ring of houses that would be the village wall.

Barbi had brought with him architects, stonemasons and engineers from all over Italy; they'd been given different parts of the village to build and the stiff breeze of competition had blown among them so that the houses had gone up in record time. Now the scaffolding had moved on and the way made clear for the procession that would take Dimitri and Lara to their wedding.

As he walked, Marchese Longo looked around him and was impressed. He hadn't visited the south of the island for many months and he could scarcely believe the progress that had been made.

'Luke, Benedo, this is nothing short of miraculous,' he was saying, 'but what of this extraordinary decoration on the walls of the houses?'

'Ah, lord,' said Barbi, 'now that was the villagers' idea. We encouraged them to paint the labyrinth onto the walls of their houses and they came up with these strange designs which they call *ksista*. They're attractive, are they not?'

'I'm not sure,' laughed Longo. 'Did they work last time?'

The last pirate raid had been a farce. Reaching the abandoned

314

old village of Mesta, the pirates had conveniently burnt it to the ground, thus giving the villagers plenty of time to prepare for their arrival.

At that time, little more than the central tower and church had been erected, so the entire village had brought their goods and livestock into the ground floor and themselves had occupied the upper storeys. As the pirates had approached the church, they'd been met by a storm of missiles from its roof and some experimental Greek fire. And when they'd tried to reach the missile-throwers, the pirates found they had joined their families in the tower. After failing to burn it down, the pirates had returned to their ships and sailed away. They hadn't been seen since.

But the pirates had been replaced by a blockade and a month ago three round ships carrying alum to Florence had been seized. The loss of the round ships was little short of a catastrophe, for each could hold over a hundred tons of alum and, with nothing able to get through the blockade, the warehouses at Chora were groaning. If the blockade continued, the Florentines would begin to look to other sources.

Longo stopped and turned to Benedo Barbi. He lowered his voice.

'The blockade is slowly killing us, Benedo. We're fortunate that the Venetian alum from Trebizond can't get through the blockade at Constantinople either, otherwise we'd lose all our markets. Did you know that two more ships were taken yesterday? It's as if the Turks *know* where to wait for us.'

He took Barbi's arm and began to walk again.

'How does your miracle weapon progress, Benedo?'

'We are not quite there, lord,' he answered. 'The mixture is volatile. We will create Greek fire again, but it will take time.'

By now they had reached the church, which was a simple,

whitewashed building with red bricks in herringbone pattern around its arched windows and a roof bright with new tiles. In front of it stood Dimitri and Lara, who were holding the plate of koufeta between them and had their wedding crowns on their heads. The sweets would be left at the church door for the unmarried of the village to take and lay on their pillows to help them dream of the one they would marry. Marchese Longo smiled.

This is what we are protecting.

After the long service and the much, much longer feast of goat and pilaf at which even Benedo Barbi had been persuaded to dance, Luke and Fiorenza found themselves walking outside the village wall under a giant moon. Marchese Longo and Barbi had retired to Luke's house and would be fast asleep by now and quite possibly dreaming of the same ksista shapes, intended to entertain by day and confuse by night, that Luke and Fiorenza were discussing.

'Quite like women, really,' said Fiorenza, who had lifted her delicious nose to the smell of mastic that hung over the fields and groves. The night was startlingly clear and star-hung and the moon made the surface of the small irrigation lake into a thing of satin.

Luke smiled and turned to her. In the excitement of recent months, he'd almost forgotten what might have happened in the mastic grove by the sea.

'I'm too young to be confused by women,' said Luke. 'They just dazzle me. Or perhaps it's just you. I'm indebted to you, Fiorenza.'

'You did it yourself, Luke. Education would have come to you like a thirsty man finds water. Lara, she's the same.'

316

'Lara?' said Luke. 'Yes, you're right. It was her idea for Dimitri to go to the Sultan's camp and mend his teeth.'

'Well, I hope he got paid for it. They'll need money now they're married. What of your money, Luke?'

Luke's fortune was still in its infancy but steadily growing. He'd discovered shoots of a sharp commercial instinct within the new growth of his learning and had applied it readily to the business of exploiting the mastic miracle. And miracle it was. Over the past months, he and Dimitri had found more and more uses for it. Not only was it a teeth-whitener, a breath-sweetener and filler of cavities, but it also seemed to work well as a wound sealant and a remedy for snake bites. Before the blockade, the ships leaving Chora with alum had begun to carry mastic in their holds as well and the first sales had been beyond their expectations.

But that was a month ago.

'We have a spy on the island,' said Luke. 'Someone who is telling the Turks when our ships leave port.'

'So it would seem,' murmured Fiorenza. 'The Medici agent perhaps? They're close to the Venetians.'

Luke shrugged. 'Did you know that they've offered to be bankers to me, as they are to the lord Longo? I'm flattered.'

'Don't be,' said Fiorenza. 'It is only because they have high hopes for you.' She paused. 'But you must watch them.'

Luke glanced at her and saw that she was looking at him with much the same curiosity as when she'd first greeted him on the steps of Longo's mansion. But now there was something else as well, something that Luke both wanted and feared.

'Shall we sit?' said Fiorenza as they reached a tree beside the lake with roots that knotted themselves together like old men's fingers.

They sat on ground dampening in the early dew, strewn with little stones covered in moss thick as double-cut velvet. Above them was a canopy of branches through which the stars winked and pulsed with the bravado of nightly reincarnation. There was the soft slap of fishes hitting water to their front. Luke knew he had drunk too much and he breathed in the night air deeply.

'I was at your new house in the Kambos last week,' said Fiorenza, who had largely been responsible for its decoration. 'I see you have rooms prepared for guests. Are you expecting anyone?'

Luke wondered at the direction her mind was taking and whether it was into territory new to them both. He breathed in again.

'Yes,' he said guardedly. 'Or rather, no. I have prepared rooms for guests but am not expecting anyone soon. Perhaps in the future.' He was trying hard to avoid her gaze.

'Are they for Anna? For your children together?' asked Fiorenza softly.

Luke didn't answer and the silence between them lasted for many minutes. Two arcs of silver rose and fell above the surface of the lake before either spoke again. Luke wondered if its water could possibly be as deep as the unspoken understanding between them, or its banks as steep.

'Where is she?' asked Fiorenza at last, gently.

'I don't know,' replied Luke. 'Still in Monemvasia, I suppose.'

'Why not go there and get her then?'

'Because they also hold my mother. It would be too dangerous.'

Luke threw the stone and the lake opened and shivered and closed again and no fishes rose for a while.

'Is she the only one you've ever loved?' asked Fiorenza.

'Yes.'

'The only one you've ever desired?'

'No.'

Now she turned to him and smiled and her face was in shadow except for her eyes which were two moons. 'That is good.'

She paused and then got to her feet. 'Now we must return to the village. It's nearly dawn.'

Very early next morning Luke and Fiorenza rode out, alone, to the new port of Limenas, which was an hour's gentle ride to the north. Longo and Barbi had left at dawn for Chora and Dimitri was presumably still abed and engaged as he should be.

The fields around the village and the mastic groves beyond were deserted and would remain so until the effects of the wine and souma had been argued away. The only sounds were birdsong and the bells of animals, the occasional cry of a rising partridge and the steady clop of their hooves on the earth. The smell of mastic had risen with the first heat from the land and with it came the scent of crushed myrtle and narcissus as the sun drew all living things towards its energy. Luke felt happy to be alive.

Fiorenza hadn't spoken since mounting her horse and her face was difficult to read behind the half-veil she wore against the dust. For Luke, the silence was welcome as it gave him the leisure to study the trees.

They seemed well tended and their ash-coloured bark had the five or six incisions, or *kenties*, low in the trunk that would allow collection of resin until October. He stopped his horse

319

next to one with a lighter bark and was frowning as he dismounted.

'What's wrong?' enquired Fiorenza from her saddle.

Luke was kneeling in front of the tree and peering at one of the incisions. 'This tree is too young to be tapped,' he said, pointing at the cut. 'Look, you can see that they've reached the bone of the tree. It's a clumsy cut. We've told them again and again that hurting the younger trees will reduce their yields.'

He sighed with frustration and picked a piece of crystallised resin the shape of a tiny pear from the circle of clay around the tree. 'This should be pale yellow or green, not white,' he said cupping the crystal in his palm and showing it to Fiorenza.

'Give it to me,' she said, leaning forward. She studied the rough, coagulated shape in her hand and began to scrape away some of the earth and clay. Free of dirt, it was still opaque and Fiorenza held it up to the sun and turned it this way and that. 'It's beautiful as it is,' she murmured. 'I shall make a necklace of it.'

'You won't,' laughed Luke. 'The penalty for theft is removal of a nose or ear, and Marchese would never forgive me if you lost those.'

'Your idea? It seems fierce.'

'Dimitri's idea. He's come to realise that this mastic just may be worth its weight in gold.' Luke wiped the earth from his hands on the sides of his doublet and remounted, waving flies from his horse's neck as he did so. 'But it will be worth even more if we can prove its use as a dye fixative.'

'A dye fixative?' asked Fiorenza. 'Like alum?'

'Like alum,' said Luke, and kicked his mount into a trot.

*　　　*　　　*

320

An hour later they were sitting on their horses on a hill over-looking the new, and still largely unbuilt, port of Limenas. It was currently made up of two large warehouses with some quays and jetties, all under construction, which stood on the flat ground at the head of a long, enclosed bay. The water was deep here and, with its natural leeward protection, the port could shelter large numbers of ships of any size and would, hoped Luke, eventually be the main place of export for his mastic.

A single square-rigged cog was being unloaded at one of the quays, which surprised Luke, who'd not believed the port yet open to business. A dark shape was in the water beside it with two smaller shapes on either side.

'Is that a horse?' he asked.

'Yes, it looks like one,' said Fiorenza, shielding her eyes from the sun with her hand.

'What's it doing in the water? I think it's coming ashore from that boat. There are men in the water with it.'

'Shall we go and look?' suggested Fiorenza and she put her heels to the side of her mare and started down the hill. Soon they were cantering across the levels towards two men who had emerged with the horse from the water and were, more or less, nude.

But as they got closer, it was only the horse that Luke saw. It was a magnificent stallion of perhaps fifteen hands and blacker than the deepest shade of darkness. It had a powerful neck that curved into a head held high, its mane clamped to it like seaweed. Beneath was a broad chest that shone with sea and muscle as the animal moved in its fear. Its legs ended in socks white as snow. Luke was transfixed.

'What is he?' he asked the older of the men, who was hurrying into a pair of cotton breeches.

But the man didn't answer and Fiorenza, looking up at the arms of the Kingdom of Seville and Leon which were emblazoned on the ship's pennant, said, 'They're from Spain.'

But one of them had understood. The younger man bowed low to the Princess, straightened and said in Greek: 'It is the Horse of Kings, Sir. The Cartujano in our tongue.'

'Cartujano?' asked Luke, dismounting. 'What is that? Is it a breed?'

'It is the horse of Al-Andalus,' said the man, 'and it is the great-grandson of Esclavo. It has been bred by monks, the Carthusians of the monastery of Cazalla in the foothills of the Sierra Morena. It is where we are from.'

'You're monks?' asked Luke, walking over to the horse and taking its big head with slow and practised gentleness in one hand while stroking its neck with the other.

The young man laughed and then said something to his companion and they both bowed from the waist so that two globes of sunburnt flesh appeared before Luke like pomegranates.

'Monks indeed,' said Luke. 'What is Esclavo, Father?'

Fiorenza answered. 'Esclavo was the foundation stallion. You can tell from the horns on his head.' She smiled and took his hand. 'Happy birthday, Luke.'

The horns turned out to be low protruberances of bone behind the horse's ears which, like the warts beneath its tail and the whorls of white hair on its rump, confirmed its Esclavo provenance. Asked to name him, Luke in his joyous bewilderment had chosen the one he already had: Norillo. It seemed appropriate.

Luke had hardly waited to thank the monks or Fiorenza before leading the horse away to the shade of a nearby tree to make its acquaintance in the way he knew best. The monks watched how the animal became still as Luke talked quietly into its ear, how its high head fell to nuzzle Luke's hair and face and how, eventually, it allowed Luke to saddle and bridle it with leather that still dripped with the sweat of another horse. Then he was on Norillo's back and patting the huge neck with his palm.

Fiorenza turned to the two monks.

'Thank you, Fathers. You have brought a horse from the sea worthy of one who will understand it like no other. Please convey my thanks to His Majesty.' Then she climbed on to her mare and, with the cry of the hunt, smacked its rear with the flat of her hand and sprang into the gallop.

The rest of the day passed as a blur of passing landscape. Leaving the juvenile port of Limenas behind, Luke and Fiorenza raced each other up the coastline with all the speed that the terrain would allow. Norillo turned out to have a balance and instinct far in advance of his three years and his reaction to even the subtlest instruction was instantaneous. Luke looked down at the ears, alert as antennae, and at the mass of black, glossy mane that submerged the proof of special parentage. He felt the muscle moving beneath him and a joy he hadn't experienced since Eskalon.

At midday they stopped by a windmill at a point that overlooked the little island of Nisaki where stood a chapel that sailors used both as a place of worship and a lighthouse. A month before, Luke had built a stone beacon next to the church which, along with a chain of others along the coast, would be lit in times of danger. Now there was no flame apart from the reflection of the sun on the sea and the tiles of the chapel roof and they ate a lunch of bread and cheese and melon in the shade of the windmill's white walls and talked, languidly, of horses.

Afterwards they slept for a while until Luke was awakened by the wet, puckered lips of a big head that leant down to him with the shyness of early friendship. Luke opened his eyes.

'Norillo!' he laughed. 'You want to go on. Of course you do.' He reached up and scratched the soft, velvety pad of the nose and then in the hollow beneath the jaw. The horse snorted and blew and tossed his head high in his impatience to be off.

'I think the message is plain,' came the voice of Fiorenza who was sitting, back against the windmill. She had been watching Luke sleep.

Luke rose to his feet and helped Fiorenza to hers. He tightened the horses' girths and held out cupped hands for her to mount. Then he swung into his saddle and broke into a gentle canter down the hill in the direction of the coastal track.

The afternoon was drawing to a close when they finally reined in their exhausted horses at the top of Cape Pari. Although no breath disturbed a hair of their heads, there was wind out on the sea before them, and the carpet of waves was patched with white as its fingers passed over it. Luke had seen dolphins here and, once, the gigantic mass of a whale. Now only fishing boats sat like fat, gaudy women with nets spread like skirts. Fiorenza sighed with contentment and leant back in her saddle.

'Trebizond,' she whispered.

'Is that where you think of when you look at the sea?' asked Luke.

'Sometimes. When I'm happy.'

Luke looked at her happiness and said, 'We've talked of everywhere in the world except Trebizond. Why is that?'

'Because to think of it in any mood less perfect than this makes me miss it.'

'So can we talk of it now?'

'If you like. But not here. Not in view of the sea.'

They turned their horses away and walked them, side by side, through a field strewn with poppies that fell gently to a thickly wooded valley. Once amongst the trees, the shock of sudden shadow left them both blinded for a moment, and the cool beneath the canopy of luminous leaves, green as if painted on glass, made them shiver. Here were ancient oaks with gnarled and bulbous branches that twisted their limbs in dark embrace like widows at a funeral. As their eyes adjusted to the gloom, they could see that they were riding on a thick carpet of fern and moss tattooed by the shifting light above them.

Further on, the gradient of the slope steepened so that they were riding into a deep ravine, at the bottom of which could be heard the rush and gurgle of a stream. As they drew closer, their horses rocking from side to side as they placed hooves amidst the pebbles of the track, they could see that the stream had high banks that were swathed in sunshine. At their end was a waterfall, its glottal sound spreading down the valley like organ chords.

Closer, where the stream gathered into pools and the banks were lower and sunlit and dotted with flowers, there were butterflies that danced in and out of the light like child ballerinas. It was a place of overwhelming beauty and Luke knew that Fiorenza had come here before.

They tethered their horses in the shade of the trees and walked out into the sunshine amidst the butterflies to sit by the side of the stream. There was a fungoid smell of earth and leaves and hidden flowers and something sweeter that must be attracting the butterflies.

'Tell me about Trebizond,' said Luke, lying back on the warm grass with his hands cradling his head. A dragonfly fanned its haphazard way through the ferns and he stretched his toes towards it.

'Ah, Trebizond,' said Fiorenza. She seemed lost in a memory and a faint smile lifted the corner of her lips and deepened her dimples into tiny dots of shadow. 'There are three jewels remaining in the imperial crown of Byzantium,' she said, 'and they are Constantinople, Mistra and Trebizond. And much the finest is Trebizond.'

She paused to pick yellow verbena from the ground beside her, crushing it to powder between her fingers and lifting them to her nose.

'Imagine a city of marble and gold rising in its own amphi-theatre to look out over a sea called Black but which is in fact bluer than lapis lazuli,' she murmured. 'Imagine it built on a table of rock which sits in front of pine-forested mountains that march inland for fifty miles. Imagine deep, wooded ravines either side that plunge to boiling cataracts, fed by springs from those mountains. Imagine walls of the purest white within which are palaces and orchards and temples and libraries and baths and everything that provides comfort for the mind and body. And imagine the smell of incense mixed with myrtle and citrus fruit and musk, and imagine it with you every day of your life.'

Luke's eyes were closed. 'I can imagine.'

'Then you are in Trebizond,' said Fiorenza.

And when she said that, Luke saw a man and woman seated on backless ivory thrones within a palace, perched high as an

326

eagle's nest, where every window and terrace looked out over golden domes and the greens and blues of forest, mountain and sea and the speckled verdigris of twin gorges full of tumbling water and birdsong. He saw, standing beside them, three women who looked like Fiorenza holding hands and waiting for something.

'I was the lucky one,' said Fiorenza. 'I was niece to the Megas Komnenos, the Basileus Alexios III, Emperor and Autocrat of the Entire East. Had I been his daughter, I would have been married to a khan or emir that threatened our frontiers. The Komnenoi are famed for their beautiful daughters and use them as coinage to buy peace with local barbarians.'

'And why is Trebizond so rich?' he asked.

'Why? Because much of the silk and spices that end up in the markets of Venice, Florence or Bruges go through Trebizond. And the Basileus takes his cut every time.'

'Could we sell our mastic there?'

'Better than that,' replied Fiorenza, gently rubbing pollen from her fingers. 'From Trebizond, you could sell it across the entire East. The caravans that come over the mountains have ten thousand camels in them and stretch for fifteen miles. They could certainly manage some mastic on their way home.'

Luke opened his eyes and saw his dragonfly engaged in desultory dance with another of its species above a rash of pink clover. It hummed above the agreeable burble of the stream and the music of the woman by his side who spoke of fabulous things.

'And alum?'

She glanced at him.

'You didn't mention alum,' said Luke. He rolled on to his side and rested his cheek on his palm to look at the Princess from Trebizond. He said, as if reading from a report, 'Trebizond also exports alum. A great deal of alum. Fourteen thousand *cantara* from the quarries at Karahissar every year, and its quality almost matches Phocaea's. The monopoly belongs to Venice, who snatched it from the Genoese using bribery and threat. But it's expensive because it takes longer to mine and bring over the Kerasous mountains and because the Basileus imposes high rates of duty.'

'You are well informed,' said Fiorenza, smiling.

Luke dipped his head to the compliment. 'And the price of alum is soaring because we can't get ours off our island and the Venetians can't get theirs through the blockade at Constantinople.' He paused. 'Which is why we must find ships.' He rolled on to his back. 'Or I suppose we could make it irrelevant.'

'Irrelevant?'

'What if mastic does the same thing as alum? It's certainly cheaper to produce. What then?'

Fiorenza smiled and studied the tips of her fingers, smudged with dust. 'Then my uncle would become very nervous.'

'Nervous?'

She blew the dust with the lightest of breaths so that it rose in a tiny cloud and vanished. 'Why do you think the Turks have let his tiny empire survive so long? Do you know how big his army is?'

Luke shook his head.

'Four thousand men. My uncle has survived because of the beauty of his daughters and the tribute he pays into the Sultan's coffers. Tribute from alum.'

They were silent after that, both thinking of similar things, both staring at the ground.

'What makes you think it can fix dye?' she asked at last.

'Benedo has been working on it. He thinks it might. It needs to be tested.' Luke looked up. 'Like your loyalties, Fiorenza,' he added quietly. 'Are they not tested? For Chios's gain would seem Trebizond's loss.'

Fiorenza's frown was temporary and, magically, turned into something else. She laughed. 'My loyalty is untested, Luke. It is entirely to my lord Longo.'

Luke rose. 'Then we should drink to it. Did we finish the wine at lunch?'

'I have more in the saddlebag. Lie down. I will bring it to you.'

Luke obeyed and closed his eyes. The late-afternoon sun brought forth golden dots that pulsed to the rhythm of his heart.

Fiorenza poured wine and the conversation turned, like the day, from the clear to the unclear and from the seen to the unseen. It was a conversation about love and allegiance and loyalty and about all the things that were invisible and in question between them. It flowed and divided like the stream beside them and its sound was often lost in the noise of water and the first cicadas as they picked up the song of the approaching night.

Luke had not tasted wine so good or so strong in his life before. Its taste filled his mouth and then his senses, one by one, so that he felt light-headed, with a strange tingling in his limbs. Fiorenza talked on and he tried to listen but something else was speaking to him. Her voice was an infusion of desire into his very soul and he felt alive with need.

Then it was night and she had stopped speaking and was regarding him with some calculation and her dress seemed to have slipped at the shoulder. Luke could hardly breathe.

329

'What is this place, Fiorenza?' he asked thickly. His head was swimming. 'Who else do you bring here?'

'Hush, Luke. Do not speak of such things.'

And she was next to him then and her scents were mixed with those of the grass and the river and the flawless texture of her skin was touching his and the calls of the night were muffled by the sounds she spoke into his ear.

'*My beloved is unto me . . .*' she murmured and her tongue was soft and her breath warm.

'*My beloved is unto me a cluster of camphire,*' she whispered and Luke turned his head and felt her tongue travel slowly across his cheek until it found his mouth.

Now she was lying beneath him and the masterpiece of her beauty looked up at him in its calm perfection.

'I . . . I can't,' he breathed.

'You can, Luke. And you must.'

He felt her legs open beneath him and her lips brush his and then stay there should any word escape.

You must.

CHAPTER EIGHTEEN

CHIOS, SUMMER 1396

Luke had no idea how or when the complicated business of separating their limbs had taken place, but when he awoke to sunshine and headache and deafening birdsong, Fiorenza had gone. And such was his state of bewilderment that he wondered, with some hope, if she'd ever been there at all.

But she had. Because beside him the grass was flattened and at his feet were two cups resting on their sides. He sat up and held his head in his hands and let his tongue explore the bitter residue of wine in his mouth. Then he looked carefully around him. Her mare was no longer tethered, so she was not somewhere in the valley gathering their breakfast.

She had loved him, and left.

Luke sat up and reached forward to pick up a cup. The smell from it was not entirely of wine and he examined the inside more closely. On its curved bottom, amidst the spots of pooled liquid, were gathered the smallest of white lumps. Luke put in a finger and drew it to his lips.

Mastic.

Mastic as aphrodisiac. He'd never believed it, thinking it a

331

placebo for the ravenous harem, but perhaps mixed with something other?

Luke pushed his hands through hair that still smelt of her and thought of Anna. He rose and walked unsteadily to the stream and lay down in it, gasping at the cold. He rubbed his arms and legs and cleaned between his thighs. He put his head against the flow and scratched his scalp with his fingers. And he drank until his cheeks were frozen and his teeth ached. Then he climbed on to the bank and lay in the weak sun and tried to think of what to do.

What have I done? Oh God, what have I done?

A whinny from the trees reminded him that he was not alone. Norillo was there and was nosing something on the ground: his clothes. He got up and walked over to the stallion and placed his cold cheek against the warmth of its neck.

'Norillo,' he whispered, 'where did she go?'

He stooped to his clothes and pulled them on over his still-wet body. Something remained where they'd been. It was a small phial and it was nearly full of a clear liquid. He removed the stopper and lifted it to his nose.

Mastic as aphrodisiac.

He untied the horse and began to walk back up through the trees and into the field of poppies that led to Cape Pari and where it had all begun the evening before.

He reached the top of the hill and stopped, staring out to sea.

There, sailing gracefully south, oars moving in perfect unison, was all that was left of the once-magnificent fleet of the Byzantine Empire.

Ten ships. Ten triremes flying the yellow and red of the imperial pennant, the *basilikon phlamoulon*, from their mastheads.

Ten where there had once been hundreds. If ever there was proof that the Empire was in its last days, it was surely here in these ten, lateen-rigged triremes that had rowed themselves away from the Ottoman fleet besieging Constantinople but had still managed to punch their way through the Ottoman ships encircling Chios.

Luke leapt on to the back of Norillo and shouted and waved but they were too far away to see him and the drum would anyway drown the sound of his voice. So he dug his heels into the sides of the horse and raced back down to the track in the direction of Chora.

Norillo needed little encouragement to stretch himself and it was only three hours later that Luke found himself trotting through the outlying streets of the capital towards the seafront. Word had got out that the fleet was approaching and there were excited people all around him moving in the same direction. When he reached the broad boulevard that skirted the bay, it was already thronged with citizens of every age.

Luke steered Norillo towards the castle at the north end of the bay, passing between windmills that turned their latticed blades to the breeze that crept in from the sea, and was soon riding across the moat and through the Porta Maggiore with its gaudy Giustiniani arms above.

Luke looked down and saw grass stains on his hose. He had not shaved and, despite his bathe in the stream, could still smell the scent of Fiorenza on him. The Adorno Palace was nearby and he knew that Signor Gabriele's stout wife had a fondness for him and that her husband was most probably on his estate on the Kambos. He would find fresh clothes there and tools for shaving. He turned towards it.

An elderly servant answered to his knocking and seemed

unsurprised to see him. Opening the door, he bowed as low as he was able and ushered Luke past him and into a large hall ringed with tapestries of the hunt. Its floor was of black marble and provided Luke with a clear reflection of his appearance.

'I wondered . . .' he began, but the man put his finger to his lips and beckoned him towards the stairs where a second servant was offering a glass of something that Luke didn't want to drink.

Again he tried to speak but was hushed politely and the finger pointed upstairs. It seemed there was someone asleep, or perhaps at prayer, above who was not to be disturbed, although the palace was large and on at least three levels. Luke made signs to leave but the retainer was insistent that he follow him and Luke agreed, straightening his pourpoint and checking his buttons.

At the top there was a curving balcony and several closed doors and one that was slightly ajar, and which had voices coming from the other side. The servant gestured towards it and Luke walked forward and opened the door.

The first person he saw, seated with others around a large mahogany table, was Marchese Longo. By his side, in clothes he did not recognise, sat his wife, the Princess Fiorenza of Trebizond.

The others around the table were all male and constituted a gathering of the shareholders of the Campagna Giustiniani. There were the signori of the Banca, the Campi, the Arangio families, and all the rest, and at their head sat their solid host, the elderly Gabriele Adorno.

He rose when Luke entered. 'Luke . . . a surprise,' he said bowing slightly and smiling with what seemed genuine pleasure. 'We hadn't expected you, but it is fortuitous that you have heeded the call. It is your navy that we expect at any hour to grace our harbour and we have assembled here to agree what is to be done.'

Luke realised that he'd been staring at Fiorenza. He recovered and allowed himself to be led to a chair. 'Forgive my appearance, my lords,' he said, sitting down. 'I have ridden fast.'

He looked around the table. Fiorenza was looking at him with one eyebrow raised and the ghost of a smile playing at the edges of her lips.

Gabriele Adorno nodded absently and then turned from Luke to the business of the meeting. He addressed his fellow signori.

'My friends, the galleys of the Byzantine fleet will be in our harbour by nightfall. We need to agree how we will receive them. Marchese, please.'

Longo got to his feet and walked over to where a large map of the Middle Sea had been pinned to an easel. He drew his dagger and used it as a pointer.

'The fleet has come from the port of Palea, above Monemvasia, where it has sheltered since learning that the Ottoman fleet is equipped with cannon,' he said. 'We don't know its destination but we can suppose Constantinople. The arms they carry on their decks would suggest that they mean to have another try at breaking the blockade, despite the cannon.'

He paused and his dagger travelled the map. 'Gentlemen, we Genoese have created a trading empire across the eastern Middle Sea and up into the Black Sea. Its centre has always been Constantinople, or at least our port of Pera, across the Golden Horn, and we have been a good ally to the Empire.'

He stepped back from the map and lowered his dagger. He looked at the men gathered around the table. 'But we have to acknowledge the possibility that Constantinople will fall, and may fall soon. And we have to recognise that the Turks may become a naval power to rival ourselves and Venice. They have already approached our brothers in Genoa about the possibility of us building ships for them and they'll be doing the same at the Serenissima.'

He paused and lowered his voice. 'But perhaps the worst thing we must face, gentlemen, is that we may have been backing the wrong party all these years, and the Venetians may now be backing the right one.'

Marchese walked over to the table and placed his two fists on it as he leaned forward.

'If I may put it plainly, signori,' he said softly, looking from one to the next, 'if Constantinople falls, then next to fall will be our island and the Turks will have a ready ally in Venice. It is on this basis that we should decide whether or not to give shelter to the Byzantine navy.'

There was an uncomfortable silence around the table broken only by the asthmatic breathing of Adorno. 'But our tribute, Marchese,' he said. 'Would the Turk so readily risk such a source of revenue? The Venetians are hardly reliable.'

'No?' answered Longo. 'We've always believed that. We've always thought that only we Genoese understood the alum business which pays our tribute so handsomely. But look at Trebizond.' Here he turned briefly to Fiorenza as if she were its embodiment. 'The Venetians cheated us out of the alum monopoly from the mines at Karahissar and have learnt how to ship and trade it from Trebizond. They could do the same here. Why not?'

Still none of the signori spoke.

'So, I ask again: are we about to antagonise the Turk by revictualling the navy of its enemy?'

Then Zacco Banca spoke. 'We may not be able to pay the tribute at all if we can't ship our alum. Remember, the Turkish pirates captured three of our round ships last month and another two last week. Now we have this blockade and no way of getting to our markets in the west.'

'Indeed,' said Giovanni Campi. 'So what, Marchese, are you proposing that we do?'

'I don't see we have any choice, my lords,' he said quietly. 'I fear we must refuse entry to this fleet.'

Fiorenza said softly, 'My lord, this is unworthy.'

Longo gazed down at his wife and there was love and sadness in his eyes. 'Unworthy? Yes, lady, it is unworthy. But what else would you have us do? This Empire is doomed and our duty must be to Genoa. To Chios. To ourselves and' –he glanced at Luke – 'to our children.'

The sadness in Marchese Longo's eyes was in those of every other one of the Genoese sitting around the table and the noises of the city outside were suddenly inside the room amidst the long silence. A decision had been made about loyalties and honour and every one of the signori wanted to be somewhere where they might better convince themselves that it had been the right one.

Then Luke spoke. 'There is another way.'

The heads turned to him with impatience. The difficult decision had been made. And he was not one of them, not of the Campagna Giustiniani.

'Let Luke speak,' said Fiorenza. 'It is his island too.'

Longo looked from his wife to Luke. 'By all means speak, Luke,' he said and sat down.

Luke rose to his feet and walked the length of the table until he reached Fiorenza and the map. 'My lords,' he began, 'I have lived amongst you now for some time. You have been kind to me and I hope that I've done you some service in return. I know you to be worthy men and that any decision you make today will be as honourable as the times allow. But there is another way, which will serve all parties, I believe.'

'Another way?' asked Longo.

'Yes,' said Luke. 'What if the fleet is, in fact, admitted to the harbour here at Chora, and the Megas Doux and his captains received with all the pomp we can muster? What if we then offer them an alternative as to where they might go next? The Empire needs two things to survive: success for the crusade that is assembling in the west, and money. What if we persuade the Megas Doux to instead take his ships to Venice, and to go with their holds full of our alum? From Venice they can put themselves at the disposal of the Duke of Burgundy's crusade and the Empire can take a generous share of the proceeds from the alum.'

There were frowns on every face around the table now, except that of Fiorenza. Gabriele Adorno's frown was the darkest of all.

'But, Luke,' he said, 'I can think of at least two reasons why this is a bad idea. First, why would we want to lose profit on our alum? Second, why would the Turk be any less annoyed with us if the fleet goes to support the crusade being sent against them?'

'My lord,' Luke went on, 'surely it's better to make *some* profit on our alum rather than the none we'll make if it rots in our warehouses here? In former times you might have expected help from other Genoese carriers, but they are all in the Black Sea and cannot get past Constantinople.'

'All right,' said Longo, 'but what of Gabriele's second point? Surely the Turk will punish us for giving the fleet shelter?'

'Possibly,' acceded Luke, 'but he may punish us more for not giving him his tribute. And we can only do that if we sell the alum which, you must be aware, is reaching record prices since the Venetian convoys from Trebizond can't get through.'

Now the first of the nods began and, Luke was pleased to see, it came from Longo, who said, 'Am I right in assuming your mastic plays a part in this somewhere?'

Luke nodded. 'Yes, it does. We've discovered that the mastic works well as a sealant for wounds. Very useful for an army. It may even do what alum does. It will fetch a good price in Venice.'

The nods were universal now. No matter how hard the signori poked at it, the plan seemed sound – even brilliant. It would allow them to do what they most desperately wanted to do before knowing the outcome of the impending crusade: remain neutral.

Marchese Longo rose. 'Let us prepare ourselves for the Megas Doux then.'

What Luke knew, Fiorenza suspected and the signori didn't, was that the Megas Doux had never had any intention of going to Constantinople. It had always been his plan, indeed his orders, to go to Chios and then on to Venice and the support of the Crusade.

Standing at the top of the long ramp down to the sea, Luke was studying the impressive heavy artillery on board the ten galleys that had dropped anchor in the bay. He smiled in anticipation of meeting certain members of the party now being rowed towards him in the best of the campagna's barges. He thought of that meeting with Plethon all those months ago.

The Venetians only listen to money and that's the one thing that the Empire doesn't have.

The barge was a gilded affair and, curiously, modelled on the Venetian version. It had eight oarsmen to a side, all in Giustiniani colours, and a low silk awning at the back beneath which the Megas Doux and his entourage would be sitting in great comfort. Above the tall rudder flew two flags, those of the Campagna Giustiniani and the Empire. The flag of the Empire was on top.

A pale moon had risen above the bay and the sun was setting in a riot of red and orange that threw its colour across the water like spilt paint. A dozen ducks rose and arranged themselves in formation and headed noisily inland and everywhere was the low burble of excited talk. This was an event not to be missed by the people of Chios. Or Scio.

'They're taking their time,' said Longo irritably, who stood beside Luke dressed in magnificent black and gold figured silk.

Luke stared out across the water. He would have to find the right moment to tell them of his decision to leave, although he suspected that one of them, at least, already knew it. He looked at Fiorenza and saw that she was entirely composed. She was dressed in the Trapezuntine, rather than Genoese, style, in a high-necked, narrow gown of pale cream damask with buttons of embroidered silver at its front. The cloth glowed slightly in the last light of the sun and its long, fluted sleeves half covered her folded hands, corded with rings. Her expression was unreadable.

Soon the barge was close to the quay and its oars were in the air and a trumpet sounded amidst the banners behind. The reception party readied itself to receive the Admiral of the Byzantine fleet.

The Megas Doux turned out to be a small man of middle age weighed down by cuirass and gold and, perhaps, the responsibility of preserving his little fleet. Nevertheless, he was a man of energy and he leapt nimbly from barge to quay and the welcome of the twelve signori of Scio.

But Luke hardly glanced at him, or at the ten captains that followed him. Instead he looked into the dark area below the awning for its other passengers. Then there they were, emerging one by one and dressed as he'd never seen them before.

Matthew, Nikolas and Arcadius. All in the uniform of the Varangian Guard.

It was two years since he'd seen them last and the tread of seasons seemed to have left little imprint. Matthew had a new beard, a thin thing of no direction, while Arcadius was stouter and limping. Luke had seen him in boats before and suspected a heavy wave. Nikko, finally, had less hair and seemed to be going the way of the entirely bald David. But all were ruddy-cheeked and filled their fathers' Varangian armour to an inch.

Luke was behind the reception line, watching them search the crowd for him and whisper to each other. The Admiral and his captains had been properly greeted and were now moving slowly up the ramp towards the gates, led by Longo and two Genoese soldiers with flambeaux held high.

'What took you so long?'

'Luke!' cried Nikolas, spinning around.

'And what are you wearing?' asked Luke, stepping back to take in the Varangian splendour. 'They *gave* you those?'

Then the four of them were laughing and huddled together in a circular embrace and were boys again. And as they laughed and jostled each other, Luke felt a wave of love and memory break over him. They were boys without brothers who were

341

better brothers than any he knew. They had shared stories and girls and blows on the training ground since they'd learnt to walk. They had a friendship that was higher than mountains and deeper than oceans and were any one of them to call out in need, be it only a whisper, it would be heard by the rest.

Luke remembered a rain-lashed jetty and a girl he'd meant to escape with. A girl they'd yet to mention. Did he dare? Not yet.

'So you delivered the message?'

'The Admiral didn't think twice,' said Matthew happily.

'And the holds are empty?'

'You can put in as much alum as you want, and there will still be room for all your money. I hear you're rich.'

'Not yet, but I'm practising,' said Luke, still whispering. He paused. 'But you've not told me of Anna. Where is Anna?'

The jostling stopped.

'We don't know,' said Nikolas. 'She went with Suleyman. It was part of the deal struck by Zoe to save our lives and to let Rachel leave the palace and go home. She's probably at the camp at Constantinople.'

'With Suleyman?'

There was silence in the huddle and Matthew was the one to break free. He stood in front of Luke and held his friend's arms above the elbows. It was almost dark now, the flambeaux having gone with the signori, and they were enveloped by the deep shadow of the citadel wall.

'You should know,' he said quietly, 'that Prince Suleyman is enamoured of her. I don't know why . . . something to do with their first meeting at Mistra. And I don't know if he's even touched her yet. If he has it will have been against her will, you can be sure.'

Luke shook his head, unbelieving.

Anna at Constantinople. With Suleyman?

'I shall go and get her,' he said.

But Matthew shook his head. 'From the Sultan's camp? That's impossible. You'd be killed.'

'I have to try! What else can I do?'

A voice came from the shadows. 'You can go to Venice, Luke. As you intended.'

Luke turned and saw the woman who, last night, had lain beneath him. Now she was half in shadow and that part of her face lit by the moon was solemn. She moved away towards the gate and Luke followed her.

'That was prettily done, Luke,' she said softly when they were beyond the hearing of the Varangians. 'Getting a message to the Admiral via your friends. You knew the fleet was going to Venice anyway?'

Luke was silent.

'What would Marchese say if he knew you were deliberately diverting Giustiniani funds to aid the Empire?'

'He would approve,' answered Luke. 'He is a good man. And a wise one.'

'And would he approve of what happened last night?' she asked.

'No. He loves you.'

'And I him.'

'So why . . . ?' asked Luke.

'Can't you guess?' The Princess from Trebizond reached up and put a soft hand to Luke's cheek and let her thumb gently stroke its curve. There were tears in her eyes. 'You've been used, Luke, yes. And you will hate me now and forgive me later.

'So that's why you must go. You must go to forget and, I

343

hope, to forgive. You must go to Venice where Plethon awaits you. He'll need you there to sign over to the Empire your profits from the mastic, as I know you've determined to do. And then you'll go to the crusade with your friends and you'll win. And when you come back, you'll bring Anna and you'll be rich, for the signori have, this afternoon, agreed to make you one of their number.' She paused. 'And, God willing, you might even greet our son.'

Then the Princess from Trebizond stood on her tiptoes to kiss him on both cheeks.

'You are *Escrivo*, Luke,' she said, and turned to go.

Three days later, Luke was standing on the stern deck of a trireme galley as it rowed to the beat of a drum out of the port of Limenas. The wind was boisterous under a leaden sky and his hair and cloak snapped in the blow as he watched the island of Chios, his home for two years, blur into distance.

Next to him stood the captain, his hand raised to deliver the order for the oars to be shipped and the two giant lateen sails raised. Luke looked up beyond the mast basket and saw the pennants of Byzantium stretch and buckle and point back towards the island. Towards Fiorenza.

Then the order was shouted and carried through the ship by others and the galley shuddered as the sails broke out and bellied, and 170 rowers, three to a bench, bent over their oars in relief. Luke looked down the long central gangway to the marine crossbowmen gathered on the fighting-stage of the prow next to a single catapult. He thought, without connection, of Eskalon. This galley was a *katergon* rather than a *taride* and therefore not adapted to carry horses. He'd had to leave

Norillo behind and he'd been surprised by how little it had mattered to him.

Eskalon. Are you somewhere in this world?

Luke looked out at the grey expanse of sea, at the curve of the waves as they rose, white-tipped, in a rising wind and pounded the sides of the ship. They were alone in this sea, the other galleys having left, with his friends aboard them, from Chora two days before. Nine galleys with holds crammed with alum while his was filled with bales of mastic. All were headed for Venice.

And, as agreed with Marchese Longo all those months past, the entire profit from the sale of this first shipment from the new port of Limenas would go to Luke. He smiled.

Or to the Empire.

Luke knew that Plethon would be in Venice. He'd worked with Benedo to create a compound of mastic and other elements that might or might not work as a dye fixative. They'd know for sure in Venice since it was the colour capital of the world. If it did, then the profits could be enormous and Plethon would know how best to use them to the Empire's advantage.

The reunion with his three friends had been, at least in part, joyous. He'd learned that his mother, while still a prisoner, was now at least imprisoned in her home. He'd make sure that a small part of the profit from the mastic would somehow get to her. He'd learned that Monemvasia was little changed by the presence of a regiment of janissaries within its walls and that the little city on the edge of the sea continued to prosper as it had always done. But over everything had hung the cloud of Fiorenza and what he'd done with her, and of Anna, whom he'd betrayed.

345

Anna who was now with Suleyman.

Luke shivered and drew the cloak around him.

'Sad to leave?'

It was the captain who'd spoken and Luke turned to a handsome man of middle age who was watching the sails and testing the tension of a stay. He didn't have the air of a sailor, being neat in quilted surcoat beneath his cloak. His boots were long, expensive and wet.

'I was asking myself the same question,' replied Luke.

A sudden surge caused the galley to lurch and Luke took hold of the deck rail. Rain had begun to fall in bursts, carried by the gusting wind, driving his cloak against his legs. 'Should we go closer to the shore?' he asked.

The man shrugged. 'There is no shore. It's all open sea from here to the straits between Negroponte and Andros. But this is a good south-westerly and it will take us there in two days.'

'And if the wind drops?'

'Then we row. At twenty strokes a minute, we can cover six miles in a day. We'll be home in two weeks.'

'Home?'

'I am Venetian, can't you tell? Or did you miss the horns?'

Luke smiled. He said, 'We have two weeks together. Why don't we begin by assuming that we know nothing, good or bad, about the other? Then perhaps we will enjoy two voyages: one to Venice and another into each other's story.' He paused. 'I would like to hear yours, at least.'

The captain looked at him and his eyes were half closed against the rain. Water rolled down his cheek and collected in a fold in the coat. 'I have some good wine in the *scosagna*. We can't do more here. Let's go below.'

Inside the cabin it was warm and cushioned and there was

a fug that came from a wood-burning stove, which was slightly smoking. Light was diffused through small windows and a latticed lantern had been lit which swung heavily in the swell. Several good pieces of furniture occupied the low space that had the musky air of a seraglio. A flask of wine and several tin cups sat on a battered oak chest.

Luke walked in and removed his cloak, then his boots, and accepted a cup. He sank into deep, tassled cushions.

'You have two questions in your mind,' began the captain after emptying his cup in one gulp and wiping his beard on a sleeve. 'First: why is a Venetian *sopracomito* in the employ of your empire, and second, why is Venice apparently supporting both sides in this impending crusade? Am I right?' As he spoke he removed one of his gloves, finger by finger, to reveal long and delicate hands that might have belonged to a harpsichord-master.

'More or less,' said Luke.

'Well, it is the circumstances which answer them,' said the captain. 'But first, names. Mine is Niccolò di Vetriano, Knight of the Order of San Marco.'

'And mine Luke Magoris, born in Monemvasia and latterly of the island of Chios.'

They nodded to each other and Luke raised his cup from his cushion. So this was a Venetian nobleman. He was different in tone from the preposterous Rufio, but was he different in morals? Was each Venetian as venal as the next?

The captain studied him through narrowed eyes as he removed his other glove with his teeth and unbuckled the belt that held his *cinquadea* short sword at his hip. Then he unbuttoned the front of his surcoat and poured himself some more wine. He sat on a low stool and leaned forward from the waist.

347

'So, why is a Venetian sailing this ship?' he went on. 'Why do Byzantium and Venice have bad blood between them? Questions.' He paused. 'Another question. Is it not usual for a father and son to both love and hate each other at the same time as one takes over from the other? Especially if they are alike?'

The Venetian drank more wine. 'So it's the same with Byzantium and Venice. Everything we have, we have from you. Our clothes, our titles, our buildings, our rituals. Even our horses. The four horses on top of our Cathedral of San Marco? They came from your Hippodrome. We owe you everything, yet we can no longer support you in your old age. We are not a good child.'

Luke was silent, swaying with the movement of the ship. It was rolling heavily now and he could hear the sounds of a sail being lowered outside.

'Then there's the thorny issue of the Crusade. Imagine. We ferried the robbers and rapists to your walls and then demanded money to pass you by. And when you couldn't pay, our blind doge led them over the walls. Even your fierce Varangians couldn't stop the slaughter that night. You still hate us for that and you're right to.'

A large wave made the boat heel over and some wine lost itself in the rich reds of the carpet.

'That night we took away your empire and created our own. A third of all your territories went to us. We took all your islands and trading posts so that we could dominate the trade of the Middle Sea. We snapped up your colonies on the cheap. We bought Crete for thirty pounds of gold. Have you seen the Sposalizio?'

Luke shook his head.

'It's the ceremony of our marriage to the sea. Every year we throw a ring into the lagoon and everyone cheers. We got that from you, too. So why don't you do it any more? Because you have ten galleys and we have two hundred. Because you don't have any sea left.'

The captain lifted his short sword and placed it on a chest from where it slid noisily to the floor with the next roll. He trapped it with his foot.

'So now there are some new robbers and rapists who wear turbans and fight with swords that aren't straight. And they're not even Christian. But that hasn't stopped us from plotting with them to bring about your final downfall. From which, of course, we expect to do well.'

He paused again. 'But we've come up against a problem. These new robbers in their turbans seem to want boats. This isn't as it should be; they were always *gazis* of the steppe, not mariners. *We* are the mariners. And doesn't that mean that they can now reach all those islands and trading posts? Suddenly we feel nostalgia for our father's tiresome rituals and old-fashioned manners.'

He looked directly at Luke. 'So now we talk to the Duke of Burgundy about his crusade. But *sotto voce*, of course.'

'While you make cannon for the Turk,' said Luke. 'Cannon big enough to bring down Constantinople's walls.'

'Do we?'

'You know you do. And the Turk has promised you Chios in return.' Luke paused in his turn. 'What do you know of this crusade?'

'Only that it may fail,' said the Venetian. He didn't sound particularly disappointed. 'There's no unified leadership,' he went on, 'and the Comte de Nevers is wasting his time jousting with the German princes instead of hurrying to Buda to join up with the Hungarian army. The crusaders may be the flower of French and Burgundian chivalry but they're too vain, too complacent and, worst of all, are giving Bayezid time to prepare. Are you determined to join it?'

Luke nodded again. 'I'm a Varangian,' he said simply. 'I can be useful.'

'I don't doubt that. Your three friends were on my galley on the way to Chios. I saw them practise with their axes. They are fine fighters.'

'We were taught well,' said Luke, and then added pointedly, 'and we listened to our fathers.' He paused. 'So what will Venice do for this crusade? *Sotto voce*.'

The captain shrugged. 'I dare say we will carry provisions up into the Black Sea and sail down the Danube to meet the army. Perhaps we will give them your mastic for their wounds.'

That halted the conversation.

'You will get a good price for it,' said the Venetian, 'especially if it fixes dye as well.'

Luke frowned. How had he known this? But then, how could he not? The compound had been put in separate jars and Limenas was a place of gossip. He changed the subject. 'The Christian army will be large. France, Burgundy, Hungary, Germany, Austria and the Knights Hospitaller. An alliance like this has never been seen before. The Turks will be stopped.'

Di Vetriano managed a smile but it was bleak. 'Perhaps, perhaps. I hope so.'

'So that's Venice. What about you?' asked Luke.

'I am doing penance,' said the captain sourly.

'Penance? Penance for what?'

'I was the captain of a great galley once,' said the Venetian.

'It was, perhaps, the finest *galera* ever to come out of the Arsenale. Four banks of oars; four hundred rowers. It could cover eighty miles in a day and turn back to front on a ducat. Magnificent.'

Luke had seen the great galleys of Venice off Monemvasia. The entire population turned out to watch them come in. It was one of the greatest spectacles on earth.

'Mine was called the *Vetriana*. Did you know that all sopra-comiti call their ships by the female version of their name? It was used for all our important dealings with the Turk,' he went on. 'I spent much of my time sailing between Venice and Edirne, ferrying men to meetings to discuss new ways to dismember your empire. I got to know the Sultan's court well.'

'So what happened?' asked Luke.

'I got carried away. I learnt their language and made friends with a eunuch in the harem, bribed him to let me see inside it. Just see, that was all. But we were caught and he was stran-gled with a bowstring and I was demoted. Now I am on secondment to your empire.'

'And what did you learn at the court of Bayezid?'

The Italian looked up slowly. 'That the Sultan is a man of strange desires which are too often frustrated by toothache.' He smiled. 'So Chios is spared for now. Because of a man who can fill holes.'

The Venetian was yawning now, showing unfilled teeth between lips half hidden by a fringe of tailored beard. 'You probably know him.'

Luke didn't answer because it hadn't been a question. He felt dog-tired and the effects of the wine were creeping over him. The cushions beneath were soft and there was a skin on the floor that would cover him. He lowered his head on to velvet and closed his eyes.

It was sometime after dawn on the second day that he and the captain were awoken by the news that two Saracen galleys were approaching from the Negroponte Straits.

'What are they flying?' asked di Vetriano, climbing the stairs to the aft-deck and rubbing his eyes.

'No crescent, lord,' said the boatswain. 'Anyway, the Sultan's fleet is at either Constantinople or Chios.'

'Mamelukes?'

'That or corsairs, lord. Shall I run for shore?'

'Do we have time? I doubt it.' The captain had, by now, buckled on his cuirass. He turned to Luke. 'There's armour in that chest,' he said. 'Put it on and join me on deck.'

Luke emerged on to the deck to see the rowers pulling hard for the shore and the marines, all armoured, crowding the foredeck with crossbows at the ready. Out at sea, to their front, were two Turkish galleys driving fast across the water to cut them off. It seemed likely that they'd succeed.

The ships were low, sleek and built for speed. Their sails were furled and they each had a small boat slung between mastheads crammed with bowmen. The ships' sides glittered with bright, turbaned helmets and chain mail and there was no doubt at all of their intention.

Luke was standing next to the captain. 'Isn't Negroponte Venetian?' he asked.

'It is,' said the captain. 'It seems the pirates do not respect Venetian authority.'

The two galleys were now directly ahead of them and close

enough to hail. They had stopped and a bristle of oars hung either side above the water.

Now Luke could see more. There were bombards between the soldiers at the sides, their barrels pointed downwards. And at the bow and stern were bigger cannon, aimed higher, at their rowers.

The captain swore softly at his side.

'Can we fight?' asked Luke.

'Yes, and we can be blown to bits by those cannon.'

'What do we do?'

'We see what they want.'

He hollowed his hands to shout. 'By what authority do you prevent our progress? We are under the protection of Venice and these are Venetian waters.'

At first there was no answer but something moved behind the serried ranks of men at the ship's sides. Flashes of more opulent colour appeared behind them and a small man with a pumpkin for a turban climbed the steps on to the stern deck. He looked more like an official than a soldier.

'You have one they call Luca on your ship?'

The captain lowered his loudhailer and looked at Luke. 'What do I say?' he asked.

'My name is not Luca.'

The captain looked at him without expression. Then he raised the loudhailer again. '*We have no one of that name on board!*' he shouted.

The turban rose again. 'We have cannon. You cannot win this battle. You can only drown. Give us Luca and you can go on your way.'

The captain looked at Luke. 'I don't think we have any choice.'

Luke glanced at the shore. 'I could swim,' he said. 'If they see me in the water they won't fire at you and I might just make it.'

The captain looked at the islands ahead. 'You'd never make it,' he said. Two marines had moved silently behind Luke and now stood either side of him. The captain nodded to the boatswain who turned to the ship's longboat.

And then Luke understood. This had been planned. A Venetian captain and a course set for Venetian Negroponte.

'You bastard,' he said quietly.

The captain looked unembarrassed. 'I cannot endanger my crew,' he said. 'And they have cannon.'

Niccolò di Vetriano, Knight of the Order of San Marco, had turned his back and the two marines took Luke's arms. He was led to the side and below him the small boat was being lowered into the water.

He would not join the crusade.

CHAPTER NINETEEN

CONSTANTINOPLE, SUMMER 1396

Passing the ruins of Troy by night, Luke dreamt of Achilles whose ghost travellers sometimes claimed to see stalking the shallows there.

The following day and night took him through the Dardanelles and into the Sea of Marmara and, as the first tentacles of dawn crept over the rim of the world, he found himself awake and attentive to the splash of the oars and the staggered pull of the boat as it made its way towards Constantinople.

For a while he lay still in the cabin and enjoyed the luxury of a goosedown mattress made for someone of greater consequence than he. The room was heavily perfumed by small braziers of lavendered wood and the noise outside was muffled by thick damask hangings that covered the door and windows. He was able to think clearly of the past five days when, having been relieved of his sword and armour, he'd been given freedom to move around this ship. The plump official appeared to be the only other speaker of Greek on board and had kept steadfastly to his cabin, leaving Luke to his thoughts.

And his thoughts were in turmoil. His carefully laid plan to go to Venice and sell his mastic was in ruins. But Plethon was there and knew what he wanted to do. His determination to go thence to Monemvasia to find Anna had been disrupted by the news that she was with Suleyman. But wasn't Suleyman at Constantinople conducting the siege?

That way lay hope, for Luke had guessed from the stars where they were going.

Constantinople.

Constantinople. City of the Thrice-Blessed Virgin, ex-Tabernacle on Earth of the Bride of the Lord. Once the greatest city on earth, whose wealth had shimmered in the beaten gold of its domes and the veined marble of its palaces. Constantinople. Built between two continents and two seas, frontier of both Christendom and Islam.

Constantinople: Kizil Elma, the Red Apple.

Now, as they approached it, Luke could hardly contain his excitement. He rose, put on his shirt and hose, pulled a cloak around him and walked out on to the deck. The sea around the galley was indigo and dolphins surfed its waves, chasing the oars and diving across the bows. Up ahead was a mass of land turning to orange with the new light rising in the east.

A sailor approached him with a plate of bread and salted fish and he ate hungrily. Then he knelt to splash water from a fire-bucket over his head and shoulders. He scratched his cheeks and chin, shivering beneath the wet friction of beard raked by nails.

Whatever was awaiting him could wait; he was to see the glory of Constantinople. Or what was left of it.

An hour later he was there.

A low mist was suspended above the water like a skein of spider web, its tendrils reaching into the Asian land mass and the sunlight spilling across it like dappled gold. Then its surface was ruptured by soaring walls of striped stone, with giant towers which rose even higher and on whose tops could be seen the flash of shield and spearhead.

Constantinople.

Luke held his breath and stared.

Was this the same sight seen by Siward on a dawn three centuries past as his ships swept up towards Mikligard? How wide would the tired eyes of those five hundred first Englishmen have been when they first looked upon those walls?

He was so lost in thought that the man next to him had to repeat himself.

'Do you see that tower?'

Luke turned to see the fat official leaning over the rail with one arm pointing towards the city.

'That's where the land walls join the sea walls. The land walls were built by the Emperor Theodosius and are said to be impregnable. The sea walls were where the crusaders got in two centuries ago.'

The man was short but wore a turban of such size that, upright, he might have been taller than Luke. His beard was long and manicured and moored him to the deck like an anchor. He seemed inclined to talk.

'Normally there would be quays and jetties all along these walls,' he continued, his arm sweeping across the distance, 'but of course they've destroyed them all to prevent us doing what the Venetians did.'

Luke could see nothing but mist clinging to the walls.

'The blockade has stopped any food getting to the city by sea. Look, are they not magnificent?'

They were passing the first of the Ottoman galleys, the sun

catching the shields slung over the *impavesati* parapets which protected the oarsmen. There were two bombards in the forecastle and Luke turned to the city walls to see their effect. Tiny pockmarks pitted the surface; tiny blemishes on a smooth, sun-kissed face.

'The cannon seem to have done little harm,' he remarked.

'They have hardly scarred the walls,' replied the official. 'But they have kept away your navy and prevented the Genoese bringing in supplies.' He paused and his smile broadened. 'And they have persuaded the Sultan that he needs bigger ones.'

The mist that hovered above the water was beginning to fragment and was pooled with fire. Looking down the line of towers that were now aglow and seemingly without end, Luke could see more of the Ottoman galleys at anchor, their bows towards the walls and their pennants limp on their masts. Theirs was the only vessel in movement and, as it swept on, it seemed as if all the world was watching them pass. Luke's mouth was dry.

He looked further along the walls and saw their striped surface jut out into a colonnade of grand, pillared arches dressed in white marble. There was a sea gate with two lions on guard either side. A church's dome floated above like a papal hat.

'That is the Boukoleon Palace,' said his companion, 'used by the Latin emperors while they were here. Now a ruin, I expect, like everything else.'

They had turned north and the sun was shining directly across the ship. There was no sound beyond the dip of oars and the cry of birds. Ahead of them rose the Great Palace and its tiered gardens with Cypress-spears thrust into the sky. The white curve of the Hippodrome sat at the summit upon shaded vaults, its top pitted with broken masonry.

The galley was now rounding the tip of the peninsula and there was a flash from above as the sun caught the column on which stood the bronze figure of the greatest of all the emperors, Justinian, his right hand raised and pointing to the east. By his side rose his masterpiece, the many-domed Church of Holy Wisdom, the Hagia Sophia. Luke clutched the rail and stared in wonder. He knew there to be cracks in its walls and few tiles on its roofs, but it was still one of the most magnificent sights in the world.

The rowers had seen it before and obeyed the quickened tempo of the drum. The galley lurched forward and soon they were passing Acropolis Point and the Golden Horn was opening up to their left and Luke could see the giant chain suspended just above the water between the northern walls of Constantinople and the Genoese colony of Pera, with the tall Tower of Gelata rising above its walls.

'Where are we going?' he asked, looking across at the turban.

The water was busier here and, beyond the chain, small craft were shuttling between the two shores. The sun blazed a pathway down the length of the Horn and birds rose in silhouette from its waters.

'We go north, beyond the city. To Prince Suleyman's lines.'

The following day, Luke was standing in the tent of the Sultan Bayezid's eldest son with a janissary on either side of him.

They had landed a mile north of Pera where Suleyman had pitched his tents on a hill overlooking the city. His father and the rest of the army were well to the south, strung out behind the siege works facing the Theodosian Walls. Bayezid had arrived a week earlier to join his army and his eldest son had immediately ordered his headquarters moved as far away from his father's as possible.

Since landing, Luke had been given comparative freedom to wander around the camp, although he'd never been out of sight of two janissaries who'd followed him without discretion. He'd spent much of the time just staring down at Constantinople, lost in wonder at its scale and magnificence. This city had stood for a thousand years, the eastern heir to the Roman Empire, and had repelled every attempt to take it except one. And on that night, when Armageddon itself had come to Constantinople, his royal ancestor had brought away a treasure that might still save it in this, its most perilous hour.

He'd thought about a sword that might hold an answer and was no longer with him.

Now he saw it in his captor's tent, leaning against a shield suspended from a pole. Suleyman was seated on a curved, backless throne of a width that required him to stretch out his arms as if in greeting. He was wearing a coat of gold tulips and a single thick, leather glove reaching far up his arm that was spattered with bird-droppings. Beside him, standing haughtily on a perch of ivory, sat an unhooded peregrine, chained at the ankle.

Luke studied the man in front of him with care. The heir to the Ottoman throne was a more manicured creature than he'd imagined, but that he was a man of infinite danger, Luke was in no doubt.

Suleyman, meanwhile, was regarding Luke with less interest.

'Luke Magoris. You have a friend here in the camp,' said the Prince, picking some offal from a plate and stretching his hand towards the bird. 'In fact you have two.'

Luke didn't reply.

'I would not count myself among that number, though,' he went on. 'There's not a great deal in you I can find to like.'

The peregrine got bored and turned its head almost fully about, shrugging its folded wings.

'You don't know me, Majesty,' said Luke.

'No, that's true,' murmured the Prince.

There was a pause in which Suleyman lifted the ungloved hand and the janissaries bowed and disappeared. They were alone in the tent.

Suleyman rose and went over to a table on which stood an elaborate jug.

'One of the few vices I've inherited from my father,' said the Prince, pouring and returning to his seat. He drank, watching Luke closely over the rim of the cup. 'Now, let's see,' he went on. 'Firstly, you were on your way to join a crusade intended to crush us, not so?' He didn't wait for an answer. 'Next, you're masterminding new methods of defence on the island of Chios which have baffled our corsairs and given the islanders, alas, no further cause to rebel against the Genoese.'

Luke remained impassive.

'Finally,' said Suleyman, now looking at him with dark intensity, 'you're daring to impose yourself on someone far above your rank and currently under my protection.' He paused. 'And that, I should tell you, is by far the worst of your crimes.'

For the briefest of moments Luke felt elation. Anna was here in the camp. The emotion must have swept across his face because Suleyman's eyes flashed black, their hoods closing in menace.

'So I would like nothing more than to see you executed. But I fear that such an action would do little to foster my relationship with the Laskaris daughter. And then there is your other friend, Zoe Mamonas.' He looked down at the curling tips of his shoes. 'So, what would you do if you were me?'

'I would fight me, lord,' said Luke calmly. 'Single combat, man to man. That would be the honourable thing for a prince to do. Let Allah decide.'

'Hah!' laughed Suleyman. 'A duel! But I cannot see the benefit of such an arrangement. If you kill me, the Sword of Islam is without anyone to wield it. If I kill you, it's of no consequence.'

Luke supposed he was in no immediate danger or he would be dead by now. 'Then send me to the crusade,' he said. 'If you're so certain of victory, I'll probably die there.'

Suleyman pretended to consider this. 'That would certainly get you out of the way. But I quite like the thought of you here for now, watching Anna Laskaris adapt to the life of the harem . . . prepare herself for motherhood . . .'

Luke flinched and found his fists clenched. Despite the clumsy provocation, his anger was rising.

'My mother was Greek,' went on Suleyman genially. 'Did you know that? I've always vowed to myself that the sultans who follow me should also have Greek blood in their veins. And hers is the best.'

Luke found his voice. 'She would never submit herself to you willingly.'

'No?' Suleyman arched a black eyebrow. His voice was a whisper. 'Not even if *your* life depended on it?' He came very close. 'Tell me, Luke Magoris, you're a merchant now, aren't you? You like money, the money you will make from selling all that alum in Venice. How much more would you make if I went on stopping the Venetians from bringing in their alum from Trebizond yet let yours from Chios through?' He paused and his smile was wafer thin. 'That could be arranged . . . for a price.'

362

Luke moved fast. His hands were around the Prince's neck almost before the sentence was out, dragging him to the floor of the tent. The two men hit the carpet with some force, Luke's thumbs digging into Suleyman's windpipe and the Turk's hands gripping his arms, trying to relieve the pressure. They rolled over once, twice, before Suleyman managed to angle his head and sink his teeth into his attacker's forearm. Luke loosened his grip as the pain hit him and it was enough for Suleyman to pull a dagger from his sleeve. But Luke had seen the move and rolled away, coming to rest within reach of the peregrine's stand. As he grabbed its base, the bird tried to escape, shrieking as it reached the limit of its chain.

There was the sound of metal from across from the tent. Luke looked up. Suleyman's guards had entered, swords drawn.

Suleyman yelled something and they stayed where they were. The peregrine, still chained, sprang at Luke, its claws splayed for attack. But Luke was beyond its reach and it screamed its rage as it pawed the air, the chain taut behind it.

Luke rose and looked around the tent. His sword was tantalisingly close. He glanced back at his enemy.

Suleyman had risen too and pulled another dagger from the belt and it was a long, vicious thing that might have gutted a leopard.

He lunged at Luke but met only air as Varangian training produced a sidestep of precision. Suleyman spun round, panting, the dagger thrust out before him.

'Oh, let me kill you, Luke Magoris,' hissed Suleyman. He was close enough for Luke to smell the wine on his breath. 'Please give me an excuse to kill you. It would solve so many problems.'

363

There was a rustle behind him. Someone was standing between the guards.

'*Prince Suleyman!*'

Suleyman sighed and lowered the dagger. 'Ah, your other friend.'

'You said he would not be harmed,' said Zoe.

'And he has not been. He attacked me as I was in the middle of discussing my plans for the Laskaris girl.' He paused and tucked the dagger in his belt. He felt his neck and tested his head from side to side. 'Does he know the penalty for assaulting the son of the Sultan?'

Zoe glanced at Luke and then, unexpectedly, knelt. 'Lord, he is impulsive. He was always thus. He feels deeply for the Laskaris girl and doesn't realise you mean her no harm.'

Suleyman was looking at Luke with malevolence. 'He threatened my life. He must forfeit his own.'

Zoe prostrated herself on the carpet, her forehead deep in its weave. 'Majesty!' she whispered, her voice muffled. 'He acted rashly and he will not do so again. I will take him into my household and guarantee that you need not set eyes on him again.'

Suleyman sat on the chair with one hand on his neck and stroked his beard, examining Luke with malice. The silence in the tent was broken only by the uneven breathing of the two men.

Then Suleyman said what he was meant to say. 'Very well. He will be your groom. But I will look to you to guard him well.'

A short while afterwards Zoe and Luke were sitting in front of her tent on cushions, sipping cool sherbet in the mid-morning heat and looking out over the Bosporus. The channel was alive with craft ferrying people and goods to the villages further down its shores or beyond into the Black Sea.

Luke looked at the palaces that lined both sides of the water, most set back with lush gardens that ran down to the water's edge. They were abandoned now or occupied by Ottoman generals.

Zoe asked, 'Suleyman offered to keep the Venetian alum from getting through?'

Luke nodded.

'And in exchange?'

'You can imagine. That's why I attacked him.'

'That was a mistake.'

'You saved me. Thank you,' Luke said. He watched a Turkish galley intercept a round ship from Genoa. Bales of something were being transferred to the lower vessel. 'Why am I here?' he asked.

'You are here because of what you've been doing on Chios,' replied Zoe. 'Your success there has made you conspicuous. The Turks want the island for the Venetians. They give them Chios and get cannon in return, cannon big enough to bring down Constantinople's walls.'

'So why not simply kill me?' asked Luke.

'Because I persuaded him that you'd be more useful alive than dead,' said Zoe. 'But it's precarious. You cannot afford to cross him again.'

'But I will,' said Luke. 'I mean to take Anna.'

'Then you're a fool. If you try to take her from him, he will kill you. Both of you . . . I would not advise going anywhere near Anna. Let me be the go-between.'

'You? Why should I trust you after what happened in Monemvasia?'

Zoe looked sharply at him. 'Your friends must have told you of my part in Plethon's visit, my part in saving their lives? Anna trusts me and so should you.' She paused. 'Anyway, what choice do you have?'

Luke rubbed his chin. He'd managed to shave and wash himself at last in Zoe's tent and was enjoying the breeze on his face. He was wearing new clothes and his feet were in soft leather. He looked down at them and wondered again why Zoe wanted to help them.

'I am already the go-between,' continued Zoe. 'And I know about the treasure.'

Luke looked up.

'I know that Plethon wants you to find it. For the Empire.'

Luke stared at her. This was unfamiliar territory.

'Has it occurred to you, Luke, that I might not entirely agree with my family's plans to protect its wealth? After all, I've little incentive given that Damian will inherit it all.'

'Your interest is power and money,' said Luke. 'It always has been.'

'And you. My interest has been you.'

'Only because I denied you.'

'Am I that shallow?' She smiled. 'All right, let's just talk about power and money. Why shouldn't my interests now coincide with that of the Empire? It seems to me that I might gain more from a grateful emperor if I were to help you find the treasure than from Mamonas primogeniture.'

Luke considered this. He'd been prevented from going to Venice and the crusade. He was at the gates of Constantinople. If he could just get in . . .

'There is a sword,' he said at last.

'Ah, the sword. Siward's sword. Is it important?'

Luke ignored the question. 'Suleyman has it.'

'I know. He showed it to me.'

'Can you get it for me?'

It was a week later that the siege was raised. The Crusader army was on the Danube and it was time for Bayezid to march against it.

It happened with the silent purpose that characterised all Ottoman military manoeuvres, so that when Luke rose one morning and came out of his tent to wash, only a handful of tents were still standing. One of them was Suleyman's.

The Ottoman army, forty thousand strong, had already assembled in the Valley of the Springs and was awaiting the Sultan. It was strung out along the northern shore of the Golden Horn and its banners fluttered in a light wind from the sea, sunshine glancing off helmet and shield. The army would take the road west to Edirne before striking north to meet up with Prince Lazarević's Serbs at Tarnovo in Bulgaria.

'We should ride to the head of the valley,' said Zoe, emerging from her tent. 'Watching them march out is a spectacle. Get our horses.'

Luke walked to the paddock where their horses were tethered. Both had been saddled and he led them back to where his mistress stood, watching the Sultan and his retinue emerge from Prince Suleyman's tent. Surely, thought Luke, the Prince was to join Bayezid on this campaign? But there he was, bowing deep to his father, without a scale of armour on his person. If he was going to war, it would not be today.

Soon he and Zoe were riding west along the northern ridge of the valley to where it ended above the mouth of the Horn. They came to a grassy defile through which the army would pass and where musicians had set out their drums and trumpets and bells to play their brothers to war. Black-skirted dervishes were there, practising the spins and whirls that would be their dance to the music, their dance to Allah. It was the dance that would remind the soldiers of their gazi roots and of the ferocity that flowed through them from the red earth of the Anatolian steppe.

Towards the east they could see a haze of dust greying the horizon and could hear the deep percussion of thousands of feet on the march. The distant beat of drum and crash of cymbals kept their horses' ears alert and sent tiny tremors up their flanks.

Then Luke heard the sound of closer hoofbeats and looked up to see two riders approaching the opposite hill.

'*Say nothing!*' hissed Zoe.

Prince Suleyman had stopped his horse on the hill across from them. Beside him, Anna was dressed and veiled as an Ottoman consort and mounted on a pretty palfrey of white and pink. Her head was lowered and if she'd seen Luke, she didn't show it. As they drew up, Suleyman turned to her and said something in her ear; Anna nodded and kept her head bowed. Then he walked his horse forward and looked directly across at Zoe and Luke.

'How does your new groom do, lady?' he called.

The musicians and dancers around them had prostrated themselves on the grass. A drum rolled gently down to the road at the bottom of the defile.

'Get off your horse,' whispered Zoe from the side of her mouth.

'No,' said Luke, quite loudly.

There was a short laugh from the other side. 'He is insolent! No doubt you will beat him later?'

'Undoubtedly, Majesty. But it is my fault. I have asked him to remain mounted since my horse is skittish this morning. The music, lord.'

'Ah yes,' said the Prince, 'the music.' He looked round at the discarded instruments.

The army was approaching beneath its cloud like a winding snake of many colours. The noise made Zoe's horse start and Luke leant across and took her bridle.

Suleyman nodded and the musicians collected their instruments and began to tune them. The dervishes stood and bowed and swept the grass from their robes. Someone went to retrieve the drum.

'You will see something unforgettable in a moment, Luke Magoris!' he shouted. 'You will see an unbeaten army on its way to win another battle. Mark it well and be thankful that you don't have to face it.'

Luke was about to reply when Zoe's hand gripped his arm like a vice.

'He will mark it well, Majesty, and his *silence*,' – the grip tightened – 'will be proof of his astonishment.'

Across the other side of the defile, Anna walked her horse forward and undid her veil. For the first time she looked up and her eyes locked with those of Luke.

In the look that passed between them then was fear and joy and, above all, certainty. Whatever happened, whatever the lies, the forcing, the blackmail, there would be no other love in his life or hers. In that gaze was a longing, a longing grounded in something sublime that happened in a cave. Anna strained to search every part of his face, to store the memory of it to be unpacked, if it had to be, every remaining night of her life. She lifted her hand as he lifted his and the world beyond them was, for that moment, somewhere else.

But the army was there.

First came the flags, yellow and red and covered in holy writing, borne on lances. Behind them rode the *ağa* of the janissaries and his captains and companies of dervishes whirling in their wake. Then, marching in loose order, came the ranks of janissaries in their tall white hats and long red coats, stepping out with their swords slung low from their waists and their most precious regimental badge, the cauldron, held between the two biggest men of each company.

After them it was the turn of the court to pass. The White Eunuch, the Kilerji-bashi, in charge of the royal household, was in front, and behind him marched the Ilekim-bashi, the Chief Physician, and the Munejim-bashi, the Chief Astrologer. On either side trod the *peik* halberdiers, smart as buttons in their long swaying coats and plumed hats and between them came all the cooks, bakers, scullions, confectioners, tasters and musicians that created, approved or dismissed the Sultan's food.

The Pages of the Inner and Outer Chambers came next, each with his little golden bow, and the *solaklar*, the veteran janissary archers that surrounded the Sultan in battle. The high-stepping white horses of the Grand Vizier, suspended nightly by ropes to tread that way, all richly caparisoned followed, and behind them his own pageboys in matching livery. The Grand Vizier himself rode next, with his heron plume bobbing on his vast turban, smiling and nodding to right and left.

The green banner of the emirs appeared and there rode Yakub, dressed in magnificent furs, and with him all the beys, pashas, kadis and other rulers, great and petty, of the Anatolian steppe with their wild moustachios and tilting turbans. Then came rank upon rank of the sipahi light cavalry in their skins of wild animals.

The corps of the ulema came next: the imams, among whom were the Sultan's confessor and the muezzins who would chant from the Holy Book. All were serious men, weighed down with age, beard and wisdom, and looked neither to right or left as they rode to holy war.

At last there was Bayezid, dressed in shimmering silver mail and wearing a helmet, pointed at the top, from which a purple plume bounced with the steady tread of his splendid white stallion. He rode just ahead of an umbrella of green silk held high by one of his Kapikulu household guard. Beside him was carried the tall lance from which hung the three Horsehairs and, next to it, the great flag of the Prophet.

Luke had never in his life seen such a spectacle. His mouth was choked from dust and his eyes dazzled by the pageant of banners and spears and turbans and nodding horse heads. His ears rang with the sound of cymbal and trumpet and the throb of the earth as boot and hoof pounded their way to battle.

But there was more. After the Sultan came the irregulars, the thousand upon thousand bashibozouks who marched for no pay but the promise of plunder and, if truly valiant, a chance to become a sipahi with rights to land and chattels. These were a fearsome force, some hardly dressed, most without proper weapons and all with an ardour to die for their sultan.

'Let's go,' shouted Zoe.

She pulled hard at one rein and her mare spun around. Luke

waited a minute, searching through the dust for the figure on the other hill.

But there was no one there.

Later that night, Luke was sitting with Zoe in her tent. It was not large and much of the space was taken up by a bed as wide as it was long. Above the bed was a hexagonal lantern with candlelight playing through a filigree of thorned rose, and around it were layers of diaphanous fabric, all of different colours, which seemed to move to the flickering light. Cushioned divans were set against the tent's walls with tables before them. On the tables were bowls of herbs and multi-coloured stones. The floor was strewn with carpets and furs and an open stove smouldered in the centre.

Luke sat against cushions on a divan with Zoe facing him across a table, kneeling and leaning forward on her elbows, her face in her hands. The tent was warm.

'I want you to wait here,' said Zoe. 'I will go and get the sword. I know where it is in Suleyman's tent.'

'What happens if he finds you?'

'He won't. He's gone to look at the city walls. He will be away a week. He's taken Anna with him.'

'Anna? Why has he taken Anna?'

Zoe shrugged. 'He takes her everywhere with him.'

'Leaving you behind?'

Zoe looked at him evenly and there was something hard in the gaze. 'This is the tent of a courtesan,' she said very softly. 'We are all courtesans, just with different skills.'

Ten minutes later she had returned with the sword hidden beneath her cloak. She removed the bowls from the table and placed it between them. Her body cast a shadow over it so she moved to kneel next to Luke. The light from the lantern moved across the pitted surface of the metal like rain and the gold dragon's head glowed as if on fire.

'What do we do now?' asked Zoe.

'We see if any part of the hilt comes apart and we look for hidden inscriptions. God knows, though, I've examined this sword often enough.'

He leant forward and pulled the sword across the table towards them, then held up the hilt to the light, turning it.

'Wait,' said Zoe. She rose and went over to the bed, parting the veils and reaching up to unhook the lantern. She brought it back to the table and set it down. 'Now we can see properly.'

Their cheeks almost touching, they peered at every inch of the sword, but there was nothing that Luke had not already seen.

'Try twisting the pommel.'

'I already have, countless times.' But Luke put one hand around the grip and with the other tried to turn the dragon's head. There was no movement.

'Let's try this.' Zoe leant across to the bowl of herbs and thrust her hand in. When it emerged it was shining. 'Olive oil,' she said and wiped the hilt between the pommel and grip. Her fingers brushed against Luke's, leaving traces of oil.

Luke tried to twist it again and this time there was some give. Just a fraction, then a fraction more. Then nearly a full turn. Nothing more.

'Try again,' whispered Zoe and put her hands over his to help him.

It wouldn't shift.

'Perhaps it's only supposed to turn that far,' said Luke.

She leant over to the lantern and moved it closer to the pommel. Luke looked down at the brilliant sheen of her hair and the river of light that flowed across it.

'Can you see anything?' he asked.

'No. Yes . . . perhaps. Just some scratching in the metal, I think.'

Luke picked up the lantern and held it just above where she was looking. 'Wait. I think they're letters. There's something written here. A word.'

She peered closer. '*Sepultus.*'

'It's Latin,' said Luke. 'It means "buried". Is there anything else?'

'There are some numerals. I can see an M and a one. The rest is too worn.'

'A date?' Luke turned the metal further to the lamp.

'I suppose so. It's difficult to tell.'

'Well, Siward was buried in the Varangian church in Constantinople. If he took the treasure with him, perhaps he meant to tell us that the treasure would be buried with him.'

'But how would he know the date?'

'We need to go to the church,' said Luke quietly. 'We need to go into Constantinople.'

On the following day, the city of Constantinople opened its Golden Gate. It was still the most famous meeting place in Christendom and Luke and Zoe arrived there at midday when the sun was at its peak.

The fields around the walls had been burnt by the Turks and bore all the imprints of a besieging army. There were empty trenches and broken palisades and the ruins of siege machinery

374

lying everywhere in smoking piles. The road was dense with traffic as local villagers poured from the city to find what was left of their homes.

The gate itself was still magnificent. For centuries, it had been the great ceremonial portal from which emperors had left for their campaigns and under which they'd celebrated their triumphant returns. In contrast to the brick and limestone of the walls, it was built of white marble and had gigantic doors studded with gold. On its top was a monumental *quadriga* with elephants and two statues of winged victory looking out with optimism.

Now the two of them joined the queue of people waiting to enter the city and soon were being looked over by guards with the double-headed eagle of the Palaiologoi on their hauberks. The Turkish army had marched away but it was just possible that a few of their number had been left to enter the city as spies. Once they had satisfied the guards that they were Greek and had been let through the gate, Luke and Zoe entered a landscape of cultivated fields, hedgerows and men bent low over the plough. The ground either side of them was a patchwork of neat furrowed paddocks with the ruins of houses and churches providing the only clue that this had once been the busy suburb of Studion. There were wooden windmills dotted between the fields and donkeys waiting to take their grain, with birds hovering to pick up what was left.

They rode past the fields and orchards and ruins in a state of wonder, seeing for themselves how a population of a million shrinks to one of fifty thousand. Another line of walls, this time in ruins, rose up before them and they were told that these had been the walls of Constantine and once the limits of a smaller city. They passed through another gate and the broad Mese, its flagstones lined with grass, began to fall away. They came to a large deserted square and a canal that ran beneath it to the harbour of Theodosius down to their right. Then the ground rose towards the second hill of this seven-hilled city and they found themselves in a place where, at last, there were signs of habitation. Around the circular, colonnaded square, with its heroic pillar at the centre, were palaces and people and the beginnings of bustle. A market had been set up around one side and every kind of vegetable was on offer.

This was not, thought Luke, a population that was starving.

The Mese ran straight now and had fewer weeds between its stones. It rose gently towards a big triumphal arch with scenes of war carved on its walls. On its top was a gold pyramid.

'The Milion,' said Zoe, pointing. 'All the distances to the important cities in the Empire are inscribed on its sides. Most of them aren't ours any more, of course.'

Behind it was a throng of people and they stopped one to ask what was going on. The man pointed to the great aqueduct that could just be seen beyond the third hill. The cistern had been closed during the siege when water had been rationed. Now it was open again.

Soon they were among people queuing around the main square of the city, at the centre of which rose the great column that Luke had seen from the sea. There were more markets here and many more people. Yellow-hatted Jews sat behind abacuses at tables piled high with coins. By their sides sat Armenians with square beards writing on parchment. Moors and Syrians chatted with fat merchants from the Levant and everywhere were the black doublets of Venetians and Genoese who eyed each other with distrust. Constantinople was open again and the many nations that had sheltered in their various ghettos and *fondachi* warehouses during the siege had re-emerged to do business. Zoe stopped to ask one of them for directions.

'This way,' she said.

They turned north along the side of the Hagia Sophia and were soon plunged into the shadow of its great walls. Beyond it, the streets were narrower and seemingly deserted and they dismounted and led their horses past doorways with cats in them and others where dogs stood guard. Then, ahead of them, was a small church, crumbling at every corner, which looked as if it had not seen a congregation in years.

'The Varangian church?' asked Luke.

'I think so,' said Zoe and they emerged into a tiny, sunlit square, with a dead bird lying next to a fountain. They tied their horses to a carved stone fish.

It was now late afternoon and they would not have much time to examine the church's interior before the light began to fade. The little door was unlocked and opened on creaking hinges and a bird startled them as it made its escape. Inside, there was more light than they'd predicted because great holes gaped from the roof, framed by blackened roof struts, with shafts of sunlight reaching in. An oak beam lay at an angle across the nave, its end disappearing through a high window where plants grew. At the end of the nave, a broken rood screen separated the chancel and two tiny side chapels opened up either side, their interiors lost in shadow.

Luke's eyes grew accustomed to the light and he began to make out features within the church. There were frescoes covering nearly every wall but of what was difficult to judge. Age and indifference had combined to fade the colours and chunks of plaster had fallen to reveal the stone beneath.

'Didn't you say there was a sword?' asked Zoe, walking forwards into particles of floating dust.

'Yes,' replied Luke. 'Over the altar. My father told me that the sword of St Olaf hung there.'

They approached the rood screen and went beyond it and there was the altar but no sword.

'In Venice probably,' said Zoe. 'Like everything else.'

'Look for a tomb,' said Luke. 'Siward's. It's here somewhere.'

They separated and looked around the base of the altar. There was no tomb.

Luke called to her. 'Come and look at this.'

He was standing below a fresco painted on to the domed walls of the chancel that was different from the rest. A shaft of sunlight showed that it was in much better repair than the others.

'What's it of?' asked Zoe, joining him.

'It looks like the Resurrection,' replied Luke. 'Look, you can see the Roman soldiers asleep around the tomb. But . . . that's strange.' Luke had stepped closer and was shielding his eyes from the glare of the sun. 'I've seen paintings like this on Chios,' he said, 'but they always have the figure of Jesus above the tomb.' He paused and looked at Zoe. 'Here there's none. And another thing: this painting is much later than the others in this church. That's why it's in such good condition. The colours are hardly faded.'

Zoe nodded. 'And look at the soldier in the middle. Look what he's wearing.'

Luke peered closely at the picture. The soldier was lying slumped against the side of a tomb whose stone lid had been slid to one side. He was wearing a corselet of gold and blue

378

scales partially covered by a dark blue chlamys, clasped at the right shoulder. On the ground on one side of him lay a two-handed axe. In his hand was a sword.

'I suppose it's natural for the soldiers to have been painted as Varangians,' said Luke slowly. 'Or would have been if all of them were. But he's the only one.'

The light shifted again as the sun sank lower and Luke felt Zoe tense beside him. Only the head of the Varangian Guard was in light. It shone with an ethereal glow. It was someone both of them knew.

'*Look*,' whispered Zoe. 'Imagine him younger, without the beard.'

They both gazed at the face, entirely still.

'It could be you,' she said softly.

Luke pulled away from the painting and found that his hands were trembling. He suddenly felt cold although the afternoon was still warm. 'The sword – look at its pommel,' he said.

The dragon head was aglow. Alive.

'It's my sword,' whispered Luke. 'Siward's sword.'

Then he said, 'Perhaps it's pointing. What's it pointing at?'

Zoe's gaze travelled the length of the blade. 'Well, that answers that,' she said. 'It's pointing to where the painting has worn away. Look at the corner of the picture. It's worn through to the plaster beneath.'

'And beyond?'

'Into the side chapel.'

There was no sound in the little church beyond their breathing. The light was almost gone now, a frieze of dust motes suspended above the ground like things discovered. They felt their way into the chapel. As their eyes accustomed themselves to the dark, they saw tombs, the black shapes of

379

sarcophagi with one, much larger than the others, rising up at their centre.

'Siward's tomb,' said Luke.

'How can you tell?'

'I just know,' replied Luke quietly. 'I must write to Plethon. He'll know what to do.'

CHAPTER TWENTY

VENICE, AUTUMN 1396

At the new headquarters of the Banco dei Medici, situated discreetly above their Hanseatic friends at the Fondaco dei Turchi on the Grand Canal, there was mixed reaction to the news.

The Ottomans had lifted their siege of Constantinople.

Of course it meant that alum from Trebizond could now get through and prices to the Arte della Lana would fall. On the other hand, it meant that the considerable outlay they'd made to the Campagna Giustiniani on Chios looked a little more precarious.

On the Rialto, all was joy. The news lifted the ducat ten against the écu, and the *cortigiane di lume,* those bawds who plied their trade in those and other parts, lifted a celebratory toast.

But then this was Venice and celebration was in the air.

Except, it must be said, for Murano. That five-fingered island, second in the Venetian constellation, its hundred glass foundries belching smoke into the gassy air, was a place of serious industry. It looked with contempt at the goose-masked, all-night revellers who rowed their unsteady way across the lagoon each dawn. Its foundries were at full blast, the scarred, glistening

381

bodies of their *maestri* toiling with tongs and bubbled rods in the bloody glare of the kiln-vents, tweaking, shaping and rolling end-jewels into weightless circles of nothing.

Leaving such a factory were its owners, the father and son Mamonas, whose palace on the Goulas of Monemvasia contained, it was said, the very finest of its produce. There was, between them, an air of smug satisfaction only slightly tempered by the thought that a dearer ducat would narrow their profit margin. Both were wearing the sober black damask that signalled wealth and probity.

They were surprised to see, waiting for them at the quay, a barge sent by the Serenissima to gather them to her bosom.

A man, also dressed in black, bowed to them as they approached.

'Niccolò di Vetriano, Knight of the Order of San Marco, at your service,' he said between lips pressed into the tightest of smiles. 'I am to bring you to meet His Serenity, the Doge.'

Father and son bowed in return, assuming their names were known.

'We are honoured,' said Pavlos, 'but we are not dressed to meet the Doge.'

'We will go to your fondaco first, signori,' said the man. 'When you are prepared, we can go to the Arsenale.'

The Mamonas exchanged glances.

'The Arsenale?' said the older. 'But we understood that His Serenity never stepped outside the palace.'

The Venetian captain smiled and examined the neat tips of his gloves. He was a handsome man of dark and manicured menace. His voice was soft and dripping with condescension. A bejewelled short sword hung at his side. 'Indeed. The Doge will leave the palace only in exceptional circumstances.'

Pavlos Mamonas inclined his head. He'd expected to meet the Doge but not so soon, not like *this*. He and Damian stepped into the boat and walked to the stern where cushions were arranged beneath a tasselled awning.

As the barge moved away, he screwed his eyes against the sun and looked across the milky surface of the lagoon towards the skyline before him, elaborate with campaniles, domes and crenellations. There was Venice, the supreme mistress of trade, reclining scented in her lagoon. There, across the water, was the flamboyant city of festivals, water parties, music and masquerades. There was the place of barter and procession and entertainments of more intimate nature conducted behind the silken curtains of gondolas. There, in all her eccentric glory, was the Bride of the Adriatic, the Eye of Italy, who counted, among her hundred thousand amphibious souls, no fewer than ten thousand prostitutes. Pavlos Mamonas smiled.

One in ten.

They were passing the island of San Michele now, the Camaldolite Monastery squat behind its walls, where the pious but worldly monks supplemented their income by making the finest maps in the world. The waves from their oars rippled against the little jetty and a monk carrying a basket of fish looked up with little interest.

Another emissary. Another alliance to allow this fair but ferocious republic to carry on its divine right of trade.

'Ah, your escort,' remarked di Vetriano. He was pointing towards the docks and wharves of St Mark's Basin from where two golden barges were rowing in leisurely tempo towards them. 'Twenty years ago,' he went on, 'I was fortunate to witness the King of France sail in on a ship rowed by four hundred slaves. He had an escort of fourteen galleys and there was a raft on which glass blowers made objects from a furnace shaped as a sea monster. Had you heard of this?'

It was clumsy and neither Mamonas did more than smile thinly. The captain spoke again.

'You will be pleased with the news of alum shipments at last getting through from Trebizond, no doubt?'

'The alum is but a small part of what we do,' Pavlos replied easily. 'Frankly, I'm more amused by the new appetite for our Malvasia wine amongst the English. Their nobility drink it by the gallon. They call it Malmsey.'

Di Vetriano laughed. 'I drink it too,' he said. 'It's a lot more gratifying than this new mastic drink.'

'Mastic drink?' asked Damian, too quickly.

The Venetian arched an eyebrow. 'Had you not heard? I brought the shipment in from Chios myself last week in one of the Empire's galleys. The rest brought alum. They broke through the Turks' blockade of Chios. Since then all the talk has been of mastic. Its applications seem limitless.' He was watching them carefully. 'They say it even fixes dyes. Surely not, for then what need would there be for so much alum?'

Pavlos Mamonas gripped his son's arm before he could answer. He looked hard at the Venetian.

Why has the Doge sent this man?

He turned towards the scene opening up in front of them. They were coming in fast with the race of the tide and the escorting galleys were finding it hard to turn to station on either side.

'Slow down!' yelled the captain to his oarsmen. 'Wait for our escorts to form up, damn you!'

The oars lifted as one and the barge slowed. Mamonas leant forward to gaze along a shoreline he knew better than most in the world. There was something about the melancholy of this marshy home to waterfowl and fishermen that he found reassuring: a refuge in a world that suddenly felt less secure.

Ten minutes later they had passed the bar and were sweeping in past the Piazza San Marco with its twin pillars from which the winged lion of the city's patron saint and his predecessor, St Theodore, looked down with hauteur. As they drew nearer to the entrance to the Grand Canal, they found themselves amidst a bustle of boats: passenger skiffs, lighters, vessels laden with fish and vegetables – all of them manned by half-naked men yelling greeting or warning to each other. Some of the ships entering were deep-keeled, seagoing vessels, pulled by tugs, which would travel past the opening bridge of the Rialto to reach the small docks fronting the fondachi further down the canal.

The Grand Canal opened up before them and soon they were passing a parade of palaces, shimmering in pink self-satisfaction, with restless coveys of boats nuzzling at their water gates and sunshine blushing their pillared loggias. This was the central artery of the city from which smaller canals branched off; it was an esplanade of wealth and splendour, a dazzling repository for the booty wrenched from Constantinople.

The canal curved its way through the length of the city and, at its second bend, came to the bridge of the Rialto where the bankers had their stalls, the merchants their offices, the slavers their auction yards and the whores their love potions. On the quays were barges from the mainland, moored in their hundreds, waiting to ship cargoes from the ocean-going ships. And it was here that the Mamonas family flag, the black castle, flew high above their splendid fondaco.

As they glided towards its jetty, two trumpeters, winged

lions on their tabards, stood at the front of the barge to herald
their arrival. A gondola, gilded and tasselled and poled by
liveried negroes wearing the Loredani badge, slowed to let
them pass.

On the jetty stood the Mamonas factor, a small man of some
girth. He was flanked by two fat sons and a fatter wife, all
dressed in black and looking nervous and hot beneath the
afternoon sun. Pleasantries were exchanged, travel enquiries
made, two heads patted and then the party walked up the steps
and into the loggia that ran the length of the building.

'I'm told all the talk is of mastic?' said Pavlos as they walked.

The factor was rubbing his hands as if the substance was
stuck to them. 'No one knows what it can do, lord,' he said.
'Aphrodisiac, wound sealant, drink, tooth filler . . . every day
it seems they have a new use for it. Some even say it will fix
dye. The market is excited. It will calm.'

'I think not,' said his master. 'And Chios is the *only* place that
can produce it?'

'It seems that way, lord,' said the man uncomfortably. 'Or at
least the sort of mastic with these properties. It would seem
that the island has a unique climate.'

Mamonas was silent for a while and the sound of their boots
on the stone echoed beneath the arches. The children were
hurrying behind, dragged by their ample mother, and one was
grumbling too loudly.

'Have you bought the land there?'

It was the question the factor had been dreading. 'Lord, there
have been difficulties . . .'

'Difficulties? It's a straightforward transaction. I told you to
pay what they wanted for it.'

'The Genoans have control of the island, lord. They will

permit no sale of land to anyone outside their campagna. It didn't matter what sum I offered.'

Mamonas cursed silently. Despite the blockade, any further pirate raids on the south of the island had been expressly forbidden by the Sultan on pain of the bowstring. Meanwhile the Genoese were consolidating their hold. He would need time to think before his meeting with the Doge.

He stopped and turned to the factor. 'Please go and thank Signor di Vetriano for his courtesy. My son and I will walk to the Arsenale.'

An hour later, the two men were walking across the Piazza San Marco. The square was full to bursting point and they were jostled as they walked. There were the booths of trade guilds collecting their dues, shipmasters recruiting crews and the perennial tourists, money changers, souvenir sellers and those of nobler rank, black-gowned and heavy with brocade. It was alive with dialect and the scents of several continents and it was, for Pavlos, close to paradise.

This was where the Mamonas family belonged. This was where an empire, built from alum and wine but now encompassing much, much more, *should* have its headquarters.

But what of my heir?

Pavlos glanced across at Damian, struggling to keep up, his head dipping with the drag of a foot.

They say Temur is lame.

The Arsenale of Venice was, undoubtedly, one of the great wonders of the world. Surrounded by two miles of stout walls, it contained the secret of Venetian power and it was a secret jealously guarded. The walls were patrolled by crossbowmen and today their red and white striped jerkins were spotless and their breastplates polished to a blinding sheen.

They, and the other sixteen thousand *arsenalotti*, were to receive their doge.

In fact he was already there. Standing in front of the ranks of his guard, the *excusati*, was the sixty-third of that office: Antonio Venier, His Most Serene Prince the Doge, Duke of Dalmatia and Istria and, to the eternal shame of every Byzantine, Lord of a Quarter and a Half-Quarter of the Roman Empire. He was a tall man of erect and patrician bearing who looked born to rule such an empire. A man of seventy-two years, with an enigmatic mouth, prominent nose, sallow skin and contempt in his eye. A man of implicit control whose only unruly feature was a beard of some bushiness.

A man unlikely to mire himself in the sweaty friction of trade.

And yet here he was, in his ermined cloak and long, Byzantine robes, grave and aquiline, the pragmatic master of a pragmatic empire. He bowed very slightly to the Mamonas couple; if he was pleased to have escaped the confines of his palace, they weren't to know it.

Father and son had seen this man before and they'd been ignored. Now he opened his arms to them.

'Welcome, Pavlos. And you, Damian. What a pleasure it is to welcome you back to Venice, which I hope, like me, you regard as home.' He stepped forward and raised the older Mamonas to his feet by the elbow. 'Come, no kneeling! We are a republic and all men are equal.'

Pavlos Mamonas rose. He remembered a room in the Doge's palace where maps on the walls told of a trading power greater than any the world had yet seen. He remembered a Carpaccio lion with its feet both on land and water signifying sovereignty over two empires. He remembered kneeling before a man who didn't know his name.

'We must talk as friends, Pavlos,' the Doge continued in his *basso* voice, turning and leading them up the steps and into the building. 'And we must talk where we shall not be overheard.'

They walked the length of a chequered hall and came to a vast door guarded by stone men with fish scales for armour and tridents for weapons. Opening it, the Doge brought them into a tall room, panelled with oak and red damask and lined with candle sconces and the portraits of former Doges. There was a row of high windows on one wall, all of which had been shuttered. Models of galleys and barges stood on plinths below the portraits and a scale model of the complex of boatyards, slipways and factories that made up the Arsenale occupied a wide table at one end. At the other end, a colossal fireplace burnt logs the size of trees. They were alone.

The Doge walked over to the model of the Arsenale and pretended to examine it.

> *'One makes his vessel new, and one recaulks*
> *The ribs of that which many a voyage has made;*
> *One hammers at the prow, one at the stern,*
> *This one makes oars, and that one cordage twists,*
> *Another mends the mainsail and the mizzen . . .'*

His murmured words faded and he looked back at the Mamonases. He removed his cloak and set it down on a map chest. He beckoned to them.

'Come over, please. Not to hear any more Dante, I promise. No, I want to show you a secret.'

The two men walked the length of the room. The model of the Arsenale was presented at thigh level and was a mass of shadow. The Doge went over to the wall and took a candle from its sconce.

'This is our secret,' he said softly, lifting the candle high above the buildings and cradles and canals. The Arsenale was a city within a city. 'No one, not even the members of the Great Council, is permitted to know how this miracle of human ingenuity is arranged. That is why the windows are shuttered and will remain so.'

The Doge spoke in a whisper. He spread an arm above the scene like a man throwing seed. 'Look at it. It is a revolution. At any one time there may be fifty galleys within its walls in different stages of production, from great galleys to *rembate*. We're even building round ships for the Genoese now. See how we use these canals to bring the boats to the workers rather than the other way round? It's a form of industry seen nowhere else in the world.'

He paused and looked across at the two Greeks. 'They tell me that in ten years we will be building a ship a day. Imagine that . . . a ship built every day of the year!'

Pavlos thought of the antiquated boatyards north of Monemvasia. The fastest they'd ever built a ship in was five months.

'And, of course,' the Doge went on, 'our method of building from the frame first means we use much less wood. That is good for the city's purse and the poor trees of our Montello hills.' He pointed at a building. 'This is the largest rope factory in the world, this a *cannello* for lifting boats from the water and this' – he looked up at them – 'is where we make

390

cannon under the expert eye of gun casters from Budapest and Ragusa.'

They peered down at a part of the model constructed of newer wood. It was a long building and had tall chimneys at one end.

'Here we are making bombards and culverins and ribaudekins and *pots-de-fer*.' He stroked the roof of the building with his fingers. 'And of course cannon to go on ships.' He looked up at the two Greeks. 'And now, it seems, we are persuaded to make cannon big enough to bring down the walls of Constantinople. There is no one else the Sultan can go to for these cannon. But of course you know this.'

Hat in hand, Pavlos Mamonas suddenly felt at a disadvantage. He left the model and walked over to the largest of the model ships, a gorgeous thing of swirling gold, canopied stern and long banks of oars poised like spiders' legs. He turned to the Doge, pointing at the model. 'Every year, Your Serenity throws a ring into the sea from this floating palace. The Romans called the sea *Mare Nostrum*, and it was truly theirs. But it's not your sea yet and nor will it be unless the Sultan allows it.'

The Doge smiled. He walked over to the model of his barge, the *bucintoro*, and stooped to look carefully along the lines of miniature oarsmen. 'There are no slaves in Venice,' he said calmly. 'Every man in the galley is a volunteer. We part the sea because we want to and it is our strength.'

'And yet the Rialto parades slaves daily. It seems you exercise your tyranny by proxy.'

'Ah,' said the Doge looking up. His smile was glacial. 'Now that's a good word. Most apt.' He placed the candle on the plinth beside the barge. 'Signor Mamonas, we are a merchant nation and cannot afford to take sides. We are unique among nations: half eastern, half western; half land, half sea; poised precariously between Christendom and the lands of the Prophet and trading indiscriminately with both. We are a place of silk and velvet and soft fumigations and we are a place of hard porphyry and marble.'

His look was now sharp, the smile gone. 'Above all, signore, we are pragmatic. We are like a hunting dog. We point to best advantage. Now, which of these sultans are we to deal with? The one ruling, or his heir?'

Pavlos Mamonas stood very still. The room was not cold but the skin beneath his doublet was pricked as if the lightest current of air had crept through the shutters. It was fear of course. He heard Damian shuffle behind him.

'My son finds standing difficult,' he said. 'Will Your Serenity permit him to find a seat outside?'

'Father—'

The Doge raised a hand. 'I would insist,' he said.

Damian stayed where he was. He looked from one to other of the older men.

'Leave, Damian,' said his father quietly.

The note of the heavy door shutting stayed with them for some time and, after it had subsided, there was no sound in the room except the crackle of the fire. Antonio Venier gestured towards it. 'Shall we warm ourselves?'

Two chairs, not three, had been placed on either side of the fireplace. They were high-backed and padded with embroidered velvet. With a screen, it might have been a confessional.

Both men sat.

'So which sultan is your master, signore?' asked the Doge. 'Is it Bayezid or Suleyman?'

Pavlos Mamonas suddenly wanted wine. His mouth was dry

and he needed something to do with his hands. He hoped they weren't trembling.

He said, 'The Sultan's heir, Prince Suleyman, has been tasked by his father with the capture of Constantinople. There is division within the Sultan's court as to where to go next for conquest. He leads the faction that would go west.'

The Doge nodded slowly, his old eyes alert above steepled fingers. 'We know this. The philosopher Plethon has been in Venice for some time now. He argues that Venice is committing suicide by building ships and cannon for such a prince.'

Pavlos Mamonas sighed. He'd hoped that Plethon had left the city by now.

The Doge continued: 'His case is strengthened with the offer of gold.'

'Gold?' asked Mamonas. 'The Empire has no gold.'

'Ah, but that's where you're wrong. A young Greek has sent us a galley filled with mastic. Do you know the price mastic is fetching on the Rialto these days? It's extraordinary.'

Pavlos shook his head slowly, his mind working.

A young Greek.

'But what is more extraordinary is that this Greek has instructed that the entire profit from the mastic go to Plethon to use in the service of the Empire. So I now have a counter-offer for my cannon.' The Doge furrowed his brow. 'Difficult.'

Pavlos Mamonas asked, 'Am I permitted to know the name of this generous Greek?'

'His name is Luke Magoris. He is from your city of Monemvasia. You may know him.'

'And he is here in Venice?'

'Alas no. He was captured by pirates and taken to Prince Suleyman's camp at Constantinople. We don't know why.'

Where Zoe is.

Pavlos Mamonas took a deep, but silent, breath. The feeling of unease that had entered him since leaving his factory on Murano had suddenly strengthened.

But the Doge hadn't finished. 'Then there's this crusade,' he said. 'They say that Burgundy has emptied his considerable coffers to put a vast force into the field. An unbeatable force.' He paused. 'Again, difficult.'

Pavlos Mamonas was only half listening now. Part of his mind was considering what he'd just discovered about Luke Magoris and the implications of telling Suleyman that he'd not get his cannon. Of Suleyman telling Bayezid. He felt ill.

But, he thought, I am here. If the Doge's mind is made up, why is he talking to me?

He decided to be direct. 'What do you want?' he asked quietly.

The Doge's beard looked like spun silver in the glow of the fire. Pavlos Mamonas waited and was suddenly glad he had not been offered any wine. The Venetians were said to strengthen it when it was served at negotiations.

'We want Chios,' Venier said at last.

Pavlos said, 'Your Serenity has already instructed me to include Chios in the negotiations. But there is a complication.'

'I know it,' murmured the Doge. 'The Sultan's teeth.' He put a finger into his mouth. 'I must go there myself one day.'

'With the alum from Trebizond now coming through, I had assumed the Chios trade less urgent.'

Venier raised his hand. 'Please, signore. The alum trade is not the issue. We want Chios, not its alum. And we want it quickly if we are to work hard to perfect a cannon big enough to bring down Constantinople's walls.'

394

The Doge affixed his eyes to Pavlos above the most sparing of smiles. He was stroking his beard, smoothing its chaos into something more akin to his speech. 'Do you want to know *why* we want that little island so badly?'

Pavlos shrugged slightly. 'Because you want to be able to say *Mare Nostrum*? Because you own every other island from Corfu to Negroponte to protect your trade routes? Because the Genoese like it so much? There is likely to be more than one answer.'

'Yes, but there is something else. Come.' The Doge had risen and was making his way to the other end of the room, where stood the model of the Arsenale. He lifted the candle and pointed to a small collection of buildings that seemed unconnected to the purpose of ship building. 'Every civilised place of work should have an infirmary, don't you think? All those accidents that can happen in a shipyard.'

'Infirmary, Serenity?'

'Yes, infirmary. I want to take you to see it, Pavlos. Come.'

A short while later they were there, without guards and without Damian, who seemed to have been magically removed. The building was entirely without character or embellishment of any kind. Two soldiers of the arsenalotti stood to attention either side of the door.

Inside was a small anteroom, whitewashed and unwindowed, in the middle of which stood a long table with two sets of strange clothing laid out. There were two overcoats, coated in wax, two pairs of long leather breeches that would stretch up to the groin and two wide-brimmed hats. All of the clothes were black. Beside them were two masks with long beaks, also in black, and two sets of gloves.

Pavlos Mamonas suddenly felt cold. 'These are the clothes of the plague,' he said.

'Indeed, and I will ask you to put them on. As you do so, I will explain why we are here.'

Mamonas hesitated. It was only fifty years since the Great Plague had left half of Europe dead and it had reappeared every five years or so since. It was an invasion far more deadly than even the Mongols could aspire to.

'Please. You will be quite safe, I promise you.'

The Greek stepped forward slowly and began to dress. His heart was beating fast. Venier joined him.

'Half a century ago,' he said, 'Venice lost two-thirds of her population in less than a year from the plague. Like most things bad, we have the Genoese to thank. A month before, the Mongol Jani Beg had been besieging their colony at Jaffa when he had the inspiration to catapult the bodies of plague victims over the walls. The Genoese fled in their boats and those that didn't go to Sicily, came to us.'

He paused to fasten the breeches tightly around his waist. 'We weren't much worse off than most. Florence's population halved in less than two months.' Now he was donning the long coat and small pieces of wax fell away as he pulled the sleeves over his arms. 'We both know what happened after that. Chaos. Jews and lepers were massacred, there were crop failures and famines because of labour shortages, flagellants were every-where. And our city, famed for its cats, lost them all in one bloody night when the populace remembered that they were in league with the Devil. Worst of all, trade seized up. The blood in this city's veins coagulated to a standstill.'

Venier had dressed completely, including the hat, and was studying the beak of his mask with distaste. Two red glass eyepieces stared back at him malevolently. 'I'm told they first thought it spread through migrating birds, hence the shape of this thing. At least the herbs inside it will provide some benefit.'

He turned to Mamonas, who was by now dressed. 'Do you know what's really interesting?' he asked suddenly, his voice lower. 'What's really interesting is the places the plague *didn't* reach. The Pyrenees, Santiago de Compostela to name two.' He had come over and was helping Mamonas tuck the cowl of his hood behind the mask. 'And yet it leapt from island to island in our Middle Sea like a grasshopper. Especially those with ports.' He had tilted the beak of his own mask to peer into it and check that the herbs were in place. 'Except one. And can you guess which one it was?'

Mamonas, giddy from the fumes in his mask, didn't answer. He'd guessed which one.

'Yes, Chios. It never reached Chios. The population of that island was, at the end of the plague, slightly larger than it had been at its start. Shall we go in?'

The Doge opened the door on the other side of the room and led Mamonas into a long corridor along which were a dozen cells. Each had a grille at eye level through which the visitor could see into the room. Penetrating the smell of herbs was the stench of sulphur and something indefinable.

The air was full of low, unhappy monologue.

'We should not talk,' whispered the Doge, turning. 'It distresses them.'

The two men walked the length of the corridor, stopping at every door to look inside. In each cell was a man, half-naked, skeletal and pale, with deep, sunken eyes ringed with shadows. Their bodies were clean and their heads had been shaven. They either sat or lay on straw pallets; they looked vacantly before them or talked to themselves. Their bodies were a mass of coruscating scars, dried abrasions where there had once been pustules and buboes, and they scratched at their necks and armpits where the scars were most closely gathered.

Mamonas reached the end of the corridor without vomiting and, even when they had come into the clean air of the outside, he did no more than remove his mask and retch. When he had collected himself and straightened, he found himself staring into the face of di Vetriano.

'You have met, I think,' said the Doge, calmly removing his mask and gloves. He placed them in a tall butt containing a grey powder. 'Captain di Vetriano will now explain further why we are here.'

The man in front of Mamonas was a more serious creature than he'd been in the barge.

'Signore,' he began, 'I don't know how much you know about the plague but I will tell you anyway. The first stage begins with buboes in the groin, neck and armpits that ooze pus and bleed when opened. After two or three days, the second stage sets in when black spots, small and large, appear all over the body. The victim then begins to suffer additional fever and vomits blood. His breathing becomes laboured. He develops a raging thirst and will drink anything. In a further two days he is dead. It is always so.'

Mamonas nodded. He'd seen it once.

'I told you that I brought in the first shipment of mastic from Chios. It was a week ago.' Di Vetriano was watching him closely. 'Unfortunately, mastic wasn't the only cargo I brought into Venice.' His voice was grave. 'I also brought the plague. We picked up some crew at Negroponte, men who had been aban-

398

doned by a Genoan galley. We needed rowers but I should have checked them more carefully before bringing them aboard. In three days it had spread throughout the crew. We were throwing men in the sea by the dozen. We limped into Venice and the ship was placed under quarantine.'

The Venetian paused and looked at the Doge, who was motionless and staring hard at Mamonas. A seagull called above them and was joined by others.

'The men died one by one, out there in the lagoon. They went from tumours to black spots and then died in agony. I myself only survived by barricading myself in my cabin. But for twelve men it was different. These were those whose duty it had been to guard the cargo. They'd been close to the mastic throughout. They developed the buboes but never reached the stage of the black spots. They'd also been consumed by the usual thirst and, in their madness, drank a compound of the mastic that had been formulated to fix dye.'

Di Vetriano looked back to the door through which they had just come. 'Those are the twelve men in there.'

For a long time, none of them spoke. Mamonas felt his heart hammering against his ribcage and his mouth was dry. He looked from captain to doge. 'A . . . a cure?'

Venier shrugged. 'Perhaps. It is too early to tell. It may be coincidence, but I think not.' He walked over to Mamonas and put his hand on his shoulder. 'You can see why we want Chios,' he said gently and smiled. 'A cure for the plague will pay for a thousand armies. It will make us invincible.'

'But first, signore, we need Luke Magoris,' said the Doge. 'We need him to tell us what was mixed with the mastic to bring about this miracle.'

Mamonas swallowed. Two masters, Ottoman and Venetian,

each as dangerous as the other. He needed time to consider this new information. But the Doge went on.

'Di Vetriano knows this Magoris by sight and is the best captain in my navy.' He bowed slightly towards his fellow Venetian. 'We need you to deliver Magoris to him. Can you do this for us?'

Mamonas was thinking hard. 'And if I do?'

'Then the alum monopoly from Chios will be yours. We will be happy with the mastic . . . once, of course, we have the island.'

Suddenly Pavlos felt very tired. He had just heard something that could transform him from a man of great wealth to a man of limitless wealth. But it was dangerous. Venier saw his struggle.

'Come,' he said. 'Nothing need be decided today. Let us return to my palace and drink some of your excellent wine.'

The two men turned towards a guard of excusati that had mysteriously appeared at the end of the street.

As di Vetriano bowed his farewell, he spoke. 'By the way, you'll be pleased to hear that it doesn't fix dye. We brought in the best chemists from Florence. The experiment failed.'

Four days later, Suleyman was standing at the top of the Gelata Tower in Genoese Pera and thinking about Zoe. It was an evening of moon and stars and bats flitting around the tall silhouette of its hat like bloated moths.

He'd been admitted to the tower by a Genoese nobleman who knew perfectly well whom he was admitting and had asked no questions. If the heir to the Ottoman throne and his companion wanted privacy, then they'd find it in this, the most obvious of places.

Suleyman hadn't joined the army marching north because its departure from Constantinople gave him the perfect opportunity to study the city's defences incognito. So he'd moved his tents further north of Pera, to a place where they couldn't be seen from the walls, donned the disguise of an Arab merchant and ridden forth with a small bodyguard.

And Anna.

And it was as he was riding back from the Theodosian walls, his map-maker by his side with a tunic stuffed with drawings, that the message had reached him that Pavlos Mamonas needed to meet with him. Urgently.

He'd been delighted by the choice of meeting place. The Gelata Tower offered unrivalled views of Constantinople's sea walls as well as the full length of the Golden Horn where the Empire's shipping had remained secure behind its chain throughout the siege.

The chain.

Something would have to be done about that chain. It was infuriating that something so simple could prove so effective. If he could somehow break or remove it then the sea walls beyond were the weakest part of the city's twenty miles of defences. But that meant taking Pera and, apart from the nobleman standing guard below, every Genoan seemed staunch in their allegiance to the Empire.

Now he turned to the man next to him, his two eyebrows arched in surprise. 'Pavlos, am I to understand that the Serenissima is attempting to change the terms of our agreement?'

Pavlos Mamonas had ridden without stopping from Venice. He'd not slept for forty hours and was more exhausted than he'd ever been but he needed to choose his words with care. He took a deep breath.

'They have been offered a better price for the cannon they're building,' he said. 'By the Empire.'

'The Empire? But it's penniless.'

'They have found money.'

'So give them more money.'

Mamonas scratched his chin. There was three days of stubble on it. 'It's not so simple. The Venetians have persuaded themselves that this crusade will succeed. They are nervous.'

'They are fools,' Suleyman snorted. 'We will beat this crusade and punish them for their cowardice.' He paused. 'So what do we do? I want Constantinople. How do I get my cannon?'

'You wait, lord. Crush the crusade and then talk again. Meanwhile . . .' Mamonas was looking beyond Suleyman to the door to the staircase, checking they were alone. He'd heard that Anna might be with him.

'Meanwhile?'

He turned to look Suleyman in the eye. 'Meanwhile, you give them the Magoris boy. They want him.'

'Why would they want him?'

'They wouldn't tell me.'

Suleyman frowned.

Why does everyone want Luke Magoris?

But then why did it matter? The more he considered the idea of handing Luke over to the Venetians, the more he liked it. It would remove him from Anna.

But what about Zoe? What about their agreement?

Suleyman's mind wandered to his usual picture of Zoe: naked on the bed beside him. No other woman had engendered such hunger in him. He wanted to keep Zoe.

But hadn't he fulfilled his side of the bargain? She had given him Anna and he had delivered her Luke Magoris. He'd never promised that she could have him indefinitely. And this was an affair of state. He wondered, briefly, how much of his daughter's activities the man standing beside him knew.

'When do they want him?'

'As soon as possible, lord. It could happen tomorrow or when you go north. There will be Venetians with the Christian army.'

Suleyman considered this. If he handed Luke over tomorrow, there would be difficult questions to answer from Zoe. Better to do it later.

Then Suleyman's mind moved on to a new idea. Having Luke escape and be taken by the Venetians might prove very useful. Especially if he then took certain information to the enemy.

'All right.' He turned towards the door. 'I will take him north and arrange for him to escape. I will tell you where your Venetians can pick him up.'

PART THREE

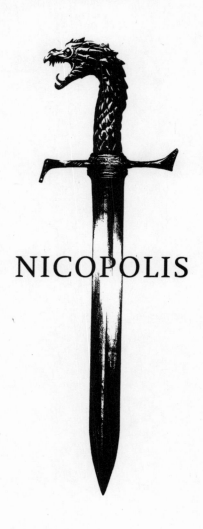

NICOPOLIS

CHAPTER TWENTY-ONE

NICOPOLIS, BULGARIA, 24 SEPTEMBER 1396

The great fortress of Nicopolis stood next to the Danube at a point where the river was nearly a mile wide. On this evening, the standard that flew sluggishly from its tallest tower was the flag of the Prophet, topped with a moon, which meant that its experienced commander, Dogan Beg, had yet to surrender to the two crusader armies encamped to its front.

Watching the armies from the prow of a hill was the heir to the Ottoman throne. Behind him and flanked by Kapikulu cavalry, was Luke.

The armies were as impressive as they were different. That commanded by the Comte de Nevers was the more flamboyant, with a vast green tent at its centre surrounded by sixteen magnificent banners given by his father, the Duke of Burgundy. Each bore the image of the Virgin Mary, patron of crusaders, and beneath it the Count's motto '*Ic houd*' or 'I never yield'. Surrounding it were the pavilions of the other French and Burgundian commanders: the Admiral de Vienne and Marshal Boucicaut; the Comte d'Eu and the veteran Sire de Coucy. Further out, a sea of gaudy silk washed across the wasted fields like a quilt and beyond stood a tilting ground with stands and emblazoned shields and pennants and all the accoutrements of the joust.

Suleyman laughed. 'This is more Lenten fair than army camp. All that's missing are the dancing bears! Where are the scouting parties, the sentries? Where are the siege engines?'

Luke rose in his stirrups to see better.

Yes, where are the siege engines?

The camp was positioned out of arrow range of the fortress walls and in front of it were some desultory earthworks but no catapults or battering rams or siege towers. And there were certainly no cannon of any size.

The other camp was better. Here flew the flag of Sigismund, King of Hungary, and alongside it fluttered the standards of Wallachia and Transylvania. The tents there were less colourful and there was no tilting yard, fewer banners and much less silk. It was the nearer of the two and Luke could hear the sound of hammer on anvil and see the smoke of campfires curling into the sky as soldiers prepared their evening meals.

The land around the fortress consisted of blackened fields lined with charred stubble, in one of which stood a scarecrow dressed in Saracen armour, a donkey's tail attached to its turban. Surrounding these was a landscape of gently rising hills and scattered woods from which clouds of starlings exploded like rain-bursts.

Beyond both armies and the fortress lay the mottled brown of the Danube with its marshy islands and, across it, the plains of Wallachia marching north towards distant mountains. The water looked sullen in the late-afternoon sun and upon it, lying at anchor, were ships flying the flag of Venice.

How many men are there in these armies? Enough to beat the Turks?

Luke heard his neighbour's stallion snort and its rider's mail clink with the movement. The day was still hot and flies gathered on the heads of the animals to be shaken aside. These Kapikulu had been his silent companions on the long ride from Constantinople along with other, more talkative sipahis from Anatolia. Zoe had explained to Luke that the sipahis were akin to the feudal knights of Christendom in that they held a plot of land, or *timar*, directly from the Sultan and were expected to come to war with retainers equipped at their expense. They were magnificently dressed in richly decorated mail and plate armour, with chest medallions and pointed turban helmets, and they carried maces and bows and had large quivers of arrows slung at their sides.

Suleyman had chosen to take just Anna with him to the crusade. But Zoe was unpeturbed. She didn't enjoy life on the march and staying behind gave her the opportunity to further investigate Siward's tomb before Luke's letter arrived with Plethon.

Throughout the journey, Anna had remained hidden from view inside a carriage at the rear of the column. If the thought of Anna so close had raised Luke's spirits, the country they'd travelled through, the woeful evidence of an empire in its final days, had lowered them again.

To begin with, they'd ridden across Thrace, a land where birds had taken the place of people. It was a flat, open country, crossed by rivers and mirrored by lakes, which had once been rich in corn and wheat and where the peasants had lived in prosperous villages with fat churches and fatter oxen in their fields. Now it was desolate and the fields were choked with weeds and the villages abandoned, their churches open to the sky.

As they rode further west, there appeared the first signs of change. People of darker skin were rebuilding the villages and pointed minarets were replacing domes. With them were groups of black-coated Bektashi dervishes who would provide the religious nucleus of their new communities.

One night they stayed at a *zaviye*, or hospice for travellers or settlers from Anatolia. Luke had usually slept with the horses, often with no dinner inside him. But that night, a sipahi knight had taken pity on him and had brought him roasted bird with a sauce of saffron and mushrooms and unsmoked honey and Luke had slept deeply and dreamt of Anna.

The next day they came to villages being built by people of lighter skin who didn't seem to want a church or mosque, people who dressed in simple robes and wore no crucifixes or other ornamentation and barely looked up as they rode past.

'Bogomils.' It was the sipahi knight who'd given him the food. He spat.

'What are they?' asked Luke, wondering if the man spoke Greek. 'They don't look as if they've come from your homeland.'

'They haven't. They're from around here. They're heretics to your church but suitable to us for repopulating these lands. They're insolent but they understand the country and work hard.'

'Why are they heretics?'

'Because of what they believe. They think that God had two sons, one bad and one good. The bad one created the world, so all material things are evil. They don't like priests or popes or churches or any form of authority. So they were persecuted by their Christian lords. But we leave them alone as long as they pay their taxes. And they don't believe in fighting.' He spat again.

'They won't fight for their beliefs?' asked Luke.

410

'Not here. But in France they did. They were called Cathars there and your pope launched a crusade against them two centuries ago. He razed whole cities to exterminate them in the name of your God.'

The sipahi knight had turned in his saddle to look at Luke, his dark eyes bright beneath the shadow of his helmet.

'Do you know what this crusade has done so far to win the hearts of the people they are liberating from us? Since crossing the river at Orşova, they have harassed and murdered the local peasantry. They massacred most of the citizens of Rahova even after they promised to spare them. Is this your God of love?'

Luke looked to the sky as if He might defend himself.

But all he saw were birds. So many that it seemed that heaven had sent a plague. There'd been herons, cormorants, ibis and white-bellied geese. Kites and falcons had ridden the currents while swifts and warblers darted and screamed their way low across the fields and lakes around them. Many of the birds were on their way south ahead of winter. Others had chosen to stay in this land devastated by war.

An empire of birds.

That evening, north of Kazanlak, they'd reached the foothills of the mountains and the guards had donned their cloaks and wrapped them tight against a chilling wind, their heads sunk deep into cowls and their eyes searching the landscape for bandits. The mountains here rose through pine-forested sides to snow-capped peaks where eagles circled on their giant wings spread out in benediction.

They had ridden down into Tarnovo as the sun fled west, turning the meandering Yantra river below into spilt honey. This city had once been the 'Third Rome', the capital of the Bulgarian Tsars that, three years ago, had held out for four

411

brave months against the Turkish onslaught. Now it was the meeting point of armies.

The road was narrow, allowing only pairs, and Luke found himself again riding beside the sipahi knight who seemed to have attached himself since giving Luke food. In front of them rode Suleyman and he was talking to his companion loudly enough for Luke to overhear.

He was talking about the Christian commanders. The ones he claimed to respect were, on the French and Burgundian side, the Admiral Jean de Vienne and Sire de Coucy and, on the Hungarian side, King Sigismund himself and the Voivode of Wallachia, Mircea, whose army had defeated the Turks at Rovine a year beforehand. He also admired the Grand Master of the Hospitallers, Philibert de Naillac, who had sailed there from their fortress in Rhodes with a detachment of monk-knights.

'If they have any sense,' Suleyman had said, 'they will listen to these men. But they won't. De Nevers is vain and stupid and thinks only of Burgundian glory and he has the right of what they call the *avant-garde*. His knights will charge and our Serbian knights will stop them. You'll see.'

And Luke had listened and remembered what he'd heard.

He was thinking about it now as he stared down at the two Christian armies outside Nicopolis.

The Serbians will be in their front line.

He didn't know why, but he felt that this information would be of importance to the crusaders. He looked over to the tents of Burgundy. Somewhere in there would be men like de Vienne and de Coucy who would know what to do with it.

But how could he get it to them?

412

Luke didn't sleep at all that night. It wasn't just that he had not been given a tent, being tied instead to a wagon wheel where the camp dogs fed on the scraps from janissary cauldrons and howled and fought their way through the night. It wasn't that a gentle drizzle had begun shortly after nightfall and continued ever since, soaking him to the bone. Luke had not slept because he kept turning over in his mind what he now knew of the battle to come..

The Serbian knights will be in their front line.

Luke shivered and drew the sodden folds of his cloak around his shoulders. He thought about the French knights of his age who'd be lying in their tents listening to the rain. How many, like him, would be facing their first battle tomorrow? How many, like him, would be thinking of the long training that had brought them to this point? How many were worrying whether it would be enough not just to survive the battle but also to uphold the honour of their calling?

He looked down at the plate next to him where his untouched food sat like an island in a sea of brown water. Around him, the campfires of the army had long succumbed to the rain and the dawn was still some way off. He could just make out a shape moving slowly, hesitantly in the dark before him. He closed his eyes and then opened them, wiping aside the rain and straining to see what was out there. He heard a sniff, and then a growl.

It was a dog. A large dog was coming towards him. Had it smelt the food?

Luke was seated on the ground next to the wagon wheel and his hands were bound either side of its axle, the chains reaching through its wooden spokes. He edged closer to the hub and felt the manacles around each wrist. They were immovable. He

413

tried to shift himself sideways, to get to the other side of the wheel, but the chain was too tight. He turned back to the dog and could now see its size and hear the rasp of its breathing. The animal had stopped and its head was just above the ground It was watching him with yellow eyes that flickered through the rain.

It wanted the food and Luke was in the way.

Luke tensed himself, readying his legs to intercept the creature in its leap, to somehow kick it away. He thought of dodging the impact but the chain made movement to either side impossible. But if he could move forward, if the chain would slide . . .

The dog sprang. With a growl, it leapt through the air and Luke flung the top of his body forward, joining his fists and pushing them out so that the chain scraped up to the hub. The dog smashed into the wheel rim above him, its jaw scraping his knuckles, its hot breath on the back of his neck. He heard a crack, a crack not of bone but of wood. The dog had missed him and he could see its black shape rolling away on the ground. He flung out his legs and his boots hit something hard: a head. He kicked again and this time the crack was of bone.

The dog lay still.

The wheel was at an angle. The animal's charge had broken the axle at the hub. He pulled the chain towards him and heard another crack. He pulled again and the wheel came away and the wagon crashed to the ground, narrowly missing him. He was still chained but he was free.

Luke waited in the darkness to hear if the sound had alerted anyone.

There was nothing. Just the sound of rain.

He could feel his heart beating against his chest and his

414

breathing was uneven. He began to crawl away from the wagon towards where he'd heard the sounds of horses earlier. He got to his feet and began to run slowly in a crouch, the chains dragging between his legs. He heard the whinny of a horse.

He reached a rail and saw movement beyond. He ducked beneath it and held the chain still as he whistled softly into the dark, turning his head to left and right. Then he heard the pad of hooves on wet earth and a horse trotted out of the night, its head held high with uncertainty. Luke lowered himself to his haunches and offered his chains and the horse's head stretched out to sniff and inspect. Then, slowly, Luke took the long nose in his hands and stroked it and his mouth came close to the horse's ear and he whispered into it and the horse nodded and Luke knew he was trusted.

Luke led the horse by the mane, feeling his way along the rail until he came to a gate. Only then did he mount the animal, talking to it as he did so. He listened for a while, judging the direction, then kicked its sides. It had stopped raining and the first light of day would soon outline the hills to the east.

But he had been heard.

He saw movement out of the corner of his eye. Riders taking shape in the darkness. Riders coming towards him. Silent riders who knew what they were following.

Luke dug his heels in, grabbing the horse's mane with both hands to keep himself on. He leant forward and whispered again into its ear and it started forward down the faint outline of a road at a trot. He looked over his shoulder and saw that his pursuers were following but making no attempt to catch up with him. Who were they and what was he to do? Any thought of going back to find Anna would have to be abandoned. He'd have to try and make it to the crusader lines.

Before him rose a darker mass. A wood and a chance, possibly, to hide. He slowed as the first trees loomed up around him, weaving his way between their trunks and ducking to avoid branches. He heard the soft crack of twig beneath his hooves and then the same noise behind him as the riders entered the wood. They were closer now. Was this another of Suleyman's games? Was he watching it all from somewhere with his cat-eyes, his night-eyes?

Who are you behind me?

The wood was dark inside and got darker as he went further in. His horse seemed to have picked out some path between the trees and Luke lay low, breathing in the comforting smell. He glanced awkwardly up at the stars, now visible through the branches, and the parting clouds. He thought he saw the North Star ahead, which meant that they were going towards the crusader camp. But the Christian army was three miles away and his pursuers just behind.

The warm, earthy scent of early autumn was all around him, a smell of pine essence released. All he could hear was the horse breathing and the steady drip, drip of rain.

Then his world exploded.

Something living landed on his back and his horse reared and he was thrown to the ground with his assailant on top of him. The air was punched out of him and he was pinned to the earth with a knife to his throat.

'If you want to live, don't move,' hissed the man through the cloth that masked his face. The language was Greek. 'Don't move at all.'

Luke lay rigid, feeling the cold of the blade against his neck. His cheek was against the ground and he could see other men emerging from the trees around, men with bows. He heard the sound of arrows being released and shouts in Italian and a scream where an arrow found its mark. The riders that had been following him were wheeling their horses, trying to escape, black shapes buffeted by panic.

'*Venetians!*' hissed the man on top of him. He was wearing the padded, buff leather of the gazi and he smelt strongly of horse.

They lay there together for a while, both breathing hard, as the riders fled and the archers returned, forming a circle around them. One of them lit a torch. The man got up and put his dagger into his waistband. He took a sword from one of his companions, broke Luke's chains, then walked over to one of the horses and found a thick pelt, which he threw at him.

'There is an hour before it is light enough to move,' he said gruffly. 'Sleep, if you can. Then I have something to show you.'

Of course Luke didn't sleep. He lay on the soft pelt in wet clothes and watched the dawn light creep slowly into the shadows around. The sky through the leaves was grey and without colour, as if uncertain what to do. Then, gradually, it turned into blue, a blue pregnant with the promise of sunshine held just below the horizon. Rain dripped from the branches.

He turned his head towards the sound of footsteps. The man was approaching; his companions had stayed sitting around the fire. They were talking in whispers and poking the embers with branches. The man knelt on one knee beside him.

'You are Luke Magoris,' he said, 'and I am Yakub, chief of the Germiyan tribe.' His face was dark and worn by sun and wind and his heavy beard was streaked with grey. He looked old but was probably no more than forty. 'You will want to know who I am and whom I rescued you from.'

417

Yakub swept away some debris with his palm and sat, lifting his sword to rest across his legs. 'I am a gazi, a gazi from the Germiyan lands in Anatolia.' he said. 'That means that I have even less love for Bayezid than you Greeks because I have already lost my lands to him.' He paused. 'The men following you were from Venice. I don't know why they want you.'

From Venice. Luke frowned. Why would Venetians be so close to the Ottoman camp unless they were supposed to be there? Had they been waiting for him?

'You were meant to escape,' said Yakub as if Luke's question had materialised before him. 'The wagon's axle was sawn through so that one hard pull would dislodge it. In the end they had to send a half-drugged dog to persuade you.'

Luke found his voice. 'Why?'

But before the word was out, he knew the answer. He thought about the unlikely generosity of the sipahi knight, of how he'd attached himself to him and brought them both to ride just behind Suleyman as they'd come down to Tarnovo. He thought about some information he'd been meant to overhear.

As if to himself, Luke murmured, 'The Serbians will be in the front line.'

'My guess is that the Venetians were to take you to the crusader commanders so that you could tell them that.' Yakub picked up a twig and began prodding the ground. 'The Turks want the crusader knights to charge first. They know that they'll like nothing better than charging other knights. It's a trap.'

He paused and looked up. 'There won't be knights in our front line but hyenas. The akincis are like hyenas, snapping and snapping until you go mad. We use them to lure you in, to tire you out with pretend charges and waves of arrows. Then we pounce.'

Luke turned this over in his mind. He'd seen the akincis as they'd marched away from Constantinople. He'd seen their small, fast horses and little bows that could fire an arrow every three seconds. But there was still a question to be answered.

'Why should I trust you? You are a gazi from the same tribes that gave us Bayezid. Why should I trust you?'

Yakub looked again at the ground. He picked up a leaf and examined it, turning it in the gathering light. 'This will be the first time that the armies of Christendom have met the Ottomans in battle. If they lose, there will be nothing to stop Bayezid watering his horse in Rome. You have heard this boast?'

Luke nodded.

'And there will certainly be no chance of the Germiyan tribe regaining its freedom.' He ran his finger along the central spine of the leaf. 'So you see, Luke Magoris, that much depends on the battle's outcome. Both of our freedoms depend on it very much.'

Yakub watched Luke carefully while he put fingers into the cowl of his cloak and stretched it away from the thick trunk of his neck, turning his head to left and right. He threw away the leaf and picked up his sword.

The gazi rose to his feet. 'I will show you,' he said. 'Now get up. We don't have much time.'

It took less than five minutes for Luke to change into gazi dress and remount his horse, which had been given a saddle and harness. It took another ten minutes for Yakub to lead him to a partially wooded ravine that lay to the front of the Sultan's army. With their four companions they were, to any onlooker, an akinci scouting party. They rode out to the front line.

There were no signs of Serbian heavy cavalry.

All Luke could see were line upon line of akincis, their bows slung low over their skins and their quivers crammed with arrows. They kept no sort of order and instead rode up and down, shouting to each other. Scouting parties were galloping in from the flanks and they rode up to Yakub and made their reports before rejoining the seething mass of horsemen.

Luke stopped and looked around him. On one side, the ground fell away into the ravine to the army's front. There was a wood there that screened any view beyond. To the east, the ground rose gently to another wood. There were no signs of any sipahis, either Rumelian or Anatolian, on either flank, but the wood could hide a regiment at least. Luke looked down the hill fronting the army.

The Frankish Knights will come through the wood and see the ravine. By then it will be too late.

Yakub had ridden up beside him. 'Come! We don't have time to stop.'

As they rode into it, the thick, screening mass of the akincis parted. The soldiers greeted Yakub but hardly glanced at Luke who, like his companions, was wearing a nose-guard and ear-pieces so that most of his face was obscured.

Then they were through the ranks of horsemen and Luke's heart almost stopped.

There, like the teeth of some open-jawed dragon, stood line upon line of sharpened stakes. There were hundreds of them, certainly enough to stop a cavalry charge of any weight, and they looked well dug in.

It is a trap.

Yakub was riding close to him. 'Don't look so surprised! Remember, you know they're there. Come!'

They rode along the back of the akincis in the direction of the hill and the wood at its crest. Yakub reined in his horse halfway up so that they were able to look down upon the army.

420

'Now look behind the stakes,' said Yakub. 'Janissary archers with all the time in the world to bring down the knights as they try to get through the stakes.' He glanced at Luke. 'Remember what I said. My akincis are no match for your Frankish knights. They're not meant to be. They are the hyenas which will send them mad with their snapping.'

He let his words sink in. Then he said, 'But this is not the main trap. It gets much worse.'

Yakub spurred his horse forward up the hill and then turned south so that they were skirting the end of the janissaries. It was now that Luke saw that the ground fell away behind the janissary lines, a feature invisible to anyone approaching from the front. And, as they approached the crest and were able to see behind, Luke reined in his horse and let out a groan.

There, hidden from view, was the main army.

There were the élite Kapikulu heavy cavalry and, beside them, rank upon rank of Serbian knights, thousands of them.

Suddenly Luke recognised the genius of the trap. By the time this cavalry charged, the crusader army, or what was left of it, would be too exhausted to fight. It was terrifying.

'Prince Yakub!'

Yakub wheeled his horse around. 'Prince Suleyman.' He bowed stiffly from the saddle. 'I was on my way to you with my scouting party. They report no movement from the crusaders yet. The two armies have formed up and seem to be deciding what to do.'

Suleyman was with a small guard of Kapikulu cavalry and had the Grand Vizier with him. He didn't answer immediately; instead looking up into the heavens. The sun was now rising in a cloudless sky and the day was getting hotter. He pushed his helmet back from his brow and put the cold mail of his hand against it.

'Deciding what to do?' he asked. 'They've already decided what to do, I think, or will do quite shortly. If it weren't forbidden, I'd wager good money that your akincis will feel the weight of the Frankish knights before noon. Are they prepared?'

'As always, lord.'

Luke was facing away from Suleyman, pretending to calm his horse and with his head low to the animal's ear.

'Good. Now, you must send your scouts out again. We need to know the minute this crusader army moves.'

Yakub gave the order and the akincis, Luke included, kicked their horses and cantered away.

They rode fast to the wooded summit of the hill and saw the ranks of Suleyman's Rumelian sipahis standing in eerie silence beneath the trees with their lance tips wrapped in hessian to prevent them catching the sun. They cantered around the back of the wood and north towards the Danube, crossing the ravine where it was shallower and where a muddy brook pooled at its centre. They came to a smaller valley and rode down it until they reached the banks of the river. Then they turned left and rode to the prow of a hill from which they could see the fortress of Nicopolis about a mile to the west.

The two Christian armies had struck camp and were formed up in two blocks, side by side, about a hundred yards apart. The Burgundian army's ranks were ablaze with colour and its front line was in constant movement as gorgeously dressed knights and their pages walked destriers up and down to calm them before the charge. It seemed as if every Christian king west of the Danube had emptied his coffers to send his nobility east to fight.

There was a patch of white at the back that Luke guessed

must be the Hospitallers. He could see perhaps three hundred knights and sergeants gathered beneath a white flag bearing a giant crusader cross. He saw that they were more ordered than the rest, sitting astride their horses and waiting patiently for their grand master's command. Behind them were the archers and crossbowmen, most of them mercenaries and some holding the deadly English longbow.

The Hungarian army had fewer knights. It was largely made up of horse archers, many of whom were little different from Yakub's gazi cavalry. Here were Kipchaks and Pechenegs, Vlachs and Wallachians and they were mounted on smaller, swarthier horses and had skins beneath their saddles and curved bows by their sides. These were the tough and fearless men of the Hungarian steppe and an obvious match for the akincis at the front of Bayezid's army.

The akincis stayed with Luke awhile, watching the scene to their front. Then one of them said something and they turned their horses and rode away. He looked down at the armies before him and wondered how he was to get to their commanders. He was dressed as a gazi and would be shot on sight if he simply rode down to them. He remembered his hair and removed his helmet so that his long fair hair tumbled down to his shoulders. Then he took off the leather armour from his upper half. Beneath was the simple white tunic that he'd worn on the journey from Constantinople. He ripped an arm from the tunic and tied it to the whip he found attached to his saddle and held it aloft.

The white flag of parley. Would it work?

Luke kicked his horse. He had a few hundred yards to ride but he knew that there were thousands of eyes watching him, the eyes of men stirred into a frenzy of blood lust.

What language was he to use? He knew Greek, Italian and

some Latin. But these men would most likely be French. He tried to remember the few French words Fiorenza had taught him.

'*Attendez!*' he yelled, waving his white flag and riding hard. '*Je suis ami! Je suis chrétien!*'

He saw heads turn and arms point. He saw swords drawn as if he might be the vanguard of something bigger. Then he saw a single knight detach himself from the army and ride forward, a mace swinging languidly from his mailed arm. The rider cantered some distance from the army and stopped. He was dressed in silver armour so polished that it caught the sun in dazzling ignition. His horse was caparisoned in gold fleur-de-lis and it trailed the ground. His visor was lowered and he looked unlikely to want to parley.

Luke slowed his horse and halted. '*Je parle avec vos commandants!*' he shouted. '*C'est important!*'

It sounded lame and the knight remained impassive. His mace continued to swing and he looked at Luke through a snout of pointed steel.

Luke considered his options. He could try to outride this fool but that would just bring others keen to spill the first blood. He raised himself in the saddle and yelled above the head of the man in front of him.

'I am Serbian!' he screamed in Greek. 'I am a deserter!'

For the first time the knight looked back from where he'd come. Luke could see some discussion in the front rank and there was a shouted command. A second rider emerged from the ranks, this time a squire in Burgundian household livery. He rode up to Luke.

'*Venez.*'

Luke followed him at the gallop. As the space between the

armies emerged, he could see that a pavilion had been erected between them and that several expensively caparisoned horses were being led up and down outside it. Men-at-arms held the standards of Burgundy and Hungary and other kingdoms. Clearly this was the place where the plan of attack was being discussed. Luke would be able to tell them what he knew.

Another knight, middle-aged, had arrived from the direction of the Hungarian army moments before. He had dismounted and was handing his reins to a page and looked up as Luke approached.

'*Qui est?*' Luke whispered to his companion.

'That is the Constable of the Kingdom of Hungary, Lord de Gara,' answered the page in Greek and bowed from the saddle as they rode up to him.

The Constable was looking at Luke curiously.

'I am Luke Magoris, lord,' Luke said in Greek. 'I bring news of the Turk army.'

The man looked over his shoulder at the entrance to the tent from where raised voices and even laughter could be heard. He took Luke's arm. 'You've seen it?'

'Yes, lord. All of it. It's not as it seems.'

'Tell me,' he said.

Luke told him and, as he listened, de Gara began to nod his head.

'Have you told anyone of this?' he asked at last.

'No, lord. Only you.'

'Good. Come with me.'

He turned and walked towards the small tent, lifting aside the flaps to reveal a space crowded with heavily armoured men, some holding helmets with tall plumes, some goblets of wine. In the centre was a table with a hand-drawn map on it. Sitting before it, looking intently at the coloured squares of wood that represented the armies, was a young man in his early twenties with a long nose and weak chin. His hair was cut short, like a tonsure, and sat between two prominent ears. His complexion suggested recent drinking.

The Comte de Nevers.

Next to him stood a man in his fifties with a shock of white hair and a broad, rubicund face lined by weather and, perhaps, experience. He looked heated and was pounding the table. 'Sire, on my sortie yesterday, we saw no sign of the Serbs. It is their irregulars that front their army. We cannot waste our knights against them!' The language was Latin.

'But, de Coucy,' said a younger man on the other side of the Count, 'are you suggesting that his highness will not lead the *avant-garde*? When we have come all this way? When Burgundy has all but *paid* for this crusade?' This man had a goblet in his hand and waved it as he spoke. Luke wondered if he was drunk.

The older man addressed de Nevers directly. 'Lord, no one doubts the Comte d'Eu's courage but we must consider our enemy. Listen to the Admiral de Vienne. He was part of the Count of Savoy's expedition in '66. He knows how these Ottomans fight.'

'Like hyenas.'

There was silence and everyone looked at Luke. The Admiral had not spoken.

Had he spoken?

The young Count looked up last and his eyes travelled, without enthusiasm, down Luke's mud-caked tunic. 'And you are?' he asked.

Luke quickly marshalled his thoughts. He glanced at the

other men in the room, most of whom were regarding him with a mixture of surprise and distaste.

'Highness,' he said, 'I have claimed to be a Serbian deserter to persuade them to bring me to you. In fact I'm Greek. I have ridden direct from the Turkish lines. I have seen how they are deployed and I know their battle plan. They would have you believe that the Serbian knights are in their front line. But it is their akincis that are there and they are there to mask sharpened stakes and, behind them, janissary archers. They mean to lure your knights into a killing ground and then attack them with their sipahi cavalry from the flanks. Then they will unleash the rest of the army, which is hidden behind the hill. It is a trap.'

There was silence in the tent as Luke's words were acknowledged. A gruff laugh came from a short, muscular man to his right. De Nevers looked at him.

'Marshal Boucicaut? You have something to say?'

'I am wondering, highness,' said the man, 'why we are wasting time by listening to someone none of us recognises and who might, for all we know, have been sent to misinform us.' He looked at Luke. 'You said you were Greek?'

'Yes, lord.'

'Ah . . . well then,' said the Marshal, and looked away. Others in the tent laughed.

Luke felt the blood rush to his face. 'Your meaning, my lord?'

Boucicaut arched an eyebrow. 'Meaning, you insolent young pup, that you are not to be trusted. Meaning that your *Orthodox* ways do not invite trust!'

There was an awkward silence in the tent.

'Or mine?' asked a voice from the other side of the tent. 'Are my Orthodox ways not to be trusted either?'

The voice came from a big, heavily bearded man dressed

from head to foot in a coat of mail. He wore a loose hauberk on which was emblazoned a black raven with a cross behind it: the arms of Wallachia. Under his arm was a helmet with a crown around it.

'Is that why your crusade has seen fit to rape and plunder its way down the Danube?' he asked. 'Because people of the Orthodox faith are not to be trusted?'

He paused and walked slowly up to Boucicaut. He stood very close, looking down at him. He was breathing hard. 'Why fight with us, then, if we cannot be trusted? Perhaps we should go home? We, the Transylvanians, the Hungarians – should we all go home?'

The silence was now oppressive. A centuries-old emnity was alive in this tent, an emnity that made these men unhappy allies, that seemed as great as their hatred of the Turk.

'Enough, gentlemen,' said a deeper voice that came from someone Luke had not yet noticed. He turned to see a man in his middle years seated on a camp stool in a corner of the tent. The man's voice was tired, as if he'd heard the argument before, but there was no mistaking its authority. Luke guessed he must be King Sigismund of Hungary.

'The decision must be the Comte de Nevers',' he said, 'perhaps advised by those of us who've seen action against these Ottomans.' He pointed towards Luke. 'I don't know who this man is, but what he says has the ring of truth. They do indeed fight like hyenas, snapping at you with their irregulars until you charge into their trap.'

He stood up and walked unevenly over to Luke, a limp, perhaps from some old wound. 'Who showed you these things?' he asked.

Luke's mind raced. 'I cannot tell you his name, lord. But I

will tell you that he is a gazi chieftain. Someone to trust.'

He heard Boucicaut snort behind him.

But Sigismund raised his hand. 'No,' he said, 'it makes sense. Most of the gazi tribes were overrun by Bayezid some years ago. They have no love for the Ottomans. It would suit them for us to win this battle.'

De Nevers was watching the King closely but also glancing nervously at d'Eu. He seemed overwhelmed by the responsibility placed on his young shoulders. 'So what does Your Grace suggest?' he asked.

'I suggest that these akincis are unworthy of the lances of your Burgundian knights,' Sigismund said carefully. 'The Voivode here' – he gestured towards Mircea – 'should meet them on equal terms with his Wallachian horse archers. I suggest using the same tactics that they use. Let us harry and provoke them into attacking *us*.'

There was silence in the tent. Outside could be heard the sounds of an army that waited for the word under a September sun that was rising fast in the sky. A nearby horse neighed and a page could be heard calming it.

De Nevers turned to a man who had yet to speak: Philippe d'Artois, Constable of France.

'Constable,' he asked, 'what is your view?'

D'Artois sighed and looked around him. He was an experienced soldier with many campaigns behind him, though none against the Turk. He walked forward to the edge of the table and looked down at the map for a long time. Then he looked straight at de Nevers.

'Prince,' he said slowly, 'de Coucy, de Vienne and their highnesses urge caution. These are men that know this enemy.' He paused. 'But I think it will be nigh-impossible to tell our knights that they must wait upon others before making their charge. However, I think we should ask the Kings of Hungary and Wallachia to send forward their horse archers with us to protect our flanks against these sipahi cavalry. And I think the knights should advance with the Hungarian infantry hard behind them.'

He looked now at Philibert de Naillac, Grand Master of the Knights Hospitaller. They were old friends. 'Philibert, do I thus speak reason?'

De Naillac had the long, unkempt hair and beard of the warrior monks from Rhodes and a reputation for common sense. 'I fear that here we see reason supplanted by some strange idea of honour, but I cannot see we have much choice. However, with your highnesses' permission, I will hold my knights back with the Hungarian main army. We may be needed later, I fear.' He looked at d'Eu. 'We of the Cross are less impeded by honour.'

D'Eu coloured and said to de Nevers, 'Sire, the Hospitallers must be their own masters, but now we have it clear. The knights will charge.'

He turned to the rest of the men in the tent and threw down his goblet. 'You have heard the decision!' he shouted. 'Forward in the name of God and St George; today you shall see me a valorous knight!'

Luke saw the man lift his helmet and turn to leave the tent. He saw the stricken face of the Admiral de Vienne, who would guard the standard that day, and he heard him say quietly to de Coucy, 'When truth and reason cannot be heard, then must arrogance rule.'

De Nevers had risen to his feet. He was flushed and reached

for his sword and helmet, which lay on the table beside the map. Sigismund approached him.

'Comte, my army is not yet ready to advance.'

De Nevers turned to him. There was something wild in his eyes. 'Then you must get them ready quickly, my lord of Hungary,' he said. 'The glory of our Christian knights must wait on nothing!' His young face was aglow with excitement. He raised a mailed hand as he walked to the tent door. 'For God and St George!'

Luke was left with Sigismund, Mircea and de Naillac. Sigismund turned to him.

'You said you were Greek yet you seem to speak Latin. You are educated but can you fight?'

Luke felt a surge of pride. 'I am a Varangian, lord.'

The effect was less than he'd hoped for.

'Ah, I'd wanted a rider.'

Luke drew himself up. 'I am a Varangian who rides. In fact I ride very well.'

'An educated Varangian that rides.' The King smiled. 'A wondrous combination.' He put his hand on Luke's shoulder. 'Varangian, I want you to follow this French army in its charge. I want you to ride behind them and, when they are engaged, come back with the news to me. I will be bringing up my army as fast as I can.'

Luke nodded.

'You will need an escort.'

Luke considered this quickly. 'Highness, there are other Varangians with one of these armies. Three of them, recently joined.'

'Yes, they are with me,' said de Naillac. 'What of them?'

'They are my friends, lord,' said Luke. 'Since childhood. I would trust none more.'

'Then you shall have them,' said Sigismund. 'Now go and find your friends and join the knights. And remember: stay alive. You are my eyes.'

Outside, all was commotion in the ranks of the French knights, with pages tightening girths and leading destriers to masters throwing back last beakers of wine before donning their helmets. The stench of defecation, human and animal, was overpowering. There were shouts of encouragement and forced jollity and curses as horse collided with horse, and a cheer went up as the red oriflamme of France was raised. Another, louder cheer accompanied the raising of the saltire of Burgundy and there was general tumult as de Vienne's men hoisted the flag of the Virgin. D'Eu, who was to lead the first battle, was already in the saddle and cantering up and down the front rank, brandishing his sword in the air as he yelled orders.

De Naillac led Luke down the side of the ranks until they came to a gap separating them from the second battle which was to be led by de Nevers. Luke could see the green hauberks and banners of the Burgundy household knights and men-at-arms who would surround the young Prince in the battle to come.

At the back of the second battle, they found the Hospitallers. Dressed in their white surcoats, they wore no other adornments and there were no pennants atop their lances. They held their helmets, square in the old-fashioned style, before them on their perfectly still saddles and the faces above the long beards were serious. Behind them, dressed in Varangian blue and with their axes slung at their saddles, were Luke's friends.

'Matthew, Arcadius, Nikko!' he yelled.

Three heads turned and three faces lit up in delight.

Then there were embraces and jokes and laughter quite out of keeping with the Hospitaller tradition, and many, many questions, which Luke cut short.

'We can talk later,' he said and gestured to de Naillac, who was standing behind him, smiling. 'The Grand Master is to give me a mount and some arms and then we are to ride out together. I will explain on the way.'

The horse was brought, then a sword without a dragon head for its pommel and an axe with two blades, and soon Luke was on his horse and cantering down the side of the two battles with his three companions. They reached a point where they were between the two armies and Luke could see how far the Hungarians had come in their preparations.

They were not ready. Not nearly ready.

He saw Sigismund in front of the horse archers shouting orders and men riding to the rear. The King turned in his saddle and waved. He looked worried.

Behind Luke, someone laughed.

'Friend of kings now, Luke?' said Nikolas. 'Does the Pope write to you too?'

By now, the French front rank was beginning to move. It was as if the four of them were standing at the edge of a beach and some Flemish dyer had thrown all his colours into the surf. Beneath a thousand bright banners, the whole line surged forward with d'Eu at its head roaring, '*Saint Denis et Montjoie!*' This army had boasted that it could hold up the heavens with its lances and it seemed that it almost could. Luke could see the Admiral and his knights raise the Virgin higher still and the shout that went up was deafening.

Luke turned to his friends. 'We are to follow the charge,' he bellowed, 'but not engage with the enemy. Hungary will be bringing up his infantry behind and we need to ride back to tell him what's going on.'

'Tell that to our horses!' yelled Nikolas.

The second battle was passing them now, with de Nevers standing in his stirrups and turning to left and right, his sword weaving circles in the air. He was shouting something Luke couldn't hear and his eyes were alight beneath the raised beak of his visor. Rank after rank trotted past and the destriers tossed their armoured heads and bit at their neighbours as they jostled for space and the ground shook with their passing.

Then they were ahead and the four Varangians fell in behind, keeping good distance between them and the last rank.

Luke knew how such a charge should go. His father had told him how the Templar knights had done it in the desert when they'd scattered the forces of Saladin. The trick was to start slow, the riders keeping rank knee to knee, to advance in close formation so that the whole line struck the enemy together. Only in the final moments of the charge would the horses be spurred into a gallop so that the impact would be overwhelming.

But this didn't seem to be happening. The horses ahead of them were moving too fast too soon. They had at least a mile to travel and would be exhausted by the time they met the Turks. And what of the Hungarians? How would their foot soldiers keep up?

Luke looked over his shoulder. The Hungarians were still forming up and it would be some time before they were even ready to march. He swore beneath his breath and kicked his horse towards the knights in front.

Slow down, damn you. Slow down!

Up ahead, the chivalry of Europe was enjoying the ride. The ground was even and sloped gently away towards trees in the

434

distance beyond which stood the infidel. The distance was great but it was closing fast and although the sun was now high in the sky, the heat was bearable so long as their visors remained open.

But some older and wiser heads within the ranks began to worry.

'Hold, d'Eu, damn you!' yelled de Coucy. He looked around him and saw the rest of the front line was made up of young knights who were as inexperienced as they were out of control. It was a stag hunt not a cavalry charge. How would these men face their first Ottoman arrows?

Now they had reached the wood and were passing amongst trees that were well spaced so that the momentum of the charge was not lessened. The young knights hacked at branches as they passed with screams of joy as if they were already amongst the Turks.

'Conserve your strength,' bellowed de Coucy.

Then they were out of the trees and, one by one, the shouts faded and the horses pulled up.

Ahead of them was a deep ravine with what looked like thick undergrowth at the bottom of it. On the other side, a hill rose sharply and on it were the akinci horsemen, wave upon wave of them, with an arrow on every bowstring.

A ravine. A ravine and a hill. A wet hill to charge up when they'd already cantered for over a mile.

The riders behind them came up and horses collided and shouts turned into curses.

But d'Eu rounded on them. 'What are you waiting for? Look at them! They're unarmoured peasants! Kill them!' So saying, he shut his visor with a sound that echoed through the trees. '*Saint Denis et Montjoie!*' he shouted again and spurred his horse into the ravine.

435

Then all the visors came down in a ripple of steel and the battle cry went up and passed from rider to rider. The front rank followed d'Eu down into the undergrowth of the ravine, hacking at low bushes as their horses stumbled their way through. Then the hill was before them and the akincis were riding forward at the gallop and shrieking their terrible war cries. The knights of the front rank now couched their lances and kicked and kicked at their horses, horses that were tired and hating this new, steeper ground, which was slick with mud from the night's rain. But their hooves eventually gained traction and the knights gathered some speed and began their long charge up the hill.

The akincis were coming down fast, expertly controlling their wiry horses with their knees as they aimed their bows. Then there was the sound of thousands of bowstrings unleashed. The arrows came low, not aimed at the knights but at their horses' chests, which were padded, not armoured, and were exposed by the gradient of the hill. Scores of horses fell and their riders fell with them, pinned beneath their bodies. The knights behind, part-blinded by their visors, crashed into those in front and men were pitched forward to land in agony on the ground. Some picked themselves up only to be cut down by arrows fired at point-blank range.

It was carnage and some of the knights at the front wavered. But men of more experience were coming up behind, men who knew that Milanese armour could withstand all but the closest Turkish arrow, and these men rallied them and helped those that could remount.

D'Eu was unharmed and still in front and was driving his heels into the sides of his horse whose white eyes rolled either side of its armoured nose. His sword had been replaced by a mace and he swung savagely at an akinci who dared ride too close, and the crack of the man's skull was loud and gave heart to those around him.

'Follow me!' he screamed as he brought another Turk crashing to the ground.

The akincis were backing off now. They had done what damage they could and knew they were no match for these knights in close combat. They turned their horses and fired arrows behind them as they galloped away up the hill and the crusaders resumed their charge, heartened by the fleeing enemy.

But as the akincis dispersed, they did so out to the flanks and d'Eu could now see for himself how accurate Luke's warning had been. Row upon row of sharpened stakes faced them fifty paces to their front, and behind them stood the serried and silent ranks of the janissary archers.

On a command, the archers released a storm of arrows, but this time high into the sky so that they fell on the knights like hail. The sound of metal on metal was deafening and the knights lowered their heads and those that bore shields raised them in cover. The arrows did not penetrate their armour but they hit and maddened the horses, which twisted and reared and tried to turn away. More knights fell to the ground, their armour too heavy for them to dodge the hooves that thrashed above them.

D'Eu was still in front and next to him was the knight with the oriflamme. He leant over and wrenched the banner away and lifted it high, swinging it in circles. He turned to the knights behind, raising his visor as he did so. 'Who will ride with me?' he yelled. 'Who will join me in these Turkish ranks? Who will help me kill these heathen scum?'

Arrows were falling all around him but he seemed immune.

His courage was contagious and another cry went up and the whole line moved forward. De Nevers was now well ahead of his battle and his household knights were still with him, some unhorsed. He raised his visor. 'I'm with you, d'Eu!'

Then there was a sound from their flank. It was a single trumpet blast and de Nevers turned towards it and his face changed.

Charging down the hill towards them, in perfect formation, were the sipahis of Rumelia and at their head was Prince Suleyman. These were not the undisciplined horsemen of the akincis. These were heavily armoured cavalry who charged as the crusaders should have charged. They were knee to knee and their lances were lowered and there were thousands of them.

Then a second trumpet sounded from the other side and de Nevers spun round to see more sipahis charging from their right. At their head was the Sultan's second son, Prince Mehmed.

And the protection that the crusaders should have had from the Hungarian horse archers was far, far behind.

The knights on the flanks turned their horses to meet this new threat, dropping their lances to the ground and unsheathing their swords. They were still the flower of Christendom and more than a match for these vermin.

'To me!' shrieked de Nevers as he wheeled his horse. 'Stand with me!'

The sipahis hit them on both sides, their lances lifting men from their saddles. They smashed into the Christian ranks, slashing with their scimitars to left and right and bringing knights down in droves. Screams of agony filled the air as the ground became strewn with fallen men and wet with their blood. The Admiral de Vienne was now holding the banner of the Virgin and around him were the corpses of others that had held it before. He thrust it aloft.

'Hold your ground!'

The knights with d'Eu had now reached the jagged lines of stakes and those without horses were pulling them from the ground, all the while rained on by arrows that fell from the air or tore into them from the front. Somehow, miraculously, they were gaining ground. The stakes were being thrown aside and the knights were engaging with the janissaries and their armour was giving them the upper hand. The Turks were falling back and no quarter was being given.

On the flanks, the tide seemed to be turning too. The sipahi charge had been halted on both sides and the knights were driving them back. But this was what the Turks had expected. Suleyman, who was in the thick of the fighting, raised his sword and signalled a withdrawal. The sipahis turned and, with perfect precision, wheeled their horses and rode away.

A cheer went up from the Christian ranks. But it was different from the cheers before. This was the ragged cheer of tired men, men who were at the limits of what they could do.

Men who wanted help from the Hungarians.

Luke and his three Varangian friends had watched all this from the wood below. They'd seen the carnage wreaked by the akincis' arrows and they'd seen the crusader knights recover and charge up the hill to the rows of stakes. They'd seen the charge of the sipahi cavalry and how it had been repulsed. They'd seen heroism and reckless courage beyond what they could have imagined and deaths that would haunt them for the rest of their lives.

Throughout it, they'd anxiously checked behind them and

had seen the Hungarian army draw closer with a slowness that was painful to watch. As the knights repulsed the sipahi cavalry and began to regroup, Luke knew that the time had come for him to ride to King Sigismund and implore him to throw forward his army.

But there was a problem.

Riderless horses, some crazed with pain, were charging back into the knights still advancing up the hill. They trampled and bit their way through their ranks and were now coming through the wood to reach the open ground beyond. Horses with their chamfrons pierced with arrows, horses with sliced, open arteries. Horses that were running in panic towards the advancing Hungarians.

Horses that would tell of a catastrophe ahead.

Luke mounted quickly and rode fast out of the wood, his friends behind him. It was perhaps five hundred yards to the Hungarians and he could cover it within minutes if he didn't collide with any of the horses that were galloping beside him. He had no time to lose.

On the hill, the knights of Christendom were preparing themselves for another sipahi charge from both sides. If they could withstand it, then the battle could still be won.

They yelled encouragement to each other from parched throats, their voices cracking with fatigue. They looked behind for reinforcements and shouted of Hungarian cowardice and they took off their helmets and wiped their brows and tried to ignore the pitiful sounds of the dying around them.

D'Eu had lost his horse. He held a sword in one hand and a mace in the other, both dripping with gore. His visor was still open and his face was caked in blood, his own and others'. He shouted to those around him to hold firm but his words were hardly audible. He looked round for de Nevers and saw the young Count not far away, also unhorsed and standing amidst a pile of bodies. The remains of the Burgundian household stood around him and the green of their livery was splashed with blood and dirt. Some held on to their lances to support them in their exhaustion. Some simply sat on the ground to recover their strength. None had mounts.

De Vienne and the Sire de Coucy were further down the slope, also standing. Together they held the banner of the Virgin aloft and together they prayed that their patron saint would send them the Hungarians they had so rashly left behind. De Coucy was wounded, an open gash visible through the mail on his arm. But he still had his voice, his deep voice of authority, and he used it to rally the men around him.

'Courage!' he shouted. 'We are Christian knights and we can still win this day!'

Then came the rumble. This was a deeper rumble than that made by the sipahi cavalry. This was the rumble of armoured knights on armoured horses and it came from the other side of the hill. Thousands of Christian eyes looked towards it: eyes that had been full of fatigue were now full of fear.

The Serbians are coming.

Luke had, by now, reached the Hungarian lines and had found the King. Riding beside Sigismund was the Voivode Mircea of Wallachia, whose troops were on the left of the column, and Prince Laczković, whose Transylvanians were on the right. The fleeing horses had reached them and were now tearing swathes through the ranks of soldiers that felt new fear for whatever lay ahead.

'Highness!' yelled Luke as he brought his horse to a halt before them. 'Highness, the battle is in the balance! The knights have broken through but they are tired. Bring forward your army and the field can still be ours . . .' He gasped for breath. '. . . but you must act quickly.'

He saw Mircea and Laczković exchange glances. He turned to them.

'Lords, this battle can still be won. But you must act *now*!'

Mircea spoke. 'Have the Serbians engaged?' he asked. His face was grave.

The answer was there in Luke's silence.

'Then the day is lost,' said Mircea. 'If the French are unhorsed and exhausted, they will not stand against a Serbian charge.' He turned his horse.

'Voivode!' shouted Sigismund at the man riding away. 'We cannot abandon them! We cannot leave our Christian brothers to the Turks! For mercy's sake!'

Mircea stopped and turned in his saddle. 'Mercy? What mercy did these knights show to the prisoners they took from Rahova? They slaughtered them! They slaughtered them before the battle began because they needed the guards to fill their ranks! They slaughtered men, woman and children. Don't talk to me of mercy, Sigismund. Bayezid will show no mercy to us when this deed is told, I'll warrant you.'

And the Voivode rode away towards his countrymen whom he would take with him back to Wallachia. Rode away to make peace, in any way he could, with the victorious Bayezid.

Sigismund turned to the Prince of Transylvania. 'And you, Prince Laczković,' he asked, 'will you desert me too?'

Laczković looked at the men from Transylvania, the men who'd hoped this Christian army would save them from the

Turk, the men who had stopped marching. 'I think, lord,' he said, his face sad and drawn, 'that my army has already decided.'

And he, too, turned his horse and rode away.

There was the sound of harness and de Naillac approached, his long face a study in calm. Behind him rode a Hospitaller knight with the standard of St George in his mailed fist. De Naillac reined in his horse and looked from Luke to Sigismund.

'Our allies desert us? No matter. We have a battle to fight. Come, my lord king, we have God's work to do this day and we cannot delay.'

Sigismund looked back at the three columns behind him, two of which were already beginning to march away. He looked at the fleeing crusader horses riding through his army in their pain and panic. 'God help us,' he said quietly.

'God will help us but only if we help ourselves.' de Naillac urged. 'Send forward your army now, sire, before it's too late. My knights are ready to ride. Just give us the word.'

King Sigismund pondered this advice. Then he turned to face his army. He stood high in his stirrups and filled his lungs with air. He threw back his head and held his sword above him. 'Soldiers of Hungary!' he yelled. 'Today we are under the eyes of God! Are we to prevail against this infidel horde or submit to its barbaric creed? Will you follow me to hurl the might of Hungary against this enemy or will you leave the field as cowards?' He paused and breathed deep. 'Will you follow your king?'

Luke looked at the ranks of soldiers behind. He saw undecided faces, questioning faces; he saw fear in them. He saw men considering life and considering death. He saw men torn between loyalty to God and King and the instinct to survive. He saw an army in the balance.

'I will follow you, sire!'

It was not a knight but the voice of a common man, a man who'd left his fields to march with this army on its holy purpose.

'And I!' yelled another, and so the cry went up. Soon the whole army was a sea of waving spears and bows. The soldiers of Wallachia and the soldiers of Transylvania were leaving the field but the soldiers of Hungary would march on.

King Sigismund turned back to de Naillac and Luke. 'De Naillac, take your knights forward and see what you can do to help the French. I'll bring up my army as fast as I can.'

'And I, highness?' asked Luke.

'You and your friends go with the Hospitallers,' replied the King. 'And use your axes well!'

On the hill the battle was going badly for the Christian army. The Serbian cavalry, with Prince Lazarević at its head, had torn into the ranks of the French and Burgundians, cutting a path of death in its wake. Now mostly on foot, the crusader knights were parrying lances with swords and those that weren't speared were crushed under the monstrous hooves of the destriers that came down the hill at a speed impossible to resist. As the knights fell back, they slipped and fell on the entrails of men and horses and they lay there in their exhaustion, unable to rise and fight again.

Behind the Serbians came the janissaries who were silent and efficient in their killing. Visors were raised and daggers plunged into eyes that looked up at their last morning. No quarter was given to any that asked for it and few had the energy to try. Screams of terror and pain filled the air and from the younger knights came the pitiful cries to mothers and to a God that seemed to have abandoned them. This was not the chivalrous adventure they'd been so keen to join. This was a terrifying, brutal affair played to rules they didn't understand.

D'Eu was still standing, his armour no longer bright and his voice no longer strong enough to shout. Around him lay piles of dead and wounded and he lurched like a drunk as he swung his mace at men and ghosts. He'd removed his helmet and his long black hair clung to the gore on his face, his eyes wild and unseeing. Part of his jaw hung open from a sword slash and blood bubbled in the neck of his cuirass. The janissaries had spared him so far and seemed reluctant to bring him down. He was a leader and leaders brought ransom.

De Vienne was on his knees. The heavy flag of the Virgin was still in his grasp, although five men had died to keep it aloft. He knew that his fifty-five years of living were nearly over and was thanking God for a good life and praying to him for a worthy death.

'Come on, you bastards!' he yelled in a language they couldn't understand. 'Come on and take this flag! You'll burn in hell for the deed and I'll be there to watch it!'

The janissaries paused and frowned at a courage that would deny them profit. Then one stepped forward and raised his sword and brought it down on the arm holding the flag and the blood from the severed limb spattered his mail. The standard fell and the janissary raised his sword again and this time it fell on the old knight's helmet and the head within it broke apart and de Vienne lay still.

It seemed, then, that a great groan went up above the clash of steel on steel. The knights of Christendom had fought within sight of this standard for over an hour, had taken heart from its message.

Now it had fallen.

De Nevers saw it come down and, for the first time, considered defeat. He looked around him at the countless dead of his household, at the Burgundian banners trampled into the ground, at the janissaries' remorseless advance and at the Serbian cavalry already regrouping for a second charge. He saw de Coucy nearby, fighting alongside Boucicaut. He lifted his visor and called out to them. 'De Coucy!' he shouted. 'Is the day lost?'

The older knight was fighting with a strength that belied his years. Two janissaries lay dead at his feet and two more were about to die. He glanced back at the Count. 'The Hungarians, lord!' he yelled back. 'Are they near?'

De Nevers looked behind him. The hill was a mass of confusion, of tangled armour and rising and falling swords and maces. If the Hungarians were there, he couldn't see them.

'We are alone, de Coucy!' he shouted. The voice was unsteady. 'Should we yield?'

De Coucy stepped back from the fight and found behind him the carcass of a destrier, a wooden stake embedded in its chest. He found a shield lying on the ground beside it which he laid as a ramp and climbed to see above the heads of the armies around him.

The crusader army was surrounded on three sides. Above them were the Serbs and the janissaries, and the Kapikulu cavalry, and on either flank were the sipahis with the akincis behind them, and all were slowly, remorselessly closing in. Only at the bottom of the hill, at the treeline beyond the ravine, was there any hope of escape and he could see scores of men who'd abandoned their weapons pouring into it.

Nowhere could he see help.

446

Had de Coucy looked a moment longer, he would have seen it. Had there not been so many men and horses fleeing in panic through the wood, he would have seen the tight ranks of the Hospitallers emerge from the trees like a white, welcome surf.

Had he waited a minute longer, he might not have turned back to de Nevers and said, 'Lord, the day is surely lost.'

Luke urged his horse into the ravine along with three hundred others, calling on the panicked men that passed him to turn and fight, crying out that behind them came more soldiers, more men to turn the tide of this battle.

Then he saw de Nevers's standard drop.

The household knights had formed a ring around their prince. He saw a man in front of them pinioned to the flank of a horse by a lance driven down through his windpipe. He saw him feebly raise his arms to beg for death and he saw a knight from Burgundy step forward, cross himself and deliver that death with his head averted. Around the knights were the enemy, many with arrows strung to bowstrings. Then he saw the knights kneel as one and lay down their weapons.

'Stop!' he yelled. 'Stop! We have come!'

But he was too far away and, even if he hadn't been, he doubted if he'd have been heard. This was an army exhausted beyond listening, an army that had no strength left to fight.

The Hospitallers saw it too and all heads turned to de Naillac.

'Engage!' he bellowed, and the knights kicked their destriers and drove them into the flanks of the sipahis. And Luke and his three friends charged with them.

Up to this moment, Luke had felt everything but fear: the sharpened focus of adrenalin, the ebb and flow of hope and dismay, but he'd not felt fear. Now, as he spurred his horse forward and lowered his lance, as he saw numberless turbaned helmets through the slit of his visor, he realised that he was about to join battle for the first time and he felt the clutch of fear deep in his stomach. He knew his father was somewhere close, watching.

For the Empire. For you.

Then they were upon the enemy and there was no time to think of anything but kill and not be killed. Luke and his three friends fought as a unit, protecting the others' flank as each discarded his lance, drew his axe and picked an opponent. Luke felt a surge of excitement, each of his senses heightened to meet the imperatives of destruction and survival. He fought with a skill his father would have been proud to see.

He was a Varangian Prince and he was the best of the best.

Soon the sipahis were falling back and some, desperate to escape this scythe of ruin, had turned and were riding over the janissaries behind. Now the screams and curses were Turkish and the banners that fell had holy verses on them.

But the rush of the Hospitaller charge was slowing.

Swinging his axe and controlling his horse with his knees, Luke could feel the momentum of the charge lessen. He felt it stall, then stop. And then he felt his horse take its first, grudging step backwards.

We are three hundred. They are forty thousand. This is madness.

There was a cluster of Kapikulu cavalry to his front, the same guard he'd seen earlier. They were fighting in close formation, protecting someone behind them.

Suleyman.

Then Luke saw him. A gap had appeared in the Kapikulu ranks and the heir to the Ottoman throne, splendid on a black charger, was there urging his men on. The flag of the Prophet was behind him. He turned in his saddle and his eyes met Luke's. A smile spread across his face.

He shouted something that Luke couldn't hear. Then he yelled at his guard and they began to fight their way in Luke's direction.

Suleyman was closer now, still screened by his men, but close enough to be heard.

'Congratulations on your escape,' he yelled, his voice booming over the clash of steel. 'The crusaders fell into our trap and the credit must go to you, Luke Magoris! You have the Sultan's thanks and, if you drop your axe, I'm sure he'll want to give them to you in person.'

'What does he mean?' cried Nikolas. 'Who is he?'

'His name is Prince Suleyman,' Luke answered, 'and he's practised in lying. Don't listen to him.'

Suleyman laughed. 'I'm sorry, Luke, I hadn't realised we would be understood if I spoke in Greek. Forgive me.'

Luke dug his heels into his horse's sides and sprang forward and, with a roar, his friends did the same. Taken by surprise, the Kapikulu fell back.

Then Luke heard de Naillac's shout from behind him. It was the command to withdraw, a command that would be obeyed without question by every Hospitaller.

'What do we do now?' shouted Arcadius, pulling up his horse. "Go with them?'

Luke looked at Suleyman, who was smiling behind his nose-guard. He was much closer now.

'Yes, Luke Magoris, what do you do now?'

Luke turned and saw Matthew beside him, loyal Matthew

already having to engage two of the enemy because the Hospitaller to his right had pulled away.

Matthew who will die if I continue this fight.

'Will you spare them if I surrender?'

Suleyman nodded. 'I will spare them. You have my word.'

His word?

Suleyman lifted his sword, ready to give the command.

Luke turned to his companions. 'Drop your weapons!'

Three faces turned to him in horror.

'Do it!'

The Varangians lowered their axes and pulled back their horses.

Luke looked back at Suleyman.

His word.

Behind them, the Hospitallers had crossed the ravine, fighting as they went, and now fifty of the knights had dismounted and turned to face their enemy. Meanwhile, de Naillac and the rest of them had galloped back to the Hungarians.

'The Burgundians have surrendered,' panted the Grand Master. 'Your Grace should retire with your army. My men are holding them at the ditch but they will soon come through from the flanks.'

Some of de Naillac's reserve had left him and it was this, as much as the news, which struck the King. Beside him was John de Gara.

'De Naillac, can we not turn it?' he asked.

The Grand Master shook his head. 'They are too many, lord. They have made prisoner some of the greatest names in Christendom. Don't give them more.'

The Constable turned to his king. 'You should ride for the boats, sire. The Hospitallers will guard you. I will come behind you with the army.'

'No,' said Sigismund. 'Why should they fight if their king deserts them?'

'Because they will live to fight another day when we can do it free from Burgundian folly!' said the older man hotly. 'Go, sire, while there is still time.'

By the time that the bashibozouks had filled the ravine with their dead, by the time that the last Hospitaller knight had fallen, the Hungarian King, together with de Naillac, had reached the safety of the boats.

His army had thrown back charge after charge by the sipahis, horse archers fighting on foot beside foot soldiers.

But then the Serbians came, ten thousand of them, and the Hungarians' last hope was extinguished. They'd fought for an hour against impossible odds and hardly a man had looked behind him. But now the line began to break and first one, then another threw down his weapon and turned for the river.

De Gara cursed and pleaded with them but it was no use. This army knew it was defeated and its soldiers thought only of their wives, their fields, their future. With de Gara were the knights of Hungary that had stayed to shield their king, knights who could at least expect some ransom if captured and who'd fight to help men of lesser station get away. They prepared to make their stand, standing shoulder to shoulder across the plain, facing both ways as the Turks encircled them, some looking back to Nicopolis where the gates had opened and another army was riding out to fight them.

'Stand!' shouted de Gara. 'Let's bring as many down as we can before they take us!'

And then it began. Sword clashed with sword and mace with mace and sparks flew into the air with the blood. The Hospitallers rejoined the fight towards the end, having delivered the Grand Master and Hungarian King to the ships. The river had been full of soldiers trying either to board the ships or swim to the other side where the Wallachians were already forming up to march away. Sigismund and de Naillac had stood side by side at a ship's rail to watch a vessel slowly capsize under the weight of men clambering up its sides.

Then they'd heard a cheer. De Gara had raised his hand and the flag of Hungary come down, and a cheer had gone up from the Turks that could be heard in Nicopolis. The battle had been won. The Ottoman Empire had proven itself superior to Western valour and the gates of Europe were thrown open.

And as King Sigismund sailed away down the Danube, past the river's islands and on to the Black Sea, his cheeks were wet with tears.

CHAPTER TWENTY-TWO

NICOPOLIS, 25 SEPTEMBER 1396

The morning after the battle dawned noisily with the harsh, scraping calls of carrion birds circling high above the dead strewn across the field of Nicopolis. From the banks of the Danube to the hill where the Burgundians had made their last stand lay bodies. And those that had not been picked clean by the bashibozouks now had their eyes pecked out by crows. The cries of the wounded rose like a dark music and the stench of decay hung heavy in the air.

The morning was a grey one, with a low mist hanging over hills and valleys drained of autumn colour. There was a light wind with a chill that presaged meaner weather to come and men shivered and drew their cloaks around them.

Bayezid stood alone in the middle of the plain on which the Hungarians had fought and died, and held a cloth to his nose. He wore a long, open coat of buff leather above a mail shirt and loose trousers tucked into riding boots, their black leather stained with the gore around him. He'd just ridden from the crusader camp where he'd spent the night celebrating his greatest victory.

He was in a dark mood.

453

He'd risen early and spent some time just looking towards the fortress of Nicopolis. There were cages suspended from its ramparts in which meat for the birds had been left: the naked, twisted remains of crusader knights who'd died in shrieking agony the night before. The birds were still there, perched on the bars and reaching in with their beaks. The walls behind were streaked with blood.

Before the walls still stood the smouldering remains of fires. The Bektashi dervishes had piled the crusader scaling ladders high and put stakes at their centres on which to tie and roast the priests and monks found in the Christian camp. They'd danced their whirling dance around the flames and been clapped on their way by the men of the victorious army.

Bayezid's temper since rising had been such that his retinue stood at a prudent distance: his three sons, the Grand Vizier and a bodyguard of Kapikulu.

'How many dead, Vizier?' he shouted across the bodies.

'Ours or theirs, highness?'

'Ours, fool. I care not how many *Christians* lie on this field.'

The Vizier looked around him as if in calculation. In fact the dead had already been counted and he knew their number by heart, dreading its disclosure.

'Over twelve thousand of our men are martyrs, lord. It is too many.'

Bayezid groaned. *Twelve thousand.* A quarter of his army.

'And theirs?' he asked. Now he cared more.

'Half that number, lord,' the Vizier replied and then: 'Their armour, highness. It stops our arrows.'

Bayezid was silent. He thought of Constantinople with its walls of double strength. He thought of scaling ladders and the men needed to mount them.

Twelve thousand!

The Sultan knelt beside the body of a young sipahi, his eyes still staring into the heaven he'd gone to. Was he, even now, in the arms of the promised virgins? Across his legs was strewn a Hungarian archer, one side of his head removed by a sword blade.

Bayezid stood and watched as a blackbird landed. He kicked out at it.

'Vizier!' he shouted. 'I want this sipahi taken from the field and a mausoleum built. Find his family and give them money.'

An hour later, Bayezid's mood was darker still. He sat, slumped, in a high-backed chair of burnished gold with piled cushions spilling out either side of his great frame. His boots had been replaced by soft slippers that rested on a little stool. One hand held a goblet while the other was poised above a low table on which a bowl of sugared fruits had been placed.

The Sultan sat beneath an awning that had been erected on some open ground beside the Ottoman camp. Sharing it were his three sons, the Grand Vizier and Yakub. Anna stood next to Suleyman. Behind them were the imams, who had been summoned for a reason: Bayezid wanted interpretation of the law of Islam.

There were hundreds of chests before him and piles of gold and silver plate. Some were open, their contents spilling out over the ground. The treasure had been brought from the crusader camp and its value was beyond measure.

Also in front of him was a young woman kneeling on the ground, her dress torn and her hair matted with filth. Anna was staring at her in shock, her mouth slightly open.

'They did this as well?' said Bayezid. His voice was barely controlled.

The Grand Vizier nodded.

'Give her money,' said Bayezid, turning away.

'So, Majesty,' said the Vizier when the woman had left. 'We now know that these knights slaughtered all their prisoners before the battle began. They killed not just men but women and children too, people who could not have offered them any resistance. And the only ones kept alive were those pretty enough to slake their wretched lust.' He paused. 'You have heard it from her lips, lord.'

Bayezid nodded darkly into his wine.

'You wish, therefore, Majesty, to execute as many of these infidel as is permitted under our law.' The Vizier turned his vast turban towards the imams beside him. 'I have consulted with the ulema, lord, and they tell me this. Prisoners are the property of those who capture them, to do with them as they wish. However, the law also says that one-fifth of all prisoners will belong to the Sultan, God's shadow on earth.' He bowed low and Bayezid waved impatiently for him to continue.

'Your Majesty has seen fit to interpret this in the past as the means by which we can claim the strongest prisoners for the Devshirme. In consequence you have generally sent your share to the villages of Anatolia to begin their education in the ways of Islam.'

Bayezid's impatience was visibly growing and the Vizier hurried to his conclusion. 'So the judges are unanimous, Majesty, in deeming it proper for you to execute one-fifth of the Christian prisoners if you so wish.'

'I do so wish. How many are there?' asked Bayezid, wiping his lips with the back of his hand.

456

'We have ten thousand in all, lord. So two thousand will die.'

'Good,' said Bayezid. 'Prince Suleyman, Prince Mehmed, you have prisoners?'

The brothers looked at each other. Mehmed stepped forward.

'Father, we each have prisoners.'

'Then you will kill them,' said Bayezid flatly. 'Kill them all. And do it here. I want an example set to the army.'

Mehmed bowed. 'Yes, Father.'

Bayezid threw back the remains of his wine and looked at Candarli. 'Vizier, my sons will bring their prisoners here and will be the first to execute them. Tell others that have prisoners to bring here those they have selected to die. Remember, it is to be one in every five.'

The Vizier bowed.

Suleyman stepped forward. He gestured towards Anna. 'Should the woman retire, Father? It is not seemly.'

Bayezid shrugged. He'd barely been aware of Anna's presence. Suleyman quickly nodded to the guards, who lined up to escort her away.

The Vizier said, 'Lord, the Comte de Nevers, Marshal Boucicaut and the other leaders of the Christian army await your pleasure.'

The Sultan turned to his sons. 'These men we will spare, and twenty others of rank that de Nevers will identify. These men we will keep for ransom. Now, go and fetch your prisoners.' He looked back at the Vizier. 'Bring the Burgundy Prince.'

A short while later, de Nevers was standing in front of Bayezid. He was still wearing his armour but it was pitted with dents and the arms of Burgundy had vanished beneath the filth of his hauberk. His face was bruised and unshaven and seemed

457

much older than the day before. But the gaze that came to rest on Bayezid was still proud.

He, and a dozen of the highest-ranking survivors of the French–Burgundian army, had been led before the Sultan with their wrists tied and heavy chains dragging behind them on the ground.

De Nevers spoke in Greek. 'Highness, we are noblemen of the highest rank and should not be chained. We have given our word not to attempt escape.'

Bayezid scowled. 'Kneel.'

De Nevers looked bewildered.

'Kneel!'

De Nevers was kicked behind his knees by a guard and he knelt. De Coucy and Boucicaut started forward but they too were brought down by the guards.

Bayezid's scowl deepened.

'It seems to me, Count, that you are a proud and stupid man. You must be to have led an army to such a defeat.'

De Nevers blinked up at the Sultan. 'Sir, I am—'

'You are nothing!' yelled Bayezid, flinging his cup to the floor. He glared at the Prince through hooded eyes, his face flushed with anger. 'Since crossing the Danube, your army has murdered and raped everything in its path. This person' – he gestured towards the terrified woman still standing at the edge of the tent – 'was kept as a concubine in your camp, her body defiled by your knights.'

De Nevers struggled to rise. His face was white and a film of sweat covered his brow. 'Lord, I—'

'Silence!' roared Bayezid.

De Nevers's eyes had lost some of their pride.

'What did your army do to its prisoners on the night before

battle?' the Sultan asked softly. 'Tell me, Comte de Nevers from this small place called Burgundy, what did you do with them?'

De Nevers was silent. He looked at the ground and then behind him at the knights kneeling to his rear. Beyond them, in the wide, open space before the pavilion, he could see other knights, pages, archers, being assembled, all tied to each other by thick ropes attached to their necks. At their front were a man and a boy dressed in gold mail to whom others bowed.

He turned back to the Sultan. 'These men, you mean to enslave them?' he asked slowly.

'No,' said Bayezid calmly, taking the new cup offered him. 'I mean to execute them.' He took a long draught of wine. 'As you executed your prisoners before the battle. Is it not just?'

The young Prince's eyes widened in disbelief. His hands had started to shake.

'The difference, of course,' continued Bayezid, taking a sugared fruit from the bowl, 'is that these men are not innocent. They have fought against me and killed too many of my men. I do not wish that to happen again and this deed might prevent it.'

'But . . . that's barbaric!' shouted de Nevers, his voice too high.

'Barbaric?' hissed Bayezid, leaning forward. 'More barbaric than the massacre of every man, woman and child in Jerusalem three hundred years ago?' He paused. 'You see: we of the Faith have long memories.'

De Nevers heard a throat clear behind him. Prince Suleyman stepped into the pavilion and bowed to his father.

'My prisoners are assembled, lord,' he said.

'And mine, Father,' said Mehmed, walking up to stand beside his brother.

Bayezid's eyes were glassy and the flush on his cheeks high. He took time to shift his gaze from de Nevers to his sons.

'Prince Mehmed,' he said, 'I anticipate you enjoying this process rather less than your brother, so you will go first. Is your sword sharp?'

Mehmed looked at his father. His sword was drawn. 'It is sharp, Father.'

'Good, then you may begin.' He turned to the man kneeling at his front. 'Comte de Nevers, I desire you to watch these executions. Get up.'

De Nevers was lifted to his feet. He pushed away his guards. 'You cannot do this!' he yelled. 'It is against every rule of war!' He took a step towards Bayezid, who rose suddenly from his chair and slapped him hard across the face.

'You will turn and watch or it will be worse,' he hissed.

Out in the open a thick chopping block had been placed on the earth and beyond it stood the silent line of knights awaiting their fate. The first was being brought forward and offering no resistance to his guards. Mehmed had moved to the side of the block and was running his thumb down the blade of a vast scimitar. The knight calmly knelt and placed his head on the block. Mehmed lifted the sword high above his head, both hands on its hilt.

De Nevers looked around him in panic. 'De Coucy, Boucicaut!' he shouted. 'Say something! We cannot let this monster do this!'

Bayezid lifted his hand to signal a halt. He stood there for what seemed like an age, swaying slightly and staring out at the scene before him. Then, very slowly, he turned to the Burgundian Prince.

'What did you call me?' he whispered. 'Monster? Is *that* what you called me?'

De Nevers took a step backwards. There was sweat coursing down his unshaven cheeks.

Bayezid turned. 'Vizier, ask the learned men of the ulema to step forward.'

Luke watched the scene unfolding with appalled fascination. He was to die, along with his friends, any hope of reprieve having been dashed by Suleyman who'd come up to him and spoken quietly into his ear.

'This is a pity, Luke Magoris. I had given my word to Zoe that you would come back alive. Now it seems that a higher power has intervened.'

Luke had looked back with loathing. He was to die at the hand of this devil and he would never see Anna again.

'You'll not see me beg,' he had said evenly. 'Just do me this small favour, Suleyman. Release my friends. They have done nothing to deserve this fate.'

But Suleyman had laughed and turned away without answering.

By now the imams had arrived. They were elderly men with heavy beards and heavier robes. They stood uncertainly in front of their sultan and looked at him quizzically. Did he require further interpretation of the ulema?

But Bayezid had had an idea.

'Give them swords!' he shouted, waving the goblet in the direction of the old men. He went back to his chair and lowered his bulk into it. He turned to the ulema. 'You will show us how to kill these men. Please proceed.'

The imams glanced at each other. Swords were being thrust into their wrinkled hands and they looked at them with distaste.

The eldest stepped forward, shaking his head. 'Highness, we are men of the law, not executioners. We do not know how to kill.'

Bayezid laughed. 'Then you can learn as you go along, old man. Come, it's not that hard!'

No one moved. The knight with his head on the block looked up and now there was fear in his eyes.

'Begin!' yelled Bayezid.

And so it began. So began the clumsy slaughter of knights from Burgundy by men hardly able to lift the swords to do it, by men whose hands were used to writing, to explaining, not to meting out death.

They did their best. They worked hard to kill with some precision. And the knights' determination to die well, to show no resistance, helped. But the sword blows were weak and missed their targets and necks were left half severed, spewing blood while the executioners paused to draw breath or vomit.

Mehmed, de Nevers, even the guards tried to intervene again and again, but every time they stepped forward, Bayezid would raise his hand and fix them with a glare that left no doubt as to his will.

The massacre went on for what seemed hours. The old men slipped and fell in the blood they were shedding; knights tore off their mail to offer easier flesh to strike; men knelt to offer themselves to their God and to beg, silently, for a killer with some strength or at least sight.

At one point, a sudden ray of sunshine pierced the clouds and the knights took it as a sign from heaven and a great cry went up as men called out to one another to take strength, to trust in their God.

At last it was over. The final pitiful groan subsided and the imams, their robes crimson, sat on the ground and stared at each other in horror. Their limbs ached and their breath came in spasms and sweat trickled its way past the blood and dripped on to the sodden earth around them.

Bayezid was drunk. He had enjoyed himself, laughing and clapping as the murders went on, roaring insults to de Nevers and impervious to the disgust around him.

Then it was the turn of Suleyman's prisoners.

Luke had braced himself to face death with the same courage as those who'd gone before. Now he turned to his friends and saw the same determination in them and he drew them all to him so that they formed a circle, their arms entwined and their heads pressed together.

'We are brothers,' said Luke quietly, 'brothers and Varangians, and we will die as such. Let's show these bastards how a Varangian dies.'

'Just one last question, Luke.'

It was Nikolas.

Luke looked at him. Nikko. The one never far from a joke.

'Did you actually . . . you know, with Zoe?'

The arms gripped harder with the laughter.

'You can't die without knowing that?'

'No.'

Luke smiled. 'I'll tell you on the other side,' he said.

The imams looked at the next group being brought forward and they looked at Bayezid, who could have been asleep. His eyes were closed and his huge chest rose and fell and his goblet had fallen from his hand.

Suleyman and Mehmed looked at each other.

'We must stop this madness,' whispered Mehmed.

Bayezid opened his eyes. 'We will continue, Prince Mehmed,' he said quite calmly.

'I will not continue.' The oldest of the imams had risen. 'This is ungodly cruelty and I will have no further part in it. Great Sultan, you may kill me, but I will not go on.'

He threw down his sword and one by one the imams rose and did the same. They faced their Sultan, their backs as straight as they could make them, and they defied his will.

The only sound came from the sky and the birds of prey that had gathered to circle these new pickings. The sun emerged from behind a cloud and bathed the scene in a warmth that belied its savagery. Bayezid stood up and moved to the edge of the pavilion and looked up, enjoying its heat on his face. Then he smiled and shrugged; he beckoned to a servant for another goblet, which he lifted in the direction of his heir.

'Very well,' he said. 'Prince Suleyman, you may continue. Perhaps rather quicker, if you will.'

Anna had heard, rather than seen, the dreadful spectacle. And, because of the courage of the Christian knights, she'd heard little beyond the exertions of old men and the soggy connection of blade with skin.

She was sitting in a little tent to the rear of Bayezid's and beside her sat Devlet Hatun, her elbows resting on a table and her palms to her ears. Since their first meeting at Serres, the two women had come to trust each other. Anna knew that much of what she confided to Devlet Hatun was passed on to her brother Yakub Bey and that this was all part of a wider plan to connect good with good.

During the journey north to Nicopolis, Anna had barely slept and now she clutched the older woman's shoulder as much for

464

support as comfort. She was dizzy with exhaustion.

The uncomfortable ride had given her time to think, to let logic push Luke from her mind. At Monemvasia, she'd agreed to go with Suleyman to save the lives of Luke's friends. Now the Turks had won a great battle and nothing stood between them and Constantinople. They would win and she would be forced to marry Suleyman. She had to banish Luke from her thoughts.

But logic couldn't push him from her dreams, and the little sleep she'd had had been devoted to him.

Now she stood, swaying and praying that he had survived the battle.

Then someone spoke.

To begin with, she couldn't place the voice. Then she could. *Yakub.*

He was standing at the entrance to the tent. 'You should come.'

Anna let go of Devlet Hatun's shoulder and walked to the entrance. Through it, she could see the side of Bayezid's tent, and beyond it, an open area littered with bodies. In the centre, in the midst of death, knelt Luke, his head on a block. Above him, sword raised above his head, stood Suleyman.

Now she was running, running towards the scene before her. Everything else was a blur. Bayezid had turned in his chair and was moving his head. The Vizier's head was bent, listening to one of the imams. De Nevers was being supported by Boucicaut, vomit at his feet.

She reached the open ground, stopped and swung around to face Bayezid. 'Stop this.' She paused, recovering her breath. 'This is unworthy of you, lord.'

Bayezid was looking at her as if he wasn't quite sure who she was. His head was on one side and there was spittle gathered at the side of his lips. An empty goblet was in his hand.

'I think not. Please proceed, Prince Suleyman.'

Anna spun and looked around her. Then she ran over and picked up a sword. She held out her arm and put the blade to her wrist. She stared at Suleyman. 'If you do this, if you harm one hair on his head, you will never see me alive again.'

'No, Anna . . .' It was Luke.

Bayezid leant forward in his chair. 'And if you don't do this, Prince Suleyman,' he growled, 'you will not rule this empire after me.'

Suleyman looked from Anna to his father, his sword still raised.

'You will submit!' screamed Bayezid, flinging his cup to the ground.

Suleyman didn't move. There was a silence so complete around them that the sudden shriek of a carrion bird came out of the sky like a thunderclap.

Anna walked over to him and, very softly, so that only he and Luke could hear, she spoke.

'Spare him, Suleyman, and I will submit.'

Suleyman did nothing. Then, very slowly, he lowered the sword.

But someone else was speaking. It was Yakub: he'd moved to stand in front of Bayezid. With him was the Vizier and one of the imams. He turned to the imam. 'Tell your sultan. Does not the law forbid the killing of prisoners if they are below twenty years of age?'

The imam's hands were still stained with blood. He stared at them, then looked up. He nodded.

'Majesty.' Yakub now faced Bayezid. 'You cannot kill this boy. The Book forbids it.'

'Cannot, Lord Yakub?' growled Bayezid.

But the imam had recovered himself and came to Yakub's aid. 'Highness, the lord Yakub is right. Allah has granted you a great victory and perhaps it would be wise to regard his law. It is forbidden to kill child prisoners.'

Bayezid slumped back in his chair. He shook his head as if to clear it. 'And what should I then do with this . . . *boy*, lord Yakub?'

'Send him to the tribes of Anatolia, highness. Do what you always do with your share of the prisoners. Send him to our homeland to be taught how to be a janissary. He will make a fine one.'

Behind him, Suleyman had recovered some of his composure. This was not as it should be. Luke was going somewhere he didn't want him to go. He watched Yakub as an animal watches another steal its prey.

He turned to be sure de Nevers was watching. He wanted to be heard by him.

'Father,' he cried in French, 'the law may spare his life but this one we cannot send away. He speaks languages and has the Varangians' skill at arms. He would be valuable to us here.' He paused and looked directly at Luke. 'After all, he was the one we sent into the crusader camp.'

Luke leapt to his feet. 'That's a lie!'

Scores of Christian faces were turned to him.

Suleyman addressed de Nevers. 'Did he not ride into your camp with news of our battle order, my lord Count?'

De Nevers was looking strangely at Luke.

Marshall Boucicaut spoke. 'Indeed, sire. You will remember. He claimed to be Serbian. We didn't trust him.'

Luke reeled. This was madness. He'd told de Nevers everything that had then come to pass. But who here knew this except men who had everything to gain by shifting the blame for this catastrophe?

Bayezid was getting bored. He didn't know why Suleyman wanted this prisoner or why he was speaking in French but his son had publicly challenged him and he was in no mood to favour him. 'Lord Yakub? You were the one to point out the law that has saved this boy. You will send him to one of your villages and make him into a gazi.'

Suleyman strode over to his father. 'Father,' he said in a voice that only Bayezid could hear, 'I have reasons for wanting this boy to stay.'

But Bayezid had had enough of his eldest son. He said softly, 'You have humiliated me before the army. I care nothing for what you want!

'Yakub, you will do this?'

The gazi bowed. 'I will do this, highness.'

CHAPTER TWENTY-THREE

EDIRNE, OCTOBER 1396

The party that left Edirne with the Sultan Bayezid a month after the Battle of Nicopolis was a varied one. This was especially true in the matter of age: Luke found himself the youngest by some years, the pretty page having been made to stay sulking in the capital.

The oldest person present was a man he'd never seen before but who'd joined them at the city gate, slipping quietly into the column behind the ranks of the imams. He was tall and gaunt and rode badly, his simple white robe rucked up to reveal legs spotted with age. His beard was as white as his caftan and was shaded by a beak that an eagle would have raised with pride. He wore a turban of green cotton from which grey hair hung like netting. He seemed to be known to Yakub, who rode next to Luke, and brought his horse up to the gazi's other side. He glanced at Luke, nodded and said to Yakub, 'we should talk, old friend. Shall we fall back a little?'

Anna had remained in Edirne, imprisoned in the harem, and Luke had not set eyes on her since she'd put a sword to her wrists. Matthew, Nikolas and Arcadius had stayed with her and become part of the Court Guard. If he couldn't keep Luke, Suleyman would at least have the Varangians who, with some polishing, might make a fine embellishment to his retinue one day. Luke was relieved.

They'll be close to Anna.

Suleyman himself had gone to straight to Constantinople, partly to resume the siege and partly to escape the necessity of explaining to Zoe why he'd not returned from Nicopolis with Luke. Suleyman had missed Zoe. He'd not taken her on the campaign because he believed carnal diversion before battle to weaken the sword arm. After it, he'd wanted nothing more than to lie with her.

Bayezid's party came back through Thrace and the birds had seemed to travel with them, or at least those that had not already gone south for the winter, and they were fat, black creatures that had perhaps gorged themselves on the flesh of two thousand Christian martyrs.

Luke knew that the memory of that slaughter would stay with him forever, that his worst nightmares would be of men kneeling silently on blood-soaked ground, of exhausted executioners turning their old eyes to their sultan for some small measure of mercy and finding none within those cold, blood-shot eyes.

Approaching the town of Stenia, they'd seen the walls of Constantinople in the distance, defiant above the mist of an autumn morn. Here they'd crossed the Bosporus and ridden down its banks to the new castle of Anadolu Hisar, built four years past to stop help coming from the Black Sea.

Now it was a prison.

As they rode up to its gates, men were being paraded along

the cliffs overlooking the channel and many were familiar to Luke. De Nevers, Boucicaut and d'Eu were standing in chains and all had days of dirty beard on their faces. Their once-splendid hauberks hung from gaunt bodies stripped of armour and they were wrapped in filthy bandages still black with their blood.

Their guards pushed them into line and the Sultan drew aside his curtains and laughed at their misery and drank toasts to the ransoms they'd fetch. And these men who'd once commanded armies turned their heads to look at the tall Greek who rode with Bayezid in clean clothes and no chains and their hearts were filled with hate.

The Sultan had come here for a purpose. Helped from his litter, he walked over to where he could see the waters below. Then he clapped his hands, toothache forgotten. 'Is that him?'

A long line of ships was making its slow way down the channel.

'Yes, lord. In the front boat.'

Bayezid clapped his hands again and turned to the line of chained men. 'De Nevers!' he shouted in French. 'See! Hungary still comes to your rescue!'

The Turks roared at that; even the grave imams raised a smile. The guards slapped each other on the back and yelled insults and challenges to the boats below, and in the first of the galleys, the King of Hungary clutched the foredeck rail and looked up at his former allies through a film of tears.

Luke could do nothing except look as well but he'd have given his fortune to be somewhere else. He saw Sigismund below, his long cloak wrapped around his hunched frame, and he saw de Naillac by his side: two men sailing home to tell of the catastrophe that was Nicopolis.

A voice came from the line of prisoners behind him. 'Traitor! May you rot in hell!'

Luke turned and saw Boucicaut staring at him.

Then de Nevers spoke. 'We will get home one day, Greek. And when we do, you will pay for what you have done. This I swear.'

In Edirne, Anna was sitting in misery with Suleyman's grandmother.

The Valide Sultan Gülçiçek, now seventy, was a woman smelt but seldom seen. Among the many scents of the harem, among its shifting essences of food and flowers and mastic, hers was a very specific smell of decay.

It was autumn when the Valide Sultan became most tetchy, being prone, at this time of year, to confront the issue of her age and, in confronting it, to banish the younger women from her presence.

It was also the time of year that the Chief Black Eunuch, the Kislar Ağasi, spent most time planning how best to distract his mistress by way of entertainment. In a month's time, winter furnishings would be introduced to the harem, soft velvets hung in place of sullen linens and the calm of milder weather would descend like manna upon the rooms, pools, courtyards and lawns of his little kingdom.

Until then, he needed to extemporise.

On this particular evening, he'd invited a travelling bard-poet and his apprentice to give of their best. First, the *ozan* had told amusing stories to the strum of his disciple's *bağlama*. Then he'd dared suggest a musical rhyming contest between the quartet of wives allotted to Bayezid by the Koran. Each *kadin* had embellished the game further by suggesting forfeits for

472

those unable to find a suitable quatrain for the rhyme. There was little love between them.

The mother of Bayezid, unquestioned ruler of the harem and much beyond, was sitting on a low couch in the shadows of a little alcove before a tall window covered by an intricate wooden grille. Behind her, the evening light was caught in coloured glass and horn so that it arrived around her as tiny shards that exploded among the beads and sequins of the cushions.

She was, as she liked to be, almost invisible.

The room outside the alcove was blue and gold. Tiles from Iznik rose in patterns on all four sides to a height where gold mosaic took over. Above the mosaic, on a frieze beneath the dome, the calligraphy of earnest Koranic injunction swirled. In the centre was a small pool, strewn with the flowering of late roses and, drinking from it, a child sambar, its spindly legs mirrored in the water. Around the marble floor were bowls of apples and almonds and clear mastic sweets. A single cushion was propped against the pool's wall and on it rested a zither, a tambourine and a little drum. Carpets were hung on the walls and before them knelt bare-breasted servant girls who stared at the ground. They were young and had gold bands on their upper arms and had, it seemed, escaped the Valide Sultana's injunction on youth.

Anna had no idea why she'd been summoned to this room. She sat in uncomfortable silence next to the alcove listening to the ozan's game and smelling the smell of Bayezid's dying mother.

Then there was a cough and quiet fell upon the women.

Gülçiçek spoke. 'You do not like this game, Anna Mamonas?' The voice was muffled by its journey through the veil but no softness had attached to it. It was low and there was malice in every word.

'I am sorry, highness, my mind was elsewhere,' she said into the stillness.

A pause. Only the sambar dared lift its head, its tiny horns hooped in question.

'I think you were thinking of a Greek. Am I right? One who betrayed his kind at the field of Nicopolis?'

There was stifled laughter from within the alcove. It belonged to Nefise, the Sultan's aunt and Gülçiçek's constant companion.

Anna didn't reply. She had heard Suleyman for herself. She didn't believe it.

The ozan and his apprentice were quietly gathering up their instruments and preparing to depart. Gülçiçek addressed them.

'You haven't finished,' she said sharply. 'The lady wishes to play our game. Give her a rhyme.'

The older of the men looked at Anna and then round at the kadins. No one spoke or moved. The apprentice carefully lifted his instrument.

'Give her a rhyme about the Prince Suleyman since he is to be her husband. What could be more fitting?'

The ozan sat and gazed at the floor. Then he lifted his head and cleared his throat as his apprentice began to strum the strings of the bağlama.

He sang:

> *The prince before the city walls*
> *Calls out to those that guard*
> *This gilded shadow of ancient Rome . . .'*

There was silence. The rhyme was deliberately easy. Three lines were all that Anna had to give, three lines of poetry that would deny what was left of her empire.

Three lines she could not say.

The silence rose into the dome and stayed, pregnant, above them. Anna felt her anger rising.

'A forfeit, I think,' came the voice from within, soft with satisfaction. 'Now, what would be appropriate?'

There was a rustle in the dark and a whisper met by a wheezing laugh.

'Yes!' came the voice. 'That's it! A question that demands the truth.' She paused. 'Are you a virgin, Anna Mamonas?'

Anna recoiled.

'The marriage to the Mamonas boy,' continued the Sultana. 'An unconsummated pleasure, he tells us. So the answer must be yes, surely?'

Anna still could not speak.

'It seems simple enough,' came the voice from the darkness, soft and full of hatred. 'Will my grandson have a virgin for his queen, as he believes he will? Or will he have a whore?'

'Highness,' Anna whispered, looking into the darkness, 'what do you want of me?'

But the answer came from someone else.

'Enough!'

It was Suleyman and he was striding into the room. He wore a riding coat that billowed behind him and high boots mottled with dust.

'Enough, Grandmother,' he said more softly, turning to kneel before her.

'Enough?' asked the woman from the shades. 'Would you not like to hear the answer to that question?'

The heir to the Ottoman Empire bowed low. He was breathing deeply. 'It is, I think, a question better put to her by the man she will marry,' he said calmly. 'I will take her to a place where we may speak with greater ease.'

There was a snort of displeasure from the darkness and Suleyman rose. He bowed again, then turned to Anna and stretched out his hand. 'Will you come with me into the garden?'

She rose and went before him from the room, not bowing as she left.

They stepped into a scene of moonlit geometry. Low hedges of yew enclosed beds of flowers that had been coaxed to the challenge of providing autumnal scent by expert gardeners. Around them were lawns and a perimeter of fruit trees that almost succeeded in masking the high wall that was the limit of the harem's world.

The lawn was scattered with the shadows of sleeping animals and, between the trees, the domes of smoking leaves. A sudden breeze carried their rich smell to Anna and she shivered.

In between the hedged borders were four terraced walks that converged at a tiny lake where stood an island with a chiosk enclosed by a lattice interwoven with jasmine and honeysuckle. Around it, the waters were strewn with lily pads and leaves and an arched bridge connected the island to the garden.

Suleyman was leading her towards it and soon they had crossed the bridge and were sitting on a stone bench within. The smell of burning leaves was fainter but still with them and Anna closed her eyes and filled her lungs with its unpainted goodness.

Suleyman said, 'An oasis, I should imagine.'

Anna opened her eyes. 'This island? Yes, lord.' She was trying to keep her voice steady. 'An oasis within the desert that is your father's harem.'

'A desert?' he asked. 'Is it not a place of beauty?'

'No,' replied Anna. 'It is a dry place of scheming old women and it is strewn with the carcasses of those they do not like.'

'I suspect she just was trying to frighten you.'

Anna looked out through a gap in the vines to the lawns. She saw the trees beyond and she heard something faint within them. 'Did you know that there are caged birds in those trees?' She laughed softly. 'You have your walls and you almost manage to disguise them with trees. But then what do you do? You put caged birds in their branches!'

Anna looked over at Suleyman and saw his profile against the fading sky. She saw that he was without fight that night.

They were both quiet for a long while, thinking of what had nearly happened on a bloody piece of ground.

'Would you have done it?' Suleyman asked.

'Yes.'

'You love him that much?'

'Yes.'

'And yet he betrayed an army.'

'Did he? You let him escape. It seems careless.'

Suleyman didn't answer. Luke Magoris was removed, Anna had submitted to him and Constantinople would fall. Nothing else mattered. It was victory, so why did it not feel like victory?

'You can do a lot of good as the wife of the Sultan . . . Save whole populations from the sword. Constantinople's, for instance.'

Anna flinched.

Damn you, Suleyman.

The Prince sighed. 'I merely tell you what is true.'

'So tell me something more. Did he betray the army?'

Suleyman rose. 'I said what I said to keep him here. Surely that should please you?'

'You said what you said because Zoe wants him here. It is your agreement.'

The harem had given her much time to think. He shrugged.

'Well, whatever the past, you submitted to me and I lowered the sword.' He looked out again over the garden. A sambar stirred and called out in its sleep. 'How long will it take for you to come willingly?'

Anna breathed deeply. The smell of the leaves was fainter. *You can do a lot of good as wife of the Sultan.*

She looked back at him. 'Willingly?'

'Willingly.'

'Six months,' she said. 'It will take me six months. Then I will come willingly. But tomorrow I want to ride as far from this place as I can. And I don't want to come back inside these walls. Ever.'

Suleyman waited.

'There's more. I will not marry you until my marriage to Damian is annulled. It must be set aside in the eyes of the Church. *My* church.'

Suleyman seemed to be lost in thought, but then he laughed. 'Well, it's not the language of poets,' he said, 'but I dare say I can agree to these things. Where would you like to ride to?'

'I don't care. Tomorrow?'

'Of course. You have demanded it.'

'Can I go alone?'

'Ah, no,' said Suleyman. 'You will be escorted.'

'By your Varangians?'

Suleyman laughed again.

'I think not. By my sipahis.'

Suleyman was as good as his word.

Anna was woken at dawn the next morning and escorted to the Gate of Felicity. Two black eunuchs threw back the bolts of the giant doors and pushed them open. Outside was a saddled horse and a troop of sipahis wearing silver mail and turbaned helmets.

Anna had chosen to dress as her new freedom permitted. She wore clothes she had not worn since leaving Monemvasia. Gone were the diaphanous veils and silken pantaloons of the harem and in their place was a buff leather jerkin covered by a woollen surcoat. On her head was a velvet cap with a jaunty feather piercing its brim.

'Where do we ride to?' she asked the nearest of the men.

'We go north into the hills, lady,' said the knight from behind his nose-guard. 'The lord Suleyman is to meet us there later.'

Anna leant forward to pat the neck of her horse. The horse was young and strong and still smelt of its stable, and Anna felt the curve of its belly against her legs and breathed in its scent with pleasure.

Then they were in motion and the five sipahis closed ranks around her as they trotted across the square.

Anna reined in. '*No.*'

They stopped.

'Know this,' she said. 'You will tell me where to ride and I will ride there, fast. If you can, you may follow me.'

At exactly that moment, Suleyman was woken by a servant to bad news. The woman lying by his side heard it too.

Bad news from Chios.

'Sunk?' said Zoe, raising herself on to her elbow and pushing the hair from her forehead. She rubbed her eyes. 'How?'

'A sudden storm,' replied Suleyman, putting on his slippers. 'It comes off the land at this time of year.'

'How many?'

'Half the fleet. We won't have enough ships now to enforce the blockade. Their alum and mastic will get through.'

'Have you told my father?'

'It's he who is telling me. He's waiting outside.'

As soon as Suleyman had left the room, Zoe rose and went over to the place where she knew there to be a spy hole from which he could see those who awaited audience. She rose on tiptoes to look through it. In the room were her father and a man she didn't know. He was handsome.

Suleyman was pouring wine and talking. 'You are hardly in a position to complain, di Vetriano. Your city played quarter-master to the Christian army.' He turned to her father. 'Pavlos, do you speak for them still?'

Pavlos Mamonas bowed. 'The Serenissima wishes to convey its regret over its part in the crusade.'

Silk on silk.

Suleyman frowned. The full enormity of the disaster at Chios was coming home to him and he would have to explain to Bayezid why the ships were there at all. He needed Venice more than ever now.

Mamonas continued. 'The Doge has instructed me to enquire whether you wish them to resume the arrangement.'

Suleyman looked up sharply. 'You know damn well I do,' he said crossly. 'Is it as before?'

The man di Vetriano spoke, joining the tips of his fingers as

480

if in petition. 'It is as before, lord. Venice wants Chios, as soon as the fleet is re-equipped.' He paused. 'And a person.'

Suleyman raised his finger to his lips. He glanced behind him and then ushered the two men through the door they had entered by.

When the door was closed, Suleyman said, 'I gave Magoris to you before Nicopolis, and you managed to lose him. Anyway, I don't know where he's going. Only Yakub knows that.'

'But, lord, you will know the route he's to take,' said the Venetian, 'should we want to . . . *intercept* him.'

Suleyman was silent, thinking. He'd already decided on something else, something that he'd thought of every moment since Anna had done what she'd done at Nicopolis. This might be the time. He glanced at the door, then turned back to the two men.

'We will talk of this interception.'

From Anadolu Hisar, Bayezid's party had ridden south and east along the shores of the Sea of Marmara and then on to Bursa, once capital to the Ottomans until Edirne had supplanted it and shown the direction of their territorial ambition.

Bursa was the end of the Sultan's journey and the place where Yakub would leave his retinue to travel on to his capital at Kutahya. Bayezid had come to Bursa to commission a new mosque to thank Allah for the great victory at Nicopolis. On the eve of the battle he'd promised to build twenty new mosques if victorious but the Vizier had whispered in his ear of campaign and sundry other costs and now there would be twenty domes on this single mosque instead.

Much of the last part of the ride the Sultan had spent in conversation with the old man who'd joined the party late and, like everyone else, Bayezid seemed to hold him in the greatest respect.

So it was with some surprise that Luke saw the man leaning over his bed the next morning.

'Luke Magoris,' he said, 'it's time to rise. Your first lesson begins today.'

Luke swung his legs over the side of the bed and rubbed his eyes. 'Lesson? Lesson in what, sir?'

'Well,' he said, 'firstly in who I am, I suppose. Do you know who I am, Luke?'

Luke shook his head.

'My name is very long and I won't try to teach it to you. I am a *sufi*, a mystic, and I come from the holy city of Konya. My friends, who include Plethon, call me Omar. You may call me Omar since we will be friends.' He paused. 'You've heard Rumi?'

Luke shook his head.

'Well, he was a great thinker and poet, a man of great wisdom. All Muslims revere him, even Bayezid. He was buried in Konya and I watch over his tomb. Before that I was in Kutahya.'

'So that is why you know Yakub?'

Omar smiled. 'I have known Yakub for many, many years. You might say we think alike about things. We want you to help us.'

'Help you? By becoming a janissary?'

Omar laughed. It was a deep laugh, full of warmth. He tapped his long nose. 'That's what Bayezid believes, certainly. But I think Prince Yakub may have different plans for you.' He paused and looked hard at Luke, suddenly serious. 'A great many people are depending on you, Luke.'

An hour later, Omar led Luke down into the city streets, which were already busy. As they walked, he talked of Islam.

'If you were to be trained as a janissary, as Bayezid wishes, then you would be indoctrinated in our faith. Whatever you now think, believe me when I tell you it would happen. It always does. But instead I shall explain the Faith to you and why I choose to follow it.'

Around them thronged men and women of every colour and dress. There were Arabs, Turks, Georgians and Jews, and no one bowed and no one gave precedence to anyone else. All seemed equal in the city of Bursa.

'I choose to follow Islam because its rules are reasonable and uncomplicated and much to do with allowing courtesy to our fellow humans. There are five pillars to our faith: belief in Allah, prayers five times a day, giving money to the poor, making a pilgrimage to Mecca and observing Ramadan. Within everyone's grasp, you would think.'

Luke thought of Christian Europe where the Latin word of God was denied the ordinary man and the Church grew rich by selling the way to Him.

The day was cold and without sun and they stopped at a stall where a man sold chestnuts roasted on a grill. Soon they came to a large mosque in a courtyard with buildings surrounding it. A fountain played at its centre and around it sat men and women washing their feet.

'This mosque was built by Bayezid's grandfather Orhan, founder of the Ottoman Empire. It is not just a place of worship, but also a place of rest, of learning, even of commerce. Here there is a hospital, a dormitory for travellers, a school, a soup kitchen. And over there is a market. Look, you can see that a caravan's just come in. It is late in the season.'

Omar pointed towards the arched entrance to what looked like another courtyard. There were people crowding through it, eager to see what had arrived on the camels. He turned to Luke and winked. 'I love markets. This is Han Bey, the best of them. Shall we go and see?'

Inside was chaos but, through the bustle, Luke could see that the courtyard was surrounded by an arched colonnade under which the merchants were selling their wares. The press of people was a river of colour and, miraculously, the river seemed to be flowing in a single direction.

With vigorous use of his elbows, Omar worked a passage to the front, Luke hard behind him. Soon they were able to see the merchandise on offer under every arch they passed.

One man sold caged birds of exotic hues that spoke in different languages. Another had gracefully carved lyres, tambours and a *kudüm* inlaid with mother of pearl; he played *neys* of a different sizes to the delight of watching children. They saw trays of spices and bales of exquisite silks and tables on which leather-bound Korans were opened by men with gloves. There were weapons from Persia and fireworks from China. There was silver from Bohemia and gold bands from India which women held out on their wrists to admire.

The merchants were resplendent in silks of every colour, paragons of fat prosperity with their beards combed and their turbans flashing with jewels. Coins were piled high on tables covered with rich kelims and behind them stood big men with arms folded above belted daggers.

It was overwhelming and exhausting and after an hour Omar pushed their way back to where a walled fountain played beneath a tiny mosque raised on stone pillars. They sat on the wall next to a family eating something wrapped in vine leaves.

'You've heard of the Mongols? Of Genghis Khan?' Omar asked.

Luke nodded. All the world knew of Genghis Khan.

484

'Well, the only good thing that he did,' continued Omar, declining a vine leaf offered by his neighbour, 'was to bring the East under one rule. Trade has flowed freely ever since. Look at it!' He waved his arm over the scene before them. Then he leant back and trailed a finger in the water, lifting out a leaf that dripped into his lap. 'There's a new Mongol leader now who is just as terrible,' he said quietly. 'Temur the Lame. Have you heard of him?'

Temur the Lame. Tamerlane. He had heard of Tamerlane.

'What Temur decides to do next will decide the fate of empires. Yours included.'

Luke was about to ask more when he saw a commotion in a part of the market they'd yet to visit. There were shouts of anger and a stick was waving in the air.

Omar rose. 'So much for the peace of Islam,' he said and began to make his way towards the disturbance. This time the crowd parted before him like a sea.

At the far end of the square, a little semicircle had formed in front of an arch under which were tables arrayed with trays and jars and scales next to piles of lead weights. There were lumps of something white and grey and sometimes translucent lying on the tables and to Luke they were familiar. The merchant had his back to him and was remonstrating with a stout woman, who was livid with rage and shouting without pause.

For the crowd, this was entertainment at its best. The more that the woman shrieked, the more they laughed, some so helpless that they were hanging on to their neighbours for support.

Then Luke recognised the back.

'Dimitri!' he shouted and stepped out into the open space,

clapping a hand on to his friend's shoulder. 'What's going on?'

Dimitri swung round. 'Luke! What are you doing here?'

The two embraced.

'Thank God you're safe.' said Dimitri, stepping back.

The woman had stopped yelling, momentarily diverted by this new arrival. Then she started again.

'Oh, shut up!' shouted Dimitri. 'Go and look in the brothels!'

The crowd roared at this.

'I don't really understand what she's saying,' said Dimitri with a shrug. 'It seems I sold her some aphrodisiac yesterday which she gave to her husband last night. She hasn't seen him since.'

Another man emerged from the shadow of the arch behind. He was bald and smiling and holding a set of bronze scales. He held out his hand. 'Luke, I heard your voice. What happy chance!'

'Benedo Barbi!' cried Luke, taking his hand. 'What brings you to this chaos?'

Barbi laughed. 'I am to visit the Hospitallers at Smyrna and teach them about Greek fire. We go there next.'

'You've perfected it?'

Barbi nodded. 'Better than that. I've developed a hand-held siphon.'

The Hospitallers at the fortress of Smyrna were the last Christian stronghold in Anatolia. Bayezid had tried twice to take it and would try again now. Greek fire would be useful there.

Then Luke remembered that he was not alone. 'Omar, these are my friends Dimitri and Benedo Barbi from Chios. Dimitri sells mastic.'

'So I see,' said the old man happily. 'It seems to work.'

Dimitri grinned and shook his hand, ignoring the woman who was now being led away by the crowd. He turned to Luke. 'Can you talk? We have things to tell you.' He glanced at Omar. 'Forgive me, sir, but this is unexpected.'

Omar nodded and walked over to the stall. He picked up a lump and examined it carefully. 'So this is the cure for the Sultan's toothache. We have much to thank you for, Dimitri. You go and talk and I will keep your stall. But don't be long, I'm a poor haggler.'

Dimitri and Barbi led Luke back through the arch and into a cavernous warehouse full of kneeling camels being unloaded. The air was thick with the smell of dung and spices and dust rose from the straw on which the animals lay. The November grey entered through windows high in the wall and struggled to make headway through the gloom. It was a place to talk and not be heard.

Dimitri sat down on a bale of cotton. He unbuckled a flask from his belt and offered it to his friend. 'So what happened?' he asked. 'The last I heard you were on a ship bound for Venice.'

Luke drank the water and wiped his mouth with the back of his hand. 'The captain of the ship was Venetian.'

'So you were given to the Turks?' asked Barbi, who'd sat down as well.

Luke nodded. 'Then taken to Nicopolis as their captive. To watch.'

Dimitri took the flask and seemed engrossed in it. When he spoke again, his voice was low. 'I hear it was a massacre. And worse. I heard that Bayezid murdered thousands of knights who might have been ransomed, that he got old men to do it.' He looked up at Luke. 'Is it true?'

Luke nodded again. 'What else did you hear?' he asked softly.

487

Dimitri and Barbi exchanged glances. News of Luke's treachery had reached Chios already.

Luke leant forward and took Dimitri's arm. 'Dimitri, what you've heard about me isn't true. You know me. I'm no traitor.'

The two men looked at each other for some time and then Dimitri smiled. 'Marchese will be relieved. It was the only thing clouding his happiness.'

'His happiness?'

'Of course, you don't know. Why should you? Fiorenza is with child.'

Luke stared at him. 'With child?'

'Yes. After all these years, their prayers have been answered. The whole island rejoices.'

Luke felt weak. Fiorenza with child? With *his* child? Of course it was his child. Marchese was incapable.

Dimitri frowned. 'You've gone white, Luke. Is the news so bad?'

Luke forced himself to smile. 'No, of course not. It was a surprise, that's all. I thought . . .'

'You thought Marchese too old? We all did.' He was looking at Luke quizzically. 'It would seem a miracle, no?'

'A miracle, yes. Please tell them how happy I am.' He changed the subject. 'How did the alum and mastic fare in Venice?' he asked. 'Did we get a good price?'

'The very best.' Dimitri said. 'With no alum yet through from Trebizond, we got what we asked for. And the Venetian fleet took pounds of mastic to dress the crusaders' wounds.'

'And does it fix dye?'

Dimitri shook his head. 'Alas no. The Florentine chemists saw to that. But it didn't matter. We sold it before the markets heard the news. The price was astronomical. Do you know how rich you are, Luke?'

Luke didn't answer. Dimitri didn't know that every penny of that profit had gone to Plethon, to the Empire.

But Luke wasn't really considering that. He was thinking of the vines of Sklavia and the orchards of the Kambos and of a child that would grow up there thinking another man his father.

Then he remembered something and turned to the engineer. 'Benedo. How is the building? How are the villages?'

'The villages are good. They're coming up fast and the mastic is reaching its markets. The blockade is no more.'

'No more?'

'There was a storm. The Turkish ships were scattered, many sunk. And then the Empire's fleet appeared and sank what was left.'

Chios delivered.

In a world that had deprived him of Anna, of his freedom, of his good name, of his child, this was a rare bit of good news. Perhaps one day, when he had done whatever he had to do, he could bring Anna there.

One day.

'I should go back to Omar.'

Dimitri asked, 'Why not come with us?'

'Escape? No, they have Anna and my friends. Anyway, where would I go? Christendom thinks me a traitor.'

Back in the courtyard, Omar was haggling for his life. It wasn't so much the price as the sheer number of people desperate to buy the aphrodisiac now that word had got round of its effects. Luke wondered if the brothels of Bursa would be able to cope.

Beneath an arch on the other side of the square, a dark man

in darker clothes was watching the scene, his hand on a short sword at his side.

Luke didn't see him; nor did Omar or Dimitri.

But Benedo Barbi saw him and he frowned. He'd seen him somewhere before.

It took no time at all for Anna and her escort to reach the walls of the city.

The only creatures abroad at that early hour were dogs and cats and bakers stoking the ovens that would make the city's bread. Their hooves echoed against the walls of sleeping houses and through the narrow streets that led out of the city. They met a line of donkeys plodding moodily along, their heads sunk low and their backs piled high with the stuff for building. A turbaned man walked in front and stopped to bow deeply as their little calvacade passed.

Then they were out on the plain and around them was all the melancholy of a spent summer. The fields were bare, scraped clean of their harvest and black with the stumps of blasted crops. They passed vineyards shorn of their bounty, with row upon row of stiff yellow leaves that only waited for a passing wind to lay them to rest.

Anna rode with all the energy of uncloistered joy. She swept off her cap and allowed her hair to cascade behind her. She felt the sun on her cheeks and lifted her palms to wipe the tears from her eyes. She felt the thrill of horse between her thighs and the smell of leather filling her nostrils. With every perfect stride stretched out beneath her, the memory of the harem grew fainter.

Whatever the future, for today I am free.

By mid-morning they had reached a small town where a

490

market was in progress. Soon they were passing between stalls of hung game and trussed fowl, between copper utensils and carpets of herbs. There were baskets of over-ripe fruit and vegetables bursting from their skins. They passed forges and entered streets thick with the sawdust of wood carvers and lined with the kiln-fires of potters. The air was heavy with yeast and cow dung and carob and blood.

At midday, they were riding through a landscape of lakes and marshes. There were flamingos and black storks and pelicans strung out along the shores and a blizzard of cormorants taking wing. Anna stopped her horse and watched the sunlight dance across the water and listened to the talk of a million birds.

An hour later they had reached the valley of the Mariza River and its sides were thick with forest. The road they travelled was lined with trees aflame and the floor beneath them was hoof-deep in leaves crisp as parchment. She slowed her horse to a walk and the leader of the sipahis caught up with her.

'Lady,' he said as he came to her side, 'from here we turn south.'

A track ahead branched off to the left and they took it, rising with the hill towards a forest of oak. Soon they were among gnarled, arthritic branches twisted with age and a silence broken only by the soft fall of hoof. As they crested the hill, Anna drew her horse to a standstill and stared at the beauty before her. The path ahead broadened into an avenue carpeted in gold. The trees on either side were beech and their tall trunks rose to form a vaulted roof above. She was in a cathedral through which heaven shone its individual eye.

The sipahi knight rode up to her and coughed politely; she nodded and gently kicked her horse. It was late in the day and

491

the shafts of sunlight shone low through the branches, turning the carpet to a weave of richer reds. Then they were entering the hills where the air was milder and the sound of water could be heard all around. Through the trees they could see the glint of waterfall and the velvet of washed, mossy rocks. They saw deer between tree trunks and once they saw a single boar that stared at them, legs astride, on the path ahead. Anna raised her hand to stop a sipahi arrow and it cocked its heavy head, turned and trotted away.

Then, quite suddenly, they were there.

At the top of the slope, the wood ended and below lay a meadow halved by a tumbling brook. Stretching into the distance were fold upon fold of wooded hills with all their reds and yellows glowing like a pathway of embers towards the setting sun.

And there, pitched next to a little waterfall, was the tent that Suleyman had given her at her wedding. It was open on three sides.

She dismounted and walked slowly towards it and a delicate music came over the meadow to meet her. With it came servants who carried jugs of sweet wine and sherbet.

Anna entered the tent, sat on the cushions and watched the sun complete its progress to the west and she listened to the zither and thought of Mistra.

She thought of the Evrotas River twisting its way through the valley beneath the city walls. She thought of Mount Taygetos behind, always topped with snow. She thought of autumn in Mistra, of the St Adrian's Day market where roasted chestnuts would be tossed from hand to hand as they cooled. She thought of grumpy praetors lighting the evening lamps along the narrow streets. She thought of her mother hanging tapestries on the walls of the triclinium against the winter cold. She thought of a little city on a hill that would, quite soon, fall to the Turks.

You can do a lot of good as wife of the Sultan.

The sun was almost set now behind the hills. It was a dazzling display of beauty put on by whoever's God was up there, and its finale was an explosion of oranges and reds and yellows witnessed by an audience of tiny clouds basking in its brilliance.

Then all was violet and people with lamps appeared from nowhere to unroll the sides of her tent and to cast rose petals over her bed. A servant appeared at her side and refilled her glass with wine and another offered a plate of quail's eggs and the roe of sturgeon. She ate and drank and wondered, with mild interest, when the Prince would arrive.

And then she thought of Luke.

Where are you? Where are you now?

He was as good as dead. She would never see him again. She closed her eyes and let the fatigue steal over her limbs. The questions came and went with images in their wake. Then they slowed and finally stopped on one single image that filled her mind as it had done every night for so very long.

Like this, she drifted into sleep, soothed by the lullaby of a zither.

She awoke suddenly. It was morning and she was in the bed and clothed in a gown of finest lawn. Someone had done this. A servant, she hoped.

She was aware that a voice had awoken her and it was a voice she knew.

Then she heard the voice of her future husband. He was

talking to somebody close to the tent. But she knew it wasn't his voice that had woken her.

There was a dressing gown hanging over a chair beside the bed and she quickly rose and put it on. She would not greet him from her bed. Her head was still heavy from the wine and the deep, deep sleep that had followed it and she found a little basin and splashed water over her face, blinking open her eyes.

Whose voice woke me?

Anna left the tent to find Suleyman outside but not the answer. The Prince was sitting at a table admiring the view. The horse from which he'd just dismounted was being led away by a groom and behind it followed a larger creature, stepping out elegantly. At its rein was a tall sipahi knight with gold mail and a gyrfalcon held high on his wrist.

Whoever had woken her was no longer there.

Anna walked over to the table and sat down. On it were bowls of fruit and dahl and honey and rose petals strewn between them and a small vase of lilies whose milky filaments bowed under orange stamens. For a while, neither of them spoke and the only sound was the gurgling stream and the music of morning birds.

Eventually Suleyman said, 'I have brought a poet with me.'

'A poet? For me?'

'For us both. He will recite to us as we take our ease.'

'But I want to ride. You've brought a gyrfalcon. We can hunt.'

Suleyman looked up from the peach he was quartering.

'I told you,' she continued calmly. 'that I want to ride.'

Suleyman smiled and lifted the peach to his mouth. 'And I want to listen to poetry. We disagree so soon?'

It was Anna's turn to smile. 'So let's take the poet with us. Does he ride?'

494

At that, Suleyman laughed. 'All right, we will ride. When would you like to go?'

Anna rose. 'Now,' she said.

Suleyman watched her for a moment; then he shrugged and rose and walked with her up the meadow, the long grass brushing their ankles. There was a little waterfall near the trees at the top and he knelt to fill his water bottle.

Then she heard it again. The voice that had woken her. It was within the trees.

She turned and walked up to the wood, leaving Suleyman at the stream. She entered the trees and peered into the sudden gloom and saw that he was standing there alone, his two eyes separated by a band of silver metal.

Eskalon.

He was the captain of the guard's horse, the one she'd seen led away. His long nose was protected by a shaffron studded with jewels and at his haunches hung embroidered cloth of gold.

Eskalon.

She breathed his name and stepped forward as the great head came down to meet her. She lifted his chin and rested hers on the bridge of his nose so that they stared at each other, eye to eye.

'Where have you been?' she whispered, but she knew it was the wrong question.

His eyes were near to hers and they had tiny pools of light at their centre.

'Where is he, Eskalon?' she whispered.

The two pools moved a fraction as if the door to another world was opening. She looked into them and the trees grew still around her, the canopy above closing out the sun and birdsong. Then she was looking around a landscape of swirling gasses and there was someone coming out of the mist towards her, someone she knew, someone she still loved and who still loved her.

Luke.

The shape of him was vague but unmistakable. In a moment the face would appear and she was dizzy with longing. He drew closer and she lifted her arms to him.

'Anna.'

It was Suleyman's voice.

Anna turned to him.

He said, 'You are pale.'

She took a deep breath, feeling the warmth of Eskalon's breath on her neck. 'Prince Suleyman, I want to offer you a wager.'

'A wager? It is forbidden for me to accept wagers.'

'And it is forbidden for you to drink wine and for your father to fornicate with boys from Trebizond but it happens. Call it a challenge.'

'And it is what?'

'A race. On horseback. You and me, back to the gates of Edirne,' she said.

'And the prize?'

'If I win, this horse – which, by the way, I will ride.'

'And if I win?'

She looked at him and her hand came up to touch the lily at her ear.

'You win me,' she said. 'I will marry you without divorce. I will turn to your faith. You can have your red-haired heir within a year.'

CHAPTER TWENTY-FOUR

EDIRNE, OCTOBER 1396

In the Year of Our Lord 1354, an Islamic God had stamped his sandalled foot and the walls of Gallipoli fell like a camel sinking to its knees in the sand. A passing Ottoman war band then skipped into the fortress and so began the stream of Turkish men, women, children, sheep and saints that, ever since, had poured across the Dardanelles up into the fecund valleys of Thrace. Their ferries had been Venetian.

In that year, too, a philosopher called Plethon had been born in a city not far to the north. Adrianopolis, city of Hadrian. Now Edirne, city of Bayezid.

In that city, on the day following her race with Suleyman, Anna sat on a stone bench in a little courtyard made by Murad for his wife, the Byzantine Princess Gülçiçek Khatun, and stared at a pillar.

The courtyard was colonnaded with Roman columns resurrected from the earthquake and each one was different. A single tree stood at its centre, planted to mark the birth of the Princess's first-born, Yildirim.

So absorbed was Anna that she did not hear the soft tread

of the philosopher until he was next to her and had spoken the word of the Prophet.

'"Cursed be the man who injures a fruit-bearing tree."'

Anna swung around. 'Plethon!' she cried, jumping up from the bench and hugging the togaed midriff of the man before her. The sunshine glanced from his balding head and two cats tiptoed away to sleep in the trimmed borders that ringed the square. 'Are you really here?'

'In person,' said the sage, performing a little bow. 'It is, after all, my home. Or was.'

Anna smiled. She was dressed, from head to toe, in the whitest gown and her hair tumbled to her shoulders in waves of copper. Her face had thinned and there was shadow where once there'd been curve. Her eyes held something distant in them as if her mind was elsewhere.

Plethon took her hands and gazed at her, watching the colour creep slowly into her cheeks. 'Anna,' he said at last, 'are you very unhappy?'

She laughed, but it was a thin sound. 'I am well,' she said with conviction. 'I eat, I sleep, I live.' She smiled. 'No, I live in luxury and have iced sherbet on call. And I have a horse.'

'A horse?'

'Eskalon. He was Luke's but he lost him. Now he's mine.'

Plethon opened his mouth to speak but she put her finger to it and leant forward.

'And he told me something.' It was a whisper.

'The horse?'

'Yes. He told me that I must go to Luke and that he would take me to him.'

Plethon watched her for a moment, wondering if, perhaps, her mind had finally succumbed. How would she take the news he had to give her? Gathering the folds of his toga, he lifted his long beard free and sat down on the bench, patting the space beside him.

'Anna, you have agreed to marry Suleyman. The world knows it.'

'I have agreed to marry him in six months' time if there's been no word from Luke. There's been word.'

'From a horse?'

'From a horse.'

Plethon frowned. 'Luke's destiny . . .' he began, but then stopped. For a moment he wondered what right he had to say what he was about to say.

'Luke's destiny is to be with me.'

Plethon looked down at his hands, at the fingers that had too often pointed to false truths. But this one he was certain of. It was time to be brutal.

'Perhaps,' he said, looking up. 'But there is something he has to do before he can be with you. I thought it was a question of treasure. Now I see that it's also something else.'

Anna sat very still, dread climbing up her like a weed. She had given so much to this empire; given her brother, her freedom, nearly her mind to its ravenous maw. Must she now give Luke?

She looked away towards Yildirim's tree. 'What does he have to do?'

She looked back at him, the misery clouding her eyes a darker green.

'You've not mentioned Prince Mehmed,' she continued. 'Mehmed would take the Turks east, away from Constantinople. Why not talk to him?'

'Because Tamerlane is not ready yet. He needs to be persuaded that he wants to fight Bayezid. Mehmed is not the prince to do that.'

'So find another prince.'

Plethon took her hand. 'Anna,' he said softly, 'Luke *is* that prince.'

She frowned. Luke was no prince. He was a Varangian. The numbing dread was in every part of her now.

A Varangian sent to persuade Tamerlane. Luke is going to Tamerlane.

She had to think of something else. 'Will Constantinople hold?'

'Constantinople will hold until the Turks get their cannon. I come from Venice where I tried to persuade the Doge to sell them instead to the Empire.'

'And will they?'

'Before the crusade, perhaps. Now, no. They are Venetians.'

She frowned. 'They're also Christian . . . And the Varangian treasure, have you given up on that?'

Plethon shook his head. 'While you were at Nicopolis, I entered Constantinople to search Siward's tomb which is in the Varangian church there. But someone had been there before me.'

'It was empty?'

'No. The top had been removed. It was full, but with a body. There was no room for anything else.'

'So where do you look now?'

'Mistra,' he said. 'I go there next. There was a mural in the church that had been covered over with recent paint. Whoever did that wanted to hide its message.' He paused and smiled. 'I expect a proposition quite soon.'

Anna only half heard him. She was thinking of Mistra and of her yearning to be there. She said, 'Tell me, Plethon, what is *my* destiny?'

'To marry Suleyman.'

Anna shook her head. 'Not if I can be with Luke.'

Plethon said nothing.

'So you are on your way to Mistra. Why have you come here?' she asked.

Plethon saw the fragility of her mind and the despair that made it so. He had dreaded this moment. 'To take you with me.' He paused. 'Anna, your father is dead.'

At first the words held no meaning for her. Then they did. Of course he was dead. He'd been dead since Alexis had gone. He'd been dead when she'd seen him at Serres.

I shall never speak with him again.

Anna rocked back on the bench, embracing herself.

Plethon continued, very softly: 'I've come from the Emperor Manuel to seek peace. To see what can be rescued from the ruins of Nicopolis. I've also come to ask the Sultan if I can take a daughter to Mistra to see her father interred.'

Anna tried to smile but the ice that had entered her soul froze it on her lips. 'And what does the Sultan say?' she whispered.

Bayezid had been drunk when he'd received him. The fair page from Trebizond had supported his more extravagant gestures of contempt as Plethon had argued the case for peace. But he'd agreed to Anna leaving because it would upset his eldest son.

'He said yes.' Plethon unravelled a fold in his toga. He put two fingers to his closed eyes and rubbed them. Anna saw how tired he was. 'He even agreed to allow Matthew, Nikolas and Arcadius to come with us: a Varangian escort. He must want to annoy his son very much.'

Plethon glanced around the courtyard. He'd seen movement among the tulips but it was only a cat, its grey-silk body flowing from the flowers like mercury. He rose and took Anna's hand. 'We leave tomorrow at dawn. The funeral is in three days. We'll have to ride fast.'

Later that night, in that part of the palace reserved for honoured guests, Plethon's drift into platonic sleep was disturbed by the arrival of a woman in his bedroom.

At first he thought he was dreaming. He sat upright in his bed, drew in his exposed stomach and rubbed his eyes. When he reopened them, she was still there.

The room was big and cool and had two large windows that looked on to a little garden of scented flowers. Diaphanous curtains filtered the moonlight into gently moving squares of white that stretched across the room to the foot of his bed. Standing, silhouetted in one of these, was the woman, and the moon made a mockery of her caftan as a thing of modesty.

He had guessed immediately who she was.

'Zoe,' he said.

There was no answer. He wondered how he would react to an invitation. She was rumoured to have a taste for the bizarre and it was just possible that she saw philosophers as such. A waft of jasmine travelled to him on the slightest of airs. The curtains moved fractionally.

'Am I to be blessed?'

Now certain that she had entered the right room, Zoe glided down the path of silver that led to the bed and sat on it.

'Unlikely,' she replied. 'Not, you understand, on account of your years. It's the beard. I can't manage beards of such length.'

Plethon smiled. He reached over and took his toga from a chair by the side of the bed. 'How can I be of assistance to you, Zoe?' he asked, wrapping the folds around his released stomach

'If it's not my body you want, am I to presume it's my mind? Shall we light a candle?'

'No. Too dangerous and I will not stay long.'

The girl drew her knees up to her chin and hugged her shins with her arms. Her long black hair followed the curve of her back like oil and the profile of her face was sharp with concentration. Her eyelashes curled above her eyeball and she seemed to Plethon like a cat-goddess.

'You saw Anna this morning,' she said.

Plethon didn't answer.

She sighed. 'I don't expect you to like me,' she said, resting her cheek on her knee and looking at him. 'I am a Mamonas and therefore beyond redemption. But I have helped Anna in the past.'

Plethon still made no comment. He let her consider her next words.

'I can help you.'

Plethon smiled. Then he said, 'Anna told me you've been away.'

'The Prince Suleyman desired my presence.'

'To fire cannon or climb scaling ladders? Your gifts are endless, lady.'

The girl's face hardened. 'We all do what we have to, to survive,' she said quietly, 'even you. Why else are you here?'

Plethon nodded and pulled the toga tighter around his shoulders. The night breeze was slight but he had shivered. This was a strange world of ever-present danger and he felt it all around.

'I was in Venice two months ago,' he said. 'Your father and brother were there. Did you know that?'

'No.'

Plethon believed her.

'I saw them in the Doge's barge. A great honour.' He paused. 'They were with a man called di Vetriano.'

Zoe looked up sharply. She frowned.

Di Vetriano.

'Why is this interesting?'

'Because he is working with your father and brother to supply Suleyman with the means to take Constantinople. But then you'll have worked that out, as you'll have considered that it may be time to look to different alliances.' He paused while they studied each other in calculation. 'You opened the tomb,' he said.

Zoe breathed deeply and looked away.

'As soon as Luke left with Suleyman, you went into Constantinople and you opened the tomb. You found something and now you want to make a bargain.'

She released her knees and turned to face him on the bed. 'I know where to find the treasure in Mistra.'

Plethon considered this. She might just be telling the truth. But, if so, why had she not gone to get it? He lay back against the pillows, putting his hands behind his head. 'I assume that it's occurred to you that it might not be gold that lies there?'

She smiled. 'Of course. The legend has it that it was a single casket that was buried. That wouldn't be enough gold to be interesting. Certainly not to me, anyway.'

'So what do you think it is?'

'I've no idea. Something that will save the Empire, they say. Anyway, that's where you come in. I take you to the treasure, you make use of it in any way you want and I take my reward from a grateful Emperor.'

'And what would that reward be?'

'I don't know yet.' She got up to leave. 'I will see you tomorrow dressed for the ride to Mistra.'

The following morning, Luke was riding behind Omar through the hills east of Bursa, leaving the snow-capped peak of Mount Uludağ towering behind them. This was rich farming country, land that had been held by Byzantium for centuries until taken by the Turk. It had been held by *akritoi*, Greek frontiersmen who'd been exempted taxes in exchange for guarding the border. Many of them were still here, tending their fields next to more recent sipahi settlers. It was a country of hard fields and skeletal trees, a country with its produce stored, a country waiting for the first snows of winter.

Luke pulled his cloak around him. 'Where are we going, Omar?'

'We're going out into the steppe where the nomads live and you're going to live with them.'

Luke was baffled. How could this be useful to the Empire? 'But I'm not a nomad,' he said. 'I know nothing of their ways.'

'So you'll learn.'

Luke thought of his life in Monemvasia and Chios, his life of comfort and friendship and learning. His easy life.

'Will you be there?' he asked at last.

'No, you'll be on your own. You'll learn more that way.'

'But how will I talk to them?'

Omar laughed. 'Really, Luke, how do you think? You'll learn their language.'

Luke considered this. He wanted to know more. 'Tell me about the Germiyans.'

Omar brought his horse to a stop and leant forward in his saddle, both hands on its pommel. 'The Germiyans were just

505

another tribe of Oghuz Turks that were driven west from their lands around the Caspian Sea,' he said. 'But they were well led and expanded their territories under Yakub's grandfather. His generals established their own beyliks, which took their lands from the Byzantines and stayed friendly with the Germiyans. For a time it seemed that they would become the dominant clan. But then the Osmanoğlu produced one truly inspired leader in Osman and the Ottoman dynasty was born. Four years ago, the Germiyans finally succumbed to their rule.' Omar smiled. 'So you can see why Yakub hates Bayezid.'

'But what of the tribes further to the east?'

'The Black and White Sheep Ilkhanates? They are what's left of the Mongol Horde that swept west two centuries ago under Genghis Khan. They are nomads of the same stock as Tamerlane but have settled.'

'So they'll not welcome Tamerlane?'

'No, but they may give him the excuse to invade. Both he and Bayezid count them as vassals.'

Luke pondered this. He asked, 'So will Tamerlane come?'

Omar lifted his palms to the heavens. 'That, Luke, is what the world is asking. Tamerlane has unified the Mongol Horde again and broken out of his lands in the east with a savagery never seen before. Great cities have been laid waste as far west as Baghdad, their citizens butchered and towers built of their skulls. No one knows where he'll go next.'

That night Omar and Luke stayed at a monastery where Christian monks welcomed them with generosity. They ate roasted quail and cabbage and Luke was given hot wine. The monks talked to Omar around the fire and Luke fell asleep to the murmured debate of learned men who wanted to find things to

506

agree about. He didn't remember being put to bed or the sound of the wind that blew in from the steppe.

They left early and rode all of the next day through land that was unfolding into plain and Omar talked unhurriedly of Islam. Luke listened and thought of Plethon. Two teachers. Two teachers of kindness and patience. Two messages of surprising similarity.

At length they came to the city of Eskişehir, said to be the loveliest in all Anatolia. It had been the birthplace of Osman. They rested there in the caravanserai and shared a meal of roast partridge with men travelling east for the haj.

From Eskişehir they turned south and headed further out into the steppe.

The steppe.

Luke had grown up in a small city on the edge of the sea. He was used to narrow streets and the noise of human exchange. Now all around him was nothing. No buildings, no people, no sound except the wind. There were no towns or villages on the steppe, no trees or fields, no farms. There was nothing but mile after mile of grass and rock and low, sweeping hills, fissures scarring their sides like claw marks. So vast was this land in every direction that it merged with the sky.

Which was why they saw the riders.

They were far, far behind: tiny specks that never got closer. When they stopped, the specks stopped too. There were many.

'They're following us,' said Luke.

'Yes, and not caring much if we know it.'

'Who are they?'

Omar shrugged. They had stopped side by side and were looking back at their pursuers. 'One of the tribes curious to know why we're here? I don't know.'

It was late afternoon and the day was beginning to darken. A sudden gust of wind lifted the horses' heads and Luke looked into the distance. Curtains of rain were moving fast towards them, their shadows mottling the ground like a disease. Lightning branched out across the sky and the horses pricked up their ears and pointed their noses towards the danger. Luke leaned forward and whispered words into a quivering ear and the ear was still.

Omar spoke. 'We are still far from our destination. We need to hurry.'

It took three days of hard riding for Plethon, Anna and Zoe, and their Varangian escort, to reach Mistra. They'd left Edirne at dawn and ridden without conversation all day. The others had changed horses but Anna had Eskalon beneath her and he'd looked ready to ride the same distance again when they stopped at an inn south of Corinth on the first night.

The truth was that Anna hadn't really known what to say to Zoe.

Certainly, Zoe had helped her in the past and she'd believed her a friend. But she'd lied to Anna about Suleyman, whom she now knew to be her lover, and she was certain that her interest in Luke went beyond concern for his welfare.

So, at the first opportunity, she'd gone to find Plethon. He was washing his face from a bucket outside the inn.

'Why is she here?'

Plethon's face had been pressed to a towel. He emerged, blinking. 'Because she may or may not help me to find the Varangian treasure in Mistra,' he said. 'Her interests may just coincide with mine.'

'She is Suleyman's lover,' said Anna.

'And you are to be his wife. We are not all free to be what we want to be.'

The conversation had ended there. They'd gone to bed, slept for a few hours, and been back in the saddle before dawn, so it was in a state of some exhaustion that they dismounted to enter the little city of Mistra on the following night, leaving their horses at the city gate. Anna bade farewell to the Varangians who were to stay at the palace barracks, while she, Plethon and Zoe would sleep at the Laskaris house.

All except Anna were entering for the first time. Plethon's travels had taken him everywhere except, surprisingly, Mistra, and for some time he'd longed to see the place that some were calling the Empire's finest jewel. Zoe had found no cause; her family did little business with the city and, in recent times, no Mamonases would have been welcome there.

Anna had not seen her home for two terrible years and her tired eyes strained to conjure memories from the shadows around her. It was approaching midnight and the streets were deserted apart from the cats darting from door to door like messengers, their tails aloft. The street lights were newly extinguished and a faint smell of resin hung in the air. There was a cry from an upper window, perhaps a dream of a time when Suleyman had stood before their gates with a young girl before him on his saddle.

The moon emerged from behind a cloud. Plethon had stopped and was looking up at the dark mass of the Despot's palace. There were lights in its windows.

'The Despot works late,' said Anna, stopping beside him. Zoe had wandered on ahead. 'We go there tomorrow.'

They walked on and caught up with Zoe and were soon turning into the street where the Laskaris house lay.

Approaching the door, she saw a small woman standing alone beneath a street lamp, bent with waiting. The light from it turned the woman's hair into a long, disordered veil of mourning white, ribboned by scissors. Not the colour of her mother's hair.

When she got closer, when she realized that it was Maria standing there, she let out a cry and brought her balled fist to her mouth. Then she was running, running as fast as her tired legs would allow to reach this woman who had suffered two deaths and then a third: her very will to live.

Moments later Maria was in Anna's arms, and in her raised face, wet with tears, Anna could see the deep scars of her pain. She held her mother's head between her hands, the white strands of hair spilling through her fingers, and whispered the four words she knew might bring her back from the dead.

'*I am in love.*'

That night was the last that Omar and Luke would spend together before reaching the tribe.

They had arrived at an old Byzantine monastery perched on a hill above a small village called Seyit Gazi. It now held a mosque with outbuildings gathered within stout walls. They had ridden up the path to its gate in the rain and dark on horses whose heads hung low with fatigue.

Omar was both well known and loved by the men of this place. As soon as they'd ridden through the gate, they were surrounded by torches held high above faces shining with relief that they'd arrived late but safe.

One came up to Omar and embraced him as soon as his feet touched the ground. He seemed to be of similar age. 'Welcome, old friend!'

Omar kissed both of his cheeks. 'There are men following us, Abraham.'

'Then we will bar the gates and post guards,' said the monk. He gestured to another, who hurried away. 'This monastery is difficult to break into.'

While Omar went into the mosque to pray, Luke was led across the courtyard by Abraham and down some steps into a large vaulted room with cells on either side. In the middle of the room was a long table with plates neatly laid out and a cup by each place. There were candles in wooden holders and baskets of bread and earthenware jugs in between.

Abraham sat and gestured for Luke to sit beside him. 'We were worried for you. The steppe is not a place to spend the night if you are not a nomad.' He lifted one of the jugs. 'And there is more rain coming. Much rain.'

Luke looked around him. Some of the cell doors were shut.

'Each door leads to a *cilehane*,' said Abraham, '"a place of suffering", in your language. Men come from far away to live in them and, while here, they will fast, talk to no one and read only the Koran.'

'As I did,' said Omar, who'd arrived to take the seat next to Luke, 'for five years; with Abraham, who chose to stay.'

'Why?' asked Luke. 'Why here?'

Omar leant over and took a basket filled with bread. He offered it to Luke. 'Because it has special significance. It is the shrine of one of our saints, Battal Gazi. He was a giant Arab who fought the Greeks many centuries ago and ran off with the Emperor of Byzantium's daughter. Theirs was a great love. Her tomb lies next to his in a vault below.'

He looked around at the cells, then he turned to Abraham. 'The cells are taken?'

'Many already. People come early.'

Omar turned to Luke. 'It is the saint's birthday tomorrow and there will be a vigil in the crypt tomorrow night. Many pilgrims have come already. More will come tomorrow.'

Much later, when they had eaten hot food and the last of the monks had gone to bed, Luke and Omar walked across the rain-splashed courtyard to the room they would sleep in. There were two beds in the room and a fire in the grate and a stone canopy above it shaped like a holy hat. Chairs had been placed before the fire and a jug of wine sat on a low table between them.

'I don't usually drink wine,' said Omar as he sat, 'but tonight I'll make an exception. I'm sure Allah will overlook it.'

Luke shook the rain from his cloak and laid it next to the hearth. Then he poured wine for them both. It was hot and strong and tinctured with cinnamon and Luke felt warmth flood through him. He stretched out his legs and closed his eyes.

'Don't go to sleep,' chided Omar gently. 'I have much to tell you and this will be my last chance to do so.'

Then Omar began to talk and his deep voice rose above the wind and the rain outside and Luke sat forward and stared into the fire and listened to every word.

Omar spoke of Battal Gazi, who had loved a Byzantine princess with a passion that had transcended creed; then he talked of other things. And, as he spoke, Luke began to know this wise and funny man who'd forced his gentle way into his existence and why he'd cared to do so.

At last he said, 'That is why we've come to this place, Luke. Because its beauty lies in the love that is buried deep within it.' Omar prodded the embers with the tip of his shoe. 'Like you.'

'Me?'

'Yes, you, Luke. You know love without question. That is rare.'

The fire was bright in Omar's eyes, casting miniature dancers in his pupils. His beard had been touched by the alchemist's hand and ran in silver to his waist.

Luke said, 'But many people love.'

'Yes, but not like you. There is great power in such a love. Power that can be used for good.'

Luke leant back in his chair and stared into the fire as if it might hold answers amongst the embers. He suddenly felt tired and perhaps a little drunk. The jug was almost empty and Omar hadn't touched the cup beside him. The walls around him were now almost lost to darkness, and he heard the noise of the wind and rain beating against their ancient stone. There was one question still that needed answering.

He said, 'Why are you helping me, Omar? You're a Muslim like Bayezid. Why are you helping a Christian?'

'Religion is not the point, Luke. *Reason* is the point. There is a new flame of reason that's been lit in the West among the city states of Italy. People there are beginning to think in new ways and show it through their art, their writing, their systems of government.' Omar sighed. 'But there is also a darkness coming in from the East, two monsters who would extinguish that flame, who would drag us back into another dark age. Bayezid and Tamerlane must be made to destroy each other. It's the only way.'

'Which is what you and Plethon want to bring about. But I am confused as to my part. Is it to find a treasure or to meet a madman?'

Omar turned to the fire. His eyes had taken its embers. 'Which would you like it to be, Luke?'

Luke shook his head. 'I was left a sword,' he said. 'A sword to take me to a treasure.'

'Or to remind you that you are a Varangian? A Varangian prince?'

Omar rose and went over to his bed. His back was to Luke. He turned.

'I have your sword here,' he said, lifting it so that the fire made a river of its blade. He lowered it and walked over to Luke. 'Here, it's yours. Yakub brought it from Suleyman's tent. He thought you might need it.'

Luke took the sword. He looked down at the dragon head, at its open maw.

A Varangian sword. For a Varangian quest.

'Well, I can't go back anyway,' he said. 'I am a traitor in the west.'

Omar shook his head. 'I could pretend so, but I won't. Sigismund of Hungary has told Emperor Manuel the truth about Nicopolis. You may not be welcome in Burgundy, but you can return to Mistra.' He paused. 'Anna is there now. With Plethon.'

Luke stared at the old man. 'In Mistra? Why?'

'Because her father is dead. She will attend his funeral. She will be there for some weeks.'

Luke felt a wave of happiness break over him. He could walk out of the monastery that very moment, ride to Mistra and find a future with Anna. Somewhere. Somehow.

He took a deep breath. 'Why have you told me this? You could have kept silent and I'd have done what I had to do.'

'No, Luke.' Omar shook his head. 'That is the old way; not the way of *reason*. You must make this choice for yourself.'

Luke looked further into the fire, into its endlessly shifting centre. So many questions.

Much later, when Omar had gone to bed and the wine jug was empty, Luke sat with the sword in his lap and stared at it.

He'd looked again at what was scratched into its hilt. He'd read the word 'seputus' and seen the date below it.

Except that it wasn't a date. It was a name.

Mistra.

Outside the walls of the monastery, on a low hill to the west, twelve men were preparing for sleep.

They had ridden all day and kept the two men they were following always in their sight. Now, as they spread their bedding out on the ground, they looked up at the sky and swore beneath their breaths. The rain was closing in and it would be a hard one. Most were men of the steppe, of the Karamanid tribe, and they could feel its rhythm in the earth beneath them.

Two of their number were not of the steppe. They lay apart and looked not at the sky but at the black hulk of the monastery that broke the darkening horizon. One of them smiled. He'd watched the two men enter earlier and had seen the gates bolted behind them.

The men were exactly where he wanted them to be.

He yawned and drew his cloak around him. Tomorrow would be busy. For now, he would sleep.

CHAPTER TWENTY-FIVE

ANATOLIA, OCTOBER 1396

Luke pulled up his horse. The thunderclap had been endless, rolling back and forth to reach a crescendo of deafening percussion. The animal had stopped suddenly, its body rigid with terror. Luke whispered into its ear, his hand massaging the wet down around it. At last it calmed and Luke felt the tension seep through his legs.

It was a good horse, intelligent and strong. It had understood perfectly the need for silence as Luke had saddled it at dawn and led it out of the still-sleeping monastery. That had been eight hours ago.

Before the rain had come again.

Now it fell in torrents, hitting the dry steppe around like a drum-roll, making Luke's cloak a thing of weight rather than warmth. He was wet to the bone.

He hadn't slept at all in the night. He'd gone to bed with two words jostling each other in his mind.

Mistra.

He would leave at dawn, ride back to Mistra, tell Plethon of what he'd found written on the sword. He would see Anna and tell her that he'd come back to her from wherever it was he had to go, tell her to wait for him. Then he would return to Omar. His note explained it all. He'd be back at the monastery in ten days, maybe less. Omar must have faith in him. He'd even left his bag as hostage.

But now, as the landscape around him became less certain through the rain, as the warnings crashed out from the heavens, as the varied smells of the steppe combined into a single stench of wet leather and horse fear, he was not so sure.

Have I done the right thing?

He looked around him. It was as if he was separated from the world by this curtain of grey. He felt water course its way down his spine and thought of the spiced wine of the night before. He looked down at the sword by his side, saw the rain hitting the dragon head pommel in tiny explosions. He shivered.

Then he heard something beyond the curtain, something faint that wanted to get through: a shout.

Immediately he thought of the group that they'd seen following them on the previous day. It must be them. But where to hide? There were no hiding places on the steppe.

He stopped and listened.

The shout came again, this time closer – in front. Luke strained his eyes, wiping the drips from his eyelashes and nose.

There. A rider. Just one. Approaching fast.

A rider in a hurry.

Luke waited for the man to draw up to him. He was cloaked against the rain and had large saddlebags strapped to the horse's flanks. Luke couldn't see his face.

'Friend,' the man said. He spoke in Turkic but it was not his tongue. 'Is there a monastery ahead?'

Luke uncovered his head. 'Benedo Barbi,' he said, smiling. 'You followed me?'

517

Just then the sky delivered another bone-jarring crash and Barbi's horse reared. The Italian swore and grabbed hold of its mane. For a moment, Luke thought he might fall.

When he'd come back to earth and settled his horse, Barbi said, 'I followed you from Bursa. It wasn't difficult. You and the old man make strange companions. I came when I remembered where I'd seen the man before.'

'What man?'

'One of the men following you.'

Luke frowned. Unease had settled on him like another cloak.

'His name is di Vetriano,' said Barbi. 'He's Venetian. I saw him watching you in Bursa.'

Di Vetriano.

'You know him?' asked Luke.

'He's an assassin. I met him in Cairo. He tried to kidnap one of the Mameluke chemists I was working with. He'd been sent to get what we knew about Greek fire.'

'By the Doge?'

Barbi shrugged. 'Probably. Anyway, he's following you and that can't be good. You've not seen him?'

Luke nodded slowly. 'Yesterday. We saw him yesterday. With others. I must have passed them when I left this morning.'

A sudden gust of wind blew the cowl up over Barbi's mouth. He pulled it down. The rain was harder now, almost blinding.

'Where are you going?' he asked.

But Luke was already turning his horse. 'Later, Benedo. For now, we have to ride fast. There's a good man in danger.'

In Mistra, the Despot was wiping away a tear. The tear was of happiness, of grief, of guilt. Anna, whom he'd last seen two years past at Serres, who'd probably saved his life then and whom he'd not expected to see again, was sitting across from him.

With her was Plethon. Zoe had been left at the Laskaris house with Maria, who was still sleeping. She and Anna had talked quietly through much of the night of the one thing that mattered most, that gave hope.

I am in love.

Maria's mind had been more fragile than Murano glass and anything that might shatter it – Alexis, her father – had been put to one side to be looked at later when the time was right. Instead they'd talked of Luke, and Anna had woven a tapestry richer than any the Laskaris house possessed. She'd created a fair Varangian, a prince of *England* as Plethon had told her, taller than most, who rode a horse named Eskalon and wielded a sword with a secret. She created a man who could speak languages and dream labyrinths into life. She talked of how he'd saved her life once and then nearly brought her across the sea to Mistra. Her threads were of the real and unreal until they joined in a single weave, as Anna had intended, and her mother fell into the first sleep she'd had in weeks.

Finally, when she'd gently kissed her mother's forehead and put a blanket over her, Anna had sat and listened to the air around her still ringing with her song of Luke, played to a distant, eastern drum.

Now she sat with Theodore and Plethon at the end of a long table in the Despot's palace. The windows beyond them were canvasses on which an autumn sky was painted. A fire burned noisily in the grate and warm wine was laid before them.

The Despot spoke. 'So the Emperor's given up on negotiation?'

'There's no point, Majesty,' said Plethon. 'The Sultan laughed at me when I saw him in Edirne. Bayezid has resumed the siege and means to take Constantinople. Then it will be Mistra.'

Theodore sighed. He'd been feeling much older lately, as if the season's decay had entered his bones. He missed Simon Laskaris with an intensity that had surprised him. He cried a lot these days.

'How long will it be, do you think?'

'No time soon,' said Plethon. He'd not met this man before but had heard much to recommend him, especially from Anna. 'They need cannon of a size as yet uncreated to bring down the walls.'

'Which the Venetians are building for them?'

Plethon nodded. 'Yes, but not always successfully. The casts are too big. They blow apart.'

'And you encourage this . . . combustion?'

Plethon smiled. 'I do what I can. I have a little money.'

Theodore rose and walked to one of the windows. On one side of the mullion, a pattern of leaves had arranged themselves across the glass. He breathed and rubbed his sleeve across its surface.

'I'm told you do wonders,' he murmured. He turned. 'I've long wanted to meet you, Plethon I hope you will do me the honour of staying at the palace tonight? I would talk with you further, alone.'

The philosopher dipped his head. 'The honour would be mine, Majesty.' He paused. 'The Emperor wishes me to go to Methoni. There is a bishop there.'

Theodore nodded. 'The Bishop Adolfo. He is a Venier, cousin to the Doge of Venice.'

'He is sympathetic to the cause of union,' said Plethon. 'He has the Pope's ear, and his cousin's. May soon be made cardinal.'

'But you cannot believe that another crusade is possible? Not after Nicopolis?'

'The Christian princes are competitive, lord. Where one fails, another may succeed. It is possible with the Pope's blessing.'

'And the price?'

'The union of the Churches of West and East. As you would expect.'

'Which,' said the Despot, 'I am told you support. But it is not popular with the people. They would see it as another conquest. This time the Pope's.'

Plethon nodded. He had placed his palms side by side on the table and seemed to be studying nails that needed some attention. 'The talking may be enough,' he said at last. 'If the Venetians see another crusade as a possibility, then they may be persuaded to blow up more cannon. We need time.'

'Time? Time for what?' asked Theodore.

There was silence then. It was Anna that broke it.

'Tamerlane.'

She had hardly moved during the conversation. Now she rose from the table and went over to stand next to the Despot. 'Tamerlane to come to our rescue. One tyrant set against another. We are all pawns, aren't we?'

Theodore took her hand. The tears were already in his eyes. 'I'm sorry, Anna.'

Anna turned to the man sitting at the table. 'Why him? Why must Luke do it?'

'Because Luke *can* do it. He has the talents and he has the will.'

'And will he return?'

'I hope so. And when he does he will be a hero. The truth is now known about Nicopolis.'

'Then I am released from Suleyman?' she asked quietly. 'If the Sultan goes to war with Tamerlane, what point is there any more in me marrying his son? Perhaps I can marry the hero instead?'

Plethon spoke with care. 'Anna, much has to happen before Bayezid meets Tamerlane on the field of battle. We cannot afford to anger Suleyman or Mistra may fall before Constantinople.' He paused. 'You must go back.'

Anna nodded. She'd known it must be thus. They'd talked of it only days ago. She went over to a chair on which her cloak had been laid. Her voice was dull. 'We should leave for my father's funeral. Plethon, will you come with me to collect my mother?'

In the little church of St Sophia, the body of Simon Laskaris had been dressed in a long tunic of brushed silk of the deepest red dye. His face shone with the embalmer's oil so that he seemed to be perspiring. He was laid out on a bed of velvet supported by trestles and behind him was a board on which the Laskaris arms looked out with dignity for the last time. There would be no heir to this illustrious name.

Anna had walked to the church, hand in hand with her mother, the Despot and Plethon either side of them. Black hung from every window and whispers hung over the people lining the streets like a shroud.

Simon Laskaris was to be buried at last.

For most, it was a relief. Since Serres, he had acted as a man deranged, walking the streets at night in his bedclothes, his white hair unkempt, his beard brittle with food. People had ached to see such a man shorn of his dignity and they remembered the cause of it and wept.

Tonight, they stood beneath their torches until the Despot's party had passed and then followed them up the hill to stand in silent vigil around the church of St Sophia.

Those inside the church took their seats in the side chapel where the leaders of Mistra had been buried for generations. Anna, Maria, Theodore and Bartolomea sat in the front row. Behind them sat the highest-ranking men of the court and their wives.

Now the singing began and the incense swirled and the candles fluttered in the small draught that came through the windows high in the chapel's walls. The Despot rose to stand beside the body of his oldest friend and spoke a solemn eulogy that told of greatness and friendship.

And Anna watched it all with dry eyes.

Simon Laskaris dead. Alexis dead. Luke as good as dead.

For no reason, she thought of Zoe. Had she come?

Zoe had come. Her rank permitted it and she was deemed unguilty of the sins of her father and brother. She had crept into the chapel after the service had begun and now stood at the back. Her eyes were fixed on the wall behind the altar.

It was dark by now and difficult to see much above the weak light of the many candles. But she could just make out a figure, then another.

Yes.

It was a scene she'd seen before, a scene she'd covered with paint in a Varangian church in Constantinople..

It wasn't identical, but the composition was the same: the open tomb, the guards lying asleep around it; one guard, his sword pointing. But there was something new in this picture.

She looked up. Her heart was beating fast.

Yes. There it was. The risen Christ.

She had lied to Plethon. She'd found nothing in Siward's tomb in Constantinople. She had come to Mistra hoping to find something.

And there it was.

Luke and Benedo Barbi rode into the village of Seyit Gazi beneath a steady cascade of rain that drilled into their backs without mercy. By now, the steppe around them had turned into a brown glue that gripped their horses' hooves and made every step a journey. Sound, at least, was obliterated by the downpour. They felt invisible.

Above them, somewhere, was the monastery, but the rain was too dense for it to be seen. They reached a little square where the bulbous dome of a mosque could just be made out on one side. There was a man beating his fist against the door.

Luke kicked his horse and rode up to him. The man was dressed as a monk and his sodden robes clung to his body like a second skin.

'Are you from the monastery?'

The man turned and began to back away.

Barbi said, 'We are friends. We're not with the Venetians.' He wondered if he understood Greek.

The man stopped and stared up at them. He was shaking with cold and fear and rubbing his palms against the sides of his tunic as if they might somehow dry.

Luke asked, 'Are they inside the walls?'

Now the monk stepped forward, bringing his hands to his head and pushing his long hair away from his eyes. His face was shiny with wet and filth. 'They were dressed as pilgrims. For the vigil. The saint's vigil.' He looked from Luke to Barbi. 'We thought they were pilgrims.'

Luke dismounted, unsticking himself from the saddle with pain. The insides of his legs were raw. He approached the man. 'How did you get out?'

The monk looked behind him, up at the louring bulk of the monastery somewhere beyond the rain. 'I swam,' he replied. 'There is a cistern and a pipe to the outside for when it over-flows. I came out through the pipe.'

'And the others? Did others manage to escape?'

The man shook his head. 'Only me. It's too dangerous now. All this rain will fill the pipe.'

'How many Venetians are there?'

The monk considered this. 'They're not all Venetian. Just two. The rest are of the Karamanid tribe.'

Luke had heard of the Karamanids. They were the neigh-bouring tribe to the Germiyans and their enemies. They had yet to succumb to Bayezid. He walked back to Barbi, who was still on his horse. He looked up, shielding his face from the rain. 'Can you swim?'

Barbi shook his head. 'Never learnt. Can you?'

Luke grinned. 'Like a dolphin.'

Barbi dismounted. 'Luke, you heard him. It's too dangerous.'

Luke shrugged. 'It's the only way in. They'll have barred the gates and manned the walls. It's the only way to get inside and you can't swim.'

'But you'll drown.'

'Not if we hurry.' Luke turned to the monk. 'Father, can you show us this pipe?'

Minutes later they were leading their horses across the square to the edge of the village where they tied them to a fence post. Luke patted his animal and then stopped. He'd had a thought. He walked over to Barbi.

'Have you got the Greek fire in your saddlebags?' he asked.

The Italian nodded. 'I have two siphons and the solution inside it. Do you want them?'

'Bring them.'

The monk leading, they began to climb the hill, their feet slipping in the mud. The siphons were heavy and Barbi struggled to keep up.

Then they were there. The monk stopped. He was kneeling next to the opening to a clay tunnel. It was not much more than a man's width across.

'It's still dry,' said the monk. 'But the moment the water inside the cistern reaches its level, it will come out in a rush. You'll need to be quick.'

Luke had taken off his cloak. 'Give me one of the siphons,' he said to Barbi. 'Help me to strap it on to my back.'

The engineer lifted the siphon and helped Luke into its harness. Water was drumming against its metal and splashing into their eyes. Luke tested the straps, then: 'Let me tell you my plan,' he said.

But Barbi was shaking his head. 'I already know your plan,' he said. 'And it's insane.'

Inside the monastery crypt, all was yellow. Tall tallow candles cast their unreliable light over the tombs of the saint and his Byzantine princess, bathing them in a wash of quince. Around the tombs were low arches supported by stout pillars and the floor was squared by flagstones rippled by the flow of time. The only metal objects were rings, some driven into the beams above the tombs and one large one in the floor. Around the walls, half in shadow, stood men dressed in the clothes of pilgrims, their hoods drawn back. All had the wind-blasted features of men of the steppe.

Suspended above the tombs in the pose of crucifixion, with his hands inside two rings, was Omar. He was naked to the waist and, in the candlelight, his skin had the texture of unfeathered chicken. His feet were resting on the giant's tomb.

Before him stood the Venetian di Vetriano. He had his short sword at his side and was holding a crossbow that was pointed at Omar's heart.

There was a sudden gust of wind as the crypt door opened and the candles jumped and cowered. One went out. A man dressed in black had entered and shook the rain from his cloak. 'We found nothing,' he said to di Vetriano. 'Just his bag.'

'And you searched it?'

'Nothing. No capsules, nothing.'

'What of the monks?'

'Locked in the refectory. They're not talking. I don't think they know where he's gone anyway.'

Di Vetriano frowned. He turned to Omar. 'It would seem that he's done it again. Magoris seems to have infinite cunning when it comes to escape. First Monemvasia, then my friend Rufio's boat. Now this monastery.' He paused and walked up to Omar, his head the height of his waist. He looked up. 'Where is he, old man?'

Omar didn't answer. He was looking at the Venetian with calm and some interest. He knew him now. 'Di Vetriano.'

The Venetian performed a little bow. If he was surprised by the acknowledgement, he hid it well. His face, pointed and sallow, was a mask. Venice was good at masks.

Omar continued: 'Why would the Serenissima's most infamous sea captain be looking for Luke Magoris?'

This time the Italian didn't respond. He didn't know who Omar was but he felt a power emanating from the old man that was beginning to unsettle him.

Omar said, 'Why would this sea captain, the same that brought Luke Magoris's mastic from Chios to Venice, be searching my young friend's baggage for a *capsule*?' He paused. 'A capsule of what?'

Di Vetriano frowned. 'You ask too many questions, old man,' he said. 'It will be my turn soon.' He turned to the other man. 'Fabio, take some of these animals and make another search of the monastery.'

His companion gestured to two of the Karamanids and left. Another candle went out with the draught.

Di Vetriano went over to one that was still alight. He set down the crossbow and prised the candle from its holder with both hands. Hot wax dripped on to the back of his hand and he swore. He returned to Omar, climbing to stand on top of the saint's tomb so that they were facing each other.

'I'm told that old men's skin burns like parchment,' he said genially. He was holding the candle in the space between them and lifted it so that the flame was almost touching Omar's nose. 'Now, once again, where is Luke Magoris?'

Pieces of Omar's beard and eyebrows were curling and there was the acrid smell of burning hair. The only movement in his face came from the clenching of teeth. He stared straight into the Italian's eyes. 'I don't know. He left this morning without saying goodbye.'

Di Vetriano laughed softly, a dry sound. He broke off a piece of wax from the top of the candle, studied it for a moment and then pressed it to Omar's cheek. There was a smell of scorched flesh and the old man flinched but no sound came from his lips.

'Do I have to ask you again?'

Then Omar blew. He lifted his beard and puckered his lips and the candle went out. Di Vetriano stared at the smoking wick in amazement.

Omar said, 'You need to listen, not talk, di Vetriano. You've made a mistake.'

The sopracomito's smile was, just for a moment, unfastened from his face. He took a step backwards, lifting an arm to keep his balance on the curve of the tomb.

'It doesn't do what you think it does,' said Omar.

Di Vetriano had gone very still. 'And what do I think what does?' he asked slowly.

Omar didn't directly answer the question. He shifted his weight and looked up at an arm. A trickle of blood was running down from his wrist. He looked back. 'I was in Venice when your ship came in,' he said. 'With my friend Plethon. We were there to meet with your doge. We saw your ship held in St Mark's Basin flying the flag of plague. Yet there were men brought ashore. We speculated why.'

Di Vetriano was watching the man in front of him closely, his arms folded tightly to his chest. He had not relit the candle.

Omar shifted his weight again. 'You will permit,' he continued, 'that the lands of the Prophet have been far more advanced in the field of medicine than Christendom? Indeed, remain so, yes?'

Di Vetriano didn't answer.

'We have long understood that a mixture of mastic from Chios, orange blossom and other ingredients can offer some amelioration against the onslaught of the plague.' He paused and then he said, 'It can delay the plague's advance for a matter of weeks, but it can do no more.'

There was sweat now on the Venetian's brow. A bead broke free and ran unrestricted to the bank of his moustache. His eyes were unfocused.

Omar spoke again, quietly and with sympathy. 'Signore, your agreement with the Serenissima would seem voided.'

Below the crypt, below the flagstone with the ring at its centre, the cistern was filling fast.

Luke was in the tunnel with the siphon on his back, the straps biting into his shoulders. At his waist was an oilskin containing the stuff to make fire. The pipe was bigger than he'd thought it would be but it was dark and slippery and rose at an angle that meant he had to use his elbows to make any progress forward. The pain was excruciating.

He stopped, closed his eyes and listened.

Nothing, except the steady fall of water into the cistern ahead. He adjusted the siphon on his back and inched forward. Around him was a black woven so dense that it seemed palpable. For a moment, he thought of the labyrinth and a dream that had brought forth a village. Without darkness, there could be no light.

He stopped and listened again. The sounds ahead had changed. There was silence now. No water meeting water. Just silence.

530

Then something else.

Water was coming towards him and was approaching fast. It sounded like a huge snake slapping its flesh against the sides of the pipe. He took a deep breath and ground his body into the sides of the pipe.

Coming. Coming. Com . . .

Then it was upon him. He just had time to brace himself before it hit, pushing him backwards so that he had to use his knees as well as his hands to stop himself from going with it. It filled his nose and his ears and plastered his hair to his skull. The noise was deafening. It went on and on.

Luke felt himself slipping and his lungs ready to burst. The straps of the canister were like knives in his shoulders, pulling them from their sockets. He pressed every part of his body into the wall in one last effort.

Hold on.

Then it was gone.

As quickly as it had come, the water vanished and Luke opened his eyes, shaking his head and blowing water from his nose. He was breathing hard, the sound filling the space around him.

It will come again. I must move fast.

Taking another deep breath he began to edge forward. He could feel air on his face. He must be almost there.

Then he was. He could see nothing but blackness but his head and shoulders were suddenly in a bigger space and there was an echo to his breathing. He'd reached the cistern. He pulled his body through the end of the pipe and down into the deep water, his legs working to keep him afloat. It was bitterly cold.

He reached up and found only air. Then he crouched down

and launched himself up as high as the siphon on his back would let him. This time his fingers touched stone. He sank back into the water and listened, clamping his teeth together to stop them chattering. The only sound was the rush of water into the cistern.

I don't have much time.

He looked up, his eyes raking the darkness. Nothing.

Then he saw it. A tiny sliver of light that meant a wellhead.

The crypt.

Shifting the siphon into a more comfortable position, he swam towards it. The sound of falling water was lower here and he could hear faint voices above. He looked beyond. There was another sliver of light, just as the monk had said. It had to be the refectory where the other monks were being held.

He paddled over to it and waited. He could hear nothing above.

He ducked deep under the water and brought his fist into a clench. He rose and his knuckles hit wood.

Now there were voices. It was so, so cold. His teeth were hitting each other so hard he felt they must break.

Hurry.

He punched up again. There was a pause and he heard the sound of wood shifting, of a rope straining. The slice of light grew into an oblong and then, slowly, into a square. Within the square, circled, were the faces of men.

'Help me up,' he breathed, his voice almost taken by the cold. 'I'm heavy. I've got something on my back.'

In Mistra, it was an hour before dawn and the night was clear and bright with stars. There was a quarter-moon which gave small light to the little city on the side of the hill. But then no one was abroad except the messenger cats.

It was some hours since the Despot had emerged from the church of St Sophia and told the people still keeping vigil to go home. Now, even the breeze had gone, perhaps taking the soul of Simon Laskaris to some other, kinder world.

The church was quiet but some light could be seen in the little windows high in the side chapel where he'd been buried.

Anna looked up at them and rubbed her eyes. She should feel exhausted, she knew, following her ride and the long talk with her mother. But things had happened to keep her awake.

First, she'd felt the presence of Luke. Not there, but in her bedroom where she'd lain, trying to sleep.

He was coming to her, she was sure of it.

She'd risen, put on a shawl and crept past the room where Zoe was sleeping to tiptoe down the stone staircase and out into the street. She'd walked to the city gate where the stables were and she'd found Eskalon. It was dark and difficult to tell stall from stall, but he'd called to her and she'd found him. She'd taken his big head between her hands and lowered it so that she could look deep into those brown eyes. Where she'd seen him before.

He wasn't there.

Then she'd sat on a bale of hay and wept for a long, long time. Luke was somewhere far away and was going further. And she had to marry Suleyman.

She looked over to where Eskalon's head was turned towards her, watching her, and she felt a sudden longing to lead him from the stable and let him take her to wherever Luke was. Eskalon would know where to go.

She even rose and walked over and closed her eyes and put

her cheek to his neck, breathing in his horse-smell; the smell of Luke.

Where are you?

Finally, she'd left and slowly, slowly walked back to the house, every footstep pulling its chain of misery. But as she'd approached the gate, she'd seen movement in the little square behind it. A figure, definitely female, was hurrying across. Anna stepped back into the shadows.

Zoe.

Anna sank further into the shadows and drew her shawl over her head. Where was Zoe going at this time of night?

Why do I even need to ask? You're going to the treasure.

She heard soft footfall drawing nearer. Then Zoe was passing her, almost at a run. Anna waited a while, then followed her.

Zoe was climbing the streets of the city with the stealth of a cat, keeping to the shadows and constantly turning her head to left and right. Once she stopped and turned and Anna just had time to back into a doorway. Had she been seen?

When Anna stepped out into the street, Zoe was no longer ahead.

Where did you go?

Anna lifted her nightdress and quickened her step, passing the shadows of shop booths on either side. She rounded one corner then another, going faster all the time.

Still no Zoe.

She came to the big square on which the palace stood. Two guards were bent over a brazier, warming their hands against the first chill of winter.

Then she was across it and still climbing. Was Zoe ahead of her or had she stopped somewhere?

Anna reached the little square in front of the church of St

Sophia. She saw the dark bulk of the cistern and the well by its side, shadowed by a yew tree between. There was light inside the church.

Anna considered what to do. If Zoe was in there, it was because she thought the treasure was there too. And if she meant to remove it, she'd need help. Male help. Were there others in there with her?

She turned and began to walk back down the hill. She would need to find Plethon quickly and Plethon was asleep inside the palace. Ahead of her, she saw the guards huddled around the brazier. She walked up to them.

'Which of you is in command?'

The guards looked at each other. Had they understood? Then one of them stepped forward. 'I am in charge.' The accent was thick.

Albanians.

Anna took a deep breath. 'You know the one they call Plethon?'

The man nodded.

'Go into the palace and find him. Tell him Anna is in the church. With Zoe and others. Do you understand? Zoe and others.'

The man nodded again, then leant down to pick up his helmet. Anna turned and began to climb the hill again, reaching the little square with the yew. She crossed it and tiptoed up the steps to the church's door. It was fractionally open. She pushed it, praying that it wouldn't creak, and listened. No sound, just the sombre stillness of an empty church and her own, careful breathing. She walked in.

Inside, there was some light. It came from the side chapel at the end, the chapel where her father lay. It was a soft, unwavering light and it held her gaze for some moments before a shadow passed before it.

You're here.

Anna crept along the wall of the church, placing one foot in front of the other with infinite care, until she reached the altar where she stopped and crouched low. She could smell herbs now, the thyme and rosemary that had been laid either side of her father's body when he'd slept on his velvet bed. An owl cried outside and was answered by another.

She rose slowly and edged along the side of the altar until she could see inside the chapel.

Zoe was kneeling on the floor with a candle in one hand. She seemed to be reading the inscription engraved on the marble tomb below. Simon Laskaris's tomb was on the other side of the chapel, an open grave with its slab to one side, awaiting its own inscription.

Zoe looked up and stared for some time at the mural above the altar. Then she rose and walked towards it, holding the candle aloft.

As the light approached the mural, Anna could just see the painting of figures surrounding a tomb, a tomb that had been opened. One figure lay propped against its front: a soldier asleep, a sword in his hand. Zoe lifted the candle and its light fell upon the sword.

Anna gasped and clutched hold of the altar. She held her breath, the blood pounding in her temples. Zoe stood very still in front of her, the candle held high.

Have you heard me?

But Zoe was still studying the painting. Anna narrowed her eyes to see what she was seeing. It was Luke's sword. There was no mistaking it. The dragon pommel, the hilt. It was Luke's sword.

And its blade was pointing towards the tomb where Zoe had knelt.

Anna's mind raced. Plethon had talked of a mural in some church in Constantinople, a mural seen by Luke and Zoe. A mural with a question. Was this the answer?

Zoe stood for a while more, staring up at the mural. Then she turned and walked back to the front pew of the chapel. She reached down with one arm. When she rose again, there was a loaded crossbow in her hand. She was pointing it to where Anna was crouching.

'Come out, Anna,' she said quietly.

Anna didn't move. She was still shielded by the altar and the door to the church was not so far. She could run but then . . .

But then what?

This has to happen.

Slowly she stood. She walked forward into the chapel and stopped in the aisle. She was at one end and Zoe at the other. And Zoe held the crossbow.

Anna asked, 'Whose grave is it?'

'Manuel Cantacuzenus. Some say the greatest of the Despots. And his wife Isabelle of Cyprus.'

'And the date?'

'The year of his death: 1380. The year Siward left.'

Silence.

Then Anna said, 'Why did you lie to me?'

'About Suleyman?' Zoe shrugged. 'It was necessary.'

'You've always been his lover?'

Zoe said nothing.

Anna said, 'And Luke?'

Zoe shook her head. 'It would have been nice. But no.'

Anna thought back to the cave and knew this to be true. That had been Luke's first time, she was certain. But she had no doubt that Zoe had tried. She looked into eyes that were harder than stone.

'Have you ever loved?'

Zoe laughed. 'Loved? Why would I have loved? It ends in nothing.'

Pavlos Mamonas. Of course.

Zoe had been her father's son, the one he should have had. She had been the child with the genius for trade. He'd sent her abroad to learn more, and she'd learnt. Then he'd taken it all away.

Anna said softly, 'You cannot have that empire so you want another. Suleyman's. And I'm in your way.'

Zoe was watching her through half-closed eyelids. Her head was to one side as if Anna was a thing of interest. She seemed amused.

'But why the treasure?' Anna asked. 'Why is gold important? Suleyman has gold. He doesn't need more.'

Zoe smiled then. It might have been a smile of friendship were it not for the crossbow. 'You think that's what's down there? All this trouble for a little gold? Plethon sent by the Emperor to dig up a single casket of gold? I don't think so . . .'

Anna waited. There was more to come.

'The legend has it that whatever's down there can save the Empire,' continued Zoe. She looked down at the tomb. 'But whatever can save, can also destroy, if given to the right person, wouldn't you think?'

Anna understood. 'So you give it to Suleyman who takes Constantinople, becomes Sultan and marries you,' she murmured. She was staring into a candle, into a single tongue of flame rising above its wick, rigid with certainty. She looked up. 'You would betray your empire.'

'This Empire that devours its children? Yes, to gain another. It's not a difficult choice.'

'And the treasure, or whatever it is? How will you get it up?'

'I have friends. You remember the Albanians that Alexis took to Geraki? The ones that disappeared? They're inside the city.'

Albanians. The guards around the Grazier. Plethon won't be coming

Anna slowly nodded. She needed to escape. She needed time. 'You know, I actually thought you cared for Luke. I was even a little jealous.'

Zoe was looking at her as if in wonder. 'We are so different,' she murmured, shaking her head. 'You have the heart of the man who will rule the world and yet you want a Varangian. We are so very different.'

'Was that why you never married? Did you always plan this?'

'Something like this. And it would all have been so much easier if you hadn't arrived.'

Zoe looked beyond Anna.

'Richard, tie her up.'

Before she'd had time to react, Anna's arms were pinioned to her sides. She felt breath upon her neck.

'We'll not kill you yet,' said Zoe. 'You can see what we bring up before you die. You can tell your father when you see him.'

Anna's hands were pulled behind her back and she felt the bite of rope around her wrists. For a moment she thought about screaming, but a gag was now covering her mouth. She was pushed forward on to a bench and Richard Mamonas appeared before her.

Zoe pointed towards her cousin with the crossbow. 'Did you know that he killed your brother?'

Anna clenched her jaw. Alexis, his pale, anxious face set in entreaty, rose up before her. She closed her eyes but he was still there, this time straining to tell her something, to tell her of cannon.

This Empire that devours its children.

She opened her eyes and looked up at the painting. It was Luke lying there. Luke in a place with another open tomb. How could she make him wake up and come down with his dragon sword to help her?

Richard Mamonas was now tying her to the bench. When it was done, he checked the knots, straightened and walked over to join Zoe. He'd not looked at Anna.

There were footsteps in the church outside and two men walked in, one of whom she recognized. They held torches and carried the tools for lifting.

Then the three men got to work. Chisels were inserted into the sides of the stone and hessian applied to their tops to muffle the sound of the hammers. Soon, they were levering the stone up with iron bars until it broke free of its mortar and bigger bars could be put in to lift it. The men's faces were taut with concentration and shone with sweat in the candle-light. Then the top of the tomb was free and had been lifted to one side. Zoe picked up a candle and stepped forward to peer inside.

'Lift them out.'

Richard and one of the Albanians lowered themselves into the hole and lifted one, then two bodies out. They were wrapped in a heavy material bound by ropes and they scattered earth as they came.

Zoe said, 'What else is down there?'

'Just earth,' said her cousin. Only his chest, shoulders and head were visible above the hole.

540

'It must be beneath.' She looked up and gestured to the other Albanian. 'Give them spades.'

The two men began to dig, throwing the earth on to a pile on the chapel floor. It was not long before Richard Mamonas stopped. 'I've hit something. Metal.'

Zoe knelt down. 'It will be heavy. Can you get ropes around it?'

'Yes, with more digging. Get them to bring the pulleys.'

Two more Albanians entered the chapel and set up lifting pulleys at each end of the grave. Richard Mamonas dug further and then disappeared to tie ropes to whatever was in there. After a while he reappeared, nodded at Zoe and climbed out of the hole.

'Lift,' Zoe said, signalling to the Albanians.

Four men bent their backs to the ropes, placing hand over hand to pull them. There were squeaks and groans and curses when, once, the object snagged itself on the grave's walls.

Bit by bit, something came into view and Anna leant as far forward as her ropes would allow.

It was a casket, perhaps six feet in length, which had once been made of wood but was now a series of metal bands holding together its splintered remains.

Slowly, slowly, they lifted it from the grave and then swung it sideways to allow it to come to rest beside the hole.

No one spoke. The Albanians recovered their breath and looked at one another. Zoe and her cousin just stared at the casket.

'Get rid of them,' whispered Zoe, not moving. 'Tell them to go.'

Richard Mamonas said some words to the soldiers and they picked up their tools and left. There were just three of them in the chapel now.

Zoe said, 'Bring her over here.'

Mamonas crossed to Anna and untied her from the bench. Then he pulled her to her feet and led her over to stand at the side of the hole.

Zoe looked at her. Her eyes had a curious light in them. 'Do you remember me washing you in that cistern below the palace?' she asked. 'Just after Richard here killed your brother?'

Anna remembered the cistern and a woman that had brought her a bath and the stuff to wash herself. She remembered steam and the sting of cuts dabbed by a gentle sponge. She remembered the comfort of disclosure.

You are scared of being buried?

Something like that.

Then she remembered a dread, a familiar dread that was now rising inside her.

'Well, I remember it well, anyway,' continued Zoe softly. 'I remember when you told me about your deepest fear.' She looked into the hole. 'It's in there, isn't it?'

Anna felt faint. Her head was swimming. She was standing on the edge of the grave and, looking down, could see nothing but black. She closed her eyes and saw a hole beneath a tree, a box that smelt of fish, a cave with a lamp that had gone out. They couldn't be thinking . . .

'Get in,' said Zoe. 'Or I'll fire this crossbow and you'll fall into it. It's up to you.'

Anna's legs nearly gave way. She felt that every nightmare she'd ever had was gathering in that chapel, gathering amongst the saints and sinners on the walls, amongst the visions of hell and damnation, crowding in to finally drive her into madness. She swayed.

'Get in.'

Then she was pushed.

Her head hit the side as she fell and her breath left her in a rush as she landed at the bottom of the grave. She felt the cold earth against her cheek as she lay there between its steep walls, winded and dizzy. She couldn't move. She was paralysed with fear. The fall had taken the gag from her mouth but she couldn't speak.

Then the first earth landed on her. She heard, dimly, the scrape of spade on stone above and felt the first gritty clod on her face. Still she couldn't move. She could only stare out at walls that towered above, up, up . . . going on forever.

The earth kept coming, more and more, heavier and heavier, a blanket to cover her. Then her eyes were covered and she could no longer see. She could only smell the blood-scent of the earth. Something moved over her gagged lips: a worm. A worm to crawl into her brain.

Her ears were filled with the sounds of the lost, the damned. She heard praying and screaming and the sounds of wild animals trapped in their cages. A convulsion overwhelmed her body, coursing from her toes to her shoulders, one last spasm. She felt herself falling, falling, falling.

And then she screamed.

Inside the palace, Plethon was woken for a second time in a week by the presence of a woman in his room.

At first he thought her veiled. She was sitting at the end of his bed, her head slightly bent and her long hair falling into her lap like moonlit rain. She had made no attempt to touch or speak to him.

'Maria?' he whispered.

The woman turned to him and he saw her eyes as two points of light between the strands of her hair. She didn't answer.

Plethon sat up. He leant forward and took her hand. 'Why are you here, Maria?'

There was no reply. The woman lifted her head and glanced around the room; once, twice.

'Are you looking for someone?'

Her eyes came back to his. 'Anna.'

'But she's with you, Maria.'

The woman shook her head. 'No.' Certain. 'No, they've gone.'

Plethon frowned. 'They?'

'Anna, the other one. They've gone.'

Plethon felt something cold trace its way up his spine. He'd seen Zoe after the funeral and they'd agreed to meet the next day to go to the treasure. Had she gone already?

With Anna?

Something was wrong. He let go Maria's hand and got out of bed. 'You must be cold. Take my bed, here. I will go and find them.'

Plethon put her to bed and arranged the blankets to warm her. Then he leant and kissed her forehead, his beard against her hair; silver on silver. 'Don't worry. Anna will be back.'

She's all she has.

He went to the door, opened it and walked along the corridor to the stairs. There were guards at the bottom, men of the Royal Guard. As he descended the stairs, they came to attention. He addressed one of them. 'Go to the barracks. There are three Varangians there. Find them and wake them. Tell them to meet me at the palace gate. Tell them to bring weapons.'

Ten minutes later, Plethon was standing, shivering, just inside the palace gate. The moon was a luminous sickle and free of clouds. The houses on the hill of Mistra were unmoored from their foundations, floating in the pale light like ships at anchor. Plethon looked up at the church of St Sophia. Were there lights inside?

Is that where you are?

He heard a noise behind him and turned to find Matthew approaching, Nikolas and Arcadius behind. They were wearing armour but no helmets. All had swords in their hands and bows slung over their shoulders.

Plethon put his finger to his lips as they approached. 'We need to be quiet.' He looked over his shoulder and then back. 'Aren't guards supposed to be at this gate?'

Matthew glanced around him. He nodded. 'Yes. I saw them earlier. Albanians.'

Albanians.

Plethon frowned. He said, 'we are going up to the church. I think Anna's inside, with Zoe and quite possibly others. Look to your weapons.'

They set off through the gate, taking care where they placed their feet. Even if Zoe was inside the church, there might be Albanians keeping guard outside it. As the four of them approached the square in front of the church, they saw silhouettes of men sitting on the wall, each with a drawn sword. There were three of them.

Matthew and the other two crouched down beside Plethon. 'One each,' whispered Matthew. 'I'll take the one on the left.'

'And I'll take the one on the right.' said Nikolas. 'That leaves the fat one to you, Arcadius. Think you can manage?'

Arcadius grunted. The Varangians drew knives from their belts.

Plethon put his hand on Matthew's shoulder. 'Remember. Silently.'

The three crept forward, more silent than shadows. To

Plethon, watching with his breath held, it was as if they'd disappeared. Then, moments later, there was a small sound and no longer any silhouettes on the wall.

Plethon gathered his toga and crept up the street to the wall. At the Varangians' feet were three soldiers with their throats open. Matthew said, 'there may be more inside the church. We should arm ourselves.'

Leaving Plethon to find the steps, the three Varangians lifted themselves over the wall and fell noiselessly into the square. They took their bows from their shoulders and put arrows to their strings. They edged their way around the cistern, grateful for the yew's shadow, their bows at the ready.

Ahead of them, the door to the church opened and two Albanians appeared, closing the door behind them. The men were carrying ropes and pulleys. Matthew nodded to Nikolas. Seconds later, the Albanians lay on the ground, arrows in their necks and the apparatus for lifting all around them. They had died as silently as the Varangians had intended. Five down was good but how many more were there?

Plethon joined them, his toga too bright in the quarter-moon. He rose to go to the door. Matthew's arm stopped him. 'No. We go first.'

Plethon opened his mouth. 'But...'

He got no further. A scream rent the night. He looked at Matthew, his eyes wide with horror. 'They're killing her.'

The Varangians rose and drew their swords. Matthew leading, they ran to the door. They turned the handle. Locked.

'Arcadius,' shouted Matthew. 'Break it open.'

They heard shouts inside. Arcadius stepped back, lowered his shoulder and charged the door. It wouldn't budge. He tried again. No movement,

'Help me,' he said and the three of them lined up, shoulders down, and charged together. This time there was a crack.

'Again!'

This time the door broke and they crashed into the church. Two Albanians were there to face them but fell at the first sword strokes. Then there were two more, better fighters who managed a parry or two before they died.

Plethon came into the church behind them. 'Quick, the chapel.' He lifted his toga and ran to it, the Varangians on his heels.

Inside were a man and a woman standing either side of a casket. There were spades and a crowbar leaning against a pile of earth. The man had a crossbow in his hand.

'Duck!' yelled Matthew, pushing Plethon to the floor as a bolt whistled over their heads. Another arrow flew, this time from behind them. He looked up to see Richard Mamonas thrown back against the wall of the church, an arrow in his chest, amazement on his face. He fell to his knees, clutching at the shaft, then pitched forward onto the stone. He was dead.

Zoe was looking around for something.

'Don't' said Matthew, rising. His bow was aimed at her heart. "You'd be dead before you got to it.'

Plethon got to his feet. He raked the chapel with his eyes. 'Where is she?'

Matthew was looking at the open grave 'She's in there. Nikki, Arcadius, get her.'

The Varangians ran to the grave and Nikolas jumped in. A moment later he'd risen with Anna in his arms. Her head to one side and her eyes closed. She was a figure of clay, her hair a tangle of roots plucked from the earth. Plethon went over to her, looking down into a face without movement. There was blood on her lips.

We were too late.

'Lay her down. There.' He turned to Zoe. She was perfectly still, staring at the casket. 'Did you hurt her?'

Zoe shook her head, her eyes vacant, unseeing. 'She fell.'

Plethon knelt. He took a fold of his toga and began to wipe the dirt from Anna's face, the blood from her lips. Her mouth was open.

She's breathing.

Her eyelids fluttered. He lifted a corner of the toga to them, using it to take away the earth. She opened her eyes. She looked at Plethon for a long time before she spoke.

'Open it,' she whispered.

He knew what she meant. Plethon sat back on his haunches. He looked up at Matthew who was kneeling across from him.

'Take Zoe and the others out of the church. Make sure no one comes in. No one.'

Matthew began to say something, but stopped. Then he nodded and rose. He signaled to the other Varangians and they left the church, Zoe between them. There was a dull thud as the door closed.

Anna had risen to her feet and was sweeping the remaining dirt from her clothes. There were bruises on her arms from where she had landed in the grave. She ran her hands through her hair and more earth fell to the ground. She wiped her hands on her thighs and took Plethon's hand. 'Come.'

They found candles and brought them over to the casket. They saw that Richard Mamonas had broken two of the metal bands, leaving one intact. Plethon gave his candle to Anna, picked up the iron bar and put it between the metal and the wood. It broke easily.

Then he sat back. Anna was by his side holding the candles and the casket was ready to open. They looked at each other, saw excitement and fear mirrored in each other's eyes.

'Are you ready?' asked Plethon quietly.

Anna looked down at the casket. She took a deep breath and nodded, once.

Plethon placed his hands on the lid, his thumbs below the rim. He lifted it free and it slid to the ground. They looked into the casket.

Inside was an object wrapped in layer upon layer of coarse cloth. The cloth was ancient and frayed and smelled of must and decay. A faint cloud of dust rose from it.

The candles in Anna's hands flickered as if a wind had passed. It was suddenly much colder in the chapel. She turned to Plethon and saw, in the candlelight, that he was ashen white. She took his hand and found that it was trembling.

'Do you know what it is?' she whispered.

Plethon didn't answer at first. He seemed transfixed by what was before him. Then he nodded.

Anna looked down. 'What is it?'

Slowly, slowly he turned to her and, as he did so, a cock crew somewhere further down the hill of Mistra. The sun had risen.

'Something that will change the world.'

In the monastery of Battal Gazi, the Venetian sopracomito had not believed the old man who was straddled above him in crucifixion. He'd seen the wretches in the Arsenale. He'd drunk the mixture himself and survived the plague.

He was standing, legs apart, in front of Omar. He had removed his doublet and in one hand held a branding iron, which he was heating over the largest of the candles. The air smelt of singed flesh.

'One more time,' said di Vetriano. 'Tell me where Magoris is and all this can stop. I'm losing patience.'

A few Karamanid tribesmen were standing somewhere among the shadows of the crypt. Others were manning the monastery walls. The other Venetian, Fabio, was lounging against the door studying the pitted blade of his sword. The steady drill of rain on stone could be heard outside.

Omar's upper body was a mass of blisters where di Vetriano had applied the brand. Some were oozing blood and a yellow liquid that glistened as it ran. The old man's eyes were closed.

Di Vetriano sighed. He withdrew the brand from the flame and blew on it so that the metal glowed. He began to walk towards Omar.

There was a banging behind him and he stopped. It came from the door. Fabio straightened and glanced at di Vetriano, who nodded. The door was opened.

A Karamanid tribesman was standing there. He said something in a low voice.

'You won't believe this,' Fabio said, turning. 'Magoris is here. At the gate. He wants to come in.'

A lightning flash lit into day the courtyard outside and, seconds later, a peal of thunder exploded into the room like cannon-shot.

'He's alone?'

Fabio nodded.

Di Vetriano turned to Omar. 'Who says fortune only favours

the good? He must want to save you.' Then: 'Fabio, tell them to bring him. And search him thoroughly.'

They waited for Luke in silence. Omar's eyes remained closed and his head was slumped to one side as if he was asleep. Di Vetriano made no attempt to inflict further pain on him but sat on the tomb contemplating first one boot, then the other. The branding iron was leant against the wall.

At last the door opened and Luke walked in flanked by two tribesmen. He was wearing a long cloak that seemed more water than wool. His long fair hair was caked in dirt and straddled his face. The rain outside swept in and water quickly entered the crypt around him, spreading across the stone so that it soon seemed as if they were afloat.

He stared up at Omar. 'Cut him down, di Vetriano.'

The Venetian shook his head. 'I think not. You seem to me the sort of fool more likely to talk if someone else suffers. He'll stay where he is.' He rose to his feet and picked up the branding iron. 'We'll keep him there and you'll talk and if you don't I'll burn him some more.' He paused. 'You'll talk in the end, otherwise you wouldn't be here.'

Luke said, 'What do you want to know?'

Di Vetriano walked over and sat on the smaller tomb. He picked up the crossbow and began to examine its mechanism, his brow furrowed. He was choosing his words. 'When I last met you it was on a galley that had amongst its cargo some jars of mastic mixed with other ingredients. It was thought to fix dye.'

Luke glanced beyond di Vetriano. Omar had opened his eyes and was looking hard at Luke. A trickle of blood had emerged at the corner of his mouth from where he'd bitten his tongue.

Vetriano said, 'As precisely as possible, please tell me the formula.'

Luke frowned. Surely the information was now useless? The tests had proved negative.

What does it matter? I just have to keep him talking.

He looked up at Omar, at his body scarred by fire, and wondered if he could hold on just a little longer. He thought of another man about the same age who'd stood before a city wall on another night of storm and swung his axe.

Luke began to speak. He spoke of mastic and orange blossom and the distillations from twenty other flowers and herbs, all the while looking straight at Omar. He talked in Italian and Latin and he used his hands to clarify points. Di Vetriano couldn't keep up.

'Wait!' he said. 'I need to write it down. Fabio, bring me a pen.'

But Luke went on talking, but to Omar. He said, 'The compound mixture is complicated. The amount of each ingredient must be mixed with exactitude. It is like Greek fire, which, they say, no one man ever knew the full formula of.'

By now, the Venetian had the means to write. He bent over the parchment. 'Say it all again. Slower.'

Luke took a deep breath. At last he'd seen smoke. He felt like a necromancer summoning forth magic from the depths. He glanced at Omar. He'd seen it too, curling in wisps from the flagstones, gossamer-thin.

Omar caught Luke's eye and nodded.

Understood.

Di Vetriano was busy with his pen. 'Say it again.'

The Venetian Fabio had seen the smoke too. He opened his mouth to speak.

But Omar spoke first. He looked round at the tribesmen and shouted: 'Karamanids, you have defiled the tomb of Seyit Battal

Gazi! You will burn in hell for this deed. See, the flames come for you!'

Luke pointed to the wellhead, where the smoke was seeping more thickly through the cracks. The guards either side of him had seen it and were yelling to their kinsmen in the shadows.

Di Vetriano looked up. He cursed and got to his feet. 'What is this?' He stared at the wellhead and then spun round to face Luke. 'What have you done?'

The Karamanids were now backing away from the smoke, their boots squelching in the water that was already an inch deep. There was a strong smell of sulphur. The man next to Luke turned and began to pull back the bolts on the door.

Di Vetriano aimed his crossbow at the closest tribesman.

'Where are you going?' he shouted. 'It's just vapour!' He moved to the wellhead, slung the crossbow over his shoulder and took the metal ring in both hands. 'Help me!'

A tribesman came over and took hold of the ring beside him. They both heaved.

The two men fell back as the stone came up. Fire rose into the room with a roar, a livid tongue of orange and red that shot upwards the height of a man. When it fell back, the water around it caught fire. The floor of the crypt was ablaze.

The Karamanids were already at the door, thrashing at their clothes, desperate to escape the wrath of the saint. The door opened and gusts of wind swept in over their heads, fanning the flames behind them.

Di Vetriano had risen from the water, his clothes alight.

'Fabio, get them back!' he yelled, trying to sweep the fire from his shirt.

But Fabio had other priorities. He'd tried to stop the tribesmen but they'd ignored his crossbow and pushed him back against a pillar. Then, as his finger had searched for its trigger, Luke had rushed him.

Now the two of them were locked in an embrace, the Venetian's back to the pillar. He'd managed to draw a dagger from somewhere and held it an inch away from Luke's face. But Luke was stronger and the dagger was being forced slowly back so that, quite soon, it was pointing at the ceiling.

Luke's hand turned quickly on the man's wrist and the dagger dropped. A second later, Luke's forehead made contact with his nose and his knee came up into his groin. Fabio went down and, as he did so, Luke hit him again.

Luke spun round.

The sopracomito was standing behind Omar on top of the tomb. He had his forearm around the old man's neck and the crossbow dug into his side. Omar's face was knitted with pain but he uttered no sound. The beam above them was alight.

'Ingenious,' said the Venetian. 'You set the cistern alight with Greek fire.' He looked around the crypt at the carpet of fire around them. 'Where did you get it?'

Luke saw that di Vetriano's finger was on the crossbow trigger and that his hand was shaking. He saw something wild in his eyes. He said, 'Give me the old man, di Vetriano, and you can go.'

But the Venetian was shaking his head. There was sweat coursing down his cheeks. He pulled Omar more tightly to his chest and the old man grimaced. Still no sound came from him. 'Oh no. I will leave this place,' he said, pressing the crossbow into Omar's side, 'and the old man will be my way out.'

'You won't make it,' said Luke. 'You have one crossbow bolt and the Karamanids have fled. Be sensible, Vetriano.'

The Venetian was untying Omar's hands with one hand, keeping the crossbow aimed at Luke with the other. He stepped down, pulling Omar with him. The water was no longer alight and there was only smoke rising from the wellhead. He moved to its edge, glancing down. He brought the crossbow bolt to Omar's neck.

'Where is your accomplice, Magoris? The one with the Greek Fire?'

Luke didn't answer. He'd heard movement behind him.

Fabio.

The other Venetian had got to his knees, sweeping the blood from his nose and eyes with his arm and shaking his head. Luke could hear him searching in the water for his weapon.

Di Vetriano said, 'Fabio, go and find the man with the Greek Fire.'

But Fabio wasn't listening. He saw no reason why Luke shouldn't die before he went anywhere. He'd found the dagger and was wiping the blade against his sodden shirtsleeve. He stood up.

'Fabio?'

Fabio staggered forward, lifting the blade to strike. One step, two steps. Then he stopped. His mouth was open, blood spilling over his bottom lip. He let out a groan and fell forward into the water. Vinsanto red.

Bennedo Barbi was standing in the courtyard with a crossbow in one hand and rain drumming on his shoulders. In his other hand was a canister strap.

Vetriano laughed. 'Thank you, Barbi. I'd have done the same myself but I need the bolt. Now throw me the canister.'

Barbi didn't move. Di Vetriano pressed the crossbow bolt further into Omar's neck. 'Magoris, tell him to do it.'

Luke said, 'throw it, Benedo.' His voice was flat.

Barbi walked up to the doorway. With a metallic crash,

the canister landed at di Vetriano's feet. He kicked it into the wellhead and they heard a splash.

'You're right, of course, Magoris. I'd not get far with all those trigger-happy monks outside. So I think I'll leave in the same way that you, presumably, got in. I imagine there's an outlet somewhere. I'm sure I'll find it' He glanced down at the hole. 'The water's no longer aflame and without the Greek Fire, you won't be able to re-light it.'

He was edging towards the edge of the wellhead, the old man with him. Would he kill Omar before he jumped?

Luke thought quickly. *He has one bolt.*

'You still won't make it, Vetriano,' he said. 'I posted a guard at the tunnel entrance.'

One crossbow bolt. One guard.

Vetriano frowned, considering this information. Then he'd decided. He pushed Omar away and jumped. Another splash.

Luke span round, 'Where is it?'

It was propped up outside the door, out of sight. Barbi reached around the door and dragged it inside and over to the wellhead. He found the tinderbox in his pocket, wrapped in oilskin. He unwrapped it, fumbling.

Luke pulled the canister to the opening and aimed the tube below.

'Ready?'

The flint was struck and the tube spat flame. The water below caught fire and, out of sight, they heard the scream of a man alight. The sound came and went, loud and muffled. It went on for a long time. At last it stopped.

Barbi turned to Luke. 'It's a bad way to die. You either burn or drown.'

*   *   *

556

Later, when the fire had gone out and the rain stopped, Luke and Omar sat on the walls of the monastery and waited for a new day to begin. Luke's sword was leaning against his thigh. There was a single star left in the sky.

'Kervan Kiran,' Luke said, looking up. 'Plethon's star.'

Omar turned to him. He wore a clean white shirt and there were bandages around his head. His beard was curled and yellow at the edges and he smelt of herbs. He looked much older. 'Have you decided what you are going to do?'

Luke remembered a conversation with this man not long ago.

'I was left a sword to take me to a treasure.'

'Or to remind you that you're a Varangian prince.'

He said softly, 'the sword had Mistra written on its blade, Omar. It was a message.'

The old man nodded. Just then, the sun crested the horizon with a suddenness that made both of them look out over the steppe. There was nothing there. But above, above in a sky still flecked with scattered rainclouds, there was another world, a giant, golden sea with islands in it and, thought Luke, a longship sailing towards them. He narrowed his eyes and stared. Siward. Miklagard.

Miklagard.

He looked down at the sword hilt resting on his thigh. Siward's sword. The dragon head was alive, its eyes glowing. It was looking up at him.

Suddenly he knew.

They've found the treasure.

He turned to Omar. 'Plethon's found the treasure,' he said. 'I go to Tamerlane.'

HISTORICAL NOTE

The *Mistra Chronicles* take place in the late-fourteenth and early-fifteenth centuries and are set against a time of colliding empires. The empires were the Ottoman, Byzantine, Venetian and Timurid.

At the end of the fourteenth century, Europe was recovering from the Black Death, a plague that, in the 1360s, had killed one in three of its population. Yet among the city states of Northern Italy, there shone the new light of the early Renaissance, a light which expressed itself through ideas and art and was fostered by trade and exploration. It was the light that would lead, ultimately, to the Enlightenment of the eighteenth century.

In the east, a Turkish tribe from the Anatolian steppe, the Ottoman, had, by the time of this chronicle, conquered most of its neighbouring beyliks, much of what was left of the Byzantine Empire and crossed over to Europe. Sultan Bayezid came to the throne when his father Murad was murdered by a Serbian knight after the Battle of Kosovo in 1389, the battle at which the Ottomans first confronted Christian knights and defeated them. Bayezid then boasted that he'd sweep through Europe, that he'd water his horses at Saint Peter's in Rome. He was *Yilderim* ('Thunderbolt'), the Sword of Islam, and, after his victory at Kosovo, it seemed that he might succeed. The Ottoman Empire was on the march westwards and it threatened to extinguish the new light of progress in Europe.

But to conquer Europe, Bayezid first had to conquer the Byzantine Empire and, in particular, the city of Constantinople. The Gates of Byzantium were the gates into Europe.

The Byzantine Empire was the eastern half and successor to the Roman Empire. It had split away from Rome in the fifth century after the barbarian invasions had overrun the western part. Its capital was Constantinople, built by the Emperor Constantine in the fourth century AD and still one of the greatest cities on earth, with huge walls that had only once been breached. At one time, the Byzantine Empire had held sway over much of Eastern Europe and the Middle East. But by the late-fourteenth century all that was left of the Empire was Constantinople and the little Despotate of Mistra. Constantinople was a city of empty palaces and ploughed fields, its population shrunk from a million to just fifty thousand. (Incidentally, no one called anyone or anything 'Byzantine' until the sixteenth century. At the time of this book, they would have called themselves *rhomaioi*, which is Greek for Roman. The 'Byzantines' very much saw themselves as the continuation of the Roman Empire.)

The Despotate of Mistra covered most of the area that is now the Greek Peloponnese and, for it, this was a period of prosperity and cultural flowering. Its twin cities of Mistra and Monemvasia became rich and their citizens built beautiful churches and palaces. Mistra had been built in the twelfth century close to the site of ancient Sparta while Monemvasia had, for centuries, been an important trading port between Europe and Constantinople, famous for its sweet wine, Malvasie (or Malmsey in English). In these last decades of the Byzantine Empire, much of the artistic and cultural activity moved from Constantinople to Mistra and many important thinkers, such as Georgius Gemistus Plethon, came to live there.

By this time, the Byzantine army was no match for the vast forces that the Ottomans had at their disposal. Bayezid's father, Murad I, had introduced the *Devshirme*, by which Christian boys were forcibly taken from the conquered villages of Eastern Europe and sent to Anatolia to be trained to fight in the Ottoman army. The best of these became *janisarries,* its elite fighting force.

The Byzantines' own elite force was mostly a memory. The Varangian Guard had once been one of the finest fighting units in the world, renowned for their fearlessness in battle and use of the double-sided axe, the *distralia.* Originally recruited from Scandinavian countries, the Varangians became a largely English force after the Norman invasion of 1066 when many Anglo-Saxons fled England to seek their fortune overseas. Siward was indeed a Prince of Wessex and had sailed with his followers to the mythical city of Miklagard in the late-eleventh century to become the first English Varangians. The Varangian treasure is pure invention, although it is true that the Varangians got first pick of the spoils when an enemy city was taken and were allowed to fill their helmets with gold from the treasury at the accession of a new Emperor. They had their own church in Constantinople, and the giant sword of St. Olaf hung above its altar

The Venetian Empire, was born out of the Byzantine Empire. In 1204, Venice had persuaded the Fourth Crusade to besiege Constantinople on its way to regain the Holy Land in order to repay, from the pillage, the money owed them for the boats they'd had built to ferry the crusaders to Alexandria. When Constantinople fell, (the octogenarian, blind Doge Dandolo leading the way), Venice helped itself to a large part of the Byzantine Empire and, in particular, the coastal cities and islands of the Eastern Mediterranean that would protect its trade routes. Much of the treasure of Constantinople was carried off to Venice, including the majestic bronze horses now in St Mark's Square.

By the end of the fourteenth century, Venice was pulling ahead of its fierce trade rivals, the Genoese. Real loathing between these two republics had come to a head in 1378 when they'd gone to war. In it a Genoese fleet had actually entered the Venetian lagoon and, briefly, taken the island of Choggia. But Venice had ultimately won the war and then busied itself with trying to prise as much territory and trade as it could away from Genoa.

Chios was one of the few Mediterranean islands controlled by the Genoese, most of their maritime empire having been established in the Black Sea. It was held under a long lease from the Byzantine Empire by a joint stock company that was the first of its kind and a forerunner to Britain's East India Company. The Mahona had been formed in the mid-fourteenth century by twelve Genoese families under the collective name of Giustiniani in deference to the great Byzantine Emperor Justinian. Its purpose was to exploit the trade of alum, mined in neighbouring Phocea on the Turkish mainland, which was the valuable substance used to fix dye in clothing. Its other purpose was to trade mastic and it is entirely true that Chios produced a kind of mastic found nowhere else in the world and that it became more and more valuable as a breath freshener (particularly in the *harem*), a wound sealant, an embalmer, a medicine and for many other uses. In India it was used to fill tooth cavities but there's no evidence that it was used elsewhere for this purpose, although the explosion of sugar consumption in the fourteenth century would have made it very welcome. The indigenous Greeks who worked in the mastic groves in the south of Chios were indeed the victims of Turkish pirate attacks in which their children were taken away for slavery. It is also true that, some time during the fourteenth century, the Genoese began to build a series of extraordinary maze-like villages in the south of the island which were intended to protect their workforce from the Turks. These 'Mastic Villages' can still be visited today in Chios and are truly marvellous to behold. The kendos festival described in the book takes place every year on Chios.

The fourth empire was that of Tamerlane, or 'Timur-the-lame' as he was called at that time. Tamerlane was a Mongol, a successor to Genghis Khan who had laid waste much of the east two centuries before. His successor, Tsubodai, had brought the hordes to the gates of Europe and might have gone further were it not for the death of the Mongol Khan Ogedai which forced him to return home. Like Genghis, Tamerlane managed to unite the Mongol hordes and shape them into a terrifying and unstoppable instrument of terror. By this time, Tamerlane had swept across much of Asia, destroying everything in his path. Whether he would come west to take on Bayezid and, by doing so, relieve the pressure on Europe or turn east was the question being asked by every Christian king.

Into this mix came invention, the invention of cannon big enough to bring down the walls of Constantinople. Cannon had been around for a century at least but none were yet big enough to destroy walls of the size of Constantinople's. There's no evidence that Venice built such cannon for the Turks, although its Arsenale certainly had a cannon foundry. The Arsenale was also beginning to mass-produce ships using assembly line methods never used before. They could well have been building ships for the Ottomans. Venice was a pragmatic republic, ready to profit by any means, as demonstrated by its behaviour in the Fourth Crusade.

The Walls of Byzantium contains a cast of characters most of whom actually existed. The Laskaris family were indeed Pro-tostators (sort of Prime Ministers) of Mistra. Their house can still be seen there today. The Mamonas family were Archons of Monemvasia. Theodore was the Despot of Mistra at this time and Bartolomea was his Despoena. These days, the title 'Despot' has rather negative conotations. In fact the Despots of Mistra were invariably good, cultured men, usually the brother or son of the Emperor in Constantinople, who ruled well and embellished their magnificent capital in the Pelo-ponnese. Marchese Longo existed on Chios and was a leader of the Mahona at the time and he did have a palace at Sklavia, although the evidence for it there is difficult to find. Fiorenza is fictional.

Bayezid's son Suleyman existed as did his brothers Mehmed and Musa and his grandmother, the Valide Sultan Gulcicek. The brothers' rivalry was very real (Bayezid having murdered his own at the time of his accession), and ultimately would lead to an Ottoman civil war, the theme of the third book in the chronicles.

Yakub-Bey was chief of the *gazi* Germiyan tribe of central Anatolia and would have been a reluctant ally of Bayezid, in spite of the Sultan's marriage to his sister Devlet Hatun. Yakub's beylik had been overrun by Bayezid as recently as the 1380's and he himself had been imprisoned. The Karamanids were the Germiyans' eastern neighbours and rivals and were yet to fall under the Ottoman yoke.

As to the events described, the city of Mistra was besieged by the Ottomans in the middle of 1390s but not taken. The Archon of Monemvasia had rebelled against the Despot some years beforehand so was quite likely not to have come to the city's aid. The meeting at Serres took place in 1392 and the Emperor Manuel fled when he thought that his life was in danger. Prince Stefan of Serbia was also there as an Ottoman vassal and his sister, Olivera Despina, was one of Bayezid's wives.

In Nicopolis was one of the most important battles in history. The crusade that led to the battle was largely financed by the wealthy Duke of Burgundy whose son, the Comte de Nevers, became its nominal leader. The Christian army was said to be huge, could 'hold up the sky with its lances'. But it was also complacent and so certain of victory that jousting tournaments were held on the eve of battle. The battle that followed was as terrible and bloody as described, as was the aftermath when two thousand Christian Knights were slaughtered by Bayezid, many by his elderly ulema.

Nicopolis sent shock waves through Europe and, from that moment on, the Kings of Christendom truly feared that the Ottomans might overrun them. There were repeated efforts to raise another crusade to come to the aid of Constantinople which Bayezid put under more or less constant siege from 1394 onwards, blockading it with his new navy. But the big obstacle was the union between the western Church of Rome and the eastern Orthodox Church. Ridiculous liturgical differences, such as how the sign of the Cross should be made, had to be discussed and agreed on before the Churches could be united and the Pope sanction another crusade. Plethon, as I say in the book, was an ardent proponent of Church union as a way to save the Empire and was to play an important part in the later Council of Florence at which it was agreed.

In the final scene of this first book, I describe 'Greek fire'. There has been much debate as to how this Byzantine secret weapon was made and no one knows for sure. What *is* known is that Greek fire played a decisive part in the success of the Byzantine Empire from around the eighth century onwards and was so vital to state security that only the Emperor and a handful of others knew how it was created.

At the heart of The Mistra Chronicles are the twin cities of Mistra and Monemevasia in the Greek Peloponnese. I first saw Monemvasia at sunset from the deck of a sailing boat and it was love at first sight. I spent two days exploring the maze of its lower town and the ruins of the Goulas above. Then I went to Mistra and fell in love all over again. Both cities can be visited today. Mistra is about three hours from Athens airport and Monemvasia, which has been largely rebuilt as a Byzantine city, is an hour on from Mistra. Monemvasia has some good boutique hotels and a swim from the rocks outside the Portello (where Joseph met his fate) is compulsory.

For those wanting more general knowledge about the world as it was at this time, I can recommend John Julius Norwich's *Short History of Byzantium*, Judith Herrin's *Byzantium*, Steven Runciman's *Lost Capital of Byzantium* and *The Last Byzantine Renaissance* and, for the most evocative overview of the Ottoman Empire, Jason Goodwin's magisterial *Lords of the Horizons*.

The story of Luke, Anna, Zoe and the clashing empires that surround them will continue with the next book in the Mistra Chronicle series, *The Towers of Samarcand*.

WALLSEND DISTRICT LIBRARY.

For further information,
visit www.mistrachronicles.com